The Armalite Maiden

The Armalite Maiden

Jonathan Kebbe

HEINEMANN : LONDON

William Heinemann Ltd
Michelin House, 81 Fulham Road, London SW3 6RB
LONDON   MELBOURNE   AUCKLAND

British Library Cataloguing in Publication Data

Kebbe, Jonathan
The armalite maiden
I. Title
823' .914 [F]

ISBN 0 434 38502 6

Typeset by Deltatype, Ellesmere Port
Printed in Great Britain by
St Edmundsbury Press Ltd, Bury St Edmunds, Suffolk

To my mother, Hilde

Acknowledgements

For the interviews they gave I would like to thank Jill Kirkham, Richard Kirkham, Deirdre McCartie, Fiona Mitchell, Barrington Roberts, D. R. H., Harry and Pat; as well as the following for their valuable assistance: Millior Braithwaite, Carey Harrison, John O'Dell, Bryan O'Duffy, Vivienne Lafferty, Bernie Payne, Robin Robertson, Lillie Ross, Theo Ryan, Christianne Schirrmann and Margaret Smith. For specialist information I am particularly grateful to B.B., A.N.M.C., M.D. and John Wall. My profound thanks are due to Imogen Parker for her faith and vision, and to Laura Longrigg and all those at Heinemann who have helped bring this book into being. I am indebted to Carlos Thompson who long ago inspired and later guided me. Above all I am grateful to Christine Simpson for her graft, judgement and almost endless patience.

1

5 July, County Donegal, Eire

Four a.m., the wilds of Donegal, five miles from the Northern Ireland border. An isolated barn, two women outstretched in the dark, violating themselves.

Eileen Feeley, older, more experienced, finished quickly.

Annie McBride, who was new to it, tried once more. Spreading her long legs again, she applied more lubricant, and clutching the plastic-covered cartridge in both hands, slowly worked it up inside herself. Unlovingly prised apart, her tender flesh recoiled. The Vaseline helped and, fingering the thick slippery package further in, she drew breath. Just the string dangled, as though she'd inserted a tampon. Only this tampon was designed not to staunch bleeding, but to induce it in British soldiers.

'Get a bloody move on,' said Feeley.

Determined to prove herself, Annie sat up, fighting the pain with deep breaths. She could hear Feeley spraying herself. Waves of cheap cologne crossed the dark barn.

'Catch!'

Annie watched the dull gleam of the perfume bottle into her hands, gripped the hem of her skirt in her teeth and sprayed her thighs, crotch and the inner tent of the skirt in sickly scent.

Feeley creaked open the barn doors, introducing the first translucent hint of dawn. Clutching their abdomens, the two women eased themselves into the car – a battered sky-blue Ford Escort. Feeley hurried to start the engine. Grinding hoarsely it coughed repeatedly and expired. She kept trying, but the car shook like an early-morning dog and settled.

'Flooded,' she observed coolly, sitting back to light a cigarette. 'Dixie'll go mad . . . today of all days.'

The two women who sat in silence were very different.

Annie McBride, twenty-one, was tall and slender. With a striking face and a shock of red curls bursting from her beret, she sprang from well-to-do Irish-American stock and spoke with a soft cultured Irish accent.

Eileen Feeley, twenty-six, was shorter, stockier and more conventionally pretty. She had straight black hair and spoke with a biting, melodic Ulster accent, beaten out of the urban realities and lyrical setting of war-torn Derry city.

Annie McBride had just graduated with distinction from a remote training camp, where seasoned instructors had pronounced her the most promising material they could recall. Dubbed 'the cheetah' for her grace, skill and speed, she'd outrun, outwitted and, best of all, outshot her mostly male comrades. As a girl Annie had regularly hunted with her father. Today she was convinced she would claim her first man.

Better known as 'Black Rose' for her raven hair and cruel temperament, Eileen Feeley was already a veteran. As a teenager she'd seen the still, gaping bodies of local men, shot dead by British paratroops, and, restrained by soldiers, she'd watched her brothers dragged off in the dead of night to be beaten and tortured by RUC detectives, sentenced on the evidence of soldiers in courts which dispensed with juries, and banished to faraway prison camps for the best years of their lives. Fuelled by hate, Feeley was ready to give her last pint of blood to rid Ireland of the British. With several kills under her belt, her reputation had ghosted into barracks across the province, softening the knees of British soldiers. The whispered name of Black Rose even sent shivers down the necks of hardened IRA men.

What galled her this morning was that this cocky upper class upstart Annie McBride didn't appear to be afraid of her. She tried the ignition again. The car stuttered, rocked and fired, and crept out of the barn. Miles of broken fields shrouded in mist and darkness spread before them. As night retreated, the car, like a small hammered beetle, followed a bumpy track over a primitive patch-work landscape carved by the ice age and chiselled by wind and rain.

They reached the road, a pale scar on the land. All was still, nothing for miles, only waves of drystone walls and the distant outlines of a whitewashed farm. As they headed north, the grim profile of Douish Mountain appeared to rise out of the shimmering sea.

Picking up speed, the car splashed through potholes, every jolt sending a shaft of pain through their wombs. Feeley bore it all with pride, waiting for Annie to complain, and when Annie finally winced, Feeley smiled scornfully.

2

'You'll get used to it . . . if you survive. Few do. Most of our recruits get killed, or we trade them in. This is no ordinary unit and we don't carry passengers.'

Annie returned her gaze unswervingly, intoxicated with the knowledge that she'd been assigned to the most feared Active Service Unit in the province.

'You worry about yourself,' she smiled boldly. 'I'll worry about me.'

'God help you,' said Feeley with a cold laugh, taking a blind bend at sixty, enjoying the thrill of speed and the anticipation of carnage to come.

Just then an immense figure of a man loomed on the road ahead, stepping aside as the Ford seered to a halt some yards beyond. Hands in trouser pockets the young giant walked briskly to join the car, but not sharply enough for Feeley.

'Get a fucking move on!'

Michael broke into a run, bundling himself into the back of the car as it shot away.

'What d'you think this is, Mick – a picnic?'

Stung, Michael O'Cinneíde sat with his hands in his lap, gazing out at the dawn-lit rolling patchwork: aimless sheep, slow-drifting clouds, brushstrokes of blue-green sea. Then his eyes shifted to Annie, the brilliant profusion of red curls, her slender shoulders, her normally pale complexion tanned and freckled by sun and wind. He loved her. He'd known her four weeks and could remember the details of each love-making. But the more he loved her the more desperate he became to possess her.

Feeling the heat of his eyes, Annie smiled nebulously over her shoulder. She'd fallen for him with all the blind passion she gave to anything new that excited her. Michael was an IRA man of three years' standing, who'd 'joined the lads' after an encounter with a British patrol in which the soldiers, bitter about the murder of Lord Mountbatten and the slaughter of eighteen paratroopers at Warrenpoint, had taken revenge on the first Paddy that came to hand, leaving Michael beaten senseless, his van wrecked and his dog kicked to death.

But Michael's appetite for war had faded, and now, at twenty-nine, he could appreciate how happy he used to be, working the farm with Molly, his adopted mother, and singing ballads in the pubs most evenings.

3

Annie had loved him fiercely and briefly, as much for the romantic image he cut as rural-working-class Republican hero as for his ruggedly handsome face, powerful body and playful, vulnerable nature. But the passion had passed like a summer storm.

Feeley stopped the car on a rise a hundred yards short of the border, where the road passed from Eire into Britain without welcome or warning. In this remote boundless region where the invisible border meandered at will, a stranger could wander in and out of both countries all day and not know it.

As planned, Annie got out and picked wild flowers, scouring the rocky hillsides, scraps of woodland and murmuring scrub. No sign of anyone, yet she had the uneasy feeling of being watched.

'I don't like it,' she said, climbing painfully into the car.

'You see something?' said Feeley.

'No, just a feeling.'

'Jaysus, woman!' Feeley took the car away at speed.

'What if she's right?' said Michael.

Feeley threw back her head and laughed. 'Just like Big Mick to get scared as a rabbit on the day!'

The words were barely out when a voice boomed from the bog. THIS IS THE BRITISH ARMY . . . HALT, FORD ESCORT . . . HALT, OR WE FIRE!

Feeley slammed the brakes, pitching everybody forward. Rigid they sat, eyes flicking to left and right, but there was no one to be seen. In the dreadful silence Feeley reached inch-slow for the insect repellent, lifted her skirt, sprayed herself and passed the canister to Annie.

VACATE YOUR VEHICLE NICE AND SLOWLY . . . the hollow English voice resounded over snag and boulder. RIGHT-HAND DOORS ONLY . . .

They stood foolishly in the road, breeze nibbling at their clothes, sheep their only witnesses. The surrounding rocks were barren one moment, alive with human forms the next. Surfacing like bog-goblins, they leapt from rock to rock wearing baggy camouflage jackets and woollen caps and brandishing guns. One flourished a loud hailer.

TURN ROUND . . . HANDS ON ROOF!

Too surprised to be afraid, Annie was slow to obey.

'Turn round!' barked the soldier, running up.

4

His minions needed no orders. Two of them provided cover, two fell upon the car, one activated an HF radio, feeding the Ford's particulars to Central Computer, and the leader stepped smartly up to frisk the travellers in turn – Michael, Feeley and finally . . .

Annie felt the shock of his boot shoving her feet further apart, his gloved hands running up her legs like vermin; over her knees, thighs and buttocks – scavenging. Her blood froze. The urge to render the Englishman helpless with a back-heel in the balls was almost overwhelming.

The leader stepped back. 'Turn round all of you! Sit! Hands on heads!'

They squatted in the road. The searchers ducked from the car shaking their heads. The leader grunted unhappily. The driving licence was clean, the Ford's chassis and registration numbers had aroused no curiosity at Central Computer. The leader focused on Michael.

'Destination?'

'Castlerock,' replied Feeley lying.

The Englishman switched to her. 'Purpose?'

'Fishing.' Hate rang in her voice.

A glance at his men confirmed tackle and sandwiches found in the boot. He looked at Annie. She returned his gaze evenly. The nerve! she thought. Acting like they own this country. . .

'Very well!' he snapped. 'Eyes shut!'

They gaped, squinting into the first rays of sun.

'I said. . .'

They squatted, eyes closed, in the road. Soft footfalls faded.

'Who were they?' whispered Annie.

'SAS, you fucking eejit,' said Feeley.

'Bugger this!' grinned Michael, getting to his feet and stretching. At once a loud crack rent the air, a bullet whipped the dust between his boots, and he hurriedly sat down.

Cautiously opening her eyes, Annie found the landscape deserted. Gritting her teeth against the foreign body bruising her vagina she blurted, 'Will you look at that!'

'What?' cried Michael.

'Stalking through the stone-bramble. . .' murmured Annie mischievously.

'Mother-o'-Jaysus, where?'

A huge dragonfly was clipping back and forth below them.

'. . . blue and yellow, weaving this way . . .'

Michael stared. What kind of regiment sported blue and yellow?

'Shut it, the pair of you!' said Feeley. 'Here they come.'

Trailing dust a team of Landrovers hurtled along the road, bearing down on them and slewing to a halt at all angles. Out tumbled regular soldiers. Another English voice pitched into them.

'On your feet, legs apart, hands on heads!'

The hairs on Feeley's young body bristled with hate. She longed for the feel of a sub-machine-gun in her hands, magazine-fed bullets spewing from the death-chamber. But the fantasy was abruptly stifled by the sound she most dreaded – barking; a pair of black labradors straining on leashes, 'wagtails' as the Army called these simple allies.

Annie glanced at Feeley, but Feeley's gaze was fixed on some distant peak and Annie knew she was alone. She'd envisaged glory. Now all she could see ahead was the slow living death of a gaol sentence.

The dogs were presented first with the car, ferreting eagerly inside and out. Finding nothing they emerged with what's-next expressions in their eyes.

Whimpering with excitement they started on Michael's boots and jeans, taking lingering pleasure in farm smells. Michael's guilt-spiced perspiration drew the odd growl, but he smiled indulgently. Men he feared, dogs he loved, and one of his raised hands dropped of its own accord to stroke the animals' heads.

Finally the women, one dog dragged over to each one. Feeley struck a nonchalant pose, but her knees quivered and the fanatic reverted to the girl who once dreamed of being a typist.

This is my life, Annie reflected as the dog pressed its moist nose to her bare ankles. Given, wasted, thrown away . . .

Both dogs suddenly raised their necks and stiffened. The audience hushed. Wild barking was the signal when explosives were detected, and already deep growls were forming.

The dogs moved in a flash, leaping at the women's groins, sniffing frenziedly, jabbing, probing, alternating growls with plaintive whimpering, waves of perfume and insect repellent vying with whiffs of nitroglycerine. Enticed and repelled, the dogs backed off and sneezed loudly, triggering a chorus of coarse male laughter.

6

'Poor buggers need bitches!' observed a leering sergeant.

'They are bitches,' retorted a handler, drawing in his leash.

Two miles away, on the other side of the border, the most wanted man in Ireland crouched behind a pair of field-glasses on a dew-washed hillside.

Medium-tall, dark and gaunt, his thin strong body, deep-lined face and restless green eyes bore testimony to his hit-and-run existence. Born into poverty, educated in literature, Gaelic and revolutionary history behind the barbed wire of Long Kesh prison camp, he hated the British establishment for so tortuously dividing his country, and the British Army for the injury inflicted on his family. Today he meant to hit back harder than ever.

But what in God's name was keeping the gang, on this of all days which they knew was engraved on his heart? Every 5 July a personal score had to be settled with a passion beyond the call of duty.

The sun flashed on a far-off windscreen, a sky-blue Ford beetling over the ridge. Rolling onto his back, Dixie Ragdoll Doyle took the moving sky into his confidence.

'The blood of British soldiers will soak these hills today . . .'

2

Dixie Doyle's thoughts carried the few miles to Derry city. Drifting between rival spires of the Protestant and Catholic cathedrals, his blood vow crossed the impartial River Foyle and hovered above the barbed wire and remote-control cameras of the British base for the north-west of the province.

Below ground two officers, stripped to shorts, were playing squash at five-thirty in the morning, unaware of the shadow hanging over them.

If death could choose, it might have been tempted by the blond captain, 27-year-old Charles Winters. Well-born, newly wed and imbued with the air of a dashing cavalry officer, he had just arrived in Ulster. He actually belonged to an élite cavalry regiment, but had requested a temporary attachment to a mainline infantry regiment – 'to get a taste of action'.

But his opponent that morning was possibly the greater prize, for 30-year-old Marcus King was no ordinary soldier. The IRA had begun to notice him some time ago, not because he was black – though this was exceptional among British officers – but because he possessed two qualities they respected and feared: he was a brilliantly successful soldier, and, in striking contrast, he had developed an uncommon rapport with the Catholics of Derry. The IRA could not easily forgive him for either, and unbeknown to him he was steadily climbing the hit list.

But Marcus King's enemies were not confined to the IRA. He may have been loved by his men, but he was distrusted by many senior officers, some of whom watched his every move with keen interest, waiting for a pretext to get rid of him.

It was hot and airless in the underground court, men and walls dripping. Charles Winters, tall, smooth and athletic, hurled himself after the ball, determined to win. Marcus King, taller still and broader, stroked his shots, lithe body moving lightly, deriving pleasure more in the development of his skills and power than in the beating of an opponent.

Between games Winters subsided against a wall: 'I'm jolly glad of this opportunity to meet you properly.'

They exchanged smiles, the white man's a little awkward, the black man's a shade wary.

'Pleased to meet you too.'

The court echoed to the curious encounter of two far-removed worlds of English – the one lofty, clipped and upper class, the other deep, Jamaican and of the people.

'I say, do you mind if I ask you something?'

'Anything you like.'

'You've won a Military Cross, been mentioned in dispatches . . . I can't for the life of me understand . . .' Winters faltered.

'Why I'm still a lieutenant?'

'Well . . .' Winters coloured, and laughed. 'Yes!'

Marcus King laughed with him. Although Winters was three years younger and infinitely less experienced, he was a rank senior to King, whose promotion to captain and upward had long been imminent.

'Who knows?' said Marcus, knowing full well.

'There's no colour bar in the Army, is there?'

'Probably not officially. But invisible walls hit you just as hard. Anyway,' said Marcus, looking up at the ceiling as if he expected to see his name come up in lights. 'They got to promote me soon, seeing as I'm going to be a general before I retire!'

Driven by an indomitable spirit, Marcus King was like a runner setting the pace, always out in front; only every time he cruised into the home straight, they added another lap, leaving men like Charlie Winters to pass him on the privileged inside lane of top public school and Sandhurst.

Marcus seemed to lose himself in thought. His ambition had been to rise to Major, and then to be selected among the majors to become Colonel, the first black battalion commander in the British Army.

Glancing at King rocking lightly on his heels, Charlie Winters felt a sharp pang of jealousy and wondered would he ever be as relaxed and self-assured. But intrigued as he was by King-the-soldiers'-hero, he was wary of the rebel, and couldn't help recalling Major Draycott's warning: 'Steer clear of Lieutenant King, he's dangerous company.'

'I say, King, is it true you once led a patrol through the Catholic Bog-what's-it – ?'

'Bogside.'

' – playing the saxophone?'

Marcus nodded happily, a fond memory.

'Nobody shoot at you?'

'Too busy covering their ears!'

Winters roared with laughter. And quickly tried another angle. 'I rather get the impression Major Draycott's not wild about you?'

'Nah! He's just frustrated,' said Marcus evasively.

'What, sex?' laughed Winters.

'I wouldn't know about that. He just hates this hide-and-seek stuff, went nuts during the Falklands, wanted to be over there assaulting the beaches. Draycott's like a poor bloody Viking at the negotiating table.'

Winters wasn't interested in the Major.

'Do I understand you're in some kind of trouble?'

Marcus levelled with him, his eyes, so calm and cheerful a moment ago, fixed on Winters with dark intensity. Winters swallowed: should he tread more carefully with this fellow in

9

future? Marcus looked away with a pensive frown, taking a deep intake of breath through the nostrils, as if recalling something he'd rather forget.

'I was severely reprimanded by the Colonel.'

'The saxophone thing?' Winters straight in again. 'Was it that bad?'

'A summer's evening, people – the enemy – spilling out of doors and bars to see . . .' a little laugh and shake of the head, 'dancing to the tune of a British officer . . .'

'What on earth possessed you to – '

'Confucius say' – Marcus's grin caught Winters off guard – 'The saxophone is mightier than the self-loading rifle!'

'And they're still holding it against you?'

'There was, if possible, worse to follow. Back in England, at the end of a mess night, after the Brigadier and Colonel had left, Major Draycott started on me. I'd disgraced the battalion and all that. He'd had a lot to drink, everyone was a bit out of order, he took a swing at me, I should have walked away, but lost my cool. They piled in to break us up and I took them all on, pent up feelings. The place was wrecked.'

'Christ!'

'A good time was had by all – '

'And you carried the can – ' Marcus nodded without bitterness, 'and now you're on thin ice.'

Marcus glanced at his watch. 'Hey man, I'm on patrol in forty minutes!'

They resumed play, Winters intensifying his workrate, flaying the ball, unleashing cannonades of drives and smashes until, point by plundered point, he wrested a game from Marcus.

Marcus came to life, countering with quick reflexes, raising his game, not by consuming more energy, but alternating powerful shots with deft touches.

Committed to victory, his gentleman's face taut with concentration, Winters overstretched himself. Desperate to reach a passing drive, he lunged – a loud clap, his racket smashing into the wall, splitting the wood. Strings sagged, the racket head dangled on sinews.

'Oh fucking hell!' He swung the head viciously at the wall. 'Fucking brand new racket my father gave me . . . and what the hell do you think you're laughing at?' Winters drew himself up, pulling rank.

Marcus cocked an eyebrow. 'Pardon me, *sir*.'

Winters flushed. 'Sorry . . .' and fumbled for a friendly form of address.

'Call me Marcus.' Marcus crossed the court to offer his hand.

Winters received it gratefully. 'Charlie.'

'Long as you're in Ulster,' said Marcus on their way to the showers, 'things like rackets don't matter. They're replaceable.'

Normally free in his nakedness, Charlie Winters felt unaccountably shy in the shower, scrubbing himself briskly with his back turned. Marcus King, humming to himself to combat rising pre-patrol tension, had a feeling Winters was working up to something. Sure enough . . .

'I say Ki–, I mean, Marcus,' Winters half turned to face him. 'Mind if I join your patrol this morning?'

Marcus didn't reply at once. As he towelled himself he wondered at his hesitation. There was an innocence in Winters' question, like, Can I play with you today? Only hide-and-seek in Northern Ireland was a game of life-or-death, no place for . . . for fools, he couldn't help thinking. A chill went through him, a foreboding.

'Naturally I'll square it with the ops officer,' said Winters.

Marcus fixed his deep-brown eyes on him again.

'Why did you volunteer for Ulster?'

'Tired of kicking my fucking heels in Germany.'

'This is a dangerous time . . .'

'Wanted some action.'

'You've heard of Dixie Doyle? He likes to strike on or around this date.'

'I want to come,' said Winters, finding his authority.

3

Feeley swung the Ford into the overgrown farmyard, pulling up at the well where the arms were hidden.

The derelict farmhouse gaped, a monument to long-ago famine. Along its ivy-choked wall crept the shadows of clouds, but where was Dixie?

As Michael got out of the car and stalked through the ruins, something leapt from an overhead ledge. He gasped, as the shadow beat about his head and, spreading its wings, the raven lifted over the car and beat a slow morbid course across Thorn Hill. Already shaken by the border incident, Michael ducked through a hollow doorway and stole a swig of liquid courage from his hip flask.

In the car the women stretched out to extract their excruciating tampons. Coiling the string through her fingers Annie spread herself and slowly drew forth the bruising thing – like giving birth to death, she thought, as the cartridge slithered, greasy with blood and Vaseline, to the rusty floor. Suppressing a shiver, she looked up to catch Feeley gloating in the driving mirror. In the same moment, over Feeley's shoulder, she saw Dixie standing in the sunlight, hands in pockets, clothes crumpled from his night in the ruins, face gaunt and unshaven, vivid green eyes radiant.

Stepping cautiously from the car, Feeley spread her hands in supplication. 'SAS, Army, sniffer-dogs – you name it! And Madam,' jerking a thumb over her shoulder, 'wouldn't hurry if her arse was on fire!'

Dixie looked hard at Annie, who returned his gaze with a hardness of her own.

'It's after six,' said Dixie, 'let's move.'

Observed only by a pair of cudding cows, it took an hour to prepare the devices on the road below. Then they divided, Feeley to take Dixie into town on the motorbike, Annie and Michael to hide until their return.

As the motorbike's roar receded, Annie and Michael retired among the ruins. Checking the workings of his scarred and dated Bren gun, Michael threw hesitant glances at Annie, desiring her despite the awful itinerary of the morning. Annie had other thoughts.

'I wonder what they'll send?' She trained her field-glasses on the road below. 'Just think, they'll come into view with the sun in their eyes, roll past the first bomb and on towards the second, and just as they're well spread over the two devices, Dixie'll flick the switches . . .'

She stared fixedly at the deserted country road, thrilled and appalled, visualising soldiers rolling up the hill in armoured vehicles, breathing, joking, their brief lives ticking away

12

unannounced, ticking towards a point in time picked by an unseen enemy. Closing her eyes she tried to preview the explosions, the human debris, but her vivid imagination resisted, and all she could picture was a scene from the kind of action movies her father liked.

Looking round she studied her restless comrade, the lover in whom she'd lost interest, a simple man, big in brawn and heart, his physical presence belied by the nervous eyes of a doe.

'What was it like, Michael, the time you saw soldiers blown up?'

Avoiding her gaze. 'I never looked.'

'It's one thing,' said Annie, 'bringing down a man cleanly with a bullet . . .' Gripping him by the shoulder, she forced her wide hazel eyes on him. 'Did you know, if you're atomised by a bomb there's nothing left, not even ashes to bury?'

Mesmerised: 'For Christ's sake, Annie . . .'

She moved suddenly, snatching up her Armalite, tossing the lightweight rifle deftly into the air and catching it to her shoulder. Leaning against the stone frame of the window she took casual aim down the long grassy slopes to the road below.

'Wouldn't it be grand to take on the Brits in the old style, a guerilla army once more, raids, sniping and sabotage, blowing bridges and barracks to bits, but not men!'

'And getting ourselves wiped out.'

'Balls! We'd surprise them, outshoot them.'

Releasing the safety-catch on the Armalite, she got behind the sights, focusing, taking aim at a particular point on the road below.

'Annie? What are you doing?'

'Wouldn't you rather die brilliantly – ?'

'Annie!' Michael rose in alarm. If he wasn't mistaken, she was taking aim at the fertiliser bags, packed with explosives, stacked against the drystone wall which ran with the road. Reaching for the rifle, he slapped the barrel, trapping it on the windowsill. 'What the hell are you doing?'

She gave him a sidelong look, a provocative smile.

'Trying to imagine what it'll look like, young men blown all over this hill.'

'Brits!' he reminded her.

'Men.'

'Brits!' he insisted, towering over her, sweat breaking out on his boyish face. 'Brits hanging on to this island like the last colony on earth, Brits who've kept us at heel for as long as anyone can

13

remember, shot our people in the back and kicked my dog to death . . .!'

His face was livid, but his voice rang hollow. It was three years since he had been assaulted, his van demolished, his dog killed. It was getting harder to keep up the hate. Other feelings increasingly consumed him, softening him with longing.

'If you don't like bombs, why did you join?'

Reaching with one hand she touched his face, caressing his cheek with a tenderness which stilled him, and with a look of regret which sent a shiver through him.

'To deliver my country from the British,' she replied, 'and to unite it.'

'Then stop fussing about bombs.'

Thrusting her hands in her pockets she spoke sharply.

'So you can blow men all over this hill this morning and sleep OK tonight?'

'Sure!' he said too vehemently. 'Anyway, what choice do we have? We're under orders.'

A smile spread over Annie's face, and she threw back her head and laughed.

'What's so funny?' he flushed.

She stumbled out into the sunlight laughing and he pursued her angrily. 'I said what's so effing funny?'

She'd ceased laughing, that faraway look in her eye. He felt humiliated; women hurt him so easily. Jibes from Feeley were bearable, but from Annie . . . He hated her in that moment. Sometimes he even found her ugly, hair too red, wild and tangled, mouth too full, nose too prominent, limbs too long. But now, standing tall and straight with the sun in her hair and a secret smile on her lips, she was incomparable.

'Don't you ever want to get married and have children?'

She wasn't surprised by his question. 'I want lots of children.'

'Then you shouldn't be mixed up in this – '

The sound of a vehicle arrested them. Scurrying into the ruins they watched a tractor materialise from the direction from which the enemy was expected to come, a young farmer at the wheel, two children riding a trailer stacked with turf. Climbing past the fertiliser bags concealed behind the wall, the party laboured forty yards to reach the second device hidden beneath the road, rolled safely over it and rumbled out of sight.

Before Michael could let out a sigh, Annie had hold of him, ferociously kissing him, her mouth assaulting his, her hands in his hair, drawing him down over her. Just as his spirits were soaring and his desire swelling, he heard her voice hoarsely whispering in his ear.

'I thought you were under orders, Michael O'Cinneíde.'

His lips slid off her neck. She fell back laughing.

'Whiskey on your breath,' she chastised with mock intensity, 'sex with a comrade, what's Dixie's rule? No sex or drink before an op!'

'Ach, Annie . . .' he groaned.

She began to rise, he caught her by the wrist.

'It's not too late,' he implored.

She cocked a reproving eyebrow, but he wasn't to be put off.

'You're only twenty-one, your whole life's ahead, you've not been identified yet, you could pull out, say you can't handle the bombs, Dixie might let you, he might let me – '

'What! Speak for yourself. I'm happy in this outfit. I knew what I was getting into.' It was Annie's turn to speak too vehemently, covering her doubts.

Resuming her post at the window, she trained field-glasses across the hill towards the vast lough and distant sea. He too took up field-glasses but couldn't concentrate.

'I fancy a small farm away from here' – he tried to put a lightness into his voice – 'And a big family . . .'

'This is the life!' she countered, slowly sweeping the view. 'When I first ran away, I worked for a company selling advertising space and nearly died of boredom. Then in the drama school in London they tried to beat the spirit out of me, rebuild me in their own image and roll me out on an assembly line . . .' She gazed through the window into the middle distance. 'All my life they've tried to break me, control me, mould me to fit – parents, teachers, society.'

'I wouldn't do that,' he promised.

'Everybody tries, Michael. They can't bear you to be free.' She fixed him with a steady gaze. 'But I'm nobody's clay, I'm my own artist. No one rules me – least of all Dixie Doyle.'

Shaking his head: 'Dangerous talk, Annie, joining the IRA and turning against it.'

'Changing it,' she corrected.

He started to laugh, but the calm conviction on her face stopped him. Still, he sought a rare opportunity to mock her.

'So! Annie McBride's going to reform the Provos!'

'Transform,' she said calmly, and, finding a fresh vantage point, moved in behind her field-glasses.

Serious again: 'That the real reason you joined?'

'And to prove myself.'

'To who?'

To my mother and father, she thought, teachers, friends, enemies and most of all, 'To me.'

A Pig is a low hunched vehicle with an elongated snout, designed to move soldiers in cramped safety and minimum comfort inside its steel-reinforced shell.

A convoy of Pigs left base at six forty-five that morning, rumbling through the predominantly Protestant district of Waterside on the east side of Derry city, where kerbs painted red-white-and-blue proclaimed allegiance to Britain, and walls uttered unshakeable slogans – UNITED IRELAND IS PURE POPOCRISY – UNITE FOR GOD, QUEEN AND ULSTER – FUCK THE IRA.

Marcus King and Charlie Winters sat squashed on the petrol tank which served as a front seat in the leading Pig. Marcus was savouring a letter: Take care, honey. No heroics, I *know* you! Jamie misses you. So does his mother! Counting the days till your next leave. Love you, Marcia.

'I say, Marcus,' interrupted Winters, 'can't we open the visor? It's like a bloody sauna in here!'

Marcus replied, 'Confucius say – Visor shut; bullet foiled!'

'To hell with Confucius, I'd rather risk the bullet, old man!'

Marcus turned to the hushed throng behind. 'What about it, boys – sauna or suicide?'

'SUICIDE!'

'Fine!'

The driver thrust open the narrow hatch; a slit of cool Atlantic breeze flushed their faces.

'Glorious!' inhaled Winters, his voice hollow in the intensified silence brought on by the drumming of the bridge beneath them. They were crossing the Foyle to the mainly Catholic west side of the city. Craning forward, Charlie Winters peered across at the Nationalist strongholds of Bogside, Creggan and Brandywell, climbing in tiers to form a mountainous roofscape against the stark hills of Donegal.

Winters gaped. 'Good Lord! Isn't that an illegal Irish flag?'

Marcus squinted. A distant tricolour fluttered defiantly.

'Yep, in the Bogside cemetery.'

'Bloody cheek!' laughed Winters. Then for Marcus's ears only, 'You'd think this was Ireland!'

The river behind them, the Pigs throttled into low gear and climbed through the early traffic, ignored by the populace, finally drawing up in defensive formation beneath the seventeenth-century walls of the old city, where Marcus drew Winters' attention to a spectacular strip of graffiti: GOD MADE THE CATHOLICS, BUT THE ARMALITE MADE THEM EQUAL!

Marcus stepped into the road, sniffing the air for danger. Overhead blustered an all-seeing helicopter. Ahead lay the harsh broken lines of the Bogside, row after row of time-worn, tightly terraced streets steeply climbing, pressed from below by graceless modern flats, relieved by patches of green.

'So that's it,' said Charlie Winters at his shoulder, betraying a rush of nerves.

'They're just people, Charlie.'

'But why do they have to hate us so much?'

Marcus turned to the Pigs. 'De-bus!'

Troops spilled rubber-soled into the morning, forming four-man patrols known as 'bricks'.

'They welcomed us in '69,' said Marcus, 'when we protected them against the excesses of the RUC and Loyalists.'

'So what changed it?'

'Internment.' Marcus scanned the faces of the young soldiers, selecting a brick to lead.

'To be honest,' confessed Winters, 'I mean . . . why did they make such a fuss about internment?'

Marcus glanced at him, surprised. 'Dawn raids, hundreds of men carried off to prison camps. One minute we're drinking tea with the locals, the next we're kicking down their doors and dragging off their sons and husbands.'

Winters rallied. 'Catching terrorists, surely?'

'Some were IRA, others soon queued up to join.'

'Aha! I'm beginning to see how your mind works.'

Marcus tapped his temple. 'It's simple, Charlie. The Irish are like

17

the Caribbeans – laid back. Until you provoke them. Then they get ugly.'

Hands on hips, towering over the company, Marcus scanned the approaches once more with the air of an animal responsible for his herd. Then he gave the word, and patrols dispersed into the Bogside. Marcus quickly introduced his brick to Captain Winters. Aged eighteen or twenty, all three downtrodden privates were well known to Marcus.

Robbie McLaren was conspicuous less for his lankiness and sharp Glaswegian accent than for holding radical views, for which he was dubbed Red Mac.

Terry Noble, tough, overtly racist and easily distinguishable by his close-shaven head, was known as Bones for the bold skull-and-crossbones tattooed on his forearm.

David Rice, normally cheerful and chirpy, had lately suffered a crisis of nerves. Known as Spiky for the natural bias of his straw-blond hair, he pined for home and Lancashire.

They greeted Captain Winters without enthusiasm. Mumbling 'snotty-nosed spunk-bubble', Bones looked away in disgust. Marcus shot him a warning look and led the tense party into the Bogside.

A bricked-up street glistened with broken glass. Dogs barked, cats crawled to safety, little else but rolling litter stirred. Marcus's eyes roamed, hunting for signs of the sniper – a gaping air vent, a dislodged tile, a roof jacked up an inch, the street that's too quiet.

He was restless, even as he eased along with his deceptive loose-hipped gait. He hungered for an arms find or a lead on one of the few Provo leaders still alive and at large – like Dixie Doyle – and to show it could be done with tact and cunning instead of needless force. He longed to return to base with a fistful of vital information to slap on Major Draycott's desk.

To reduce the threat he posed he carried his rifle somewhat recklessly over his shoulder, as he led the way up one pavement, Robbie McLaren up the other. Behind came Charlie Winters and Spiky. Bones took up the rear, walking backwards in the role of tail-end Charlie, a scowl on his hard young face, fingers feverish in the trigger guard of his self-loading rifle.

They forged deeper into the urban warren, where pillar boxes and lamp-posts were painted in the colours of Eire – green for the Irish, white for peace, orange for Protestants – and where gable ends boldly declaimed: YOU ARE NOW IN FREE DERRY – UP THE PROVOS – INFORMERS WILL BE SHOT.

Beneath a life-sized mural of a monstrous British soldier was the maxim: THE ONLY GOOD SQUADDIE IS A DEAD ONE.

As though to stress the point, a solitary bin-lid began hammering a warning on a distant pavement. The thunder spread, drumming a grim tattoo through the terraced maze – The Brits are coming . . . the Brits are coming . . .

'What d'you think of Derry, sir?' enquired Robbie McLaren pleasantly.

'Not exactly Mayfair!' Charlie Winters replied cheerfully.

'Not exactly surprising!' Discarding the mask of cordiality. 'Worst housing in Britain, poorest amenities, highest unemployment, the Catholics bearing the brunt and fuck all they can do because the border's fixed so the Prods have a majority till Domesday!'

Winters flushed: was that letting off steam or insubordination?

'Fucking Red!' cried Bones. 'Take no notice.'

McLaren pursued. 'And throwing more soldiers at the problem solves nothing.'

'Right!' rejoined Bones. 'They want to drop a bomb on this place!'

Marcus had stopped to question a passer-by he didn't recognise. After Marcus had released him, the man walked on a short way, turned, shouted, 'Murdering bastards!' and ran off.

'What was that about?' said Winters.

'He's from the Rossville Flats, over where the Paras shot dead thirteen rioters on Bloody Sunday.'

'Bit of a long memory, hasn't he?'

'Memories don't fade here, Charlie, they take root.'

As the drumming of unseen bin-lids swelled, the patrol took cover at a deserted junction, backs against brick walls, radio crackling on Bones's back. Through a lull in the din Marcus heard Spiky's teeth clacking. The youth looked deathly, his nerves close to disintegration. Edging closer, Marcus hissed under his breath, 'Contemplating your boots, soldier?'

'Sorry, sir.'

'You got Provos in there?'

'No, sir.'

'Our lives depend on each other.'

'Sir.' Glued to his cumbersome rifle, Spiky looked keenly, blindly about him, at the wretched sun-streaked streets and his cocky comrades, who made him feel a jinx.

Marcus softened. 'What scares you most?'

'I'm OK, Boss.'

'Dying?'

'Yes, sir.'

'Being dead, or the business of dying?'

Baffled, the boy shrugged. 'I don't want me mates to see.'

'What!' Turning Spiky's chin and looking him in the face. 'You think you're the only one?' Aloud now for all to hear. 'Christ, man, I shit myself every time I think of a bullet breaking my skin, or a booby-trap under my feet. Think I fancy returning to my woman with no legs and no balls? Everybody's shitting themselves all the time – right, Mac?'

'Right!'

'Right, Bones?'

'Bollocks! Spiky's a wanker!'

'And you're a liar,' said Marcus. 'Charlie, do captains shit themselves?'

'Well, I wouldn't put it quite like that, but yes!'

Laughter. The easing of tension. Good man, thought Marcus. 'Anyway, fear's good!' he asserted. 'Keeps us alive.' Squeezing Spiky's shoulder, 'You're all right.'

Advancing deeper into the labyrinth, they were spared the abuse hurled at other patrols. A child would fly round a corner, stone in hand. When he recognised Marcus, the raised hand would freeze in mid-air, the child meeting Marcus's look of mock outrage. They'd ceased trying to provoke him. Youths used to shout, Wrong country! You should be swinging through the jungle! But Marcus had first won a place in local mythology the day a youth lobbed a half can of beer from a roof on the Lone Moor Road. Switching grip on his rifle, Marcus – who enjoyed his cricket – leaned onto his back foot and hit the can for a modest six into the Celtic Park.

It was seven forty-five when they started up an incline of time-scarred terraces. A big heavy-breasted woman ceased beating her bin-lid when she recognised the patrol leader.

'Take your undies off the line, girls!' she hollered. 'It's mighty Marcus and his merry men!'

Women appeared in doorways, closed faces breaking into smiles. Marcus recalled his first encounter with Big Martha. Still smarting from the indignities meted out by the previous regiment, she'd sent her children out bearing sandwiches laced with glass, and tea spiced with urine.

'How you doing, Martha? Miss me?'

'Like a hole in the head!'

A mongrel squeezed between her legs and flew at Charlie Winters' leggings.

'Come here, you bloody mad beast,' she cried. 'I said Lieutenant King – not him!'

'Thank you, sister!' laughed Marcus. Then he turned with a generous gesture to his new blond comrade. 'Allow me, Martha, to present Captain Charles Winter! He's been dying to meet you, right, Charlie?'

'Oh absolutely . . .'

'Charles, eh?' cooed Martha, pretending to tidy her unkempt hair. 'To be sure, he leaves the rest of you on the seconds rail!'

Women leaned in doorways, arms folded, enjoying the diversion. The air was bright with summer and smiling soldiers. Where was the war gone? Some boys had allowed their ball to roll down the slope. As predicted, Marcus gathered it in his feet and deftly flicked it back and forth, toying with it as though it were an extension of his boots, chatting with Martha as the boys tried in vain to retrieve the ball, exchanging banter about kids and marriage in Derry and North London – and then, without warning, 'Martha, got anything for me on Dixie Doyle?'

Silence. The air fell still.

'Before the whole place gets torn apart looking for him . . .'

Martha herded her children indoors and closed the door. Closing doors accompanied the brick all the way up the street.

'Bit of a waste of time that, wasn't it?' said Winters at the next corner.

Marcus shook his head. 'More and more Provos are turning informer, and more and more ordinary people are using the RUC's confidential phone line to give information. They're sick of it all. If we only played it cool . . .'

His attention was drawn to a woman shepherding her children from a house. Leaving his men he went after her. She turned, clutching her brood, fear and rage in her face . . . then recognised him.

21

'What's up, Roisin?'

She was Marcia's age, twenty-eight, but life had manhandled her too roughly and she looked forty – anaemic, bleached and etched with tension. For reply she dropped her case and lifted her jumper to reveal burns around her navel.

'Do you use your wife as an ashtray?'

A girl approached, Roisin's little sister Bernadette, a dark pretty sixteen-year-old, bejeaned, waspish and punky, a ferocious street-fighter.

'Thanks, Bernie,' said Roisin, leaving the children and walking off in the direction of the women's shelter.

'Mind if I talk to him?' called Marcus.

'Kill him, for all I care!'

Bernie gathered her nephews and nieces. 'Let's go before that big black bastard kidnaps you.'

'Haven't you forgotten something?'

Bernie turned. Marcus was holding up the cigarettes which had fallen from her back pocket. He made no move towards her. She had to come, taking two impatient steps, and would have snatched the packet from his hand had her eyes not been arrested by the pistol in his belt. She stood still, close to him, her fierce eyes swimming with tranquillisers, shifting from the gun to his face and back again. He watched her, hand on hips. She scratched her head, read the look in his eyes and reached slowly for the gun, her fingers feeling the cold metal, caressing the butt . . .

'Marcus, what the hell – ' Charlie Winters' voice broke the stillness.

'Your cigarettes,' Marcus reminded her. His hand covered hers. She recoiled, snatching her hand away.

Grabbing the cigarette packet, Bernie called him a fucking black bastard and strode off head high with her nieces and nephews.

Beckoning Bones, Marcus retraced his steps to Roisin's house. The hard-skulled youth crossed the road.

'Got a cigarette?' said Marcus.

Bones conjured a cigarette from his sleeve, flicked it over into Marcus's palm. Knocking on Roisin's door, Marcus asked for a light. Bones lit the cigarette without expression. The door opened, a man withdrew. Marcus followed him into the cramped living-room. Roisin's husband had resumed his seat on the sofa, head in hands.

'What happened this time?'

'Lost me temper.'

'That all, shithead?'

The man turned his head, eyes mad, fists clenched, and saw the lighted cigarette Marcus was holding up like an incriminating exhibit. The man subsided, red-eyed, unshaven.

'She's never coming back,' he said.

'You blame her?'

The man tore at his hair.

'Stop feeling sorry for yourself and do something.'

'It's all over.' Fumbling for his cigarettes he found the packet empty, screwed it up and hurled it into the empty grate.

Marcus handed him the burning cigarette. The man looked up, met his eye. A former volunteer accepting a smoke from a Brit officer. Why not? He took it and dragged on it greedily.

'What can I do?'

'Go round and see her. Leave the hammer behind this time, and swear on your life it won't happen again . . . and mean it. You're a good man sober, a bastard drunk.'

The man began to rise. 'Better clean myself up – '

'Christ, man . . .' stilling him with a firm hand, 'give the woman a few hours' break!'

Marcus turned at the door. The man was staring into the grate, smoking.

'Seen anything of Dixie?'

The man froze. He'd done five years behind the wire on suspicion of handling firearms. He didn't look round.

'You know I don't go near that crowd any more.'

'Kevin?' Now he looked round. 'I want him. If you hear anything, however small . . .'

Marcus held his gaze until he nodded.

The rising clamour of bin-lids reached Dixie and Feeley, making them pull over. Cursing, Dixie slid off the back of the motorbike and snatched a brown paper parcel from a saddle bag.

'I'll leg it. Lie low and get me in an hour.'

'Leave it this time!' begged Feeley jealously. 'It's too risky.'

He didn't need reminding how dangerous it was to visit his home. Nor were Feeley's motives pure.

'For pity's sake!'

But he was gone, scurrying down streets and entries he knew blind . . . until, minutes from home, he spotted a patrol down the end of a terrace. Almost at once a parallel patrol appeared at the opposite end. No problem – long as there wasn't . . .

A third patrol turned the corner dead ahead and started towards him. Ducking into a back lane, he squeezed into the dark shell of a gutted house. Gaps in boards emitted fingers of light, playing on something bright in the corner, a stack of crates containing – he took a closer look – Irish whiskey.

The muted tread of soldiers drew him back to the loosened boards. Armed only with the parcel under his arm, he pressed his eye to a gap and watched fascinated as the first Brit, tall and black – Marcus King! – passed close enough to him to have plucked the beret from his head.

'Freeze!' hissed Marcus.

Dixie froze. Then he realised King was addressing his own men. Suddenly, on a signal from the black Brit, the soldiers vanished over a wall.

Almost at once the inspiration for their move became apparent, the strident roar of engines announcing the arrival of a motorbike gang, pulling up with a flourish in line with Dixie's eye. As the youths dismounted and pressed towards him, he began an urgent search for a hideout within his hideout. Hands came through the boards, parting them; light and voices crowded in. From a charred beam he listened to the animated debate below. How many bottles fit in a saddlebag? How many trips would they need before the Brits arrived . . .

'FREEZE . . . BRITISH ARMY . . . ANYONE MOVES GETS IT!'

Pistol drawn, Marcus King filled the rift of daylight, ducked inside the house and herded the youths against a wall with the help of a tall blond officer.

Marcus took in the crates of whiskey and the mean lean faces of the gang. These were hoods, opportunists whose hatred of the RUC and the Army was eclipsed by their loathing of the IRA. Marcus singled out the raw-boned leader, whom the IRA had previously tarred and feathered for muggings, and kneecapped for informing.

'What do you say, Captain?' Marcus addressed Charlie Winters without a glance, 'Hand them over to the cops, or lock them in here till the Provos find them?'

The youths blanched; the leader nodded towards the whiskey. 'Don't you bastards drink?'

'At this time of the morning?'

'Take it. We never saw a thing.'

'Bribing an officer in Her Majesty's armed forces, Martin?'

The youth seemed stunned by his own name.

'Got nothing better for me?' Marcus cocked an eye.

'Like what?'

'Doyle.'

The youth considered, juggling fates. 'What's in it for us?'

'Tea with the Queen. Talk!'

Still the young man hesitated.

'We're wasting time,' Marcus told Winters. 'Let's go.'

'He's in town.'

'Where, what for, who with?'

'We just seen him and a woman going down Cable Street on a clapped-out Norton.'

Marcus blinked. Then unfolded a map.

'Can we go?' demanded the youth. Marcus nodded, absorbed in the map. The gang moved in a body and Marcus came to life, spreading himself across the exit. 'Before you go – '

'Bastard! You said – '

Marcus moved suddenly. The gang fell back and Marcus eyed Martin with menace, aiming a cocked finger like a loaded firearm. 'A gang broke into old Mrs Rooney's the other night and swiped her savings – '

'Wasn't us!'

'Could have been – '

'Fucking wasn't, right!'

'I'm watching you, Martin' – half smiling, stepping aside to let them pass – 'all of you.'

The uproar of motorbikes receded. Craning from his perch, Dixie caught snatches of Marcus King radioing Base, enough to make him scuttle away as soon as the Brits were gone, sprinting down alleys, straining lungs scarred from childhood.

He knew he didn't have long, and that now it was crazier than ever to go home. But, breathless, he reached his street and caught himself against a wall.

The odd parked car spoiled the line of the sun-drenched street.

In rain-washed potholes children played, dogs drank, a helicopter reflected incessantly. Roused by the approaching patrols the street was a hive of activity, knots of women squatting over bin-lids, shouting at children to stay close, collective rage spilling over into laughter.

'It's Ragdoll Doyle!' called a child.

A chill entered the street. The protector, the ill wind of disaster, was back. The hush pursued him to his house at the end of the street, its façade marked in a vicious graph by Loyalist bullets, ground floor windows permanently boarded. Hammering on the steel-reinforced door, he looked warily left and right, and met the eye of a pack of children come to stare unlovingly at the hero. He hammered again. Where was she? Dead? Departed? His heart pounded, he began to gasp for air. He heard the quick drawing of bolts and the door gave.

He flinched, reeling inwardly from the shock of imaginary bullets, a Loyalist trap, an RUC welcoming party, an Army surprise . . .

Mary! Dragging him inside she bolted the door. For a moment they fumbled, strangers, before painfully embracing, the pain of long separations, daily anxiety – sometimes blind panic over the safety of the other.

She broke free. She had to protect herself. Dabbing tears from the corners of her eyes, she flashed him a smile and led him by the hand. He savoured the feel of it.

'Did you think I'd come?'

'Never occurred to me! But your breakfast's on.'

He seized her in his arms and hugged her. She let him, but didn't respond.

Something bothered him, as his lips brushed the corner of her mouth. She smelled of drink.

'Will I get you some tea?'

Or was he imagining it, he wondered, watching her exit to the kitchen. She looked nice, too thin, but she'd put on a dress and touched up her face and washed her cropped hair. She also looked hollow-eyed, darkly shadowed. He trembled.

'Where's little one?' he called.

'Just coming.' He heard her telling Josie to finish up and go see Daddy, and then break off into a fit of coughing.

Something else which had bothered him now made him turn to

26

the suitcase lying open on the sofa, half packed. Heart quickening again, he took in the sad details of the room, the shabby furniture, carpets worn here and there to bare boards, the walls neatly and cheaply papered by Mary, finger-soiled by Josie. His water-colours, Magilligan prison camp in stark relief against a moonlit sea; the up-reaching hands of a prisoner clasping the snow-encrusted wire of Long Kesh. The pictures called for spotlights, he thought. As it was, the room without daylight was dreamlike, a bare electric bulb spreading its thin hopeless light. And with only the upstairs windows for air the place was stale with the smell of cigarettes, airfreshener and human stress.

'Taking a holiday?' he called. No reply. He listened to their voices in the kitchen, his wife and child, his chosen partner and the wretched fruit of their union. He listened to the rising tide of bin-lids, aware that any moment Marcus King could burst in with a horde of Brits. And it'd be over, no mercy, a collection of life sentences. He knew he was playing with fire, but he couldn't bring himself to leave, not yet, not till he'd put his proposal to Mary.

Still he shuddered at the memory of the first time they took him, the dreaded 9 August '71 – internment! police and soldiers rampaging through the night, terrorising the ghetto with echoes of the Third Reich or Latin America. Worse came two years later. Sounds and images flooded back, soldiers stampeding up the stairs at four in the morning, tearing him naked out of bed, Mary clinging to him, soldiers laughing at her bare bulging belly, as one of them broke her grip, knocking her flying into the dressing-table, where she went down in a landslide of cheap cosmetics. *She's pregnant, you bastards!* he could still hear himself screaming as they dragged him into the night.

Josie entered just then, clutching her favourite jigsaw piece and teetering alarmingly. It was her ninth birthday, but she was like an ageless gnome. She wasn't the mongol some called her, and only slightly handicapped physically . . . but oh, that strange little mind.

Mary handed him a mug of tea. 'Your breakfast's nearly done.'

'Leave it. The Brits are looking for me.'

Mary's eyes fell. She bit her lip and went out to switch off the gas.

'Hello there, sweetheart.' Dixie approached his daughter opti-mistically. 'And how's my birthday ragdoll?' She watched him

27

with her green unfathomable eyes. On his knees he kissed her damp forehead and offered the parcel. 'What's your da brought for you?' Her eyes wouldn't leave his face. He began peeling the parcel, brown paper yielding to pink tissue. Her eyes shifted to see what would emerge. A furry limb.

Her grip tightened on the jigsaw piece, eyes drawn irresistibly to the thing emerging from the folds of pink.

'Take it, sweetheart, it's yours.'

Puckering up her face she focused stonily on the floor.

'It's a koala, ko-a-la, and it wants to be your friend . . .'

Sensing her, he looked up to see Mary leaning in the doorway, arms folded, smoking a cigarette, watching. She smiled at him, a warm, bitter, regretful smile.

He tried pressing the toy into Josie's arms, but she broke free and wobbled to her mother, burying her face in Mary's groin.

Rising, he said. 'How is she?'

Mary's easy shrug meant: much the same. 'A back-firing car doesn't bother her, but she screams blue murder if I don't let her sleep with that jigsaw piece. Isn't that right, darl– '

Her chest erupted suddenly and she turned away to cough into a stained handkerchief. Dixie shuddered, felt sweat break out cold down his body.

'She's grand one minute,' she resumed, absently stroking Josie's head, 'then she's smearing her shit over the walls and calling you to come and see! Good wee girl! Budding Republican practising for the women's dirty protest!'

Dixie laughed weakly, watched Josie cross the room and climb purposefully into her high chair, where she began to rock backwards and forwards, tapping the wall with the back of her head.

'You got to go to the doctor's, Mary.'

An ironic laugh. 'Uppers for me, downers for Josie. We're a pair of zombies! I'm through with doctors. So I tried going to Mass again . . .'

'Oh, Jaysus!'

'. . . asked Father O'Driscoll why God was giving me such a hard time. I should be grateful, he says, Josie's a gift from God. I said it'd be easier if my husband was home. Why don't you come home?'

Their eyes locked. Out in the street a motorbike sounded its hooter – Feeley come for him. Already? Over in the corner Josie was working herself into a mesmeric rhythm, rocking back and forth, knocking her head against the wall – thud, thud, thud. And the bin-lids were drumming closer.

Dixie said, 'Mary . . .'

'What?'

'Let's try once more.'

'Oh, Dixie . . .' she sighed, as though it was that easy.

'I don't mean we'd love Josie any less . . . Is the back door locked?' The alertness of a hunted animal.

'Yes. Will I open it for you?'

'Wait!' He went to her, took her by the shoulders. 'Our first kid stillborn; Josie . . .' he fumbled for the right word, 'imperfect; third time lucky!'

Thud . . . thud . . . thud . . . Josie getting louder.

'We're getting out, me and Josie.'

'Sure, you need a break.'

'For good. To my sister in Dublin. I've had it, Dixie.'

He was panting for air now. 'I'll get you more protection.'

She laughed indulgently. In her eyes he could see that she still loved him, despite everything, still found him attractive. He drew her to him, her thin body against his, ran his hands through her cropped hair and touched her mouth with his. Her eyes were bloodshot, her breath stale, and as she turned away to cough, he felt the core of his life disintegrating.

Recovering, she said, 'Go now, quick, before they come. Pack in the killing and come to Dublin. Josie needs a da, I want my husband back.'

Thud . . . thud . . . thud . . . Josie making the window rattle. Dixie spun round: 'Josie, for Christ's sake!' He could witness the disembowelled death-agony of a British soldier, but he couldn't stand another minute of Josie head-banging that wall.

In the street Feeley was hooting insistently.

'Then we'll try for another?' said Dixie, animated.

'Come to Dublin. Show us you can be a father to Josie before you try fathering another. Come on, for fuck sake . . .'

Taking him by the arm, she led him to the door. He said, 'Don't go till I send you the fare, OK?'

Unbolting the door: 'OK. And you'll follow?'

'Sure . . .' He stepped outside, the street was thick with drifting smoke, an overturned car was blazing at one end and unseen soldiers were loosing baton rounds at stone-throwers.

'For pity's sake, Dixie!' Feeley yelled, revving the motorbike, looking vitriolically at Mary in the doorway.

'When?' cried Mary. 'When?'

Running for the bike: 'Soon as I can!' Spinning round, he cried 'Kiss Josie for me!' and vaulted onto the back of the bike.

'We're fucking done for, you eejit!' said Feeley, pointing out Army vehicles sealing both ends of the street. They looked both ways – trapped.

'Get back in here!' cried Mary.

Dixie looked at her, saw the horror in her face and forgot his fear. He was on the point of going to her, resigning himself to his fate, when Feeley's attention was drawn to a woman gesticulating from her threshold across the street. The front door was thrown wide and the woman was making traffic signals, waving the way through her house.

'Hang on!' Feeley yelled. The bike leapt forward, Dixie barely held on, the open doorway beckoning.

Moments later, Marcus King led his men into the lane behind Dixie's house. He was seething.

'All we had to do,' he told Charlie Winters, 'was move in quickly but casually, just us. But Major Draycott has to mount a Falklands campaign, alerting the whole neighbourhood!'

'Doyle may not even be in there,' said Winters tactfully.

Just then the Doyles' back gate flew open and a woman emerged breathless carrying a heavy child.

'Morning, Mrs Doyle,' said Marcus, as if bumping into a neighbour at home.

She backed against the wall, covering her child's head.

'Your husband home, mam?'

Mary looked the big black soldier straight in the eye. 'Yes, and he's unarmed!'

Special Branch arrived to take Mary in for a familiar ordeal of questioning. The Army laid siege to the empty house.

Two miles north of the city, a motorbike pulled up at a phone booth. While Feeley placed an urgent call on one of the RUC's confidential lines, Dixie sat stunned on the bike, immobilised by shame and rage, fingering the collection of tiny ragdolls he kept in his jacket pocket. Mary was asking him to give up the killing for her sake and Josie's, when it was for their sakes he was doing it.

He was shocked by Mary's drinking and smoking, the deterioration in her face, ashamed of himself for not rescuing her and Josie from those wretched conditions, consumed with hate for all his enemies – Loyalists and the RUC who'd met his people's call for civil rights with batons and bullets, and most of all the British soldiers whom he believed caused Mary first to miscarry and then to produce feeble-minded Josie.

God willing, today they'd pay.

And yet, as he closed his eyes and drank in the anticipation of revenge, he couldn't escape Mary's words. Why don't you come home? A father to Josie, a husband to Mary, only then would she consider another kid. Twelve years of imprisonment, hiding and fighting. What had it all been for, if he was to jack it in now? And yet, the thought of sinking into the bosom of the family . . .

Dublin called, a warm bed at night, a family, freedom to walk the streets, drop in to any bar. A terrible weariness washed over him.

Feeley returned, scarcely able to control her excitement. Dixie shook himself. Today wasn't for thinking – it was 5 July, festival of death.

08.00 Hours: Battalion Commander, Lieutenant-Colonel Gerald Stanley-Taylor moved smartly to the wall and stabbed the map with a miniature skull-and-crossbones, pinpointing a safe house by Thorn Hill north of the city. According to the tip-off this was Dixie Doyle's lair. The call to the RUC could have been a hoax or a trap. But that was for the men on the ground to worry about.

Swift response was required. Dispatch nearest available unit – by all accounts 'C' Company. . .

He turned to his ops officer. 'How quickly can we get this off the ground?'

'Twenty minutes, sir.'

'Make it ten.'

Death waited in gently sloping hills facing the sea. Dixie and Michael occupied the derelict farm overlooking the quiet road below where the security forces were expected to arrive. Over to the left Feeley lay in a cleft of rock hugging her Armalite, deadly weapon for a deadly sniper.

Over to the right her rival reclined in a hollow – Annie McBride, her back smooth against a spine of bleached rock, bare ankles brushed by maidenhead fern and mountain avens, flaming hair crushed by a brown beret.

By her side lay her Armalite. Fitted with telescopic sight, this lightweight collapsible gun was the Provos' first-choice rifle, relied on by the Americans in Vietnam, coveted by the British in Ulster. A supply of small-calibre high-velocity .233 rounds rested on a shelf of rock by her left hand. From her neck hung a fitting charm – a small silver Armalite.

Annie was a hive of nerves on this her big day, her début, her opening night. Not target practice this time, but breathing soldiers, young men from across the water, men she may have brushed past when she lived in London, men who shared with her a common language, who inhabited as she did a human body, fragile and flammable as a plastic cup. This was her first test. Would she live up to the effusive commendations of her tutors – the most promising raw material any secret training camp had turned out in years? Today was her opportunity to prove herself in the live theatre of war and, lying in her rocky niche, Armalite patient at her knee, she felt supremely confident – I can outshoot anyone – and all atremble, breathless with anxiety in case she froze on the trigger.

It was so still and quiet for miles around that Annie was able to follow a pair of local residents through her field-glasses – dusky-brown mountain hares, their blue-tinged summer coats flashing in the sun. Childhood called her back for a moment, hunting with her American father, to whom killing was an act of mercy, death mere deliverance from life. At the age of seven she'd shot her first rabbit with a customised rifle – delivered it, as her father put it. Today it would be men she delivered, not rabbits.

From an outhouse amongst the ruins of the farm, Dixie and Michael trained field-glasses on the death trap below. The little-used road was quiet, climbing through tranquil countryside. On the near side of the road huddled the fertiliser bags packed with explosives, hidden from the road by the accompanying drystone wall.

A raven, tripping carefully along the uneven wall, hopped down onto the bags and began pecking at their covering of straw.

32

'If he keeps up,' Dixie muttered, 'he'll uncover them.'

'An undercover raven!' quipped Michael.

Losing interest, the raven flapped back onto the wall to survey the scene, leaving Dixie to pull the field-glasses forty yards left to where three loaded milk churns waited patiently in a culvert beneath the road. Designed for rain-water, the culvert would shortly be diverting soldiers' blood.

Electric cable from both bombs travelled up the hill to the outhouse, covered by stones and clods. Please God, mused Dixie, they don't send an airborne reaction force. Sophisticated equipment carried by helicopters could detect disturbed ground with infra-red eyes.

On the far side of the wall a pair of cows, knee-deep in corn-poppies and purple thistle, were drinking slowly from a trough in the field. Beyond, against the glittering waters of Lough Foyle, stood the whitewashed house named in the confidential call to the RUC. But would they take the call seriously enough to send the Army? The current trend was to scale down the Army's role, pushing the police into the front line. Dixie was counting on the lure and peril of his reputation to entice the Army into the hills.

Michael kept out of Dixie's way. His role would be to maximise the effect of the bombs with an accurate hail of Bren-gun fire. Like Annie he was afraid of failing, unlike her he was not a gifted guerilla and he knew it. He glanced at Dixie, who was strangely quiet. Something was wrong with Josie and Mary. His mood would be all the more terrible if Michael let him down.

'Dixie?'

'Mmm?'

'About the bombs . . .' He swallowed bravely, 'do we really need them to fight the war?'

Dixie slowly swivelled his head, fixing Michael with a searching eye. 'Who's been putting thoughts in your head, or need I ask?'

Michael lowered his eyes, Dixie unexpectedly smiled. 'You think too much. No good for you!' He patted Michael on the back, but was really addressing himself, trying to blot Mary and Josie from his mind long enough to concentrate. How were they? Had they been harassed today? Was it his fault? Would he see them once more before they tore up their roots and went south? Should he pack in the killing and join them?

'Fucking Jeesus!' he bellowed, thumping stone, echoes of anguish drifting across Thorn Hill.

Michael paled, his fingertips seeking comfort in crevices of cool stone. Along the ridge Feeley's and Annie's heads popped up like rabbits.

Dixie's face broke into a grin. 'You better go tell them everything's OK, I was just clearing my throat! And Michael,' Michael turned in the broken doorway, 'I've some news for you.'

'Good, I hope!'

'The safe house we were to use when we escape from here fell through.'

'That's bad.'

'We'll have to use your farm.'

Paling further, 'What about Molly?' – his adopted mother.

'She's a good Republican, I'm told, like her late husband, God rest him.'

'Jaysus, Dixie, I've never even told her . . . in so many words like . . .'

'That you're a terrorist?' Dixie laughed. 'About time she knew. It'll be her privilege to billet an Active Service Unit. We'll pay our board. Now go reassure the girls and get to your post . . . and Michael?'

Michael turned round again at the exit. 'What?'

'Good luck.'

'Thanks.'

Michael hurried away, sick with anxiety. Molly lived for him. Now he was going to ask her . . . *tell* her, she was putting up the most infamous outfit in Ulster. Unless . . . an appalling thought gave a glimmer of hope, Dixie and Feeley dying in the ambush, himself and Annie getting clean away.

While Michael set up his antiquated Bren gun, Dixie checked his watch – eight-fifteen. Another ten or fifteen minutes, he predicted.

Charlie Winters was in his element, windswept in the turret of a Fox armoured car. Leading the convoy over beautifully rugged country, eyes watering, blond hair sucked back, he was furious with Marcus King for trying to steal his glory.

Twenty yards behind came Marcus King's vehicle, trailed by an RUC Landrover. Marcus, trying to remain calm in the front passenger seat, was still shaking his head at Charlie Winters' behaviour, pulling rank when Marcus had pointed out the risks and said he should lead, not Charlie.

The Fox, rapid, compact, bristling with aerials, tore along the peaceful road, its single-cannon turret revolving slowly in pursuit of sheep, crows, imaginary terrorists . . . The radio operator standing beside Winters was motioning him to slip on a protective helmet, fitted with radio. Winters, transported by the open air, refused.

'We don't bother with them in my regiment, just give us a pair of Staff Users.'

Staff Users, earphones with boom microphone attached, enable crews to converse normally over the roar of engines.

'Sir. . .?' Urgency in the radio op's voice.

'Now what?'

'The boss is on the air, sir,'

Distracted, and unfamiliar with the call sign, Winters hadn't heard Marcus calling.

'Lieutenant King suggests we take to the fields and come at the house from the rear while the RUC cover the front.'

Dropping into the baking interior, Winters snatched the map.

'Bollocks, Doyle could have escaped by then. Let's go for it!'

The steel-green Fox hurtled on, Charlie Winters' head and shoulders jutting from the turret, so that all Marcus could see when the Fox dipped out of sight was Charlie's disembodied head floating in the haze.

'Hello Tango-Three-One,' Marcus radioed, 'this is Three-Zero-Alpha, what the fuck are you doing? Stop there, stop there, over!'

Winters' radio operator looked to him for confirmation, but the intoxicated Captain, unwilling to be upstaged, replied mischievously, 'Tango-Three-One, is there a problem, over?'

'Three-Zero-Alpha,' snapped Marcus, 'let me overtake, out!'

Charlie's grin died. 'Sod that.' Over the intercom he spoke to the driver. 'Give it a bit of welly to the next bend and then slow down.'

The Fox surged forward, veering across the Landrover's path. Robbie McLaren flinched at the wheel and looked askance at Marcus.

'Overtake!' said Marcus.

The young Scot blanched, the Landrover swerved, the ditch beckoned. McLaren pressed the accelerator to the floor and aimed for the fading gap between Fox and brink. The ditch loomed, tyres pulverised the shifting verge, rocks and clods flying into fields, Marcus's men clinging to precarious steel.

'As you were!' barked Marcus. 'Bloody fool!' he hissed at the receding head of Charlie Winters.

The Landrover fell back.

In the Fox, Charlie Winters glanced at the map and saw how close he was to Doyle's hideout.

'Christ, drop anchors!'

The hill steepened, the Fox throttled down and climbed gently. Through binoculars Winters picked out the whitewashed safe house away on the right, where Ragdoll Doyle was said to be hiding. Barely visible through scrub and copse, the cottage showed no sign of life. Swinging the glasses left, he scanned the abandoned farm high on the hill.

The road was deserted, slopes basking in sunlight. On the left ran a drystone wall, on the right a hedged field and two cows grazing by a trough.

Dixie watched fascinated from the ruins, awed by his luck. A creeping convoy comprising soldiers *and* police – perfect. To guard against his recalcitrant conscience, he reminded himself that these soldiers had occupied his country not to keep the peace, but to maintain an unjust status quo, and that they were responsible for Mary miscarrying, and then giving birth to a handicapped child, whom they delighted in calling Doyle's Idiot.

As for the RUC, who worked hand in glove with these bastards, he'd never forget how in the holding pen they had selected him for experimental torture, the five techniques of sensory deprivation. Hard men cracked, confessed to anything; sheep confessed to being wolves. Dixie, who was no lamb, confessed to nothing.

Nor were these ordinary police he was following below. By their paramilitary uniforms he knew they must be from the Mobile Support Unit, renowned for their gangster-style gunning down of suspects.

Dragging the field-glasses back to the Fox, he watched it climb carefully and draw level with the fertiliser bomb. Fingering the death-switch on the command wire, he let the Fox proceed unhindered towards the culvert bomb forty yards on. Keep going, keep going . . .

Annie McBride lay flush with the ground, pressed into moss and rock, face bathed in sweat, eye resting along the sleek barrel of the Armalite, suspended above the telescopic sights, waiting.

36

She watched the Fox and the dashing blond officer roll past the fertiliser bags, and tensed in anticipation of Dixie's hand. The Fox kept climbing, and the Army Landrover took its place, a black face in front, younger soldiers peering from the back, rifles cocked at the sun.

The Fox climbed gingerly, engine softly growling, closing the distance to the culvert, the Army Landrover suspended in no-man's-land between the bombs, and finally came the RUC Landrover approaching the fertiliser bags.

Dixie's hand trembled over the death-switch, the Fox fifteen yards to go – don't stop now; ten yards – keep going, the blond officer surveying the white cottage; five . . . four . . . three – Dixie's free hand made the sign of the cross – two . . . one . . . Now!

For a moment, nothing. Landscape unscathed, Fox rolling, clouds drifting, cows grazing, heart hammering . . .

Then a blinding flash abolished the landscape and the Fox leapt inside a forty-foot flame, accompanied by a thunderclap which shook the hillside. The Fox lived a moment in the flame, then dropped into a freshly dug crater. In the field a cow, opened up by flying metal, buckled and died. In the ditch lay the Fox's sole survivor, tossed away like litter.

Mesmerised behind the wheel of the Landrover, Robbie McLaren rolled on into the heat.

'OUT!' yelled Marcus, seizing him by a fistful of flak jacket and bundling him into the road, while Spiky and Bones tumbled out of the back as bullets from a distant Bren gun struck from the hill, ricocheting off the Landrover's armour plating. Screened by the vehicle and luck, Marcus's men flung themselves into the ditch.

The four RUC officers abandoned their vehicle, scattering for the nearest safety; one into the ditch, two behind the wall and one lying very still in the road.

High on the hill Black Rose smiled righteously, and proceeded to watch hawk-eyed for any attempts to rescue her victim.

Along the ridge Annie gazed at the awesome sight below, finger frozen on the trigger of her Armalite, paralysed. The Fox lay buried in the road, mangled and blazing. No one could have survived, save perhaps the blond officer, fired from the turret like a human missile.

Dixie's eyes bulged, reflecting the burning Fox, the bullet-ridden Landrover, the body in the road. Happy Birthday, Josie. To ice the cake he only needed the RUC marksmen sheltering behind the wall to move closer to the fertiliser bomb.

When Marcus and Spiky reached Charlie Winters along the bramble-choked ditch, they found him on fire, lacerated flak jacket spouting tiny flames, flayed flesh hissing, the reek of scorched skin filling the ditch. For a moment they gaped. Then Marcus exclaimed, 'Smother him with our combat jackets!' First ripping off their Velcro-bound flak jackets, they unzipped combat jackets and fell upon the burning man, stifling the flames, smothering them as they kept reappearing.

'The cow trough!' cried Marcus.

Seizing Charlie Winters, they hauled him from the ditch into the field through a breach in the hedge, their stumbling dash shrouded by billowing smoke. As they ran Winters constantly reignited, embers fanned by the breeze, strips of flesh and fabric fusing grotesquely to weave a hideous new coat on his back. He parted his lips to scream, but without voice. And as they lifted him over the trough, they gaped together at the appalling sight which met their eyes – his feet and ankles were gone.

Charlie Winters sank gratefully, turning water to wine.

A bullet cleared the air. Marcus and Spiky threw themselves flat. Without thinking, Marcus buried his face in cool clover, as though trying to purge himself of hideous images, or have them branded on his mind for ever. Rolling over, he found Spiky lying still – too still.

'Spiky!'

The boy's eyes flickered, glazed pupils swimming.

Slapping his face, 'Charlie'll drown!'

Surfacing behind the trough, they pounced, dragging the saturated body out of the water and into the grass. A brace of bullets whistled by, a sniper finding her range through drifting smoke. As though to prove it, another high-velocity bullet penetrated the trough inches from Marcus's head, sending a crude arc of stained water into the grass. Shielded by the trough they gathered Winters in their arms and hauled him back to where a shallow dip provided cover.

'Shit!' said Marcus. 'Field dressings and morphine, we left them in the fucking flak jackets.'

For want of anything better, they tore off their T-shirts to bind Charlie's guillotined ankles.

'Think we saved him?' croaked Spiky.

'Sure.' Marcus turned his attention to the hill, from where a Bren-gunner was mercilessly scything the road. 'I'll be back with the morphine,' he said, and sprinted for the road.

Rolling into the ditch he found his discarded flak jacket and dug out the supply of morphine and dressings. Then he scrambled along the ditch and came up beside ashen-faced Bones.

'Have you sent a Contact Report?'

'Done,' muttered the soldier through clenched teeth, 'the choppers are coming.'

'Good man. Have you told them . . .?' Marcus pointed to the RUC men sheltering down the road. Bones indicated that he had. 'Then send a Cas-Rep – two dead, one critical, burns, and any RUC, OK?' Patting Bones on the back, Marcus burrowed on in search of his other man. Robbie McLaren, grey with shock, was crouched deep in bramble, rifle slanted wishfully at the hill. Marcus crawled over and slipped an arm about his youthful shoulders. A volley of bullets winged overhead.

'Run these dressings over to Spiky and keep your head down. Get back on the double. I want covering fire from you and Bones when I start up that hill.'

The young soldier inhaled deeply. Nothing had prepared him for the magnitude of the explosion, for discernible scraps of human beings smouldering in the road, the drifting stench of death.

Fingering the second death-switch, Dixie watched the RUC men working their way along the wall, probing for firing positions. Two or three, he calculated, were drawing level with the fertiliser bomb. Hand shaking, he checked his watch. He couldn't wait any longer, the sands of luck were running out. Five . . . four . . . thr –

Something moved in the corner of his eye – a fleeting glimpse of a man, shirtless and black! – breaking across the road away on the left. He was about to warn Feeley when a volley of shots from the ditch flattened him, soldiers and RUC finding their feet, hitting back. Cursing viciously he flicked the switch.

His stomach contracted, bowels stiffened, his mind conjuring a blinding explosion. But the image expired and nothing had changed. He triggered once again, and though his imagination didn't fail, there was no splash of colour, no tongue of flame alive with members of the Royal Ulster Constabulary. For a moment he stared in disbelief.

39

Then he ran, ducking from the back of the hovel, yelling at his troops as he doubled through the ruins. The escape procedure was simple – Dixie and Feeley on the motorbike, Michael and Annie in the car, both parties taking separate routes to Michael's border farm.

Annie had the furthest to run, and should have been on her way, but only now did she snap out of her spell, struck by the realisation that the ambush was over, and that she desperately needed a hit to make up for her paralysis. Recalling her skills, she took a deep breath and taking careful aim fired a single shot at a distant soldier's head. At once she felt the jolt of contact, the marksman's thrill, the shock of empathy.

Pounding pistol-drawn up the hill, Marcus heard a motorbike ignite, and drove himself harder to cut off whoever was escaping. Cresting the hill he saw the bike in full flight, ridden by a woman trailing black hair and black skirt, converging with a man clearly set on leaping aboard. Marcus stopped dead and took aim like a straight-armed duellist of old. But before he could steady on the moving target, his eye was distracted by a threat from the side.

Annie paused in her flight, surprised to encounter a towering bare-breasted black man streaming over the hill, not immediately identifiable until he stopped suddenly to aim a gun at Black Rose, squinting sideways along his firing arm, free hand on hip, chest exposed, fifty yards away.

She aimed for something round his neck that shone and squeezed the trigger . . .

Despite the disruptive effect of her running, the bullet was faithful to its purpose, trajectory near perfect in the clear morning air, arriving almost as soon as it had departed, destined for the smooth hard cavity running in sweat down his chest, which would have taken the full impact had Marcus's instinct to survive, coupled with swift reflexes, not flung him to the ground the instant the rifle was fired, the bullet skimming his shoulder without marking him.

When he looked again, the gunwoman was gone, the motorbike receding, and a car was being started somewhere in the farm. Getting to his feet, he lifted the crucifix round his neck to his lips and then sprinted for the farm. Plunging through the ruins, he was just in time to glimpse the red-haired gunwoman disappearing into the shell of a gutted house, when he faltered at the approach of a welcome sound over his shoulder, shaving the hill at such terrifying speed that he scarcely had time to turn and see it before its slipstream sucked him off his feet and bowled him over.

He was getting to his feet for the second time as the small waspish helicopter banked sharply against the blue sky. At the same moment, he caught sight of a sky-blue Ford bursting from the gutted house, and was on the point of taking optimistic aim with his pistol when the helicopter returned, skimming the roofless houses, shrieking towards him so fast he barely reacted to the machine-gun in time, hurling himself sideways and rolling over and over as the earth was opened up beside him as though by an immense airborne sewing machine.

He lay on his back, chuckling with fright in the moist grass, laughing so hard that by the time he abruptly stopped, the air was strangely still over the farm.

He sat up and looked around. The morning was soon filled again with the whine and bluster of helicopters: a Lynx landing medical teams down on the road, a lumbering Puma dropping commandos behind the ridge.

Legs shaking, he walked through the farm, restored once more to its hallowed desolation. He found the car's fleeing tracks, and further on, past the well, the fresh motorbike track, marked by a tricolour flag fluttering on a short stick. Something small lay at its feet. Close up, he saw it was a woollen doll, about four inches high, pigtails and a dress striped green, white and orange. A shiver went through him. Only one man left such a disturbingly innocent symbol. Bending to pick it up, he hesitated. Almost shot by the enemy, almost cleaved in half by his own side, he wasn't about to risk a possible booby trap. Picturing the headline – OFFICER SLAIN BY RAGDOLL – he laughed aloud again to calm his nerves . . . and stopped suddenly at the eerie feeling that he wasn't alone.

Slowly turning his head, he came face to face with a clutch of heavily armed Royal Marines, standing there sniggering.

Said the leader, 'Do you make a habit of going round like that?'

He'd forgotten he was shirtless. These white men were laughing at him.

Replied Marcus, 'Do you make a habit of showing up when the battle's over?'

Walking through them, eyeing them, daring them, he descended the hill to the road.

The Fox was still retching thick black smoke. Snatching and dispersing strands of the smoke with its twin blades, a Lynx helicopter was taking off carrying the seriously wounded RUC officer Feeley had narrowly failed to kill. Wading through the acrid choking air, Marcus came upon Bones sitting by the side of the road, head in hands, the hard-skulled, hard-eyed young warrior sobbing quietly. Marcus laid a hand on his shoulder. Bones shook it roughly off.

Marcus looked all about. Somebody was missing.

'Try the ditch,' said Bones.

In the ditch lay a body covered by a blanket, size ten boots protruding. Marcus climbed carefully down, as though afraid to wake him. Hands trembling he folded back the blanket and winced, and looked away. Still holding the hem of the blanket, he shut tight his eyes and took a deep breath before forcing himself to look again, to show Robbie McLaren the respect of not cringing from his death mask. The eyelids had been drawn shut, but he had the feeling the boy was looking at him, posing an impossible question. A single bullet had entered his neck, the neat hole cleansed by fresh blood. The sniper's accuracy and the unannounced swiftness of the death sentence made Marcus shiver, and restore the blanket. He sat a moment by the body, awed by the stillness and completeness of death. Over his shoulder he heard them starting the harrowing business of collecting scraps of men into black plastic sacks.

He climbed into the field where a cow lay on its side, pouring of itself into the grass, and walked towards a crew of medical orderlies, standing silently as though waiting for a bus. Beyond the trough he caught sight of Spiky whispering animatedly to Charlie Winters, whose head was cradled in his lap. His spirits soaring, Marcus was breaking into a run when an orderly caught him by the arm and shook his head meaningfully. Marcus stopped and looked again. Spiky lifted his eyes and smiled, and continued to stroke the dead man's head.

While Dixie and Feeley made good their escape into the hills on two wheels, Annie and Michael drove flat out for the border across a broad band of bogland.

For a time the pock-marked minor road was deserted, the landscape falling away emptily to left and right. The border was a tantalising mile away, a painfully slow dash for the shimmering belt of woodland ahead; Michael daring himself to relax behind the wheel, Annie gripping her Armalite, eyes flicking back and forth, watching the mirror, the scrubland, the sky.

She was staring into the wing mirror, something far behind hovering over the road, fixed in the lower sky like a kestrel, but looking remarkably like . . .

A helicopter! A black speck rapidly growing, hurtling towards them, skids skimming the road, blades bending trees and whipping up bushes, jaws and bulging eyes looming larger. 'Brits!'

'Jaysus, where?'

'Leave the road!'

'Where?'

'Anywhere!'

The Ford veered, shot upwards and vaulted the embankment as the road behind was lacerated with bullets. Tearing through scrub, bumping and weaving between gorse and rocks, sinking into soft ground and bucking out again, Michael urged the Ford towards the curving tract of woodland. But as the trees approached, they saw too late that a strip of shallow river lay between them and the wood. With the helicopter returning in a low sweep across the plain, Michael faltered, foot sliding off the pedal, panic moulding his face.

'KEEP GOING!'

He stamped down on the accelerator, the Ford plunged into the pebbly water, gushing wide arcs of clear spray into the air, which was abruptly torn asunder by a torrent of gunfire, striking the Ford as it leapt out of the river on the far side and surged blindly for the trees, its occupants ducking the flying glass and stray bullets.

The wood fell open, drawing them down a rough track into its broad-leafed sanctuary. The helicopter clattered angrily overhead, turning and twisting, parting the canopy up and down the wood. Like prey hiding in the darkness of the forest floor, they waited for the hunter to thresh out the furthest reaches of the wood before venturing to escape.

'Gently now . . .' whispered Annie.

The Ford crept along the misty edge of the wood before attempting a run for the indistinct border. They found a road meandering aimlessly to north and south. Michael hesitated, Annie struggled with the map. 'Just go!'

With a squeal of tyres they swung into a deserted crossroads marked by signposts in Gaelic and English. Michael punched the roof in triumph and relief; Annie punched him in the arm – danger ahead, an Irish Army unit on border patrol was coming towards them. If they stopped the car they would discover the bullet-riddled passenger side.

Ducking out of sight, Annie said, 'Arm on windowsill and look relaxed.'

The patrol was in no hurry, soldiers blankly returning Michael's smile and wave, before rolling out of sight. Michael and Annie drove for a time in silence, deeper into Donegal, while way behind them, the helicopter had been joined by another, throbbing above the wood. Michael threw glances at Annie, trying to fathom what was going on in that strange beautiful head of hers. Annie's faraway gaze took in everything and nothing. Drained by the physical pain of carrying explosives inside her, she sat numbed by the realisation that her labour had resulted in the termination of human life. She could only laugh.

'What's so funny?' said Michael.

She flashed him an arrogant smile. 'I've shot my first squaddie.'

'I thought you missed him.'

'Not that bastard . . .' Recalling to mind the splendid half-naked torso of the black officer, she wasn't altogether sorry she'd missed him. 'No, but I picked off one in the ditch.'

'Sure you killed him?'

Nodding with quiet satisfaction, she wrapped herself in the lonely knowledge of the killing.

4

Shropshire, England

Cold summer rain gathered in a gaping grave; wild cherry and silver birch moaned in the wind. Bells tolled, a saturated Union Jack clung to a loaded coffin.

Sleek black limousines crunched over gravel to the graveside. Doors smoothly opened, dispensing mourners, assembling to form a dense black throng. Press and camera crews emerged from dripping trees, dark clouds rolled overhead, lashing the bouquets with bitter rain, spattering the arrangement which read CHARLES in red and white carnations. The coffin was carried by officers, including Marcus King and Major Draycott, and also, on this occasion, by a humble private, the last man to see the Captain alive – Spiky. The bearer party proceeded with slippery care, there being nothing worse than dropping a man when he's dead. The minister screwed his face to the rain and intoned:

'We have entrusted Charles Edward Winters to God's merciful keeping, and now we commit his body to the ground . . .'

Flag rolled back, webbing bands released, the gleaming box descended into its dark hole. Watching the coffin sink, Marcus recalled counselling his squash partner about the futility of lamenting smashed rackets: In Ulster things like rackets are replaceable . . . The firing party snapped to attention and loosed a volley into the storm. Two youthful figures in austere Victorian uniforms pursed their lips and delivered the Last Post.

One or two sobs disturbed the sturdy English silence. Claire Winters, widow at twenty-four, remained dry-eyed, stiff and steadfast beneath her umbrella.

'. . . and was awarded the George Cross for courage above and beyond the call of duty . . .'

Marcus met Major Draycott's eye across the grave. The expression on the Major's formally handsome face seemed to say, This is what your attitude leads to!

'. . . and sacrificed his earthly life for Queen and country . . .'

Spiky, roused from private communion with the deceased, intercepted the looks that passed across the grave, and felt a stab of foreboding.

'. . . and may those who are enemies forget their hatred and be reconciled . . .'

Clods of earth drummed on the box.

'Lord, support us all the day long in this troublous life, until the shades lengthen and evening comes, and the busy world is hushed, the fever of life is over . . .'

The reception took place in the Regency country house belonging to the deceased's parents. The gathering overflowed into the garden, for in death Charlie Winters had attracted the crowd of his life. The storm had passed, and a fierce July sun set the lawns, steps and flagstones steaming.

Marcus and Spiky leaned on a wall, observing the elegant mourners strolling by with their drinks, fashionable touches introduced to their sombre dress, and their crisp airy double-barrelled conversation. Seeing how Spiky shrank from them, not daring to open his mouth even to a waiter, it occurred to Marcus that ordinary British soldiers had more in common with their enemies in the Bogside than with the upper strata of British society, and that Spiky would be more at ease on a desert island with a disarmed Provo than with most British officers. And yet . . .

'You liked Charlie, didn't you?'

'He was a bit of a space cadet, but he was all right.'

'He died in good hands. Will you be OK for a minute?'

Panic: 'Where you going?'

'To find Charlie's widow. Coming?'

'No thanks.'

'She'll want to thank you.'

Spiky smiled painfully. He would stay exactly where he was till Marcus returned. Marcus went to go.

'Boss, get me another beer?'

Marcus pointed out a waiter. Spiky nodded gamely. It was plain he'd rather go dry. Marcus came back.

'Listen, Shithead, you're one of the VIPs here. Half these people are hangers-on. Who was the last man to see Charlie alive, to hold the dying man's head in his lap, to ease his last moments? I think Mrs Winters would want to thank you.'

Tears filled the boy's eyes.

'OK,' Marcus relented. 'But Confucius say, No balls; no beer! So go get one, you're a fucking war hero.'

Spiky set his sights on the waiter.

Marcus hurried up the steps into the house. He had a train home to catch, and what remained of a precious weekend leave to savour. He found Claire Winters holding court in the drawing-room, seated on a couch with an array of friends sitting or standing around her. She seemed an exceptionally mature young woman, poised and very correct. He had the feeling that she had been master in her year-old marriage with Charlie. He paused on the edge of her circle, eyes only for the widow. Voices hushed, heads turned; he met her eye and smiled.

'Forgive me, Mrs Winters, may I have a word?'

The deep West Indian voice created a wider hush. Elder relatives looked across doubtfully. But the widow, faithful to his uniform, or impressed by Marcus himself, rose without hesitation. As she came to join him, he saw by her shape and the way she carried herself that Charlie had palpably left his mark, and that a child would shortly be born without a father.

Lightly touching her arm, he encouraged her to take a few steps with him into the vast chandeliered reception hall. 'I just wanted to convey from myself and all the men of 'C' Company the deepest sympathy . . .'

She was tall, fair, meticulous, every step, expression, phrase seemingly rehearsed. This, and the hollow ring of her responses, he put down to self control imposed by grief.

'I'm sure he acquitted himself admirably . . . It meant a great deal to him that his men admired him . . . Yes, he enjoyed his squash . . .'

Marcus was anxious to tell her about Spiky, the lad's courage in trying to save Winters' life, the comfort he provided Winters at the end. She listened, giving him her full attention, without any hint of emotion. He began to feel guilty, detaining a young woman evidently in shock. But something made him pursue his request.

'I wonder if I could ask you one favour. . .?'

She smiled patiently.

'Private Rice, he's been very affected . . . I mean, he experienced out there . . .' pointing with his thumb over his shoulder as though Thorn Hill was in the garden, 'a kind of bond with your husband . . . I wonder if there was something of . . . of Charlie's you could leave to him, something small but – '

'Significant. Yes, of course.' She called over one of her nieces, sent her to fetch a parcel of Charlie's personal effects returned to her from Ulster. When the parcel arrived, Marcus welcomed Claire Winters' choice of bequest, and was glad when she insisted on delivering it in person. But something in the crispness of her decision, and the way she carried it through as if following a procedure – A Widow's Guide to Etiquette – made him begin to doubt the depth of her grief.

They walked out together into the sunshine, and found Spiky looking pleased with himself, holding two glasses of beer. Far from struck dumb by the widow's regal charm, he talked incessantly about Charlie Winters, and as Marcus looked on, it occurred to him that this exacting young woman had never loved or admired Charlie, and that he'd been busting himself in Ulster trying to prove himself, trying to dazzle her.

'King!' Marcus looked round unwillingly. Major Draycott, stone-faced. 'A word.'

Claire Winters withdrew. Spiky watched the antagonists walk away from the house along the shaded avenue, and the pangs of foreboding returned.

They walked in silence as far as the ornamental lake. Then the Major, Scotch in hand, turned to Marcus.

'Things are going to change when we get back, Lieutenant . . .' The advance warning was delivered with satisfaction.

At thirty-five, Roy Draycott was conventionally handsome, thickset, immovable. A respected professional soldier, it was said he had problems at home, that his marriage was going down like the *Belgrano*.

'We're going to take those ghettos apart!'

Waiting for Marcus's reaction, he took a swig of Scotch and ran it round his mouth before swallowing. Marcus, outwardly unmoved, regarded him evenly.

'Revenge?' An ironic smile.

'Bullshit. I want that maniac Doyle caught.'

'So do I, but not by wrecking our improved relations with the ordinary people – '

'Ordinary people! Don't tell me. You think we should go in and ask them nicely to hand him over. I have to operate in the real world!'

'In the real world, Major, a backlash just gets their blood up, alienates moderates, turns rebels into terrorists. There's nothing Doyle would like better than a vicious backlash. He sits back and we do his recruiting for him.'

'Don't lecture me, King, I'm sick of your sociology.' Pointing a finger at Marcus, 'You're turning the Army into a laughing stock, your soft-soaping tactics are withering the battalion's balls! I want action, I want Doyle caught, his unit annihilated, the vermin who harbour them crushed!' Squeezing his fist tight and shaking it under Marcus's nose, 'I want our boys to walk tall again, I want the Bogside and Creggan to shit themselves when we leave Base. I'm talking about the British Army, the men who swept ashore in the Falklands and made the world sit up. No more poncing around Derry like celebrities!'

Plucking a cigarette from its carton with his teeth, Draycott lit up, sucked hard and inhaled with bitter satisfaction.

'I don't know what the hell you're so damned smug about, King.'

'You don't want them to respect us. You want them to fear and hate us, and that's all you'll get.'

'That'll do me fine.'

'Terrorists. Is that how you want them to see us?'

'You're too fucking clever for me – '

'Too clever for a black man?'

'Now you mention it.'

'Dead right. My tactics work better than your terrorism. I starve the Provos. You feed them. We were doing OK. More and more co-operation, more informers, more IRA men behind bars, the Provos desperate for new blood, hoping Thorn Hill will provide it, counting on someone like you to over-react.'

'So you want us just to sit back and take it?'

'No way – '

'Four dead not enough for you?'

Shaking his head in warning, 'Don't start, Major – '

'It's enough for me, King. Four good men wiped out, fitting testimony to your tactics!'

Marcus blinked, momentarily stunned as though by a glancing blow. His eyes hardened, nostrils flared, he closed his fists and in his mind he dashed the Scotch from Draycott's hand and pitched him backwards into the lake. Perhaps it was the thin sardonic smile on Draycott's face which stopped him, persuaded him to recoil from the bait, made him open some inner sluice gate and flood his veins with ice.

'You bastard . . .' he breathed. 'Don't tell me what to feel, I was there . . .' jabbing himself in the chest with a thumb, 'uncovered Robbie McLaren's face, carried Charlie Winters' burning body, I was there with the medics, on my hands and knees looking for Winters' feet . . . I can still smell him burning, and you insinuating – '

'Don't be so damned touchy.' Draycott drained his Scotch. 'Take my advice, drop the social work, stick to soldiering.'

An ironic smile and he turned to go.

49

'Major?'

Draycott turned. 'What now?'

'I'm twice the soldier you are, know why?'

'Pray, enlighten me.'

'I can make war, I can make peace. You only know how to make war.'

Draycott laughed and walked on. Spiky came running and found Marcus sitting by the edge of the lake.

'Guess what, Boss? I got us a lift. And look!' Proudly he rolled back his sleeve to reveal Charlie Winters' wrist-watch.

The lift from a young couple brought them to Shrewsbury, where Spiky caught a coach north to Preston, Marcus a train south to London.

The journey should have been an opportunity to relax, to get Thorn Hill and Draycott out of his mind. On boarding he made straight for the toilets and changed out of his uniform into jeans and a bright shirt. The train was stifling. He carried his suitcase to the bar and installed himself by a window with an ice cold beer and a view of picturesque countryside. He noticed his hands shaking, and that he was drinking too fast, putting both down to the conflict with Draycott, refusing to consider that the horror of Thorn Hill could still be in his bloodstream.

His efforts to relax were not being helped by the football gang in the corner, passing the odd racist remark in his direction, becoming bolder as they grew drunk. It was a Saturday, they were tailing their team to London. Marcus tried concentrating on copies of *The Voice* and *Caribbean Times* sent over by Marcia.

Shortly after Rugby, Marcus queued at the bar for another drink and a sandwich, avoiding the eyes of the gang.

'Funny smell all of a sudden,' they began, 'can you get it?'

Marcus normally shrugged off racism, only jumping to someone else's defence. But this was public humiliation. Moreover he wasn't in the mood, his mind still aflame with the bombers who'd brought Charlie's life to such a hideous end, the sniper who killed Robbie McLaren, the one who almost killed him, the helicopter that nearly cut him in half, and Draycott and the mindless philosophy he represented.

The gang, reflected in the mirror behind the barman, was five-strong, early twenties, dressed in expensive jeans, brash jackets and trainers, big, boorish and overfed, with callous loveless faces, fired-up and macho, boozed-up and restless with simmering violence. On another day Marcus might have felt pity. His turn came to order: another export ale and a cheese and onion sandwich.

'And a bunch of bananas! Yeah and something to get rid of the smell!'

Marcus's hands were flat on the bar, tacky and shaking, the barman's uneasy face a blur, the swaying carriage tense with the collective discomfort of people wishing away the episode.

'You're right, it stinks like a zoo in here – '

The word zoo was barely out before Marcus thrust himself off the bar and in one movement turned and broke out amongst the gang like a baited bear loosed against its tormentors, taking all of them on in one savage burst of violence, lashing out with rage and precision, aiming vicious slaps at faces, punches at stomachs, and slamming the biggest of them against a wall for a rapid beating, ducking beer cans and punches as he wheeled after them, absorbing the odd kick and head-butt, scattering them amongst the cowering crowd.

The carriage jolted violently, throwing everyone forward as the train jerked and screeched to a halt. For a moment, when people had regained their balance, all was still, Marcus alone in the ring, people pressed together against walls and tables, spilled drinks and plastic cups all over the floor, a few curses and whimpers disturbing the summer bird song in the open windows.

Marcus looked at the barman, standing sheepishly under the emergency lever. That's all I need, he thought, the arrival of Transport Police, arrests, questions, the weekend with Marcia and Jamie ruined. And if the Army got to hear of it, it could be just the excuse they were looking for to cashier him, destroying his dream of rising to colonel and commanding his own battalion. Panting from his exertion, he fished a fiver from his wallet, slapped it on the bar – 'Sorry about the mess!' – grabbed his suitcase and jacket and jumped off the train.

Crossing fields, vaulting fences, he came to a road. Every three or four minutes a car came by, the driver studying him from a distance, then studiously ignoring him on the way by. In the distance the train began to move, picking up speed and disappearing on its way to London.

The sun beat down on his neck, the cut above his eye from a head-butt stopped bleeding, he began to walk, shaking his head in despair, the weekend slipping like sand through his fingers and nothing he could do.

He was considering forcibly stopping the next vehicle when an old car, sturdy and well preserved, rounded the bend, an elderly man at the wheel. The driver stopped as soon as he saw Marcus's thumb and smile. 'Throw your case in the back!' Marcus got in, sat back and sighed.

'You look like you've been in an accident,' said the man discreetly.

Marcus related what had happened on the train. The man drove well out of his way to deposit him at Northampton station, where he caught a train to London.

The rails rushed south, his eyes grew heavy. Riding the rhythm of the train, he drifted away, sliding into one of the recurring nightmares he'd been having since Thorn Hill. He woke with a start, people staring at him.

London swam with heat. Marcus waded through the tide of humanity swilling round Euston Station, but finding a flustered throng pressing round the telephones, decided not to waste time, but to keep going and surprise Marcia.

Happy now, singing Bob Marley's frenetic *One Love* to himself, he shouldered his way into the filtered sun and dust of the city. He enjoyed free-wheeling through the bustle, the crowds and traffic washing over him, the auras of thousands of strangers brushing his – slick city gents and listless punks, soporific travellers and bemused tourists, aggressive young women and leering labourers. He eased along, breathing the clammy anonymity of the metropolis . . . nobody watching him down the barrel of a gun. *One love, one heart*, he sang, *let's join together and I'll feel all right* . . .

But in the Euston Road he was knocked out of his stride by the intrusion of fire engines howling through the traffic towards King's Cross. For a moment, as the sirens reached a pitch, he was back on Thorn Hill, the embers on Charlie Winters' back fanned by the wind, his severed ankles hissing in the trough. Death had been kind. Life for Charlie – and his wife – would have been hell with those kind of burns, months of unimaginable agony, years of sickening humiliation, probable nervous breakdown, possible divorce, and his days played out in a wheelchair. He'd heard of a few such cases, the forgotten casualties of Ulster.

Fucking Charlie! For the first time he allowed his anger to surface. Fearless, cavalier Charlie played the hero and took three men to their deaths with him . . .

The sirens faded. He walked on, recovering his rhythm. *Simmer down*, invited Bob Marley, *control your temper . . . you won't get no supper . . . you know you're bound to suffer . . . simmer right down . . .*

The 73 bus took him north and east to Stoke Newington in the borough of Hackney. Here he walked familiar streets, old and new, rich and poor, parks and concrete, black faces, white faces, Asian, Greek, Italian, Irish, easy-going streets where a black man could feel kind of at home, North London with the beat and heat of Jamaica in his head.

He quickened his pace past the church and into his own street, pausing across the road from his home, a three-storey Georgian terrace, council owned, separate flats on each floor, with high-ceilinged spacious rooms overlooking the park at the front, overshadowed by modern towerblocks at the back. Marcia had tried living in Army quarters and hated it. She liked her independence. Being the only black wife hadn't helped.

Longing to see his wife and son, he crossed the road and ran up the steps to the front door. Inside the cool hallway, he faltered, unaccountably afraid in case something had befallen Marcia or Jamie, or both. Chest hammering, he took the stairs two steps at a time to the first floor landing. He could hear a Hoover. Unlocking his door, he went in covered by the noise of the Hoover, and saw Marcia working with her back to him. He put his case down, relief washing over him. I'm home.

Marcia was a lovely woman even from behind – slender dark brown legs, smooth hips, long womanly buttocks filling her denim skirt, strong slim back and a full head of deep brown hair falling in curls to her shoulders.

Reaching down he switched off the current. The Hoover droned to a halt. Marcia looked at the appliance as if it had personally offended her. She tried the starter button with her stockinged foot, looked round to check the socket – and screamed.

There was Marcus, swinging the plug and cable, a wide grin on his face. 'Won't work without juice, honey!'

Her pretty face broke into a mock angry smile, they tumbled into each other's arms, Marcus lifting her up under her buttocks, spinning her round, shouting with delight, Marcia laughing one second, her face crumpling the next, clinging to him as he lowered her gently down, pressing her tear-stained face into his neck, feeling his eyes and lips and head, too choked to speak.

Over her shoulder, Marcus spied his son peeking from his bedroom, awed as ever by his father's return, faintly disturbed by the intensity of his parents' embrace.

Marcia tended Marcus's cut head, then prepared his favourite meal, while the boys went to the park. Jamie, seven, needed his father to himself, just as Marcus and Marcia would need to be alone later. Father and son fooled in the park till seven in the evening, feeding the deer, rabbits and guinea-pigs, playing cricket, wrestling, meeting friends and neighbours.

Then home, and a bath together, Jamie washing off the park, Marcus the last traces of Ulster and the brawl on the train.

'How my boys doing in here?' said Marcia looking in.

'Terrific!' said Marcus lathering Jamie's head. 'We're going to have a great weekend!'

When Marcus tried drying him, Jamie acted ticklish, resisting with hip-jerks and squeals of laughter – and accidentally slipped, his head pitching towards the sharp edge of the bath, child's skull caught at the last moment by Marcus's broad hand. Marcus hugged him, pretending to bite his neck, Jamie shrieking with delight, unaware he'd almost knocked himself out, Marcus momentarily troubled, as he had been earlier in the Euston Road. Now it was the fragility of his son that shocked him, the silken skin and lightweight bones so defenceless against the hard edges and lurking dangers of the city.

It took time to settle Jamie down, tuck him in and make him listen to a story. Marcia marched in, tidied a few clothes away, kissed her son. 'Prayers!' she reminded them, and went out again, leaving them on their knees. They only went to Mass at Easter and Christmas, but they were Catholics, and Marcia was determined to keep it that way.

When Marcus finally escaped, half closing the door behind him, he found the living-room dimly lit by the dusk, and Marcia not there, nor any sound of her.

'Honey. . .?' He went into the bedroom. By the low light of the bedside lamp he saw she was in bed, hands behind head, watching him, her faultless complexion drawing the light, her expression half shy, half brazen, her eyes, under the high arched brows, fixed on him. He stood at the end of the double bed. 'Something I can do for you, ma'm?'

'Don't you recognise a hungry woman when you see one?'

He watched her watching him undress, her large appreciative eyes taking in the full range of his body, from the broad gleaming chest and powerful limbs, to his fine hands and the unsubtle majesty of his hugely complimentary erection.

'Nice to see my property maintained in such fine condition,' she said.

'A little underused in some departments.'

'I should hope so.'

He slid under the duvet and moved beside her, propping himself on one elbow, body held inches from hers, only their heat touching. Looking sideways at him with big eyes, she said, 'You know it's not polite to keep a woman waiting.'

As his mouth came to meet hers, she saw his hand disappear beneath the duvet, and felt it materialise between her legs.

Earlier that evening, while Marcus was sitting down to eat with his family, another soldier had been coming home, his low-slung Lotus sports car weaving through the recently built estate on the outskirts of Sheffield.

Roy Draycott was jaded after the funeral, the violent row with Marcus King and the long drive. But he was hopeful about the weekend. Linda's last letter had been reconciliatory, no talk of divorce or custody. She didn't know he was coming.

It was a fine summer's evening in Yorkshire, late sun slanting into his eyes. After war-torn Derry, the trimmed estate made him want to laugh, identical crescents and houses all on parade, with manicured housewives watering manicured gardens. As he swung the Lotus into the drive, he noted Linda's matchbox Mini outside the matchbox garage. Where, he wondered, were the matchbox children? No faces at the Austrian blinds.

Feeling strangely like an intruder, he opened his own front door. Not a sound. The odour of suburban spotlessness offended him: cream walls, cream carpet, dazzling open-plan kitchen, not a magazine or cup out of place. He paused before the French windows and looked over the garden, beds of frivolous flowers divided by a bowling alley lawn.

He climbed the speckless stairs, pausing on the landing outside Linda's bedroom – his bedroom. With a soldier's caution he entered, half expecting to find her there, in bed, in the arms of a man. The bed was perfectly made, the white cover a match for the icing white walls, suffocatingly chaste.

Downstairs he caught himself in the mirror. How would Linda find him? Not bad for thirty-five, broad shouldered, reasonable looking, unsophisticated, unpretentious – a man.

He poured himself an overlarge Scotch, sank into an armchair and flicked on the TV. A smooth green carpet filled the screen, alive with blue and yellow figures and a little white ball mesmerising millions – the World Cup. Still in full dress uniform, drink in hand, eyes enslaved, Roy Draycott subsided deeper into luxury.

He surfaced with a start, expecting Army sounds and smells. He focused on the TV, and saw himself foremost in the bearer party, out of step with that black bastard King, who was clearly obliged to stoop because of his height. Pinned in his chair by the strangely unfamiliar replay of that morning's funeral, he scarcely registered the car doors and voices in the drive.

'Captain Winters, known affectionately as "Charlie" by his men, had been married for less than a year . . .' The camera faded on the buglers delivering the Last Post, the presenter in the studio repeated the night's headlines – the relentless Israeli siege of Beirut . . .

'Is that bloody all?' Draycott was saying aloud. 'Is that all Charlie Winters gets?'

He heard the key in the door, fumbled for the control unit and switched off the TV.

She was laughing as she entered, dazzled by the sunset in the french windows. A moment later she stopped with a sharp intake of breath, meeting her husband's gaze, the man at her shoulder decidedly uncomfortable.

'Well . . .' she gibbered, 'what a surprise! Let me introduce you. Roy, this is a friend of mine, Andrew Harewood from work . . .'

The friend attempted to soften Draycott's gaze with a pleasant 'Hello'.

'Shall I make some tea?' said Linda brightly. Then over her shoulder as she went through to the kitchen, 'Roy prefers tea.'

Andrew Harewood, taller and younger than Draycott, stood awkwardly. Draycott sat back, taking in the fashionable suit, expensive open-neck shirt boasting a smooth tanned chest, streamlined shoes, blithe good looks, one of the new breed of juvenile city gents taking over the country, hard-selling fast-living expense-account type, comfortable life visible in a waistline which spoiled his tapered torso.

Andrew Harewood looked to the kitchen for help.

'Linda, perhaps I should call you, or something?'

'Make yourself at . . . I'll be right with you.'

He addressed a 'mind-if-I-sit-down?' gesture to Draycott, who merely watched him with the scowl of a dog waiting for an imposter's first false move. Harewood sat down carefully on the couch.

'Just back from Ireland, are we?'

'We?'

'Well . . . you.'

'Unluckily for you.'

Harewood flushed. Rallied.

'Look, um, Roy isn't it. . .?'

'Major Draycott.'

'Very well, Mr Draycott . . .'

'Major.'

'Look,' said the executive tartly, 'don't you think you're rather jumping to – '

Linda hurried in a tray of tea and chocolate biscuits. 'Why didn't you let me know you were coming? I could have had a meal ready. You must be – '

'Where are the kids?'

'With mother.'

'That's handy.'

Linda glanced at Andrew. He read the look and drank up, scalding his gums. He rose; Draycott rose with a look he normally reserved for Marcus King, stepping over to the imposter, nose to chin, eye to eye . . .

'Roy . . .' gasped Linda.

Harewood blanched, held his ground.

Draycott clenched his teeth. 'Let me catch you sniffing round here again and I'll break your neck. Message received?'

Harewood retreated in orderly fashion, jingling his keys. 'No need for that sort of thing, no need at all. Bye, Linda, I'll call you.'

The Turbo wheeled into the Crescent and faded.

'You're screwing him, aren't you?'

She averted her eyes. He glared at her, sipping her tea, pretty as hell in a short dress and fish-net stockings, her tucked blond hair glowing in the sunset, her hot perfume meant for another man.

'The truth. No rough stuff. I'll save that for Ulster.'

'Sounds like a solution to domestic violence,' she said sardonically, 'send your man to Ulster. We've made love, yes.'

He felt the shock in his solar plexus. He had harboured some faint hope.

'Let's be honest, Roy, I haven't made you happy and you . . . haven't been easy to live with.'

'I risk my balls over there while you're having it off with that pansified prick!'

'He's not – ' she flared, and became compliant. 'I worry about you over there.'

'Between screws?'

'The children ask after you.'

'Oh they remember me?'

'Course they bloody remember you! I always talk of you – '

'And your pansy, how do they like him?'

'He's not a pansy.'

'Fucking parasite. Some of us sweat blood for this country while gin-and-tonic types like him are ripping it off!'

'He's extremely hard-working and treats us very nicely, thank you very much.'

'*Us*! Like that, is it?' Hands deep in razor-sharp pockets he turned his back and glowered across the lawn at the semi-detached house which mirrored theirs.

'We've twenty-four hours,' he said grimly, 'to sort things out . . . one way or another.'

The Holt Farm, County Donegal, Eire

On a farm straddling the border Annie lay on her back shackled on a bare bed frame, chains binding one wrist and one ankle. It was dark in the low-sloping attic, save for the glow of dusk in the skylight. Ahead lay her third night in chains.

Captivity was slow death, being chained was hell. For long hours she lay perfectly still, permitting only her eyelids to blink, resisting panic, denying herself tears. In calm moments she recalled with satisfaction how she had berated Dixie and Feeley after the ambush: This is no bloody way to fight a war . . . how can anybody celebrate blowing men to pieces . . . I've carried my last explosives, I'll have nothing more to do with bombs . . . and if you plant any I'll do my damnedest to sabotage them.

But occasionally her discipline failed her, and she broke, crying out and tearing herself against the chains. She was twisting and writhing when she thought she heard someone on the ladder and froze, wide-eyed, panting . . .

Dixie come to deliver her fate?

Michael surfaced through the trapdoor. Left to guard the girl he loved and console his mother, the young giant was in considerable distress.

'For the love o' God, Annie . . .'

'Get me out of these chains, for Christ's sake.'

'Jaysus, Annie, Dixie'd – '

'Kill you, I know. Only I heard him ride away. Where did he go?'

'Feeley took him to Derry, message from Mary. They're hunting him both sides of the border. Please God they catch him.'

'Michael O'Cinneíde!' Mock amazement.

'He's no right, chaining you like an animal, no knowing what they're going to do with you. And Molly, this is her home, she's sixty, it's a bloody disgrace.'

'I hope I look that young at sixty.' Then with a laugh, 'What do I care, I don't plan to live that long.'

'Why the hell not?'

The look she gave him – lips smiling but her eyes morbid with certainty – sent a shiver through him.

'Will you stop that nonsense!'

Slumping onto an upturned crate, Michael picked up his fiddle and plucked absently.

'Molly's sick with worrying over me. I think she always suspected I was with the Provos, but we skirted the subject. There was no chance to warn her of this invasion. When she saw Dixie without his shades and recognised him she nearly died. Since Dan's death, I'm all she's got, seeing as God, in his infinite meanness didn't see fit to bless her womb.'

'No wonder she loves you, you're a fine man.'

He smiled awkwardly.

'Better than a real son.'

'Ach, Jaysus, no. I've allowed the war to destroy our peaceful existence. She saw the news, she knows it was us, knows I've blood on my hands, and God knows, Annie, I have too . . . They showed the bits of soldiers they were picking up all over the field. You were right, it's a desperate way to – '

'I need to go,' she blurted, rubbing herself.

'What?'

'To the toilet!'

He rose to push the bucket under her.

'No, undo me, for Christ's sake!'

'You know what Dixie – '

'Michael, have some decency! Let me piss in peace for once!'

He hesitated, bucket poised between his big feet.

'He's not here anyway. Are you even scared of him when he's away?'

He produced a key and began releasing the padlocks.

'Quick!' Grimacing with the sudden onrush.

The chains fell away. She jumped up and he barred her way to the trapdoor, painful regret on his face, nodding to the bucket. 'Look!' he said brightly. 'This'll cover it!' Turning his back and scooping up his fiddle, he planted one foot on the crate and launched into a traditional ballad: *No matter where I wander I'm still haunted by your name, the portrait of your beauty stays the same . . .*

Hobbling over to the bucket, she dropped her pants, squatted on trembling knees and urinated gratefully, eyes burning into Michael's back, straying to the gaping trapdoor . . .

Standing by the ocean wondering where you've gone, if you'll return again, where is the ring I gave to Nancy Spain?

The violent shove propelled him halfway across the attic, stumbling and staggering through a thicket of bric-à-brac, barely saving his fiddle in the tumult of pots and breaking furniture.

Scrambling down the ladder she ran barefoot from the house, carrying the blanket she'd snatched from the attic, nearly bundling over Molly in the yard, fresh vegetables tumbling from Molly's basket, apologising as she ran with Michael's pleading voice in her ears. Impervious to the pain of her bare feet and stiff legs, she ran until Michael's pleas and pounding boots grew faint . . . And, blanket round her shoulders, limped into the wood.

While Annie McBride was escaping from the farm, Dixie Doyle was being spirited into Derry on the back of a motorbike.

'Roll by in an hour,' he said.

Sick with jealousy, Feeley watched him scurry away.

Imitating shadows, he came at his house down the back lane. He'd received a note from Mary saying she had to see him before moving to Dublin. He'd already sent the fare and thought they were gone. It troubled him that the courier couldn't identify the volunteer who'd given the note. But the neat writing resembled Mary's, and it had come with a coffee-stained snap-shot of Josie as proof.

Ghosting from shadow to shadow, he checked when he reached his back gate. All round the walled-in yard coils of barbed wire clawed the twilit sky. He loosened the padlock and softly entered, eyes peeled for a tripwire to eternity. Stockstill he studied familiar shapes: Josie's old tricycle, broken furniture, overflowing dustbin. Satisfied, he concentrated on the house. All dark upstairs, while pale blades of light divided the boards in the kitchen window.

Soundlessly stepping closer, he flattened himself beside the back door and listened. He grew calmer, the field-commander giving way to the husband and father.

But Dixie never succeeded in relaxing completely, and he was on the point of trying the door when he registered something wrong. One plank nailing the kitchen window had broken rank, jutting out just enough to spoil the smooth line of the house. Moving lightly along the wall, he tested each plank in turn. The offending upright was loose. His heart lurched.

Hands shaking, he eased out the tattle-tale board and stood it on its end against the wall. Behind the boards the plastic sheet which served as a window had been slit from top to bottom.

His heart stopped. He caught himself against the wall. Mary and Josie – where were they? Had the Loyalists finally got at them? Hideous images assailed him.

Parting the incision in the plastic an inch, he spied the empty kitchen, part lit by a shaft of light from the front room. He listened hard, at first hearing nothing but his own breathing. Then came a low whisper, male, from the front room. Another male replied.

Blind panic and blind hate vied for Dixie's mind, mad with the thought of what might have happened to Mary and Josie. Reason intervened – it was possible they'd already left for Dublin, that the note was fake. A trap. Please God.

Withdrawing the switchback blade from his back pocket he

placed it lightly between his teeth and, squeezing through boards and plastic, landed silently in the kitchen.

'I'll get it,' a man whispered in the front room. A chair creaked . . . footsteps . . . one of them coming. Dixie melted into deepest shadow. One of the assassins entered, prolonging his life by not switching on a light. Pocketing a revolver, he stooped to break open a pack of canned beers. Freeing two cans, he started to rise, slowing as he did so, eyes fixed on the window, the missing board. Swallowing audibly, he approached the window, not trusting his eyes in the bad light. Beginning to speak over his shoulder he got as far as whispering, 'Hey! The board's fell out!' There followed a brief tussle, a tongue choking on its own words, cans falling, a strangled expletive.

'What the fuck's going on?' hissed the second assassin, following his own shadow into the kitchen, pausing at the sight of his comrade leaning over the draining board, one hand reaching through the slit in the window as though trying to reach the plank. In the poor light it took a moment to realise his comrade's head was lolling in the sink, that he was unnaturally twisted – that he was dead.

In the split second that remained to him, he felt his nose crushed from behind by a hard glove, and simultaneously the strange separation of flesh from one side of his throat to the other.

Releasing the burden, Dixie made the sign of the cross, one for each still corpse, and taking a deep breath gravitated towards the front room, terrified of what he might find . . .

He stood in the doorway, tortured with images, which fell away at the sight of the deserted room, everything strangely tidy, but for cans tucked behind the sofa. A crushed cushion suggested a man had slept there during the day. The assassins must have entered the previous night.

He turned and went quietly up the stairs, still afraid of what he might find. The rooms echoed to his feet, beds and wardrobes stripped, Mary's dressing-table bare, Josie's toy chest hollow, save for a few wretches abandoned at the bottom. Relief and sadness washed over him.

But there remained a doubt. He wanted proof. He went downstairs, stepped over a corpse and feverishly searched until he found, stuffed under the mat, a little pile of unopened mail, including a cheque from Social Security. They'd gone. Safe.

He subsided onto the arm of the sofa, taking in the shadowy details of his abandoned home: Josie's outgrown high chair; the gaudy horseshoe Mary insisted on keeping, left over from the wedding; his own water-colours on the walls.

He may as well have been standing at a crossroads, he reflected, where diverging paths vied for his attention. Give up the killing and join us, said Mary. Stay with the war, we need you, said the IRA. A third obscure path promised to take him effortlessly back and forth between family and war, so fulfilling his first maxim – I am fighting for my family.

But he wasn't clear about that any more. Whichever way he looked at it, Mary and Josie seemed to suffer most. Mary was asking him to be a husband and father once more. It was, surely, an ultimatum. Family or war, no third path.

Derry's Brigade Commander had issued fresh orders – the elimination of a particular British officer, the Seducer of Derry, whose methods were said to be sapping popular resistance to the British occupation. Dixie's unit had been chosen for the job, in recognition of the excellent results achieved on Thorn Hill.

There and then, in the morbid silence of his former home, he made his decision. To take the killing of Lieutenant King as his final mission. Then to lay down arms and go home to Mary and Josie.

A motorbike revved in the street. He opened the door to Feeley, told her to come in. She hesitated on the threshold, never having set foot in Dixie's cursed home. Dixie was in the kitchen, taking a long look at the men whose brief lives he'd severed, their terrible stillness, the appalling expressions on their faces . . . facing them now while they were still warm, so they wouldn't return to haunt him.

Feeley entered softly, and let out a long whistle of approval. 'Who were they?'

'Fuck knows. UDA, UVF, Red Hand, young Prods come to do a job.'

'Are you getting sentimental in your old age?'

'Just fighting their end of it.'

Seeing how he stared at them, 'No, you're trying to keep them out of your nightmares, right?' She'd seen him do this before. 'You're out of your mind, Dixie Doyle! These are the bastards who've kept us down for hundreds of years, shooting and burning us when we've demanded a fair crack of the whip. I wouldn't lose a minute's sleep over any of them!'

63

He followed her to the street, pausing at the front door to take a last look. Then fishing a ragdoll from his pocket he tossed it across the room into the kitchen – his way of saying he'd been.

It was raining as they rode away. In the Donegal hills it had been raining for some time, catching Annie in a belt of woodland half a mile from the farm.

She sat huddled in the crook of a tree, bare feet tucked under her, arms about her knees, blanket round her shoulders. Cold rain seeped through her thin shirt. Closing her eyes she shivered and smiled, safe beneath the low vaulted roof of the wood.

A voice inside her appealed to her: Keep going! Escape deeper into the Republic and lie low! Invisible hands took hold of her – Run for it! It had always been her nature to run from those who shackled her, but always on impulse, and she invariably returned to the fray, taking on family, teachers, lovers – bruised, wounded, never cowed. Freedom required her to return to the farm and take on Dixie as she'd taken on all oppressors before.

So it was in the early hours that she retraced her steps into the farmyard, slipping barefoot through mud and puddles, stiff with cold, aching with anxiety. All was dark and still, rain lightly beating the flax thatch of the house, rattling shrilly on the corrugated roof of the big barn opposite where a night watch was normally posted.

Her plan was to climb the ancient rowan leaning against the house and find her way back through the skylight into her prison. But as she laid hands on the tree, a deep growl came from the barn, Michael's border collie stalking low, neck extended, teeth and eyes aglow in the dark.

'Shhh, Pip, it's me . . .'

Lifting its head, wriggling its slim flanks, it parted its jaws to bark in welcome. Annie stumbled over to quiet the animal, but a yelp of pleasure lifted over the farm. She stroked and soothed, it licked her face, and Michael's huge frame filled the barn doorway, rifle in hand.

'Annie. . .!' Drawing her in from the rain, clasping her tight as though it was he who was lost and found. She allowed herself to be held, face captured in his heavy hands, his sleeves drying her cheeks and bedraggled hair.

'They're away out hunting for you. Dixie's raging, Feeley wants your blood . . . Jaysus, Annie!' He was desperate, she was calm. He held her away, gripping her shoulders. 'Let's run for it, before they get back! Find a wee smallholding in the West, call for Molly when we're set up – what d'you say?'

Reaching for his face, she gently touched the fresh pulpy swelling round his eye. 'Did he take it out on you?' she whispered.

He smiled, calmed.

'Poor wee Michael, the life I lead you.' Turning away. 'Tell him I'm waiting.'

'Annie!' He watched her cross the yard. 'Annie . . .' he moaned, shaking his head.

The dog whimpered as Annie climbed the twisted tree, grappled with the edge of the roof and crawled over the soaking thatch. Prising open the skylight, she swung down into the attic, her scathed oozing feet glad of the dry wood floor. Her blanket and clothes were saturated, she shook with cold. In the corner lay a knapsack of fresh clothes. She began to undress.

'Don't. . .!'

A voice from the dark. She turned slowly. Dixie was squatting on a crate, back against the wall.

'What's the matter, never seen a woman before?' Breaking open her knapsack, she pulled out warm clothes and undressed, dropping her skirt and shirt in a pool on the floor, her back turned to her gaoler.

Across the dark he looked at her pale rangy body, grey against the white of her underwear. He felt a sharp bolt of desire and looked away.

'Where've you been?'

'For a walk.'

'Just like that.'

Plunging her long legs into jeans. 'It's every prisoner's duty to try and escape.'

'From the enemy, I'd have thought, not from your own.'

'You are the enemy.'

'That so?'

'Anyone who chains me is my enemy.'

'You didn't expect to be punished – '

'Punished yes, tortured no.'

'I don't think you realise the gravity of your position.'

Fully dressed, she began to towel her hair.

'Stand still when I'm talking to you.'

She fell still, maintaining a look of indifference.

'Damn it, woman, how the fuck do you think we're going to fight the Brits without explosives?' No response from Annie, only a hardening of the eyes. 'The IRA's been going for sixty years,' pursued Dixie, 'and you want to dictate policy after only six weeks?'

Rising, he came towards her. In the pale glow from the skylight they stood facing, same height, eye to eye.

'The failure of that second device left us badly exposed. Just as well Michael and Feeley were on form, because Christ knows what you were doing – two paltry rounds fired!'

'Yes, and who killed a Brit with one of them?'

His hand came up without warning, striking her hard across the mouth. The blow which whipped her face sideways might have knocked her over, but she caught herself and remained rooted, not touching her mouth, leaving a ribbon of blood to run down her chin.

'Who do you think you're talking to?' he snapped. 'And what the fuck are you so smug about, leaving us in shit and proud of it.'

'I told you, I was too stunned at first – '

'Jeopardising our lives, saving theirs, is that your game?'

'Accurate shooting is just as effective as bombs. We could have killed just as many.'

'So what's the difference? What makes you so high and bloody mighty about not using bombs?'

Stepping up to him, 'You can bury the ones I kill.'

He felt the breath of her passion on his face, the power of what she was saying. He'd killed twice that night already and almost forgotten about it. Was that because in his mind the assassins were dead and buried, whereas the soldiers blown apart in the Fox were only dead? He wouldn't confess it to Annie, but limbless men had haunted his dreams since Thorn Hill.

'A handful of us against an army. Without bombs we wouldn't stand a chance.'

'We'd adapt.'

'You may be into romantic suicide. Me, I've a war to win.'

'You won't win anything with bombs. The world's turning against us.'

'Fuck the world.'

'No! We need right on our side, we need world opinion to put the screws on the Brits. Bombs turn people off, brave deeds win them over. Look at the sympathy we got from the hunger strikes.'

He laughed scornfully. 'Was the British Government moved? They just turned up their noses while our people wasted away. "We shall never bow to terrorism," ' he mimicked a plummy English accent. 'OK, fine, we'll try peaceful protest, they can't object to us starving ourselves to death. But oh no! "We shall never talk to terrorists!" Nothing moves them!' He pointed bitterly at Annie. 'They're stone cold. The fact is, only through cold-blooded violence have we been able to penetrate their stone skulls and gain our few pennyworth of justice. Each time we tone it down, the Brits forget about Northern Ireland; they're deaf to all but bombs. The bigger the bomb, the better they listen.'

'You're just handing them a bloody great propaganda victory on a plate.'

'They can keep it. I'll win the real war.'

'So counter-violence is the only way?'

'Yes!'

'Fine!'

Her hand came up so fast he didn't see it, only felt the sharp sting and shock of the slap.

'Now we're talking the same language,' she said, bracing herself as he closed his fist to hit her. Thinking better of it he opened his hand and patted his swelling lip.

'You strike me, I strike you,' she said. 'You chain me, I fight you. I didn't join up to be pushed around. And I won't be a good little girl when it's all over either.'

'What are you talking about?'

'Wars free women. After, it's back to nappies and housework. Don't think I'm going to be wearing an apron while you bastards are running a united Ireland. And it's not just men I'm prepared to fight. When the Brits are all gone we'll still have the priests telling us what to do with our pricks, cunts and consciences!'

Dixie blinked.

'What's the matter, doesn't your wife use bad language? It's OK for me to talk about killing and maiming but shock-horror if I use a dirty word. Drawing blood's fine, but menstrual blood. . .!' Clasping her breasts in a gesture of mock outrage, 'You're all still primitives! Look at the way IRA heroes treat their women. Beat them, rape them, it's all OK because marriage is sacrosanct, inviolable, and women were meant to suffer! Well don't expect me to put up with it, nor am I going to stand by and watch it happen to others. The war has to be won *here* . . .' stabbing her head with a long finger, 'and *here* . . .' her heart, 'and *here!*' her groin.

'Stand still!' she said suddenly, voice hushed, moving very slowly closer. 'Dead still,' she whispered, reaching behind his neck, drawing him mesmerised to her, his face meeting hers, her lips landing hard and dry over his, then warm and wet as she kissed him violently, pressing herself hard against him, gripping his head in both hands, grinding her mouth into his in a kiss that was more self-assertive than sexual.

Thrusting her away. 'What the fuck – '

'Oh my God, what have I done!' Hands clasped in burlesque supplication. 'Kissing my commanding officer!' Falling to her knees. 'Take my kneecaps, but leave me my virginity!'

'For Christ's sake, woman!'

'Oh I forgot, you're a married man.' Hands clasped tighter still. 'Forgive me, father, for I have sinned, I kissed my commanding officer and he possessed a wife!'

'You're making a bloody ass of yourself!'

'Am I?' Rising, running fingers through her hair. 'You're the standard bearer of the new Ireland, the socialist Eden of equality . . . but you still do the sign of the cross as you kill, fondly imagining God'll forgive the unforgivable, and I'll bet you've got your wee wife well trained at home on her twenty-four-hour shift, unwaged and unfulfilled, and on round-the-clock standby in case you come home with your cock in your hand and an empty belly. Hail the new world!' She punched the air and snapped to attention.

He was glaring at her, speechless and disconcerted, and something else in his wild expression. Even in the dark she saw or felt she'd touched something tender.

He drew away, moved quietly to his crate in the corner. Expecting a backlash, she looked on surprised.

'Something happen to your wife?' No reply, but she thought she could hear him shivering. 'Oh, come on, punish if you must, but skip the wounded silence. I lose my respect for people very quickly. Mine for you is still intact – just!'

'She's gone . . .'

'What d'you mean, she's gone?'

'Packed up, pulled out, couldn't take any more . . . So busy fighting for them, I neglected them, left them to the devil's mercy, to drink, tranquillisers and smokes, and fucking poverty . . .'

She heard a stifled sob, the faint rattle of teeth. Was the terrible Dixie Doyle crying? Praise the Lord!

'Taken the kid and gone south . . . '

She approached carefully, slid down the wall beside him. 'Did she get there OK?'

'Hope so.'

'Can't you call?'

'No phone.'

'I'll go for you!'

He looked askance at her, picking out her face in the dark. 'Just like that!' he chuckled.

'Why not? We're comrades, you're wounded.'

He went quiet again, head forward in his hands, unashamedly himself in front of her. With a sniffle he stood up, putting some space between them. 'I was summoned before the big boys yesterday. They weren't impressed by the dud bomb, but overall, behind their solemn faces they were wetting themselves. 4–0! Our best score against the Brits in a long while.'

'You didn't tell them – '

'About you? They'd have ordered you out, or worse, to deter others. Not,' he laughed, 'that there could possibly be any more Provos half as crazy as you!'

The smile died rapidly. 'I ought to get rid of you, and I'm going to,' stepping closer, standing over her, looking down into her wide-open eyes, 'if you fail to carry out successfully the job they've given us, a job I'm handing over to you – '

'If it's to bomb somebody, you can forget it.'

'It's a sniper's mission, to eliminate a British officer.'

'What, any British officer?'

'No. The big black bastard you missed on the hill.'

'Him! Why him? I liked him. You should have seen his chest. My bullet felt the same and swerved at the last moment. Why him, for Christ's sake?'

'Bombs are out, blacks are out, anything else? You better pull yourself together, young lady . . . decide exactly whose side you're on. I'm giving you this chance to prove yourself. That man

King is making his battalion acceptable to the Nationalist community. He's more dangerous to us than the SAS. He's your man. He's also my passport to freedom, so that's two reasons why you better not miss. There are limits to my patience.'

'Passport to freedom?'

'I'm pulling out after we've accounted for King. Twelve years is enough. I'm pushing my luck, never been wounded, though I've had bullets shave me cleaner than a blade. I'm going home to my family, while I have a family. You probably think that's bourgeois and beneath contempt.'

'Not if that's what's right for you. So tell me, when do I shoot that fine specimen of an oppressed minority?'

'Soon as he gets back from a funeral in England.'

London

While Annie and Dixie were crossing a dawn-lit farmyard to snatch some sleep in the hayloft, across the sea in England Marcus was waking earlier than intended for a Sunday. Despite the late-night laughing, talking and making love with Marcia, he was wide awake, watching the first lazy paws of sunlight climb the walls, watching Marcia sleep.

She possessed an unfailingly lovely face. The high arched brows and flared nose gave her a perpetual wide-awake look, even in sleep. Even in death, he mused with a shudder, Marcia would look vital, poised to open her eyes and speak.

She opened her eyes at that moment, at once bleary, drowsier looking now than when she was asleep, patting his face curiously, as though remembering who he was, recalling with a smile his unfamiliar presence and the things they'd done in the night.

'Who are you anyway?'

'A man you took in last night.'

'What are you doing in my bed?'

'I told you. I was minding my own business, you grabbed me, took advantage of me.'

She laughed outright and slapped his arm. 'What a lie! There I was trying to get some sleep and all of a sudden there's this big bad man crawling over me. Just as well you're good looking or I'd have kicked you out!'

70

He eased himself on top of her and slow-kissed her warm sleepy mouth. 'So you do like this big bad man giving his love to you?'

Sighing, 'I suppose you're better than nothing!'

He felt her firm hands cupping his buttocks, and her body arching against his as she urged him to enter her directly. He was squeezing smoothly into her when the door quietly opened.

'Daddy, you coming to the park?'

Marcia pushed Marcus off, clutched the duvet to her and sat up. 'Jamie King! Number one, it's six o'clock on a Sunday morning and your mother's resting; number two, how many times have I told you, when Daddy's home you knock! Now get back to your room!'

The door closed on Jamie's stricken face. Marcus fell back on the pillow and laughed.

'Did you say *resting*?'

'That kid's got to learn we have our rights too!'

She flashed him an angry look.

'I know,' raising his arms in surrender, 'I'm too soft with him.'

'I'm the one who has to live with him while you're off – ' She broke off abruptly, not trusting what she was going to say.

Rescuing her, 'Maybe you'd rather I was soft on you?' he said, reaching absently under the duvet. Her eyes hardened, resisting him, and softened as he gently stirred her.

Afterwards he left Marcia to doze and, putting on a bath towel went to find Jamie. The boy's door was shut. No sound came from within. He wasn't in the kitchen, and there was no evidence that he'd had any breakfast. Marcus returned to Jamie's bedroom and knocked. No reply. He went in; Jamie was in his play corner, arranging his toy soldiers, making as if preoccupied.

'Private King reporting, sir,' said Marcus, 'wondering what the general wants for breakfast?'

No response, Jamie covering his hang-dog look with an air of indifference.

'How about we have it in here together?' Still nothing. Marcus came and knelt and slipped an arm around the boy. 'Come and help me make it?'

Jamie tightened, became still as stone. Fighting his frustration, Marcus rose to go, turning at the door to say, 'You're heading for court martial, sir, conduct unbecoming of an officer! I'll be in the canteen!'

Marcus stretched out the business of making Marcia's breakfast, hoping Jamie would appear. He wanted the brief weekend to be perfect, knowing it couldn't be. Jamie's jealousies could take hours to work through, and Marcus had to return to Ulster in the morning. Worse, Marcia was building up to something, he could feel it.

Jamie was shuffling in the doorway, bare feet and crumpled pyjamas. 'What's court martial?'

'Means you're in big trouble with the Army, and there's only one way out . . .'

'What?'

'Special mission, deliver breakfast to your mummy,' offering down the laden tray, 'without spilling a drop.'

Receiving the tray tentatively, 'She'll shout at me.'

'If she shouts at you, you and I, boy, will shoot off to the park and not come home till midnight!'

Elation: 'Promise?'

'Promise.'

He watched Jamie pick his way across the living-room, and silently prayed. Jamie toe-poked the bedroom door open and was lost from sight. Marcus listened.

Jamie returned cheerful, with a jauntiness which suggested that delivering the tray had unburdened him of something much greater.

'She didn't shout at you?'

Jamie feigned a look of deep disappointment.

They all went out for the day, beginning with a visit to the city farm in Kentish Town and the nearby street market, a boat trip on the canal and a fast-food lunch before going on to Marcus's parents in Stockwell, south of the river.

His father, an inspector with London Transport, and his mother, a hospital ward sister, welcomed him warmly, quietly, without fuss. A visit from Marcus, particularly after the horrific television coverage of the ambush in Ulster, was too great an event to be permitted to impinge too deeply on their lives. Whatever was betrayed in anxious eyes and subtle gestures, emotions were kept in check.

Mother, a large handsome woman who smiled grudgingly and never relaxed, couldn't bring herself to refer to the ambush at all. Father, a lean grey diplomatic man with a philosophical sense of humour, became serious each time he asked about the ambush, as though seeking a plausible solution to an unfathomable riddle.

'Close call, huh, Ammi, bit close for comfort?'

Ammi was Marcus's family name, the Jamaican name people close to him would use rather than Marcus.

Every now and again, without prelude, his father would become grave. 'Sounds like that business was the closest call yet, Ammi?'

'Not really, Dad. I didn't see very much. All happened so fast.'

Father nodded, contenting himself for the present with a reply they both knew to be hollow. The subsequent smile which passed between them came closer to an unspoken sharing of the truth.

Early in the evening, Father drove Marcus and Marcia back to Stoke Newington, leaving Jamie to spend the night with his grandparents. In the flat they changed to go out, waiting for their friends to pick them up.

Marcus poured a couple of rums, Marcia fixed a snack and Marcus took out his saxophone and played a slow easy-going John Coltrane number.

Elroy and Donna arrived late as expected, Marcus playing them in with a fanfare, before embracing his oldest friend, and kissing Donna. There was much warm greeting, teasing and loud appraising.

Marcia poured drinks, plump petite Donna called for another number from Marcus, clicking her fingers, slapping her hips as the deep reedy notes pumped through the flat and the perspiration played on Marcus's intently joyous face. Elroy, a wiry impulsive seductive man with keen eyes and an inexhaustible appetite for life, danced lustily with Marcia, who played her part as well as any, everyone trying to defeat the tension with bravura.

'Sounds beautiful, Ammi!' Donna praised Marcus's playing.

'Rusty,' moaned Marcus.

'Corroded!' said Elroy, himself a semi-professional musician.

They went in Elroy's car to the party off Holloway Road, a spontaneous affair arranged in Marcus's honour. The flat was teeming, good humoured people stacked on the stairs inside and on the steps outside, sliding off each other in tight passages and densely packed rooms. The heat beat a dense static rhythm through the house, it poured in like molten lead through doors and windows flung wide front and back, welding bodies together, deadening the music, suspending cigarette smoke under the ceilings.

Marcus was passed through the flat on the arms of old and new

73

friendships, cushioned from the impending reality of the morning by the camaraderie of the night. Whatever unspoken judgements he read in some friends' eyes, he was grateful to be back in the bosom of his people. He didn't try and delude himself that the love and loyalty he commanded wasn't being strained by his enduring affair with the Army. Many of the guests he scarcely knew; his circle of friends was shrinking, and some of his older friendships were drying out like neglected wells, a distant echo of former times.

Marcia looked sensational. Bathed in compliments, she drifted lightly between friends, shiny cerise dress moving on her like slow fire, dark smooth skin glowing underneath. Marcus appreciated her performance all the more because he knew she was working up to something, and had a good idea what it was. She was enjoying herself, saving her feelings for later.

Marcus didn't do so well. Normally he knew how much to drink in order to enhance enjoyment and not spoil it. That night he had to fight the urge to drink heavily, and he suspected it was Thorn Hill he was trying to flush out of his bloodstream. Twice he spilled his drinks, and his normally easy banter was rough-edged, biting, causing one or two people to move away from him. But he enjoyed himself too, drinking in the atmosphere like a man filling up for the desert, flirting a little with the women. Elroy was trying to get him alone and Marcus was making him work for it. They'd been friends since secondary school, and Marcus's continuing participation wasn't to be bought cheaply. When finally Elroy cornered him in the kitchen, he said, 'Ammi, what's up, what's the story?'

'You're my oldest friend, I don't want to fall out with you tonight.'

'Why the fuck should we fall out, man?' Elroy spread his artistic hands in genuine incomprehension.

'You're avoiding me.'

'*I'm* avoiding *you*! I'm like a dog chasing a bitch!'

'You're avoiding *me*!' Marcus flared, jabbing a thumb into his chest. 'Like everybody else here. How's your music, Ammi, how's Jamie, how's this, how's that? Nobody mentions what I do, what I am – '

'What d'you want, we praise the big hero? Sure people saw that ambush thing, we're just relieved you were OK. What d'you want us to say? We don't understand what's going on out there – '

74

'You don't want to.'

'No! We don't know shit about it. It's in our living-rooms but it might as well be on the moon. The TV don't explain it, the papers don't explain it, they only give the score. We just glad you're here!' Hands wide, big smile.

'Glad I'm here? You'd think I'm back from a world cruise. Nobody want to know where I really been.'

'I told you, they don't understand it, I don't understand it!'

'They don't like it, you don't like it, me being out there with the British Army, fighting with whites for a white country, white system, shoulder to shoulder with white Brits, friends with white Brits, betraying my black brothers and sisters . . .'

'Well now you come to mention it – '

'Then why nobody fucking say so? Everybody looking at me all smiles, good-time smiles, old-times smiles, lying smiles . . . I been in the Army twelve years and after the first year of mind-blowing disbelief, nobody says a word. When I leave town for Cyprus, Germany, Ireland, I go nowhere!'

'Don't talk shit, Ammi, I always get round to asking how you're doing wherever you are.'

'Yeah, embarrassed, like, How's it going in the Pretoria police? I used to try and explain, you turned off.'

'Like I said, it isn't easy to grasp . . . you're a gifted musician, a good father, good husband – sometimes even a good friend! So what the fuck are you doing in the Army? Christ Almighty, Ammi, the Army's for . . .' groping for a sharp, non-lethal thrust, 'for guys with something missing, their dicks or their brains!'

They glared at each other. Guests in the kitchen looked on in silence, Aretha Franklin reverberated through the house.

'What are you doing with those kind of people? And while we're on it, maybe we find it hard picturing you beating shit out of people in Ireland!'

'While we're on it, huh?' Marcus nodded bitterly. 'It's taken you long enough to get round to it . . . even now you're not really touching it . . . you never stop to think, to consider my reasons, my purpose, you just paint me white!'

'OK fine, tell me, I'm all ears!'

'Tell you?'

'Your reasons, purpose, help me understand.'

Marcus closed on him, teeth bared, eyes alight, barely able to keep his hands off his friend.

'Don't fucking patronise me! You don't know shit about what I do, but you privately tried and sentenced me years ago, and tonight you're granting me a retrial? Well that's very fucking magnanimous of you, Junior, maybe you'll reduce my sentence for good behaviour!'

Marcus turned on his heels, a path opening instantly through a throng of onlookers. Elroy tried to follow.

'Ammi, for Christ's sake, I'm listening, Brother, I'm all yours!'

Turning and pointing violently, 'Don't fucking Brother me, Junior! You've silently judged me all these years and you know nothing what goes on inside. Friendship's about trusting your mate first and asking questions after!'

People fell back. Marcus stormed down the passage. Marcia stepped into his path, eyes huge with concern, coming to him as he slowed, reaching.

Softly, she said, 'What's the matter, honey?'

Marcus, who'd turned grey, found a smile. 'How you doing, Sweetheart? Having a good time?'

'I'm about ready for home,' taking his arm, 'how about you?'

They hailed a taxi in Seven Sisters Road. Marcus shut his eyes and sank into leather, Marcia looked out at the night-bustle, shaking her head.

'Tried telling you years ago he was a shit . . . but he was your brother, so!' She made a 'that's-that' gesture. There had been nothing she could say.

They travelled for a time in silence, the Sunday night traffic thinning out in the back streets, the midsummer city sky copper and starlit over the roofs and railway arches of North London. Feeling the distance between them, Marcus reached for Marcia's hand. She held his hand and slid closer, but still he felt the tension, the lull before the storm.

'Anything you want, honey?' she said, back in the quiet of the flat.

'No, I'm fine.'

'A drink together?'

'No.'

She collected her nightie and headed for the bathroom.

'Only you!' he called after her.

'That'll cost you!' From the bathroom she called, 'I think we should talk.' She made her voice light and natural.

'Tomorrow!' he said sharply. 'This is our weekend.'

They made love slowly by the light of the city night filtering through gently billowing curtains. Naked skin glowed, Marcia's a deep dry sheen, Marcus gleaming. They kissed softly and fucked slowly, together body and heart, but alone in their thoughts. Marcia climaxed more as an afterthought than an end, and Marcus came in a frantic struggle and lay beached on Marcia's belly like a man who fears it's his last time and invests too much. It had been a long hot day. They fell asleep almost at once, buttocks touching.

Marcus dreamed of Ulster, the patchwork landscape ablaze, entire fields dancing with flames, doused by lashing rain, rekindled by the wind . . . and across the ridge against the red sky, a glorious bayonet charge led by Charlie Winters, his bleeding stumps and those of his amputated men punching holes in the bog as they ran, the sucking sound of stump and mud echoing through the smoke. Then Marcus saw a little black boy in the burning wilderness, Jamie running in circles, trying to escape the spreading pockets of fire, his hair on fire, flames licking his knees, Marcus desperately trying to reach him . . .

Marcus sat bolt upright, bare torso running sweat, eyes crazed, not sure where he was. He lay back, Marcia stroking his head.

'What did you dream, honey?'

'Jamie on fire . . . I couldn't get to him.'

Marcia got up and fixed a hot drink. They sat in bed with the first hint of dawn in the window, Marcia massaging Marcus's shoulders while he rode out the last spasms of his nightmare.

'You been getting a lot of nightmares?'

'Yeah.'

'Since the ambush?' He nodded. 'Shows your heart's in the right place, dreaming of Jamie . . . I don't mean that unkindly. Were any of those killed friends of yours?'

He considered. 'One of them was, almost.'

'Ammi. . .?'

'What?'

'I want another child.'

'I know.'

'With a full-time father . . .'

The first bird piped up in the park across the street.

'. . . and we agreed Army married quarters is no good.'

'Would you like some fresh tea?'

'Soon, I'd like it soon. I'm twenty-eight, I don't want to wait any longer. I hate putting that cap in, wanted to make love free this weekend.'

He heard the passion in her controlled voice, and felt wooden, a floating target, a duck trying to hide behind the ripples of a pond.

'Honey, I do understand how important the Army is to you, how the men look up to you, how you're like an ambassador for black people and for your two countries . . .'

'And for a civilised kind of soldiering.'

'OK, I believe in what you're trying to do, but maybe you've done enough. How about letting the young men you've inspired carry the flag?'

He gave an ironic laugh. 'I was just getting into it. I've watched and learned, bided my time, kept cool when they squeezed me out to make way for posh guys like Charlie Winters – who we buried on Saturday. I'm in my prime, honey. I feel cool on the streets of Derry. I know what I'm doing. I could run that fucking Army myself.'

'Honey,' she said, 'we haven't even talked about what happened. Imagine what I went through when the radio said a number of soldiers had been killed in County Londonderry, knowing that's where you are . . . Ammi, you put yourself in my place sometime . . . I phoned the nursery to say I wouldn't be in, spent the rest of the day on the phone trying to get through, getting through and nobody knowing, the radio on, TV, phone in my hand and any minute afraid I'd hear the news I been dreading for so long, the dread I live with every day . . . and how was I going to tell Jamie? And your mother and father? And what am I supposed to do with the bits of you they send home?' Her voice trembled, eyes awash. 'Standing there while white soldiers salute you with guns going off and everybody talking about your bravery and how you gave your life for your country . . . well fuck your country! They don't give a shit, nobody gives a shit about Northern Ireland. You'd have died for what, Ammi? To stop Irish people killing each other? To give politicians something to stamp about? To satisfy the fantasies of schoolboy generals?'

She bit her lip and sobbed quietly. She was always dignified, never more so than when she was crying. He loved her ferociously and protectively when she cried, because it was her soul coming out.

'I'm sorry, honey.' She took a breath and went on, 'I don't want to pressurise you. I knew – or thought I knew – what I was getting into when I married you, and I don't regret a thing. I'll back you whatever you do. If you feel you have to stick at it, I won't love or respect you any less. I'm not too worried about Jamie. He's better off with a part-time daddy like you than most kids, and I'm OK, even if I do wish you were around . . . But I swear to God, honey, I can't bear to think of you blown to bits in some faraway place, sacrificed for people who never knew your worth! You're just a number to them, but you're precious to me . . .'

Her words hung in the dawn-lit stillness of the room. Marcus rolled over into her lap, face buried in her thighs, breathing the warm sex odour of her crotch.

'I should be at home, and I'd like to be . . . but if you're lucky in life you do what you're good at, and I think I'm lucky . . .'

'Honey, you could turn your hand to anything, do something with your music, or start up your own business!'

'Selling? Switching from fighting for a purpose to fighting for money, one civil war to another, only here, instead of communities, it's every family against every other . . . like dogs running round trying to bite each other's tails off.'

'It wouldn't be that bad, you'd always find some tyrannical system to fight!'

'Like my family?' he laughed.

She hit him, and left the offending hand on his shoulder, her hopes rising, pulse accelerating, a whole new life to fight for. She watched him as he got up, slipped his black cotton dressing-gown over his broad shoulders and went and stood in the breeze of the long window, looking out over the silent park.

'The idea was to make it to major, then get picked out of all the majors to lead the battalion.' He looked at her over his shoulder, assuming an air of mock importance. 'Colonel Marcus King!'

'I know, honey, but face it, were they going to let that happen?'

Her words were like salt on a wound, cleansing. Running his outspread hand down a window pane, he felt a powerful urge to slam his fist clean through. A few deep breaths and then he let his shoulders drop.

'Ammi,' she implored, 'they haven't beaten you just because you quit. You stayed true to yourself. You're light years ahead, your way will come in good time.'

79

He surrendered a sigh. She held out her arms to him, he came to her.

'There's one or two things I got to sort out with Draycott, a few strings to tie up in Derry if I'm going to come home with my head up.'

Drawing him down, she held his head in her crotch, not daring to speak.

'Four weeks to the end of the tour . . . and that's it.'

'Honey,' she burst out, 'you're not fooling with me?'

He sat and restrained her by the shoulders: 'It's going to be tough having a restless tiger like me around.'

'I think I might just get used to it,' she said, her voice low and vibrant with emotion.

The plan was for Elroy to pick them up at six a.m. and drive to Stockwell to pick up Jamie and stop for breakfast. Then Marcus, Marcia and Jamie would take a taxi to the station for Marcus's train to the airport.

They lay together as late as possible, naked but not making love, drowsy, reflective. At five-thirty Marcus reluctantly telephoned Elroy. The phone rang a long time. That meant Elroy had decided not to drive them.

'Yeah?' Elroy grunted.

'Ammi . . .' He heard Elroy bestirring himself.

Falteringly: 'Six o'clock, we said, right?'

'If that's still OK?' said Marcus.

'No problem.'

'See you in a minute.' Marcus hung up, wondering if his friend had influenced his resolution to leave the Army, a decision he was still reeling from.

At six they were ready to leave, Marcus's suitcase packed. Elroy was bound to be late. Marcus went into the kitchen where Marcia was needlessly busying herself. When he slid his arms around her she thought he was merely being affectionate. But when she felt his hands crushing her breasts and then transfer their interest to the inner regions of her skirt, her heart began to race. Turning her round, kissing her deeply as though replenishing his store of her juices, he lifted her buttocks onto the kitchen table, dragged down her underpants, pushed up her skirt, tore off his jeans and pants and lowered her deftly onto his sex.

'I've nothing in,' she said breathlessly.

'Freedom!'

She wrapped herself tightly around him, hands behind his neck, legs clasping his waist, rapt expression on her wide-mouthed tear-stained face.

The doorbell rang.

'I'M COMING!' shouted Marcus, and ejaculated wildly inside her.

5

Derry

Marcus didn't arrive until after dark. The first shock was to find that Major Draycott's wish had been granted – the company had been moved across the river and installed in a beefed up RUC post in the heart of the Bogside. In Marcus's absence, the building had been transformed into an improvised fortress overrun with soldiers, teeming with searchlights, padded with breeze-blocks and sandbags, swathed in machine-gun emplacements, hugely intimidating, a massive affront to Nationalist dignity, and a tangible warning of what was to come as a consequence of the massacre on Thorn Hill.

It was five minutes to midnight, Marcus inhaling the cool night air from the roof of the fort, girding himself for the midnight briefing with the Major. All around lay the Bogside, strangely muted, cowed. His mind wandered back to London, St Pancras Station that morning, boarding the Luton Airport train, Jamie unconcerned at first, perhaps because he was anticipating having Marcia to himself again, then bawling in Marcus's arms as the guard blew the whistle . . . Marcia blithe and jaunty, even a little mad in her vain attempt to exorcise the fear that was bedevilling her, fear that was betrayed at the last moment when her face broke and she fused with Marcus on the platform. 'Honey, please be careful, no more medals, don't feel you got to leave with a bang . . .' It had struck her forcibly that in his four remaining weeks in the Army, the unthinkable could happen. 'I'm counting the days, we're all counting the days,' she said, in a way which suggested she was convinced she was pregnant already.

A minute to midnight. Major Draycott could forgive a soldier writing off a Landrover or running down a civilian, but God help him if he was late. Marcus unwillingly left the breezy roof to attend the briefing. Fellow lieutenants Warfield and Kitson would be there already, and Kitson would pass some comment on Marcus leaving it so fine. He descended into the fort, its stark passages sour with the confined sleep of soldiers. Entering the briefing room he found Warfield and Kitson stiffly waiting.

'Cutting it a bit fine, old boy!' said Kitson, consulting his watch like a schoolmaster.

Marcus laughed mysteriously.

'And what may I ask is so funny?'

'You, Kitson, you.'

Kitson repelled him: tall and spindly, with a pinched face, plummy voice and an air of perpetual self satisfaction. He was younger than Marcus, but of the old school. Never exercise initiative unless instructed, even if a tank is about to roll over your foot.

The other officer, Warfield, was a straightforward fair-minded professional, torn between loyalty to Major Draycott and a secret admiration for Marcus. Stocky, a human tank, Warfield could never quite grasp what Marcus was getting at, but usually suspected he had a point. He greeted Marcus with an affable nod.

'Had a good leave?'

'Yeah, too good.'

The triangle of lieutenants stood in silence, Warfield grim, Kitson rocking on his heels, Marcus blank, deceptively relaxed. The briefing room was uncomplicated – four walls, light bulb, table, telephones, chair and air-vents. A map of Derry covered one entire wall. The cheerless fort was a shock to Marcus after the soft lines and feminine smells of home. He missed Marcia.

Footfalls in the passage – the Major! Pulses quickened in anticipation.

Roy Draycott arrived at the briefing room at a crisp pace, private rage publicly displayed in his face. His weekend with Linda had been an unmitigated disaster. The bitch wanted a divorce, custody and alimony. He tried reasoning, bullying, even seduction. Cringing at the thought of that soft-bellied city pansy having it off with her, he tried reminding her what a real man was like. But she remained stiff and stubbornly dry. Suddenly he'd realised, lighting a cigarette in the dark of the bedroom, that she'd long been closed to him.

He paused now in the doorway, fixing his three platoon commanders with a cautionary gaze as he entered and shut the door. Then crossing to the wall-map he caned the face of Derry with his swagger-stick:

'Bogside and Creggan – poor underprivileged peace-loving folk! Never dream of blowing up a British Tom . . . but happy to harbour the bastards who do. Four Toms murdered! That's what comes from treating the Paddies with kid gloves, from poncing round Derry like pop stars!'

The room fell very still. Warfield and Kitson threw glances at Marcus, Warfield furtively, Kitson with barely disguised satisfaction. Major Draycott looked directly at Marcus, daring him to react.

Marcus met his gaze, but remained quiet, hands behind back, legs apart, apparently unmoved. Underneath he was tense and anxious. Draycott was clearly ready for him, bolstered by the backing of senior officers, inspired by cross-party declarations of outrage in Parliament, emboldened by incensed newspaper headlines. Marcus smiled to himself, like a boxer with one hand tied, faced with a free-hitting opponent supported by the officials and the crowd.

Surprised by the lack of resistance, Draycott moved in for a quick knock-out.

'In conjunction with the RUC we're compiling a list of suspects and sympathisers. You have twenty-four hours to prepare, before a full briefing at 24.00 hours tomorrow, followed by dawn raids. Any questions?'

They waited for Marcus to fill the silence with a diatribe about destroying painstakingly nurtured relations with the Catholics and driving desperate young men into the arms of the IRA. Marcus said nothing.

'Very well, gentlemen, that is all!'

'One thing,' said Marcus.

The room braced itself. Draycott tightened the grip on his swagger-stick.

'Keep it brief, old boy!' piped Kitson.

With a withering glance at Kitson, Marcus produced a bottle of Scotch from inside his combat jacket and slapped four tin mugs on the table. Unscrewing the bottle he poured generous measures under the intent gazes of the other men.

'Sounds like things are going to get hot round here from tomorrow night, but tonight' – thrusting a mug into the wary hands of each man and raising his own – 'let's remember our comrades who lost their lives on Thorn Hill.'

'Hear! Hear!' murmured Warfield, raising his mug.

Kitson, keeping his options open, waited for Draycott. All eyes on the Major, whose fondness for Scotch was well known and whose eyes remained rooted on Marcus.

'All right,' he said. 'I'll go along with that.'

'To our departed comrades,' said Marcus. 'God bless them, and may they rest in peace.'

The men drank, smacked their lips. Draycott began to relax, his victory apparently complete, Marcus King vanquished, a walkover. Marcus refilled each mug but his own.

'I'll leave you to it, gentlemen, it's on me!'

'Where are you going?' said Warfield.

'Work to do, a man to catch!' Marcus was grinning.

'What are you talking about?' said Draycott.

'An extra patrol to look for Doyle. In fact with your permission, sir, I'd like to organise a string of extra patrols for the twenty-four hours remaining, all feeding back every scrap of information on Doyle.'

'Permission denied. Waste of time, waste of manpower. I want my men fresh for tomorrow night. Scheduled patrols only.'

Marcus felt an onrush of rage, but mastered himself.

'Then I better join a scheduled patrol.'

'You do that.'

Turning at the door, 'If I find where he is, I take it the raid will be called off?'

Draycott smiled. 'Let's drink to it!' he said, motioning Warfield to fill Marcus's mug. Warfield complied and handed Marcus the mug.

'A toast, gentlemen,' said Draycott. 'to a successful raid!'

'To a devastatingly successful raid!' said Kitson.

Warfield mumbled his assent as each man, Marcus included, downed his Scotch.

'To a better way,' said Marcus quietly, and walked out.

He prowled through the fort, past the operations room where the night music of telephone traffic was arriving from patrols and observation posts across the ghetto, and on past the cookhouse

where men returned from patrol were attacking midnight breakfast, relief etched in their faces. In the washroom he found the
Company Sergeant Major stripped to the waist shaving.

'Good evening, sir!' said the big man jovially, 'knee-deep in shit
as usual?'

'Wouldn't be otherwise, Sergeant Major. I'm hand-picking some
lads for a night patrol.' Marcus reeled off a list of names; the CSM
looked doubtful.

'They've only been off the street a couple of hours.'

'They're young, they'll live.'

Marcus shivered, chilled by his own words. He ducked into
one airless bunkroom after another, choosing from heaps of
deeply sleeping soldiers. For many this was their first decent
sleep in thirty-six hours, and rousing them was like pulling men
from the sea. 'Leave it out, sir! . . . Give us a break! . . . Bugger
off, Boss!'

'Snap-patrol, move your arses!'

They stole into the night, cat-like along silent walls and alleys,
pausing and listening, merging with brick, mortar and darkness,
hands, faces and badges blackened. Since his skin shone in the
dark, even Marcus wore camouflage cream, eyes alive beneath the
slanted beret, an occasional glint of teeth.

For a time nothing stirred, only a dog going by with its head
down, breaking stride at the familiar scent of soldiers . . . and the
breeze teasing them with the scuff and scurry of litter, making
them spin round to confront a crisp packet.

Then real footsteps, seemingly near, but coming from across the
terraced maze, a young couple walking home arm in arm, stifling
giggles. Just then Marcus saw the street come alive with the shapes
of soldiers in relief against the night sky. The couple flinched,
altered direction. A brief scuffle, muffled cries. Taking one man
with him, Marcus bolted down an alley.

Fifty yards ahead the couple were spreadeagled against a wall,
legs kicked apart, the young man crying out each time his testicles
were squeezed.

'You're all alike, you murdering cunts!' hissed a corporal. He
started on the girl, crudely frisking her, hands feeling her up and
down her jeans. When her boyfriend objected, his chivalry was
rewarded with a volley of baton blows to his legs. When the girl
tried to protect him, she was pinned against the wall by two

soldiers. 'What you doing with a prick like this? Why not come back with us and – '

'FREEZE!'

'Fuck me, sir, I nearly shot you,' said a squatting soldier.

'Glad you didn't!' replied Marcus, stepping into the road. 'Thank you, Corporal, that'll do' – motioning him to release the young couple, taking the corporal aside. 'That the best way to get information out of people?'

'Just doing a P-check, when they assaulted me.'

Marcus whistled through his teeth. 'And you lived to tell the tale!'

'With respect, sir, we've just lost four men.'

'Killed by that young couple?'

'They support them that did it, don't they?'

'Not everybody here supports them, but they soon will. Somebody's boyfriend tonight, Dixie Doyle's man tomorrow. Have you got a girl back home?'

'Yeah.'

'How would you like her to be stopped and abused by Irish soldiers?'

'Lieutenant Kitson said we could give them hell!'

'And I'm telling you to use your head.'

'Fucking coon . . .' mumbled the corporal as he turned away.

'Corporal?'

The soldier turned, all innocence.

'It's fucking coon, *sir*,' Marcus reminded him.

'Sir.'

Marcus led his men into sleeping Creggan, knocking on selected doors, coaxing, questioning, watching, listening, hoping to turn the right stone.

But in the first grey wash of dawn, Marcus could only thank his silent men as they cleared their rifles and gravitated towards the cookhouse or the sack. The taste of failure was in his mouth. He headed for the de-briefing room and was surprised to find the Major waiting for him, returning a porn magazine to its pile as Marcus entered.

'What the hell are you playing at, Lieutenant? I thought I said no extra patrols!'

'A white van was stolen during the night by a slim man in shades and a woman with long black hair, also in shades. I reported it to the RUC.'

Making a note of it: 'That's not all you got up to. Undermining the authority of the Army in front of a couple of Paddies!'

'Did the good corporal give a full account of what he was up to?'

'A legitimate P-check.'

'Private parts check, more like.'

'For God's sake, King, this isn't Brixton!'

'Meaning what exactly?'

'There's a war on here,' said Draycott in a tone suggesting perhaps Marcus wasn't aware of it.

'Against courting couples?'

'Against *them*, out there!' he shouted, jumping to his feet and pointing violently.

'All of them?'

'Every war claims its innocents. At least we don't use children as human shields like your friends in the – ' Just in time Draycott repressed what he'd been about to say.

'In the what?' said Marcus quietly.

Draycott gave a little laugh and rubbed his eyes, as though tiredness explained everything. But seeing the brittle look in Marcus's eyes and the fists clenched at his sides, he resumed the security of his seat. 'I'm warning you, King,' he said with quiet menace. 'You're getting close to the edge.'

Stepping forward, Marcus spread his hands wide on the desk and leaned across into Draycott's face.

'No, Major, it's me that's warning you.'

The same dawn that found Marcus threatening his commanding officer uncovered Dixie Doyle at the wheel of a stolen van, negotiating a rutted track towards a crest of woodland.

The atmosphere was tense. Annie was on trial, Feeley wanted her to lose, Dixie wanted her to win, and Michael was trying to lift spirits with a sentimental rendering of *The Sniper's Promise*: '*The night was icy cold, I stood alone waiting for an army foot patrol . . .*'

Mist hung over the hillsides, shrouding the van as it climbed, its straining engine interrupting the vast stillness all around.

'*When at last they came into sight I squeezed the trigger of my Armalite . . .*'

'Jaysus,' groaned Feeley, 'give it a rest.'

Training began with a five mile run, broken up with exercises and sprint races. The sprints were closely contested, but Annie easily won the long distances, joking after about another five miles before breakfast. Dixie invariably trailed, determined but last, taxing his scarred lungs. Now came the serious business of the morning – the shooting contest.

Feeley, furious at Dixie's handling of traitor McBride, was doubly incensed and insulted by the decision to grant Annie the assassination of Lieutenant Marcus King. Therefore what should have been shooting practice became a competition for the right to kill the Brit, and Dixie had made it clear to Annie that her continuing membership of the unit depended on her winning.

They tacked thirteen cardboard targets to trees along the fringes of the wood, each cut-out the silhouette of a squaddie's head. Each contestant would have an Armalite, thirteen rounds – one per target – and two minutes to complete the circuit. The number 1 stood out clearly beneath the nearest life-sized silhouette, which was worth one point. The next cut-out, hung further away from the marksman, was numbered 2 and carried two points, and so on. The thirteenth and final target was so far away, it was hard to see even down telescopic sights.

Since the assassination was to be carried out from inside the stolen van, contestants would fire through a crudely opened gash in the van's side at approximate head height. Two members of the gang would keep watch for danger at all times.

Michael went first, marking up forty-eight out of a possible ninety-one points, but was penalised for overrunning the time. Dixie followed and managed fifty-six. Feeley went next. Skilled and experienced, already a legendary sniper in modern Republican folklore, her form was enhanced by personal rivalry.

With venomous spite coursing through her, she shot an impressive sixty-nine, narrowly missing two targets, numbers 9 and 13. She emerged from the van furious with herself for missing the ninth.

Annie climbed into the back of the van. Introducing her Armalite to the breach in the side, she concentrated on the intimate relationship between rifle and body, until butt and barrel became extensions of herself. Then she made herself very still, like a hunter, experiencing the same rush of nerves and energy she'd felt at the age of seven when her father first taught her to shoot. His conviction that death was deliverance from life had always given her a detached attitude to killing hares and rabbits, an absence of violent intent, and while she no longer believed in deliverance by the bullet, she had no difficulty recapturing the cool detachment of her early training.

Yet she was shaking slightly as she picked out Dixie in her sights, waiting by the first target, tricolour flag poised in one raised hand. He was consulting his watch. Once his hand came down, Annie would have 120 seconds to complete the circuit. Casting a rapid eye along the course, she could see why it was so difficult. Most targets were partially screened by mist and foliage, and when the breeze blew, the silhouettes were further obscured by shifting branches.

Dixie lifted the flag higher and abruptly dropped his hand. Annie took a sharp breath, zeroed in on the nose of the first silhouette, steadied, and pulled the trigger. A loud report rent the still mountain air and she felt the keen reflex of the stock against her shoulder. Dixie acknowledged the hit with the flag raised and moved quickly to the second target.

With each receding target Dixie became smaller, and the face and beret of the silhouette shrank. The trembling had stopped and Annie was firing smoothly and rapidly, making Dixie run from tree to tree to keep up. But as the seconds went by and the breeze picked up, the last four targets – the vital scores from 10 to 13 – seemed to sway and blur in the sights. Knowing she was ahead on time, she took meticulous aim at the tenth and knew the shot was good before Dixie raised his hand.

But distances were now so great that she couldn't make out the hole drilled by her bullet in the previous target, nor detect the silhouette shudder on impact, and as she loosed her eleventh round, she saw Dixie wave his flag low and vigorously across his body to indicate a miss. One more miss and she was beaten, and the hardest two were to come. Somewhere nearby, Feeley would be celebrating the miss and anticipating victory.

Annie checked her watch – twenty-five seconds remaining. Riding her heartbeat, she took aim at the head perched above number 12, imagined a callous British officer and fired. Dixie raised a far off arm.

Edging the rifle to the right, Annie homed in on the final dim shifting smudge that was, she assured herself, the thirteenth target. Its face was intact, no one had disfigured it. If Annie failed to now, she would lose to Feeley by two points, and Dixie would have no option but to expel Annie from the unit. With a sharp intake of breath she lined up the distant blur in her sights. With her remaining seconds running away, she slowly, smoothly released her breath and pulled back on the trigger.

Her life stood still, her future hanging on the crucial division between a near perfect shot and a perfect one.

The air cracked with the speed and power of the high velocity bullet, flying on a low trajectory across the plain and into the wood. The hills were still echoing to the shot as Dixie turned from the target and punched the air in a salute to Annie McBride.

6

11 July

Marcus was on the streets all day, following hunches, hunting for Dixie Doyle. Sun shone and rain fell in quick succession, the glistening Bogside retreated into itself as Marcus led a patrol into the concrete glare. Few women banged their bin-lids, knowing how dangerous the Army would be after Thorn Hill. They took their families indoors and fastened the bolts.

In the early afternoon Marcus halted his brick at the foot of a long familiar terrace. He knocked on a door which was usually wide open. 'Martha?'

She appeared at last, filling the doorway, holding back the mongrel which a week earlier had gone for Charlie Winters' legs.

'Go home, Marcus, this is no place for the likes of you.'

'I like it here.'

'If there were more like you, we'd like you here too. But you're on your own, son, you can't win.'

'With a little help from my friends?'

Arms folded beneath her pendulous bosom, she shook her head. 'You'll not catch Dixie.'

'What do you know about Dixie?'

Neighbours appeared in doorways unsmiling.

'Shall I tell you what I know about Dixie? Until your government sorts them lot out' – nodding towards the Protestant side of the river – 'I know we need bastards like Dixie to protect us.'

'If we don't get him soon there'll be hell to pay.'

'There's always been hell to pay, and we'll still be paying long after the next regiment takes your place.'

She went inside and closed the door.

As Marcus led his men up the hill, he spotted a number of men being spirited through the bomb grilles and heavy metal gates of a corner pub. While his men took up positions, Marcus hammered on a caged window.

'Lieutenant King, British Army, open up!'

Disregarding standard procedure, Marcus handed his rifle to a soldier and strolled into the bar taking Bones with him.

'Afternoon, ladies and gentlemen.'

Pistol holstered, he stood centre-room looking slowly round. Through the nicotine haze he recognised faces on the fringes of the Provos, their eyes lowered. The room was still, drinks frozen on tables, even the barman rooted, caught in the act of drying glasses.

'If any of you good people have any idea where Dixie Doyle might be, then for God's sake – for your sakes . . .'

A few minutes away a stolen white van crept on higher ground through the terraced maze, the most wanted man in Ireland in the cab, the most wanted woman at the wheel, the queen of snipers in the back, and a gigantic young farmer close behind, keeping look-out astride a motorbike.

'He's gone into another pub,' reported Dixie, training field-glasses across the labyrinth, 'to do another Laurence Olivier.'

Marcus emerged from the pub. A glut of confidential calls had been received by the RUC, most of them well-intentioned. But he was well aware that only twelve hours remained before Draycott unleashed the raids, destroying whatever goodwill existed between the battalion and the people. For Marcus it would be a personal blow, leaving the Army with an overwhelming sense of failure.

As he led his men deeper into the ghetto, a tract of wasteland opened out before them, peopled one minute, deserted the next. Even packs of dogs ran away, like creatures in the path of a forest fire. Marcus would normally have skirted exposed ground, but something he saw just then changed his mind, a gang of youths spilling onto the wasteground idly kicking a ball, hands in pockets, refusing to be intimidated.

He gave the signal and his men fanned out into the open. The afternoon sun was breaking through, setting the scab of land sparkling with weeds, bricks and broken glass. Marcus walked towards the youths, casually assessing them, boys in their mid-teens wandering home from school, faces marked with studied indifference, wavering on the margins of a society which seemed to offer but three options – joblessness, crime or the Provos.

The two parties converged, and would have passed cleanly through each other had Marcus not caught Spiky's eye and silently communicated instructions. As the youths' football rolled into his path, Spiky intercepted it and hoofed it forward. Marcus pirouetted round and trapped the ball neatly between his feet.

'Hey!' shouted a youth. 'Give us our bloody ball back!'

There was purpose in Marcus's piracy, a device to flush people from their homes and loosen their tongues. Juggling the ball with his boots he hoisted it in the air, whipped off his beret and headed it all the way back to Spiky.

A youth ran at Spiky, who waited till the youth was upon him before lobbing it back to Marcus. As the gang ran at Marcus, he lifted the ball over their heads to Bones's feet.

'Bastards!' The youths swarmed after the ball, the soldiers moving it quickly amongst themselves.

Marcus caught Bones by the arm and hissed orders in his ear. 'Get on the radio, send for the two nearest patrols and a helicopter for cover.'

Across the river in the main Army base, the battalion's Commanding Officer, or C.O., Lieutenant-Colonel Gerald Stanley-Taylor, was summoned urgently to the Ops Room where a screen was receiving pictures live from the Bogside by Heli-tele. At first he saw nothing remarkable, a fine summer's day over hostile territory, slate-grey roofs, the high-rise Rossville flats. Then the flying camera banked sharply and the terraced maze opened into a bomb-site seething with people. For a moment the C.O. thought he was witnessing a riot.

'Appears to be a game of football,' he shrugged.

'Take a closer look, sir.'

Obligingly the camera swooped low over rooftops and hovered.

'Why,' enquired the C.O. completely baffled, 'am I watching a game of football?'

'Because, sir, we appear to be in it.'

Uproar on the ground, outraged booing from the dense crowd, raucous laughter, begrudging applause.

'And I believe we've just gone one-up, sir.'

'You mean to tell me. . .?'

The camera swept slowly across the clearing, taking in goal-posts improvised with oil drums and dustbins, crowds undulating and troops slung around for cover. The C.O. strained his eyes. No doubt about it. British soldiers playing soccer behind enemy lines.

'Oh well played, King!' blurted a voice over his shoulder. A throng of officers had pressed into the room, appalled and excited by the spectacle. The C.O. quelled them with a scandalised look, then resumed staring at the screen in disbelief.

Half a dozen soldiers appeared to be playing a horde of boys and men, a grey-haired priest the referee. As the camera zoomed closer, Marcus King could clearly be seen mesmerising the opposition, infuriating and enthralling the crowd, blatantly enjoying himself, performing with style, the ball a casual extension of his feet. Then a shot, the ball curving dangerously, arresting for a moment the charged carnival atmosphere. A save! A just roar, the natives counter-attacking on waves of partisan hooting, sweeping through the British defences to fire at Private Spiky Rice flapping like a grotesque bird in the Army's goal, the ball cannoning off his impossible limbs and flying wide.

The crowd groaned, laughed. The shadow of a helicopter passed slowly overhead, unnoticed.

Taking a stiff pull on his cigarette, Major Draycott wearily answered the phone in the operations room of the improvised fort. It was a bad line, sounded like – Is that you, Major?

'Course it's fucking me. What have we this time, Doyle's favourite toothpaste?' The line cleared, the C.O.'s nasal drone instantly recognisable. 'Ah! it's you, sir. My apologies. We're all a bit jaded over here – '

He listened, grinning contemptuously.

'Must be some mistake, sir, not even Lieutenant King would – '

The C.O. was having a fit, something about 'watching the bloody thing live!'

Face darkening: 'I'll deal with it right away, sir.'

*

'He's mad!' Shaking his head, Dixie followed Marcus King through field-glasses.

'Bloody dangerous, you mean,' said Feeley behind the wheel of the idling van, parked on a terraced hill with a long clear view of the game below. Annie was standing in the back, watching proceedings through field-glasses, waiting for the word. Michael cruised adjoining streets on the motorbike.

A roar went up from the crowd, reverberating through the terraces. The Bogside had equalised, television crews arriving just in time to capture the moment.

'Smart bastard,' murmured Dixie, 'pretty piece of propaganda.'

'So what are we waiting for?' said Feeley.

Dixie glanced repeatedly at the helicopters, two of them now. 'When I give the word' – addressing Annie over his shoulder – 'you'll want to be sharp. If one of those bastards up there spots the rifle . . .' He trailed off to sweep the scene below once more through field-glasses, picking out crouching soldiers guarding the match at both ends of the ground. Another glance at the helicopters, waiting for them to retire a little further . . . another long look at Marcus King.

'Stand by!' Excited now, the optimum moment arriving as players settled for the restart after the goal. 'Any second now.' The line of fire would be clear, and the helicopters removed to the far side of the ground. 'One shot, McBride, that's all . . . wait for it . . .'

Annie stood close to the breach in the side of the van, clutching her Armalite, poised to introduce it, concentrating her mind like a professional, while wishing her victim was a pompous white general and not the magnificent creature she had run into at Thorn Hill. Nothing is ever simple, she told herself.

'NOW!'

Annie thrust the rifle through the breach, anticipating the ease with which her sights would locate the distinctly tall, conspicuously black British officer, already foreseeing his face marked by the telescopic cross of death. But before she could find him, an unexpected noise began to distract her – the hammering of bin-lids, tentative at first, rapidly spreading.

'Shh-it!' she heard Dixie curse. 'The fucking cavalry!'

Peering over her sights Annie saw them – droves of armoured vehicles bursting into view, converging on the wasteland from all directions.

'Shoot!' cried Feeley, slamming the van into gear.

'Get going!' Dixie told her.

Annie got behind her sights again, trying to track her victim through a human veil of fleeing spectators.

'Fucking shoot!' yelled Feeley.

'Get this bloody crate moving!' said Dixie.

Annie caught glimpses of Marcus King's head as he waded through the running tide of humanity, and though her finger was poised and willing, her mission had become more lottery than art.

'Stupid bloody bitch!' spat Feeley, taking the van away.

Dixie clung to the dashboard, the prospect of capture and torture bearing down on him.

'We'll get him,' he said, 'if not today, tomorrow.'

In the back Annie sank to the floor, exhausted with the tension of the unreleased bullet.

The tide of human panic broke over him, leaving Marcus washed up on the edge of the wasteland, gathering his men and weapons under the shelter of a factory wall. Bin-lids echoed, drowned by the swelling high-pitched whine of Saracen armoured cars, and the booming amplified voice of Major Draycott.

'THE GAME IS OVER . . . RETURN PEACEFULLY TO YOUR HOMES . . . THE GAME IS OVER . . . RETURN PEACE-FULLY – '

His Saracen drew up sharply. Leaning out, he glowered down at Marcus.

'Good afternoon, Mr King! Congratulations! Lots of fun all round, eh! The C.O. will see you at Battalion H.Q. at 18.00 hours sharp!'

He thumped the side of the turret. The huge armoured vehicle lurched forward across the wasteground in pursuit of the enemy. On the Rossville Street side a hard knot of hate had formed, hurling missiles at the advancing steel, falling back in tatters as packs of Flying Pigs charged them, salvoes of heavy-duty baton rounds whipping people off their feet, scattering others into side streets, where they regrouped to ambush the circling armour.

Marcus gazed into space. His men shifted uneasily, none more so than Spiky, who feared now for his hero and protector. It was hard-bitten Bones who broke the silence.

'Reckon your glory days are over, Boss.'

When Marcus entered the Commanding Officer's room at the appointed hour, he found the C.O. sitting forward at his desk, stiff and resolute, anxious to get the business underway and over with. Major Draycott was present, and something in the way he was standing there, hands behind back, gazing confidently out of the window, suggested to Marcus that he had carefully briefed and coached the C.O.

The C.O. glanced at Marcus and away again, shrinking from eye-contact. He was fairly tall and fairly thin, with dry slack features, lustreless moustache and a mincing mouth. Marcus saw in him a humourless military specimen unconnected with the world, inconceivable out of uniform. But what repelled Marcus were those pale, loveless eyes.

'I hope you realise the gravity of what you've done.'

There was a hollow ring to the Colonel's voice, like the tolling of a bell. Nor was Marcus offered a seat, suggesting the interview would be brief and to the point.

'You've let the side down very badly indeed. Your reckless behaviour this afternoon compromised the Army's authority and seriously endangered the lives of your men. Nor, regrettably, is this the first occasion I've been obliged to speak to you. The saxophone incident was bad enough, but this . . . was quite beyond belief.'

The C.O. spoke without emotion, keeping his eye fixed on some inanimate object over Marcus's shoulder. Marcus stood much as Draycott stood, legs apart, hands behind back, shoulders straight. His face, he believed, was calm. Inside he was quivering with humiliation.

'No doubt you thought you were improving the Army's image. To that I would say that you are not employed to run our P.R. department. And what's more, you achieved precisely the opposite. You simply exposed us to ridicule, made a laughing-stock of my battalion in particular and the Army in general. I shouldn't be surprised if you insist that your peculiar brand of fraternising is a clever means of intelligence gathering. It is not. It was a cheap publicity stunt that backfired badly.'

He looked directly now at Marcus, a glimmer of feeling in his pallid eyes. 'Do you realise your performance has gone out on television? Foreign networks were present and your antics have been beamed around the world!' His voice reached an unexpected peak, moustache quivering. Mastering himself he delivered sentence.

'You've been on a warning since the saxophone incident and the mess brawl, and one might have hoped you'd have taken the opportunity to redeem yourself. Sadly that has not been the case, and it has become abundantly clear that you and the Army are not compatible' – 'Not compatible' rang in Marcus's head – 'Today's football fiasco was the final straw and I have no further wish to see you in my battalion. My report is already on its way to the Brigadier. You have altogether overstayed your welcome in the British Army, and I expect you to do the honourable thing and resign your commission . . .'

Resign? The word reverberated through Marcus's brain. And 'overstayed your welcome' – as though he'd been some loutish guest – 'in the British Army', the stress on British, as though he was a foreigner, a colonial. He stood unblinking, stunned.

'In the meantime, while I may not be entitled to strip you of your rank on the spot, I can and do insist that you cease forthwith to carry out the duties of an officer. On no account' – he looked purposefully at Major Draycott – 'is this man to exercise command on the streets.'

Draycott nodded politely, as though mildly surprised.

'As far as I'm concerned, as long as he's still with us, he's a soldier in a brick, a dog's body.' The C.O. focused narrowly on Marcus's rigid face. 'You have forty-eight hours to think things over, Mr King. I've no doubt that you will arrive at the same opinion as mine – the only course remaining to you is to leave the Army of your own volition. That will be all.'

He looked resolutely away, waiting for Marcus to be gone. Draycott continued to gaze out of the window, glazed with victory. Marcus stared dumbly, refusing to believe his senses, blind to what had long been coming. He'd effectively been reduced to the ranks at a stroke. He felt his eyes sting. His head dropped, eyes roaming for solace over the regulation carpet. Like a chastised boy he longed to leave the room as quickly as possible. But he couldn't move. Shock was giving way to pride. Lifting his eyes to the men who had just erased his career, he found his voice.

'You can't do this to me, I'm a fucking hero!'

No response, save for a tightening of the Colonel's jaw.

'Overstayed my welcome?' He divided his savage gaze between Draycott and the C.O. 'I've sweated blood for the Army all over the world, risked my life when others kept their heads down . . . worked my balls off forging links with the people of Derry and everything was under control today until you sent in the armour. I'm telling you, I could run this fucking outfit blindfolded!'

Teeth set, eyes ablaze, he paused for breath, and for a reaction. But the C.O. appeared unmoved and Draycott merely sharpened his gaze, as though taking casual aim at something out of the window.

'You're not helping yourself,' observed the C.O. drily.

Marcus floundered in the unexpected silence. He was like a boxer who hasn't heard the verdict, stumbling round an empty ring after an opponent who is no longer there.

'You've no right,' he blurted, 'you know bloody well I'm a good officer.'

'I don't deny you possess some admirable qualities, wouldn't you agree?' – looking across at the Major.

'Absolutely.' Draycott at his most bland.

'And in some respects an exceptional record. But for some time your conduct has, to put it mildly, been inconsistent with that expected of an officer.'

'You mean I've a mind of my own.'

'Nothing can excuse what happened today – '

'There's a few things I'd like to say about that – '

'I don't want to hear.'

'Interview's over, King,' said Draycott turning sharply.

'No way!' Marcus levelled with him. 'Every man has the right to defend himself.' He rounded on the Colonel. 'I did not endanger the lives of my men this afternoon . . . I called up two sections and a chopper for cover, and slung a cordon round the area. Number two, it was good publicity for us, the supposedly brutal British Army playing football with locals in the heart of Nationalist Derry . . . good, that is, until the armour arrived. Now I know what we look like through their eyes. Are the cameras still out there recording us beating hell out of kids we were playing football with? There was no riot,' he said, pointing at the C.O. and then the Major, 'until you two panicked' – the C.O. hoisted an eyebrow – 'or was it you couldn't bear the idea that we might be getting it together with the enemy!'

'That's enough!' bawled the C.O., springing to his feet.

'If you think I'm going to resign . . .' Marcus shook his head, smiling bitterly.

'Leave the room at once!'

'You're going to have to drum me out.'

'I said get out!'

Later that evening Marcus was summoned to the briefing room. Major Draycott was on his feet in readiness, hands clasped behind his back, face firm with resolve. Beside him, formally at ease, stood Platoon Sergeant Bob Wallis, a stocky cheerful 23-year-old Geordie. When Marcus entered, Wallis glanced uneasily at him and then contemplated his boots.

'Mr King, you heard the Colonel. Under no circumstances will you exercise authority during tonight's raids. You will be in Sergeant Wallis's section, and take orders from him, understood?'

Wallis stuck to his boots. He was accustomed to taking orders from Marcus King and didn't know where to look. Marcus looked neither at Wallis nor at Draycott. His shoulders and head had dropped, the pride seemed to have gone out of him. He looked like a man who'd suffered a blow on the head. His face was immobile and expressionless. Only the ever vigilant eyes betrayed traces of shame, rage and bewilderment.

'Understood?' repeated the Major.

'Sir,' conceded Marcus in a murmur.

'Good. That will be all, gentlemen.'

Marcus and Wallis left and went their separate ways. But halfway down the corridor Wallis turned. Marcus also turned, meeting the younger soldier's gaze.

'You're all right,' said Marcus, 'don't worry about it.'

That evening, while rioting exhausted itself in the Catholic Bogside, festivities were underway in the Protestant back streets of Waterside. For it was the eve of the glorious Twelfth of July, when every year the beleaguered Loyalists of Ulster summon ghosts from the graveyards of history and make them dance to the tune of Protestant supremacy.

This was 1980s' Derry, but something of 1930s' Chicago spilled from a rowdy bar off the Dungiven Road at eleven p.m. that night. Teddy Paxton, local supremo, a heavily built man with deep voice and eloquent gestures, joked with friends and followers, rolling a Havana cigar between chipped teeth, smiling graciously as someone's handsome wife dusted ash from his ice-blue suit. Politely declining a lift, exchanging hearty goodnights, he walked homeward flanked by two silent bodyguards, the charm falling instantly from his face.

Teddy Paxton ran the local UDA – Ulster Defence Association, the Protestant Loyalist answer to the IRA. Like its enemy it accommodated a broad selection of minds, from romantic champions to psychopaths. Paxton was neither of these. A shrewd man in his thirties, he dined with politicians and drank with gunmen, and his fist-thumping Loyalist speeches were lined with rhetoric on the rights of Catholics in a future independent Ulster. Poor and prosperous, detached from the violence and steeped in it, he led a charmed and dangerous life. A clean-cut family man, he trod a path of righteousness, never straying down alleys where Republicans were tortured or bombs assembled. No blood stuck to his hands, and unlike the IRA, his paramilitary organisation operated legally.

He paused at the foot of his street, where a chanting crowd danced around one of scores of bonfires raging in the district, twenty-foot pyramids of wood, tyres and household junk setting the darkness alight and casting an orange glow over terraced rooftops. Flutes and accordions played traditional hymns, antipapist ballads drifted across the river towards the Catholic strongholds. Swapping patriotic jokes on the fringes of the crowd, Teddy Paxton strolled on to keep his appointment with the new assassins. He walked with a lordly confident air, lending a measure of grace and conviction to the public face of the UDA.

But behind the façade, Paxton was as nervous as the community he represented. Life was as hard and insecure as ever. Paxton saw the sectarian struggle in similar terms to the Great War, when terrible hardships and sacrifices were endured over many years for the capture or loss of a few paltry yards. Nothing changed. The Catholics knew who they were and roughly where they wanted to go. The Protestants knew roughly where they wanted to go but weren't sure who they were. Paxton was supposed to be British, but didn't feel British. He was supposed to be anti-Irish, but the soil which nourished his roots was Irish, and in some inner sense he felt Irish. Most of all he felt himself to be an Ulsterman, but then his Catholic neighbours across the divide were also Ulster men and women, including Provos like Dixie Doyle. And while Union Jacks would accompany the Orange Lodge parade in the morning, he reserved his deepest misgivings for the British, mistrusting their motives for being in Ulster, believing them to have more to do with exploiting a remote and ideal training ground for the most advanced anti-terrorist army in the world, and with meeting NATO requirements for a disunited Ireland, than the lip service monotonously paid to the democratic rights of the arranged majority. In short, he feared the IRA and hated the British.

As he reached his door and looked back at the silhouettes cavorting round the bonfire, one side of his burly face broke into an obstinate smile. Betrayed by Westminster, threatened by Dublin, slaughtered by the IRA – but by God we're alive and kicking!

Just then a mob turned the corner of the narrow terraced street. His guards stiffened, glints of sub-machine-guns inside army surplus camouflage jackets. Singing and swearing, the mob gravitated towards Paxton. He stayed put, and when they reached him he saw they were mere teenagers and children swinging cans and half empty bottles. A girl of no more than fourteen pitched to the ground, spilling beer over his shoes and lacerating her hand. Sprawled at Paxton's feet, she opened her eyes and screamed. A youth picked her up and they staggered on together. Bending down to wipe his shoes, Paxton experienced a sudden wave of despondency.

'You should stop it!' quailed an old woman across the street. 'Our own flesh and blood carrying on like savages. 'Tis no celebration no more.'

He turned away and beat upon his own front door.

Paxton's wife admitted him to the neat, well furnished terraced house. She made him a pot of tea and went to bed, having pressed the family's best clothes for the morning's parade in Limavady.

His office was the converted front room. A UDA banner, proclaiming LAW BEFORE VIOLENCE covered one wall, a portrait of its chairman adorned another, with TEDDY PAXTON – PROTECTOR OF THE PEOPLE – DEFENDER OF THE FAITH blazoned underneath.

Pouring himself a whiskey, he switched on the television to catch the News. *'In the World Cup Final Italy beat West Germany . . . PLO–Israeli cease-fire holds in Beirut'* – and then a familiar fatherly face filled the screen, Reverend Ian Paisley urging a Falklands spirit in Ireland, a Lebanon-type invasion of Eire to flush out the IRA – *'Unshackle British troops and the RUC . . . let there be war!'*

A car in the street. The wolfish Alsatian under the desk cocked an ear and growled, then recognising the coded rapping on the steel shutters, went back to sleep. The two assassins were admitted and kept standing blindfolded.

Paxton shuddered at the sight of the killers in his office, reminding himself that violence – even death – was a fact of life. The assassins looked ideal, nondescript and inconspicuous, single men without ties or feelings apart from a burning hatred for Fenian rebels, and reserves of pent-up violence. According to their dossiers, once pointed in the right direction they never missed. This assignment, however, was of a different calibre.

'You don't need to know who I am, or where you are,' began Paxton hoarsely, 'only that it's high time Mr D. Ragdoll Doyle was put to sleep . . .'

He thought he saw them flinch. They could not have failed to know that their predecessors – admittedly not pros – had been found in Mary Doyle's house, throats cut.

'While the Army plays football with Fenians,' pursued Paxton, 'Mr Doyle enjoys the freedom of the city, robbing banks, bombing RUC officers and bumping off prison warders. You'll get five grand for Doyle, half for any of his gang, particularly Black Rose and the new recruit, whoever she is. Keep in regular touch with this number . . .' He quoted a number and made them repeat it back.

The assassins had no sooner left when Mrs Paxton burst in. 'Do something, for God's sake, the street's on fire!'

He stepped outside. A burning telegraph pole, like a giant's torch, had set the end house alight, crowds falling back in horror and delight. He went indoors and picked up the phone. Dialling a number he gave his name and asked for the Fire Chief.

'Hello, Bill, sorry to bother you. You got a spare engine? My street's burning . . . No problem, tell the boys Teddy Paxton guarantees their safety.'

The dead hour before dawn, bonfires still smouldering on the east side, but strangely no sign of the Army.

All quiet on the Catholic west side, streets deserted, houses darkened, and here too, the fort seemingly inert. But like a tightly coiled snake, the Army watched, feigning sleep, preparing to strike.

Marcus King sat squashed among silent young soldiers in the back of a Pig, dumb with anger, grateful for the darkness which hid his shame. He felt sorry for his men, who couldn't look at him. It was hard for them to deal with his disgrace, one minute their leader, the next a fellow squaddie. A man who had demanded of them the highest military and moral standards, he was now in no position to demand anything. He had been different things to different men – elder brother, father, mentor. He was the sort of man you went to if your girl was screwing another bloke back home.

Marcus checked the luminous hands of his watch – 3.27 a.m. In three minutes' time the signal would be given and all his work destroyed.

A few streets away, someone Marcus had tangled with before watched from her window. Sixteen-year-old Bernie O'Rawe suffered from insomnia and was gazing across the night at the fires on the Proddie side of town, enjoying the way they lit up the river. In her head she was reliving the previous day's riot after the football match, the terrible thrill of fighting the Brits, the buzz she got from a life-and-limb game played out on the streets for real, and then seen in replay on TV.

The Army was in bad humour. Four dead the other day, couldn't take its own medicine. Bernie's big sister Roisin, fearing a Brit night-raid, had sent her kids over. As Bernie returned to bed, excited by the prospect of raids, she had to burrow in among her two nieces. One of them woke and they started a tickling game. Bernie tired of it.

'Stop acting the goat, Anna-Marie, and give us a song!'

Anna-Marie fell asleep, Bernie drifted back to childhood and a boy she once liked. Only later did she find out he was one of 'them'. Bernie sang tunelessly in the dark: *Holy Mary, mother of God, pray for me and Tommy Todd, I'm a Fenian and he's a Prod, Holy Mary mother of . . .*

She froze, listening intently to the night.

The signal was given, engines started up. Marcus closed his eyes and felt for the crucifix round his neck. He was going into action against people he'd worked so hard to win over. He knew all the addresses earmarked for his section. They belonged to Sinn Fein workers, known Republican sympathisers, and families of men

103

behind the wire. It was a close summer's night and people would be sleeping naked. He pictured himself in bed with Marcia, woken by the splintering of a door, soldiers swarming into the bedroom. Rash thoughts to be carrying on a raid, but they reminded him he had to call Marcia and put her mind at ease. Some of the Toms had seen the football fiasco on the TV news in the fort. Brilliant! they'd said. What a laugh! No mention of an officer being disciplined, only that serious disturbances had led to a riot. What would Marcia think if she saw him playing football one minute and engulfed in a riot the next?

The tightly packed Pigs moved off as quietly as they could, stealing across the night, stalking the urban warren, infra-red eyes giving off no light. Closing on their selected target, they lurched forward with a deafening roar of engines, soldiers stamping in the back, tyres wailing round corners. A screeching of brakes, Marcus thrown sideways, then springing into the road. This is it! he told his anaesthetised conscience. Sink or swim.

Trailed by a squad of young soldiers, Marcus bolted along the street: Check door number, grit teeth, think hate. With a deep breath he slammed the flat of his boot at the shoulder of the door, it flew open, lock disintegrating, and he was halfway up the stairs like a man possessed, bursting into the first bedroom, obliquely lit by floodlights in the street – no one there. Wrong fucking room . . . Spinning round he flung his boot at the door across the short landing and crashed into the bedroom, locating a figure watching him as he dived behind a wardrobe. Roisin Devereux sitting up in bed smoking a cigarette, looking at him as if he were late. The cigarette reminded him of the last time he'd seen her, the morning of Thorn Hill, when he'd stopped her in the street and she'd shown him the cigarette burns on her stomach, before handing over her kids to her sister Bernie and heading for the women's refuge.

'Where is he?' snapped Marcus, rifle pointed at the bed.

She looked at him blankly. She wasn't a day older than Marcia, but with her shabbily bleached hair and stress-ravaged face she could have been forty.

'OK, Boss?' Sergeant Wallis filled the doorway.

'Search the other rooms,' replied Marcus.

The sergeant was gone before either realised Marcus wasn't giving orders any more. The house shook with the violence of the search.

Marcus approached the bed. Roisin observed impassive. Whipping back the covers on the unoccupied side, he felt the sheet for body heat. There was none.

'I said where is he?'

She frowned, feigning I-don't-know-who-you-mean.

'Your husband, remember?'

'Ah! Offside.' Offside meant over the border, probably into Donegal.

'The kids?' Marcus began rooting through drawers and ripping up carpet.

'Gone to my mother's.' Humming absently, she took to reading a magazine, not looking up until she heard Marcus attacking the floorboards. 'For God's sake,' she said mildly, 'is that really – '

He was on one knee, holding something in a handkerchief. She looked at the revolver, then at him. She knew what to expect in the hands of the wrong interrogators – days and nights of bullying, threats against her children, verbal sexual abuse of the most lurid kind. Her calm evaporated, face crumbled.

'Get dressed!' he said.

'No, Jaysus, no!' she begged.

Pointing at her pile of clothes: 'Get dressed!'

'Bog off, you Brit bastard, look what the hell you've done to my place – '

'Yeah, and what about this?' snapping open the revolver to reveal three rounds in the chamber – 'three bullets for three Brits!'

'Mother o'God, believe me' – pleading again – 'it's for our own protection.'

'Under a floorboard? Get up!'

'Please!' Reaching out to him.

The sergeant barged in. 'Find anything?'

Marcus thrust the gun in his pocket. 'No.'

'We taking her?'

'No.'

'Get going then, shall we?'

'Yeah, we're late.'

The sergeant pounded down the stairs. Marcus and Roisin stared at each other.

'You'll say nothing?' she demanded.

· 'I found it in the street,' he said, aiming a vicious kick at the wardrobe, his boot smashing through the thin wood. A last look of exasperation and he was gone.

105

'Thanks!' she called after him.

He was sprinting along the street, on fire with shame and rage, the street blinded by searchlights, choked at both ends by Pigs, reeling with women screaming and swearing as their menfolk were dragged from houses and stuffed into police vehicles.

Marcus reached Roisin's parents' house, Wallis and the rest of the squad hard on his heels. Calling for the sledgehammer, he pounded on the door with his fist. 'British Army, open up!'

'That's the stuff!' – a voice from the road – 'Keep up the good work!' Kitson, newly promoted to captain, grinning sardonically from the front of his Landrover.

Marcus tightened his grip on the sledgehammer and appeared to lean back, coiling himself to let fly and perform the unthinkable. Hate gleamed in Marcus's face, terror fused with disbelief in Kitson's, and a section of the street froze in awe.

'Marcus!' Wallis's desperate intervention.

Marcus tore his eyes from Kitson and swung the sledgehammer, lifting it high over his shoulder before bringing it down like an axe on the front door, cleaving the top half in two. Inhaling swiftly, he swung again and again until the door parted company with its bolts and disintegrated. Thrusting the sledgehammer into a soldier's hands, he released the safety-catch on his rifle, burst into the house and pounded up the stairs. At the top he kicked a door open and followed it in. A sallow spiky-haired teenager was sitting up in bed – Bernie O'Rawe, Roisin's young sister, glaring at him, eyes shot with tranquillisers. From her twisted lips came a vicious torrent of expletives. Tossing his head as though to parry them, he came towards her, rifle aimed at the all too obvious human lump beneath the covers. He sprang, tearing back the bedclothes . . .

'Big bloody hero!' yelled Bernie. 'Terrifying a couple of wee kids!'

Removing the threat of his rifle he looked down at the little girls wrapped round Bernie's pale legs – two of Roisin's kids, staring at him in speechless terror.

'Relax . . .' he said, frightening them even more.

The house was in uproar. Bernie could hear her father being taken away and her mother going mad. Scrambling out of bed in her nightdress, she made for the door. Marcus side-stepped, blocking her. She tried to dodge round him, but he caught hold of her, coldly aware of his hand on her person.

'Let my da go!' she hollered. 'He knows fuck all!'

'They won't keep him long,' said Marcus weakly.

'He's an old man, for fuck sake!'

Her teeth sank into the soft underside of Marcus's wrist. He winced and lost hold of her; she barged past him and got as far as the door, where he caught her by the arm, swung her round and flung her back on the bed.

'OK, Boss?' A shout from downstairs.

'Coming!'

Bernie crouched with feline defiance on the bed. As Marcus backed out of the room, he saw himself in her hate-filled eyes.

Armed with binoculars, Major Roy Draycott scanned the Bogside from a blockhouse perched on top of the fort. In the sharp light of dawn he saw figures running and shouting. Armed with wood, wire and corrugated iron, they were setting the streets drumming with the frantic activity of a termite hill closing the damage after an attack.

So, the natives were establishing 'no go' areas, obstructing the lawful passage of Her Majesty's Armed Forces. That wouldn't do at all, he mused, shaking his head, smiling.

Below stairs, the suffocating quarters and corridors of the fort were jammed with roistering soldiers, bragging and guffawing, high on violence. And rumours were spreading that the Paddies were throwing up barricades.

In a cramped stifling bunkroom Marcus lay on his back drenched in sweat, one wrist bound where Bernie O'Rawe had sunk her teeth into him. Unshaven and shivering, he was aware of the deterioration setting in. His latest fall, he reflected, had begun on Thorn Hill. In one week he had seen comrades blown apart and Charlie Winters burn to death, he'd quarrelled violently with Draycott after the funeral and with Elroy at the party in London, he'd been stripped of officer status and given notice to quit, and to put a thorny crown on his humiliation he'd just been forced to participate in the kind of brutal raid which destroyed his hearts-and-minds method of soldiering. The thin ice had finally broken and he was sinking into dark depths of despair, fearing more than anything that he would return home to Marcia and Jamie, friends

and family, a broken man. Only two choices remained to him –
resign or permit them to boot him out.

Spiky entered, breathless. 'Draycott's issuing dick-guns and a
thousand baton rounds!'

'Great!' rejoined carousing Bones. 'Zap the cunts!'

They knew Marcus's feelings about baton rounds. Better known
as plastic bullets, baton rounds were flat-nosed heavy-duty PVC
projectiles. Almost six inches long and launched from a wide-
barrelled gun, they flew after human beings like elongated torch
batteries. Intended as last resort weapons, some thirty thousand
had been fired the previous year, a lot of last resorts in Marcus's
view. Designed to disperse mobs and temporarily disable indi-
vidual rioters, plastic bullets had a way of breaking limbs,
fracturing skulls, blinding, and worse. Seven people, children
included and all of them Catholics, had been killed by them the
year before.

Unable or unwilling to control his feelings, Marcus leapt up and
set off to find Draycott. On the way he stopped to try and phone
Marcia, but there was a queue, and he pressed on to the briefing
room. He didn't knock, he flung the door open, stepping inside
and, ignoring Kitson and Warfield, levelled with Draycott and
expansively clapped his hands in derisive applause.

'Congratulations, Major! You've got the battle you wanted!
Falklands–Ulster, Argies, Paddies, what the hell, zap the
bastards!'

Draycott paled. 'I don't believe this . . .'

'You better bloody believe it, because if we let rip now with
plastic bullets somebody's going to get killed.'

'You have precisely ten seconds to get out, King!'

The glorious Twelfth had fully dawned, the day hot and sunny. All
across the province Loyalist carnivals unrolled – pipe bands and
booming kettle drums, best suits and bowler hats, pretty girls
clapping and denim-clad skinheads, magnificent lodge banners
unfurling in the breeze, trumpets, medals and sashes gleaming in
the sun.

But while the Protestants were commemorating the 292nd
anniversary of the Battle of the Boyne, and celebrating one more
tenacious year's survival, the Catholics on the west side of Derry
were preparing for a modern day campaign.

Mid-morning, sixteen-year-old Bernie O'Rawe stepped over the debris of her front door and set out to cross the ghetto and make sure her grandparents had survived the night unharmed. She wore tight blue jeans, a sleeveless T-shirt and medium-high heels. The sight of barricades going up fired her with pride, and she experienced a rush of excitement at the prospect of a street battle, of hitting back at the bastards who'd smashed their way into her house and taken in her father for questioning. As she picked up her pace, she hardly noticed the Army helicopter passing slowly overhead, brushing her with its shadow.

A few streets away, a motorbike was creeping from the Creggan into the Bogside, having slipped undetected into the city from the hills to the west.

Dixie normally shared the bike with Feeley. Today Annie rode pillion, sitting high, back straight, red hair billowing under her helmet, Armalite folded in two inside a deep shoulder bag. They pulled up outside St Eugene's Cathedral.

'What if the Brits don't attack today?' she said.

'They will,' he said flatly. 'You know what to do. Good luck.' She climbed off, Dixie caught her wrist. 'I expect to hear on the radio that a British officer was shot dead.'

Their eyes met through open visors.

'You will,' she said with an unmistakable smile.

He rode away to try and locate her victim. She entered the lofty Gothic cathedral, dressed in clean jeans, short leather jacket and trainers. She lit a candle and sat in the stained glass light, focusing her mind on the killing job. She would wait here until a messenger arrived telling her where to go.

There was still a queue for the soldiers only telephone. Marcus sank his pride and went beret in hand to the Ops Room, requesting permission to use the phone. Warfield, embarrassed, was willing. Kitson was not.

'Out of the question. Jolly well queue up at the pay phone like any other squaddie.'

Marcus backed out, quietly shutting the door, leaning back against the corridor wall, closing his eyes.

'Sir?' A hand touched his shoulder, the Company Sergeant

Major. 'I'm sorry about what's happened. The lads are behind you, you know that.'

What use are the lads behind me?

He skipped midday dinner and joined the queue for the phone behind Bones, aware that time was running out, that any minute they'd be called to fall in for action.

'Phoning your mum?'

'Could be,' replied Bones, a none-of-your-business squint on his callous face.

Twenty minutes later, as the passages emptied in preparation for the attack, Bones stepped up to the front of the queue.

'That's your lot!' barked Kitson. 'We move in five minutes.'

Bones, receiver in hand, appealed to him.

Kitson looked at Marcus and then at Bones. 'You've caught me in a good mood, Bones. Just you then.'

The young hard-eyed soldier caught the look that passed between Marcus and Kitson, saw the torment in Marcus's eyes.

'Bollocks!' he exclaimed, slapping the receiver into Marcus's hand and storming off. 'Didn't want to talk to her anyway.'

Marcus turned his back and started to dial London. He could hear Kitson about to speak.

'Don't,' warned Marcus, 'say anything.'

He felt Kitson's eyes on his neck, felt his own heart stampeding, praying Marcia was home, aching to hear her voice, longing to reassure her he was OK – whether or not he was. He heard the clickety-click of connecting lines, a long pause and then . . . the engaged signal.

He went into action with a distorted smile on his face. High on emotion and lack of sleep, riddled with shame for his part in the night's lawless violence, he laughed at himself, riding in the back of another packed Pig, with engine fumes and the smell of unwashed males in his nostrils. As the Pig slewed to a halt and the order came to de-bus, he dropped into the sunlight flexed and numbed for action. There was no escape. Draycott and the C.O. had won, crushing Marcus the peace-maker, forcing him to join the boot-boys. Marcus could see no way out. You can't go half-hearted into battle.

Annie McBride saw them coming, felt a tremor of anticipation. Climbing the outside stairs of a block of dour flats, she reached the highest point and watched as the wide road gradually darkened with the measured approach of Army vehicles – a line of Pigs foremost, squat, square and drab with urban warpaint, steel ploughs known as Paddy-pushers fixed to the front, steel gates sticking out like elephants' ears to protect the soldiers advancing in full riot gear. Behind came the huge Saracens, armed with turret-mounted water-cannon and machine-guns.

The British force drew up quietly in the afternoon sun, while loudhailers offered the Irish lines one last opportunity to dismantle their defences and go home.

Directly below Annie's position, shirt-sleeved Bogsiders jeered and continued bolstering the barricades. Annie felt strangely calm as she trained her field-glasses into the glare, trying to locate exactly where Lieutenant King was. She thought she'd spotted him among the foot-sloggers, and was wondering how that could be, when she heard footsteps on the concrete stairs. Something in their tread made her start. Had the Army spied her? Straightening her dark glasses she turned slowly to meet them . . . four just men, and grim. Not Brits, thank God, nor Prods, but the thinner, high-boned features of Catholics. Involuntarily she smiled. They didn't.

'Identify yourself.'

Strangers were spies, she reminded herself. They closed around her, breathing down her neck. Spreading her long deep shoulder bag she let each man see its chilling burden. They stared dumbly at her. Who was she? Nobody had ever seen her. Silently they consulted each other, and then it dawned on them. Dixie's unit, the other woman. Averting their eyes, they went away.

She smiled ironically to herself. Famous already, the media full of speculation about Dixie's redhead, the one they believed killed the soldier with a single shot on Thorn Hill. She began to tremble slightly with the memory of that deed. The best way through the trauma of any reality was to return to it as soon as possible, to kill again . . . and again . . . and again.

Suppressing thoughts and feelings, Marcus trotted forward into dust and smoke. You're a robot, he told himself over and over, swearing and laughing into his visor, incarcerated in his lunar helmet, constricted by his flak jacket, weighed down by a huge transparent shield and the fat-barrelled baton-gun which launched the plastic bullets. I have no feelings, I'm a robot . . . I've no eyes, I'm a machine . . .

As they met the first rain of bricks and petrol bombs Spiky Rice, running thigh-to-thigh with Marcus, pitched on his face, scarring his visor and rattling his head. Scooping him up, Marcus plonked him on his feet and slapped him on the back. 'Onward, clockwork soldier!'

Through his shield, Marcus began to distinguish men and women behind the Irish lines, heads for riot sticks to crack, heads with savagely angry faces, people whose crime was having the gall to defend their community.

From behind came jets of water, streaming overhead and pounding a burning bus thrown across the road. Steel ploughs leapt at the hissing shell, drew back, struck again, butting and goring, twisting the bus out of the way and roaring on towards the barricades.

Marcus, taller than those around him, seemed to attract the heaviest barrage, stones battering his shield, petrol bombs exploding in his path, until finally the heat and hail beat him to a standstill. He stood stranded in a no-man's-land, drawing down on himself a deluge of missiles. From behind came the shouts of his men, calling him back. He wavered, jolted by successive blows, half hoping a brick would skip past his shield and lay him out. He felt himself seized from behind, dragged back into the baseline. Then he heard the order he'd been dreading, the sealing of his shame.

'LOAD BATON GUNS!' Kitson's shrill plummy voice.

Like an automaton, Marcus broke open his baton launcher and rammed home one fat ugly plastic bullet.

Annie had seen him, identifying him by his brown hands and dimly by his brown face through the visor. There were two other black soldiers in the company, but none with the height and posture which she recognised from Thorn Hill and the football game.

Reaching into her bag, she withdrew the folded Armalite, opened it out into its long slim lethal shape, slotted home one slender magazine, released a bullet into the breach and secured the safety-catch. Next the silencer, all done quickly and skilfully. Finally she squeezed a macabre black mask over her head and started up the last flight of stairs. I'm sorry it has to be you, soldier, but I'm going to do it . . . over and over again . . . until it doesn't affect me any more . . .

She reached the open walkway, keeping well back from the road below. A line of spectators, mainly women and children, were leaning over the parapet coughing and shouting. The first in the line saw her, and the hush travelled all along the front doors of the flats. Mouths dropped, mothers gripped their children. Annie came slowly towards them, directing everyone back into their homes with precise movements of the rifle barrel. They shrank from her, melted into concrete.

Annie slid along the wall, picked her spot, and released the safety-catch.

'FIRE!' bawled Kitson, imbued with the charisma of power. 'FIRE AT WILL!'

A deafening cannonade, a cacophony of rapid explosions as the flat-nosed plastic bullets flew at 160 miles an hour, homing in through smoke and dust to knock men down like bottles, drawing muffled cheers from the soldiers. Plastic bullets and petrol bombs passed each other in the murderous air, leaving Celtic and Saxon blood to mingle in the grit. High on the walkway, the lone sniper tracked the ebb and flow of her target through the smoke.

Marcus fired, watched his bullet fly, saw a stone-thrower whipped off his feet, clutching his leg as he fell, face transported with pain. Reloading, he heard his sergeant pointing out a ringleader in a red jersey. Marcus took careful aim and fired.

A piercing bang, the missile vanishing into the smoke. An exact shot, scrupulously pitched below the human target's waist, only the man in red was in motion, and though he may have felt the wind of the projectile, it brushed his thigh and headed for the girl crouching in the mouth of a side street . . .

One moment she was calculating her next move, the next she took the blunt face of the bullet in the head, slamming her skull against the redbrick wall.

While the man in red tried to escape from a plimsolled snatch-squad, Marcus swept forward in a wave of men and then broke loose on his own, sprinting thirty or forty yards to where the girl lay piled against the wall.

Spiky arrived, crouching down to cover him.

Marcus knelt down, pulled off his helmet, lifted the girl's face away from the wall. The shock of recognition. Bernie O'Rawe. The double shock, strangely calming, that she was dead.

Blood spilled through his fingers. Her skull was broken, but her face was flawless, only the mouth a little slack, neck limp like a doll, eyes wide staring into oblivion.

He touched her face, the skin of her sun-warm cheek. Then he drew down her eyelids with the tips of his fingers.

From the high walkway, through amassing and clearing smoke, Annie watched fascinated as he picked up the body in his arms and carried it, head dangling, back towards his own lines. Lifting her Armalite, she slipped the sights over him like a necklace and, fighting her feelings, settled on the trigger, waiting for the moment when surely he would transfer the body, permitting her, in all decency, to shoot.

The moment appeared to be imminent. A team of medics were hurrying towards him. But as they reached him, and he was relinquishing the body, a voice boomed and a Saracen armoured car drew up sharply, breaking the spell and masking Annie's view. The Major, leaning out of the turret, shouted again. 'Get your bloody arse up front, King!'

Emerging through dust and smoke, Marcus King threw himself at the Saracen, scrambling like a madman up the mesh, his murderous intentions reflected in the fear transforming the Major's face.

Annie pulled the Armalite to the right, tracking him once more in her sights, reaching him as he was falling upon the Major, trying to tear him bodily from the turret, while a host of men were scaling the Saracen, dragging him back down again by his legs and arms.

Riveted, her trembling finger poised on the trigger, Annie watched her victim tumble backwards through her sights into the throng of soldiers. Almost at once, a tall spindly officer weighed into the fray, bawling and waving. The soldiers fell back. For one perfect moment, Marcus King stood isolated and exposed in the middle of a ragged circle of men, fist waved in his face by the enraged officer.

Annie fired.

A muffled shot barely troubled the air.

*

At the debriefing in the hayloft of the farm that night, Feeley would not be calmed.

'If only I'd had him in *my* sights!' she fumed, robbed of the chance to be the sniper who nutted Lieutenant King.

The pressure was on Annie again. She argued that she couldn't very well shoot a man carrying a dead girl and obviously in distress.

'Why the hell not?' charged Feeley. 'They reckon it was him shot the girl. Madam's too fucking fussy!'

Annie lied, said there was no other opportunity to shoot Marcus King. She knew full well she'd had him at the mercy of a clear line of fire for several seconds. But at the last moment, as he'd swayed bare-headed in the dust-blown circle, she'd shot the fist-shaking captain instead. Exactly why she didn't know.

The media were agog with rumour. Local radio had speculated: Has Dixie Doyle's redhead struck again?

Feeley rounded on Dixie. 'She' – pointing righteously at Annie – 'was supposed to redeem herself by bumping off King. She had the chance and didn't fucking take it. She ought to be out on her ear. You're getting softer than shit, Dixie Doyle!'

Feeley was right. Dixie ordered Annie to get up off her backside. Then he rose and faced her, his face lean and cold, his intense green eyes seeming to convey to her a personal message of bitter disappointment, as if to say, Never mind your redemption, what about my passport to freedom? Meeting his gaze head on, she had the feeling he'd confided only in her his intention to quit after the killing of Marcus King.

Michael, on look-out duty behind the mounted machine-gun, looked round uneasily, afraid for Annie. A glance from Dixie redressed him. Feeley, squatting on a bale of straw, assumed an air of professional detachment. Annie herself seemed startled by Dixie's anger, the freckles standing out around her eyes, her face suddenly snow-white against the flames of her dishevelled hair.

Dixie was breathing hard. He had a Colt .38 thrust in his belt and looked mad enough to use it.

'You're a law unto yourself, Annie McBride, orders mean fuck all to you. I send you out to shoot Officer A, you cheerfully shoot Officer B –.'

'You wanted to hear on the radio that a British officer was shot dead. I did it, you heard it. And he was a captain!'

'Dead on!' Michael blurted, 'Jaysus, the Bogsiders took a hell of a beating in the night. I'd say they'll be toasting Annie tonight. And so should we!'

They looked at Michael amazed. He too looked dazed by his own boldness.

'Shut your face, Michael!' said Feeley, jumping to her feet. 'You're fool enough as it is.'

'He has a right to his opinion,' said Annie sharply, 'it's about time you two started showing him some respect. You treat him like shit, the pair of you. God help Ireland if tyrants like you take over!'

'You watch your mouth, young woman.' Feeley kicked over a bale and came towards her, hands closing into fists.

Dixie caught her by the arm. 'Drop it, Feeley –'.

Thrusting him off, pointing viciously at Annie. 'She's been with us six weeks, we've been together six years, and she's telling us how to operate.'

Annie didn't wait to be assaulted. 'Too right!' she said and, lunging at her enemy, caught her by a fistful of shirt, swung a leg behind her knees and dropped her flat on her back. She would have kept Feeley pinned to the floor, but Feeley was strong and flung her off, and as Dixie tried to wrestle them apart, Michael stepped in and used his size and conspicuous muscle to separate them like children and keep them all at arm's length.

'For God's sake, the Brits could creep up on us and we'd be at each other's throats!'

For a moment the loft fell quiet, everyone catching their breath. Feeley looked to Dixie for a firm lead, but he subsided onto a bale, rubbing his eyes. He seemed distracted, feverish. Nobody knew about his nightmares, the spectres of bomb victims that surfaced every few nights and made him afraid to sleep. He was thirty-one but felt forty. His appetite for war was deserting him. He wanted out, a new identity in Dublin, another child with Mary before her health collapsed altogether, and before they killed him.

'Well, Dixie Doyle!' resumed Feeley, hands on hips. 'What are you going to do about her?'

Breaking into a wry smile, Dixie started to chuckle to himself, and then to laugh aloud. 'You got to hand it to her. She couldn't get her man so she picked herself another!'

Feeley glowered at Dixie, her raging expression shot with disillusion. 'I've heard it all now. This unit's going to the dogs,

she's making fucking eejits out of us and you're letting her!'
Turning abruptly she snatched up her rifle and stormed off, calling
ominously from the foot of the ladder. 'That girl'll be the death of
us!'

There was a moment's stillness after she'd gone. Then Dixie
caught Annie's eye.

'Don't think you're off the hook,' he said soberly. 'We've orders
to get that black bastard and we will . . . or rather you will.'

He went off down the ladder. Michael looked at Annie, but she
was closed, that faraway look in her eye, and he went back to
peering out across the moonlit fields.

Annie lay back and gazed at the dimly lit, spider-webbed rafters.
She felt good. First because she was making her presence felt in the
unit, second because killing the officer had not been as bad as
killing the young squaddie on Thorn Hill, and also because she
hadn't killed Marcus King.

7

The cell, intended for six men, had but one occupant – a discredited
black officer accused of attempting to take the life of his commanding officer. It contained three sets of bunk beds, a table and two
chairs. There was one high barred window. A man in military
custody lying on a top bunk could gaze at a thin band of sky.

Visitors stepped cautiously into the cell, ostensibly to express
concern. In reality, the doctor, psychiatrist and the Battalion
Commander wanted to assess the prisoner's mental condition.
They left shaking their heads. The man wouldn't speak, eat or
acknowledge anyone's presence. Had he opted for hunger strike?
Had he gone mad? No one knew. Finally four robust regimental
policemen were sent in to remove him forcibly from his perch. He
came down of his own accord and sat facing his interrogators
without seeing or hearing them.

On the second day a subtler ploy was tried, introducing a young
soldier to coax a reaction from his mentor.

'It's me, Spiky,' said the young man, stepping cautiously into the lion's den. The rumour was Marcus had cracked. 'Wondering how you're doing . . . me and the lads all miss you . . . we had a whip-round . . .'

He held up a bottle of rum and two glasses. No reaction. Marcus lay on his bunk staring at the ribbon of sky.

'And I brought some papers . . . thought you'd want to know how the cricket's going . . .'

The prisoner moved, turning his head to look at the papers dumped on the table. Newspapers were strictly denied to him. Swinging his legs over the side he lowered himself to the floor.

'Here!' Spiky smiled nervously, proffering a packet of the long slim cigars Marcus favoured.

Marcus accepted the packet with a deep intake of breath and began peeling the cellophane. Removing the cigars one at a time, he thrust them into various pockets of Spiky's jacket and then marched him to the door and hammered on it. It opened at once. Over the shoulders of armed guards Marcus met the gaze of Battalion Commander Gerald Stanley-Taylor listening in the passage, hands behind back.

Before releasing the wretched Spiky, Marcus thrust the bottle of rum into his hands. 'Be your own man, Spiky. Never let anybody use you for their dirty work.'

Alone again he turned to the papers, and was gripped by several articles – TIGHT SECURITY FOR BERNIE'S FUNERAL – BERNIE'S AMERICAN DREAM – FAMILY DEMANDS JUSTICE. Enraged relatives and citizens were calling for Bernie's slayer to be charged with murder. He began to tremble, his fingers seeking the tiny grooves made in his wrist by Bernie's teeth.

On the third day he was led before an informal hearing. A parade of faces turned to stare. Handcuffs jarred his wrists. The dry formless voice of the C.O. broke through the whispering and pencil tapping.

'I've called this hearing, gentlemen, to judge this soldier's fitness to face disciplinary proceedings.'

Marcus, outwardly steady, reeled inwardly. After a few moments he realised he was being addressed directly.

'Do you understand the charges which could be brought against you?'

Charges? He tried replaying what he'd only half heard: disregard for standard procedures, endangering the lives of his men, conduct unbecoming of an officer, actions resulting in the death of Captain Kitson . . .

He gazed into a wilderness.

'. . . and do you deny that you attempted to take the life of Major Draycott?'

He opened his mouth to speak. The room fell so still he might have been alone, the men before him mere effigies which would dissolve into dust at a touch.

'I want to speak to my wife.'

Murmuring heads ruined the illusion of stuffed dummies.

'She is being kept informed,' said the C.O. 'Arrangements will be made for you to speak to her in due course.'

An older man in a civilian suit was on his feet.

'I should like to reassure' – faltering, looking round for guidance – 'Mr . . . King?' The C.O. nodded helpfully. 'That in accordance with Rule 9, paragraph 2, of the 1980 Amendment to the Northern Ireland Coroners Rules, he shall not be compelled to appear at the inquest into the death of Bernadette O'Rawe. I trust that will put his mind at ease somewhat.'

Marcus smiled inwardly. It was becoming clear. They weren't concerned with his killing of Bernie O'Rawe, only with his challenge to the Army. He was looking at his hands, recalling the sensation of her blood draining through his fingers. 'I want to be there,' he said quietly.

'There's absolutely no need,' said the C.O. hotly, 'the Army doesn't hold you responsible, not for that.'

'I want to attend,' Marcus raised his voice.

'That would be extremely ill-advised, playing into their hands. Isn't that right, Major Draycott?'

'Absolutely,' said Draycott rising to his feet.

Marcus started at the sound of Major Draycott's manly voice, the man who more than anyone had driven him to the edge.

'You'd be wasting your time,' said Draycott with the assurance of an actor. 'You didn't breach the rules for engagement. You fired under orders, in a riot situation, at the lower half of a specific target, at a range beyond the minimum twenty metres. It was sheer fluke you hit the girl. No member of the security forces has ever been prosecuted over any fatality by baton round, despite numerous, shall we say, dubious incidents.' Assuming a complacent smile: 'Neither you, nor the Army, has any case to answer.'

119

He resumed his seat, not taking his eyes off Marcus, who returned his gaze expressionlessly.

'I'm going to be there,' he said, meeting all the faces. 'I'm going to give evidence.'

Annie was the first to the top of the mountain. Resisting the urge to collapse, she eased the pack and rifle off her back and stood hands on hips gulping sweet Donegal air, muscles crying out from the uphill training run, body teeming with perspiration.

She sat down, forehead cooled by the breeze. Valleys of rock, splashed with lakes and split by rivers, and parcelled in every imaginable hue of green, fanned out before her. To the north she could see the Atlantic, to the west and east Loughs Swilly and Foyle, so that she was surrounded on three sides by water, dazzled by the July sun and minutely flecked with waves.

Unavoidably her eye strayed to the far off ridges of Thorn Hill, where she'd shot the young squaddie called Robbie McLaren, and then south to Derry where three days ago she had ended the life of an officer called Kitson. Both were unmarried, but they must have had mothers, and she wondered whether any cause, even the end of British rule, restoration of equal rights and a united Ireland really justified playing God with human life. Her head nodded, but her heart wavered.

The others staggered up the last stretch, Feeley grimly out of sorts, Dixie straining his lungs, Michael sprawling at Annie's feet, one heavy hand coming to rest on her ankle, fingers venturing a few inches inside the turn-up of her jeans. Preoccupied with the business of death, with the terrible intimacy of dead names, like Robbie McLaren, Annie barely felt Michael's attentions, much as she hardly noticed that they hadn't made love for nearly a fortnight.

'You OK, Annie?'

She looked at him, her wide hazel eyes transparent.

Dixie had reserved his news for the summit. 'The word is,' he panted, 'yer man's been moved to hospital – the psychiatric wing, still in military custody. Orders from the big boys are the same. They want him dead. They're not impressed with our attempts so far and don't see Captain Kitson as a remotely adequate substitute. Getting the man who killed the O'Rawe girl would have tremendous propaganda value. And they want it done now, while she's still fresh in her grave, and in everybody's mind. But it's not a job for a sniper, so' – looking directly at Feeley – 'it's you and me.'

Feeley kept her face, but inside she was euphoric.

Annie sat up. 'You're not thinking. . .?'

Dixie raised his eyes to heaven. 'For Jaysus' sake woman, don't start.'

She heard the tension in his anger and read his mind. The freedom to join his family depended on Marcus King's assassination. How he did it was his business and he didn't want her interfering.

'You're going to use explosives, aren't you?' she accused.

'She's off again!' said Feeley happily, and adopting an upper crust English accent, 'Madam McBride is altogether a better class of terrorist!'

'We're going to bomb his cell,' said Dixie with laboured patience, 'that's all.'

'A bomb is hardly going to respect the boundaries of his cell!'

'The only other casualty could be, with luck, the military policeman on guard outside. And if she's dead unlucky, the night nurse.'

'And that's a chance you're prepared to take?'

Dixie looked at her coldly, his eyes mirroring the rocky green landscape. He looked straight through her, addressing generations to come.

'In war you try and balance maximum injury to the enemy with minimum innocent casualties. Nothing's bought free, least of all a country.'

After reflection Annie said, 'How about phoning a warning?'

'Fucking eejit!' scoffed Feeley. 'The idea is to kill the bastard, not warn him.'

'A last-minute call, Dixie, timed to coincide with the bomb and made directly to the night nurse?'

Her voice, and its blatant appeal, hung in the heady air. All eyes on Dixie.

'I'll think about it,' he said.

121

8

Marcus King paced his hospital cell. It was clean and white, pleasanter than the Army cell, and more disturbing. Without any window there was no sky, dawn or dusk, no escaping the room's sanitising embrace.

By now the first shock had lifted. Grey reality had set in. He'd killed someone. Not a gunman. A girl. It would shadow him always. There would never come a day when he woke and said: that's it, it's not there anymore. Even if it faded in the minds of others, he would carry it, like an implant, beating its guilty pulse.

He heard the spy-slot drawn, sensed the intrusion of an eye. The door swung wide, admitting two Royal Military Policemen, followed by a doctor and a male nurse. Dwarfed by his military escort, the doctor was briskly formal. 'Will you undress, please. Your commanding officer is here and we are obliged to search you.'

Marcus stared at his visitors, a strange smile on his face, caught between mirth and dread. The doctor cleared his throat and repeated, 'I'm afraid we have to search you.'

Marcus's smile evaporated. Without thinking, he took a step backwards.

The sergeant drew himself up. 'We haven't all day, Mr King.'

Marcus spread his hands: 'Come on, man, be reasonable, I got no weapons' – patting himself vigorously – 'search me!'

'That's what we intend to do.'

'For Christ's sake – '

'You went for the Major.' The sergeant took a step forward. 'Your C.O. is on his way here and you could attack him, so we're obliged to search you, simple. So get your clothes off.'

'No way.' Rooted.

The sergeant turned and whispered to his colleague, who left the room hastily. Marshalling his thoughts, Marcus tried to stem the rising panic: They're trying to break you, Brother . . .

The doctor appealed to him: 'Your co-operation would make this less distressing all round.'

'My co-operation! What happened to the promised phonecall to my wife? No contacts, no newspapers, you keep me isolated and disorientated – now this!'

The military policeman was back with two hefty colleagues, making four in all. Truncheons drawn, the grim white host closed in around Marcus. 'Now then,' wondered the sergeant with a deep intake of breath, 'are we going to co-operate or not?'

'You can't do this . . .' Marcus backed away, succumbing to panic, 'I'm an officer in the British Army!'

'You are not!' The voice, nasal, high-pitched and horribly familiar, came from the door. Lieutenant-Colonel Stanley-Taylor, the C.O., the man who'd stripped Marcus of his officer status, stepped up smartly: 'But I'll tell you what you are, Mr King, you're a disgrace to your uniform!' Bristling with indignation, he appeared to draw deep satisfaction from seeing Marcus King brought to heel. As he vented his spleen his torso stiffened, his chin stood up and his eyes radiated with cold lustreless triumph. He held his head high on a sinewy neck, a vainglorious smile on his face, the inevitable swagger-stick twitching behind his back.

'The trouble with you, King, is you think yourself so ghastly superior. But the truth is you're a malicious fool with the dubious distinction of dragging this battalion and the Army into widespread disrepute!' Flecks of spittle hit Marcus's face, and the final '-pute' was delivered like a rifle shot.

'Bullshit!' stormed Marcus. 'It was your bully-boy tactics disgraced us, your thick-headed, sledgehammer mentality . . .' Mad and seething with fear and rage, he was jabbing a cocked finger in the C.O.'s face. 'I warned Draycott someone would get killed – '

The guards seized him, the C.O. exploded.

'Stand to attention, damn you, King, when I'm talking to you!' His words rose in a crescendo, puffed cheeks flushed red, quivering lips gummed at the corners with saliva.

Marcus was shaking. Held rigid by the guards, he stared feverishly into the C.O.'s odious little eyes.

'Has this man been searched?' The C.O. recovered his dignity.

'Not yet, sir.'

'Then get on with it. I'll be back in precisely five minutes.'

The Colonel turned crisply on his heels and departed. Marcus went slack, trembling as the guards gingerly released him.

'Give him room,' said the doctor, thoroughly discomforted. The guards spread their circle and the doctor stepped inside.

'You'd better undress now,' he suggested.

'You've got to three,' advised the sergeant, rolling his truncheon in his fist. 'One . . .'

'I'm quite sure there's no need for that,' said the doctor.

Marcus began to undress, shrinking within himself. His flesh fell bare, chest and tapered torso, long arms and muscular legs, a sheen of sweat colouring his dark skin. He came at last to his underpants. He removed them with the same forced calm displayed for the rest of his clothes, but he felt hopelessly compromised by his nakedness, genitals burning under the assault of countless sneering eyes.

The male nurse stepped forward gloved in rubber, also adopting a strained calm, and needlessly ran his fingers through the prisoner's public and private hair.

'Grip the table, please, and spread your legs.'

Marcus turned round to meet the table and bent over clasping the edge, buttocks jutting into the audience. Dropping his head between his outstretched arms, he could look back between his legs, past his dangling genitals, at several pairs of boots belonging to men who were silently, unashamedly viewing his humiliation.

'Wider, please.'

The transparent silence was magnified by the squeaking of rubber, alien fingers prying inside the entrance of his anus. He held his breath, clenched his teeth, shut tight his eyes. His anus instinctively resisted the violation, recoiling against the probing fingertips. He could feel the nurse's discomfort and impatience.

'Get on with it, man,' complained the sergeant.

The fingers were whipped out. 'You do it, if you're so damn keen!'

'All right, all right,' intervened the doctor, 'let's all stay as calm as we can.'

The fingers returned with renewed insistence, prising Marcus apart, forging deep into his very being.

'That's enough!' He sprang up, shoving the nurse away, floundering in his nakedness.

The guards flexed, a voice barked. 'Who are you to say when is enough?' The C.O. was back, Marcus ignored him.

'What do you think I've got up there, machetes? Jesus Christ, you could have trained a gun on me, none of this shit is necessary, I know what you're doing . . .'

124

'I'm sure that was sufficient,' ventured the doctor.

'Get dressed!' snapped the C.O.

Quivering with shame, Marcus turned his back, hurriedly dressed and found himself alone with the C.O.

'It's at least four days since my arrest' – fastening his trousers – 'and I'm still waiting to speak to my wife.'

'I've made arrangements for you to telephone London' – Marcus looked up, unable to hide his excitement – 'after your court martial in the morning.'

Marcus swallowed and looked away. Strength drained from him, he caught himself against the chair, forced himself not to succumb, not to sit down. Stand up, you bastard . . .

'When's the inquest?' he said steadily.

'Inquest?'

'Yes! Bernie O'Rawe's inquest, the one I'm going to attend!'

'You'd do well to consider your situation carefully.'

'When?'

'I haven't the slightest idea. There will be the usual delay, I shouldn't wonder.'

'You're a second-rate commanding officer, a worse liar' – the C.O. reddened – 'you're afraid of me testifying against you, and Draycott.'

The C.O. laughed shortly. 'I think you'll find we'd come out of it rather nicely, while you would be shown up for what you are – a malicious revenge-seeking mutineer! You didn't get your way, your career's in tatters and now you want your miserable revenge.'

'To hell with revenge! Won't bring the girl back.'

'Nor Captain Kitson, let me remind you.'

Marcus's turn to laugh shortly. 'Major Draycott wanted me to shoulder the blame for Charlie Winters' death, you want me to carry Kitson' – straightening – 'I've given the best years of my life to the British Army, done shit for bastards like Draycott, sweated blood for my men, fought for my country, took on the IRA right across the province, nearly had my arse shot off Christ knows how many times, saved men's lives and won a fistful of medals . . . I done the Army proud, but what did the Army do for me? I should have been captain or even major long ago, but each time promotion came round you found some Charlie Winters to take my place . . . I was ambitious, I was going to rise to C.O., turn out a crack battalion of flexible, intelligent, modern soldiers, the kind of outfit that gives Nationalists no cause to join the Provos – not the fucking thugs and vandals we were the other night!'

Coming closer, breathing down into the C.O.'s rigid face, 'But you and Draycott put a stop to all that, couldn't deal with an NCO who didn't have his brains in his boots – and a black man! Not satisfied, you cut me to the ranks. Ever think what that might do to a man? And now you want to push my head under.' Shaking his head grimly. 'I haven't given twelve years for nothing and if you think I'm going to slink off home with my tail between my legs – '

The C.O. stepped back smartly. 'You've had your say – '

'I'm not done yet,' smiled Marcus.

' – conveniently omitting the appalling details of your rebellion. It'll be a different story at the court martial tomorrow morning.'

He turned on his heels, pausing at the door: 'I'm not a heartless man, King, so permit me to offer you a piece of advice . . .'

Here it comes, thought Marcus.

'To save yourself the humiliation of dishonourable discharge from the Army, we might be persuaded to let you go on medical grounds, we might accept a plea of PTSD. Not familiar with it? In the Great War they called it shell-shock when a man cracked. In World War Two, battle fatigue. Now it's post-traumatic stress disorder. Of course it would require your positive co-operation' – raising his eyes as if to say, I trust you follow my meaning? and managing an almost avuncular smile – 'I should have a jolly good think if I were you.'

He went out, the bolts were slammed. He was heard issuing the guard with instructions. 'Make sure the prisoner is searched before the court martial tomorrow morning.'

The C.O.'s heels echoed and faded.

Marcus subsided against the door and slid to the floor, face in hands. Humiliated and crushed, he felt held together by worn threads. To live with Bernie O'Rawe's death was bad enough. Add to it dishonourable discharge . . . No wonder the C.O. and Draycott were so confident. They were throwing him a lifeline – retirement on grounds of a breakdown. All he had to do was crawl, give a good impression of a coward in court, publicly deny all he'd achieved, all he'd seen, all he believed in – deny himself.

9

The long day descended slowly into night. Hour after hour the prisoner lay face down on his bed, refusing medication.

A fresh guard took over at ten-thirty, with instructions to check the prisoner every fifteen minutes. On his first inspection through the spy-slot, he saw the prisoner slumped over the table, head cradled in arms, eyes vacant. He reported to the night nurse, who duly recorded the continuing deep depression of the prisoner.

The prisoner appeared much the same at each inspection, until at eleven-fifteen he was seen to be tucked up in bed in the pale glow of the night light.

The ward was quiet, a couple of nurses chatting in the office, rain beating on a window, sporadic laughter from the three guards in the lobby just outside the ward. To pass the time, the solitary guard outside Marcus King's cell would look out of the fire-escape door at the rainswept streets three floors below or, shouldering his sub-machine-gun, stroll down the long corridor, past the office and look in at his card-playing colleagues.

Midnight. Yawning as he rose from his chair, the guard drew back the spy-slot. Yawning blurred his vision, so that at first he only *thought* the prisoner had hanged himself.

Blinking, he gasped, and began fumbling with the bolts like a man possessed. They'd stressed the prisoner was important. On no account . . .

He burst in, the prisoner was swinging gently from an air-vent by knotted sheets, pressing forward on his weight, face contorted, bare feet loosely touching the floor, upturned slop-bucket kicked away where he'd stepped off. The guard must have hoped it wasn't too late as he took the prisoner's weight and reached to free his head. Struggling with the noose, he may have had time to wonder why there were no friction marks on the neck, when two sharp blows to his own neck rendered him unconscious.

While Marcus was making sure he hadn't killed the man, a motorbike was drawing up in the street alongside the hospital. The pillion rider, dressed as a nurse, proceeded round the corner into the building, and took the lift to the third floor.

When she reached the security ward she disturbed three Royal Military Policemen at three card brag. Succumbing readily to her looks and charm, they fell easily into flirtatious banter with her as they perfunctorily frisked her and checked her bag. They gave their Christian names unsuspectingly. Within moments she would use the authority of the sergeant's name to entice away the guard outside Marcus King's cell.

'And what about your name, darling?'

'Rose,' she said mysteriously.

Just then Marcus was himself emerging from the cell, straightening his unfamiliar uniform. It wasn't quite large enough, but it wasn't conspicuously ill-fitting and the peaked cap hid the top of his face. He didn't want the sub-machine-gun, but he was stuck with it.

All was quiet until suddenly, as he was bolting the cell door behind him, the phone rang in the office and in the same moment a shape appeared in the glass doors at the end of the corridor. Slipping into the alcove containing the fire-escape, he skimmed a look round the corner and saw a nurse enter the ward, appearing to falter while the phone was being answered in the office. Risking the inevitable clap of noise, he released the bar on the fire-escape door and stepped into the night, closing the door behind him.

While Marcus descended through wind and rain, the newly arrived nurse drifted past the office and was surprised, even disappointed, to find no guard outside the end cell. Glancing over her shoulder, she delved into the folds of her skirt and produced a small parcel on a string. Adjusting the timing, she drew back the spy-slot and peered in. The prisoner was tucked in bed facing the wall. Taking care not to wake him she slid the parcel through the slot and dangled it to the cell floor. Four minutes to remove herself, via the fire-escape.

Reaching the ground, she cursed and waited in the shadows while a Royal Military Police Landrover drove out of the hospital compound. Then wrapped in her cloak she ran round the corner. Climbing onto the back of the motorbike she encircled the rider. Together they sat riveted to their watches. Almost at once an explosion ripped through the night.

'Bang on time!' cried Eileen Feeley.

Tossing a ragdoll over his shoulder, Dixie opened up the throttle. I'm free! he thought, feeling the wind as it rushed into his lungs. He'd done twelve years' active service, capped now with the assassination of a primary target. I'm going home, he told himself. I'm going home.

Only now, as the euphoria settled and the wind-blown rain cooled her face, did Feeley experience a twinge of unease about the black face of the Royal Military Policeman at the wheel of that Landrover.

Marcus aimed for the city centre, the only place he might find a newspaper in the middle of the night, and learn the date of the inquest. The discovery of keys to a Landrover in the pockets of his new trousers had granted him unexpected mobility. He drove in a state of trembling excitement, tempered by a nagging anxiety that he'd made a mistake in breaking out. Anxiety became fear, fear of what they would do to him when they caught him, fear of public disgrace, of separation from Jamie and Marcia.

I'm free! he kept telling himself, but only like an escaped animal is free. How soon before the hunt began? Would he manage to stay at large until the inquest, when he'd materialise and tell the truth to as many journalists as possible – there was no need for a battle, no need for that girl to die. Only then could he begin to be free.

He drove in a daze, exhilarated by the power of the Landrover and his decision to break out. He drove faster, the urban nightscape parting before his eyes to left and right like a scene from an old movie. The rain was easing, traffic light, he was growing calm when suddenly the road converged towards an Army checkpoint – his own regiment, different battalion.

He slowed down, dropped gear, got close enough to distinguish shapes of troops in the rain, the dull gleam of their rifles. A searchlight opened up, blinding him. Lowering his cap further over his eyes, he climbed gear again, gathered speed, flashed his headlights and repeatedly sounded his horn – I'm Military Police, I'm in a hurry! – not letting up until he'd hurtled horn-blaring through the checkpoint, bracing himself for shots that didn't come.

Approaching the river, he found his bearings and pulled up sharply outside a taxi office in the Protestant Waterside. Shouldering his sub-machine-gun, he walked in.

'Evening. Got any newspapers?'

The drivers looked blankly at the tall black Military Policeman. They muttered and pushed two crumpled tabloids his way. Expecting him to flick through them, they were surprised when he started to walk out with them.

'What's he want with them?'

'The cricket, man,' said Marcus, 'what else?'

The papers were useless, no mention of Bernie O'Rawe, nothing on Northern Ireland. Marcus flung them down and drove on. The war could go on for another hundred years and the media would keep the British people in the dark all the way.

There was nothing for it but to swoop on a taxi office on the west side. Crossing the Craigavon Bridge, he skirted the walls of the city and headed into Republican territory. The streets grew darker, quieter. He dimmed his lights in a vain effort to become less conspicuous – a lone military vehicle in enemy territory, madness. The rain stopped; through lazily flicking wipers he watched the road intently, sudden side streets, doorways, scabs of wasteland. He drove well back from the windscreen, hoping no one would spot him and alert the Provos. The breeze blew a sheet of newspaper across the road. He thought of stopping for it, but drove on.

The taxi office came into sight, a dim light thrown into the street, a couple of black cabs parked outside, which operated into the heart of the Republican ghettos. At the last moment he changed his plan. Instead of pulling up with a screech of tyres and bursting in, he drew up quietly, left the Landrover idling and, shouldering the sub-machine-gun, strolled in. The small office was crowded with couples out for the evening. The moment his presence filled the entrance the room fell still.

'Evening. Anyone got a local paper?'

Faces stared. Nothing stirred but the low cumulus of cigarette smoke. A driver broke the spell.

'What was that?'

'A local paper, come on.'

'You got a bloody nerve.'

Marcus eyed several newspapers lying on a counter and moved to take them. The driver moved to stop him.

'You thick, or what? Don't you know where you are?'

'Get back!' He began to unsling the gun. People fell back, a dog snarled, Marcus snatched up the papers

'Thanks!' he grinned, backing out to the sound he must have feared, the revving of an engine, *his* engine, his means of escape, his Landrover! He dashed from the office just in time to see it being driven away at speed, swerving round the first corner it came to with a howl of tyres.

He stood dumbstruck on the edge of Provoland in a military uniform with a sub-machine-gun and a pile of newspapers under his arm. A throng spilled from the office. They looked up and down the street for Marcus's men, and when they didn't see any, they focused on him, smirking.

'You're in shit, mister,' said a woman drily.

'You think so?' Marcus lunged, seizing a driver by the collar, extracting him from the crowd which surged forward, waving the gun as he backed off and forced the driver into the nearest taxi, piling in after him and being driven off under a hail of abuse.

The shouts faded, the crowd receded in the wing mirror. Marcus sighed, knowing how easily he could have killed somebody, another death to add to Bernie O'Rawe, too much to carry.

'Got a map?'

'Fuck off.'

'What's that?' Rummaging in a stack of discarded packets and pens he seized a map and flicked on the light. 'Get on the Strand Road, head for Buncrana!'

'We're on the fucking Strand Road, we're heading for Buncrana.'

The panic was rising again, threatening to overwhelm him. What was Marcia doing tonight? When would he see her again? How had he got into this shit? Why couldn't he think with his knees like any normal soldier? He scoured the map. Tiredness and a sense of hopelessness were creeping over him as the taxi rattled through the night, the road darker as the city thinned out into the hills. He needed somewhere safe and soon for the night, and thought he'd found it, concentrating on a remote building marked on the map.

'OK, this'll do.' The taxi pulled up at a lonely crossroads. 'How much?' He'd found six pounds in a pocket and produced a fiver.

'Fuck off and get out.' The man wouldn't look at his passenger, let alone his money.

Half out the door, 'You know who I am, don't you?'

'What?'

Marcus was wrong. The man hadn't made any connection.

'Tell them,' said Marcus, 'that Lieutenant King broke out so he could testify at Bernie O'Rawe's inquest, because he's sick about what he done and won't let the Army get away with murder.'

Closing the door he started to walk away.

'Hey!' The driver was in the road. 'What were the papers for?'

'I want to know when they're holding the inquest.'

The driver stared at him. 'It was yesterday. They read out a statement from you. All cut and dried. The O'Rawes will be lucky if they get two-and-a-half pence compensation!'

He got back in his taxi, turned it round and roared off towards the twinkling lights of the city. The papers slid from Marcus's grip to the road.

'Bastards,' he murmured, and lashed out with his feet, scattering newspaper into ditches and fields on the breeze.

He'd been walking and running along the dark country lane for nearly a mile, wondering if he had misread the map, when he came in sight of the low impressive building cut against the night sky. His boots crunched gravel up to the door. He pulled the bell cord.

Derry twinkled across fields in the distance. He rang several more times, until he heard the soft patter of footsteps, a delicate voice asking who was there. Military Police, he said. She doubted. He unfastened the badge from his cap and pushed it through the letter-box. The door gave, a plain young nun, coat thrown over her nightdress, stood expectantly.

He was shown into a wood panelled office shelved to the ceiling with ancient books. Soon a latch turned and the Mother Superior entered noiselessly, apparently wide awake, a slight bony creature with sharp features and the bright black eyes of a crow. Closing the door, she looked up at him between the starched wings of her wimple, which kept the custody of her eyes and pressed her faded face. Her gaze travelled to the gun. He unslung it and hung it over a chair.

'How can I help you?'

'Please forgive the time, Reverend Mother . . .'

'Sit down, please.' He took a seat. 'What troubles you?'

'I've killed someone.'

Her eyes rested on his face. 'Tell me.'

He reached inside his stolen jacket and passed over a newspaper cutting. She went to her desk, found a pair of spectacles and read

132

standing. Over her head he read an inscription carved in wood: LORD OBSERVE OUR INIQUITIES – WITH THEE THERE IS MERCIFUL FORGIVENESS

The Holy Mother turned. 'But it was an accident.'

'I joined the Army, I pulled the trigger.'

She clucked her tongue disapprovingly. 'Feel sorrow, by all means, but beware excessive guilt. It's an indulgence. Ask God's forgiveness and you'll be all right.' She offered a concluding smile.

'It's not forgiveness I'm after.'

'Oh?'

'I want to atone.'

'I'm sure you will, in your own way. Why not talk to your chaplain?'

'I've . . .' he stumbled on the word he'd been about to utter, the awful truth. Surprised to find it harder to confess than the killing, he looked up and said it.

'I've deserted.'

She looked at him afresh. 'Hadn't you better. . .?' But no, she saw in his eyes and in the slow shaking of his head that he was past returning. 'I hope you're not thinking of spending the night – '

'I need somewhere to hide.'

'This place is only for brides of Christ.'

'Just tonight.'

She saw the patience in his folded hands, the tired sloping of his broad back, the pain in his eyes. Gnarled fingers to her dry lips, she pondered.

'There is a room . . .'

He followed her along echoing passages and then up a spiral staircase. At the top she showed him through a low-arched door into a high-ceilinged room. She switched on a light. One good bulb in a wrought-iron chandelier spread a thin glow. As she silently confiscated his firearm, the sight of her cradling it brought a fleeting grin to his face.

'We will talk in the morning,' she said and started down the stairs.

'Reverend Mother?' She stopped and looked up. 'I need to call my wife.'

'Use my office.'

Heart racing, he hurriedly retraced his steps down dim corridors to the office. He stood over the phone trying to recall his own number. A clock said two-ten a.m. The number arranged itself in his head. He dialled. It was answered almost at once, Marcia's voice shrill with alarm and expectation. 'Yes?'

'Hi! It's me.'

'Jesus . . . where are you?'

It was a restrained, low-key conversation conducted in unfinished sentences. Her voice, frail and breathless to start with, grew steadily stronger, surpassing his. He told her, in brief, the facts. He could hear her intake of breath, staying calm, guarding her reactions, rallying, even laughing when told where he was spending the night. It wasn't her style to panic. But she had to keep asking how he really was.

'Ammi, be easy on yourself, you didn't mean to do it. Take all the space you need, but, honey, the sooner you give yourself up the sooner we can all be together again. You haven't changed your mind about – '

'No, I'm coming home.'

'Ammi, I've been going crazy – '

'Listen, I won't call again – '

'What!'

'When they don't find me they'll tap the phone.'

'Ammi, how am I going to – '

'Marcia, please! I have to live the rest of my life with this. I don't want to be ashamed of the man I see in the mirror every morning. I don't want you and Jamie ashamed of him either.'

'I just want you . . .' she murmured, fading.

'Christ, Marcia!'

Rallying again. 'I understand, and I'm with you . . . all the way. But you still haven't said what you're going to do – '

'I won't be long.'

After he'd replaced the receiver he sat holding his head in the dark, distressed by the call, desperate to give himself up and go home. He paced back and forth, trying to talk himself into doing it. He'd taken on the Army and lost, so what? He'd done his best. Anyway, what possible form could his atonement take, now that the inquest was over? He ached for Marcia, felt sick thinking what he was putting her through. She was strong, stronger than him, but it was a lot to ask of her, to wait and wait, night after night, powerless to intervene. He closed his eyes, a Bob Marley number returned to mock him – *Oh Lord have mercy, is there a place for the lonely sinner?*

Returning to his room, he was about to lie down when flickering light alerted him to someone with a candle climbing the stairs. The nun who first admitted him entered bearing a tray. Setting it down in the bay window, she lit a second candle from the first, and left.

He discovered a jug of milk, a basket of bread, cheese and fruit, and a Bible. Tearing into the food, he picked up the Bible, opening it where a sheet of note-paper protruded. The Bible was defaced, one line vigorously underlined. By the light of the candle he read, 'I will lift up mine eyes unto the hills, from whence cometh my help.' Lifting up his eyes, he looked out at the dark formations of hills running north. Unfolding the sheet of paper, he found a hastily scrawled map describing a route north from the convent to the sea. Off the most northerly tip of County Donegal, an island was drawn, marked Inishtrahull, and beside it the name Brother Dominic.

Lying down fully dressed he drifted into a nightmare. It looked like Finsbury Park in North London, but he knew it was Thorn Hill and he was running from a helicopter, its shadow twisting and growing, blades whipping up the bushes where he was hiding. Someone was shaking him, he sat bolt upright, the young nun leaning over him candle in hand, a helicopter blustering over the convent, searchlight sweeping the grounds.

'Come quickly!'

He was on his feet, holding the trembling map to the candle, watching the flame consume his route north. At the foot of the stairs waited the holy mother. She led him to the purest sanctuary of the convent – the novices' dormitory, which smelled of unperfumed sleep.

Each bed was curtained off, unseen novices slept or listened. Halfway down the dormitory a young nun emerged from her cell in stiff calico nightdress and gown, and he was ushered in to take her place. He took off his boots and cap and climbed into bed with them. The Mother Superior handed him a frilly nightcap and was urgently called away. Burrowing into the lumpy mattress, he lay in God's hands with the summer scent of the young nun on the sheets.

Light splashed on the ceiling, a male voice was hushed by the holy mother stressing the sanctity. The officers tiptoed, flashlights weaved along the aisle. The holy mother remarked that the novices rose at five and needed their sleep. Curtains were carefully drawn back.

Rubber soles squeaked closer, curtains scratched on ancient rails. They'd reached the next cubicle. Scrunching himself up, he clung to the crucifix round his neck and prayed.

Curtain rasping, beams of searching light. They saw a frilly nightcap on a calico pillow, the sleeper breathing lightly, clothes neatly folded, wimple and veil, underpants strikingly white against the black serge habit. The curtain was drawn softly closed.

A few hours earlier, in the hayloft of Molly O'Cinneíde's farm, Annie lay awake listening to the night, Michael's heavy arms wrapped round her. He slept peacefully. Making love with her again made him very happy. What for her was a brief replenishment of love and lust, was much more for him, and he would wake with a terrible aching for her, to have and to hold her for himself for ever. She loved him in snatches, affectionate, passionate and then indifferent. He had been saddened and shocked to learn she took the pill. He wanted an accident.

Disentangling herself, she put on her top and plucked hay from her hair. The loft moaned in the wind. Peering out between warped boards, she saw the fields glistening after the rain and began to weep. She had stayed away from home for almost three years. Sometimes she drew strength from the knowledge that she was wounding her father. Sometimes she yearned to be his little princess again, tossed high in the air above his laughing face, landing in his powerful arms, crushed in a hug which smelled warm and peculiarly of him.

Armalite in hand, she crept down the ladder and crossed the starlit yard. She entered the silent wood-warm house, careful with latches, softly on creaking floorboards, so as not to wake Molly. With Michael's dog curled at her feet, Annie drank tea and listened to the radio.

The news of the hospital bomb came at one a.m. One man perished, no further details released. She felt strangely saddened. Tired but unwilling to move, she sat in a kind of stupor, until the 1.30 news and its surprising disclosure brought a smile to her face. Then she heard the motorbike, breaking the stillness.

Engine cut, silence restored. Footsteps to the front door, suppressed laughter in the passage. Dixie entered the kitchen, Feeley on his arm, dressed as a nurse, both mud-streaked and flushed with the night, Dixie sober, pensive, Feeley buoyant, frisky.

'Any news?' said Dixie.

The radio was on quietly, Annie regarded him evenly.

'A bomb went off, a man died.'

Dixie lowered his eyes, Feeley gave a hoot and punched her palm.

'Get out the glasses, girl!' she ordered, a hint of reconciliation in her voice.

Annie fetched three glasses, Feeley found three beers, the air filled with the snapping open of cans. Dixie sat down at the table, thinking ahead. Feeley was too excited to sit. 'What did they say? Did they find the ragdoll?'

'The bomb cremated a Royal Military peeler. M.K. escaped.'

A moment's silence.

'She's messing,' said Feeley hopefully.

Dixie studied Annie. 'She's not.'

Annie related all she'd heard, Feeley swore viciously, Dixie sank his head into his arms on the table.

'That guy's got informers in the stars.'

For a time no one spoke. At two a.m. the radio confirmed the escape and reported the hijack at the second taxi office. Feeley brightened, all for going after the black bastard.

'A call to the taxi office and we'll find out where – '

The phone went, startling them. They gazed at the outmoded appliance with its rustic ring. Dixie crossed the room, cautiously lifted the receiver. His face gave nothing away. He replied in monosyllables, closing with, 'OK'. He returned to the table without meeting their eyes.

'Black man in military cop uniform spotted close to a convent near Galliagh off the Buncrana Road. We might be lucky, get to him before the Army.'

'Kidnap him,' blurted Annie, 'why not kidnap him?'

'We've orders to kill him, eejit!' said Feeley.

'If they insist, we kill him after, but first we kidnap him. What a coup, capturing the man who killed Bernie O'Rawe, taking prisoner a former officer who decries Army tactics! Maybe we could even hold out for an exchange of prisoners . . .'

Feeley assumed a who-does-she-think-she-is expression, but Dixie was nodding thoughtfully: The man who stole Marcus King from the Brits.

*

137

Early in the morning a car crunched over gravel and swept to a halt at the steps of the convent. Since the owner lived in daily danger, the car was a swift, inconspicuous Vauxhall with frequently replaced number plates.

The driver climbed out. Silver-haired, heavily built, immaculately dressed, he paused to look about and sniff the air, almost as if he imagined he was being watched. He pulled the bell cord and waited patiently.

Shown into the wood panelled office, he introduced himself with old-fashioned charm.

'Please forgive the appalling intrusion, Reverend Mother . . . Frank Mulraine, Detective Inspector, Regional Crime Squad.'

She took in the heavy wedding ring, flamboyant tie, indulgent waistline, and resented the worldly invasion, particularly since it reeked faintly of tobacco. She motioned him to sit.

Frank Mulraine's smile softened most women, but not this old bird, he calculated, so he hit the point.

'A British soldier, wanted by the police and the Army, stayed here last night.' He paused for her reaction. There was none. 'Did he not?'

She sat watching him, tight-lipped.

'Reverend Mother, my men took the liberty – for which I apologise – of removing certain items from the tower room. Your guest was careless with a few stray hairs and fingerprints, belonging to a certain Marcus King, a fellow probably unhinged, who escaped last night from a psychiatric unit, leaving a Royal Military Policeman to burn to death in his cell . . .'

Ah, observed Mulraine, a flicker of reaction.

'There you have it, Reverend Mother. When he hijacked a taxi to a spot a mile from here, he was wearing the roasted man's uniform . . . was he not?'

The holy mother's pressed face faded still paler.

'Now if you don't mind, I should like to ask one or two questions.'

'One or two,' she agreed.

'D'you mind if I smoke, Reverend Mother?' he said brightly, cigarettes already in hand.

'I do.'

With a courteous nod, he pocketed them.

'Did yer man come to seek shelter?'

'For his spirit.'

'Then he unburdened himself?'

'He did.'

Mulraine twitched with anticipation. 'And was it a solemn weight?'

'It was.'

'Could you give me some idea what it was so troubled him?'

'He confided in the Lord, through me. And that's four questions.'

'May I take it he was distraught over the girl he inadvertently killed?'

'You may.'

'Did you form the impression that he was in cahoots with the Devil, if you know what I mean?'

'I don't, sir.'

'The Provisional IRA blew a hole in the hospital. Did you have the feeling that his arrival here was . . . facilitated?'

'No, I did not. But you, sir, just gave me the impression that he was responsible for a man burning to death.'

'My mistake, I apologise. Former Lieutenant King is wanted for a number of things, but not murder. But 'twould be as well to find him before he does himself or anyone else any further mischief. Where did he say he was going?'

'To make his peace with God.'

'And where might this divine encounter take place?'

'A cup of tea, Inspector, before you go?'

'Most kind, but no. I wonder if perhaps you didn't recommend some holy spot, on a slip of paper, a letter of introduction or an address quickly reduced, almost successfully, to ashes?'

Rising: 'I'm sure you'll excuse me, Inspector, I have a distressed parent to see. Sister Francis will show you out.'

Alone a moment, he made for the desk and examined the broad-leafed note-pad. Smooth sheets without indentations suggested the user tore off the top sheet and rested it on the desk blotter when she wished to write. He ran his seasoned fingertips over the furrowed surface of the blotter. He couldn't be sure, but the lab would tell. Detaching the blotter from its leather holder, he rolled it up and tucked it inside his elegant jacket.

As the front door closed behind him and he walked to his car, a time-worn slate slipped from the convent roof, shattering at his feet. Not one to be startled easily, Mulraine glanced up ironically, preferring to take it as nothing darker than a just rebuke from Heaven.

From her high perch over the drive, Annie McBride watched the silver-haired detective stoop into his car and, grinding gravel beneath her tree, sweep into the lane and disappear. Through field-glasses she picked out the cause of the falling slate – Dixie, concealing himself among the chimney pots.

They had arrived only just on the dark side of dawn. Creeping up on the convent they'd ghosted through silent cloisters, clambered over moonlit roofs, spied upside-down through windows, hurrying as daylight threatened and overtook them. They held a dew-soaked conference behind a hedgerow. No sign of their quarry. Only one option remained.

Wrapped in a dawn-grey cloak, Feeley walked innocently through the orchard and looked over the wall into the vegetable gardens where nuns were at work. One novice strayed, Feeley stalked her and pounced. Dragging her down to a bed of clover, Feeley uncovered the girl's white throat and caressed the flesh with a blade.

'The soldier, where is he?'

'Gone.'

'When?'

'This morning.'

'Impossible.'

'As God is my witness.'

'Time?'

'About half-past four.'

'Shit! Destination?'

'I don't know.'

The blade nipped, a thread of blood. 'The convent goes to heaven in five minutes . . .'

'A monastery on some island to the north . . . 'tis all I know, so help me.'

10

Stormont Castle, Belfast

Inside the debunked parliament buildings in the park, an emergency meeting was in progress in the ministerial conference room.

Presiding was the Secretary of State for Northern Ireland, representing centuries of direct rule from Westminister. As usual on these occasions, no Loyalist or Nationalist politicians were present. Attendance was restricted this morning to only two other men – Sir Ian McNab, Chief Constable of the RUC, the most senior policeman in the province, and Lieutenant-General Sir Jeremy Pemberton-Billing, GOC, the most senior military commander, each with thirty feet of polished table to himself.

The sole witnesses to proceedings were the sun-set shepherds reclining in the immense faded oil painting over the yawning fireplace.

The Secretary of State, a lack-lustre figure compared with the immaculate police chief and impeccable Army commander, sat at the head of the table. He looked haggard, having come direct from a late-night grilling by the PM in London.

'Sir Ian,' he said brusquely, 'may we leave the so-called torture-of-suspects report till Monday's meeting?'

'Leave it as long as you like,' smiled the Chief Constable.

'To the point then, gentleman, the first thing the PM wants to know is how that football fiasco was allowed to be filmed.'

He peered from one man to the other for explanation.

'The Army stopped the game as swiftly as possible,' said Sir Jeremy defensively.

'But the media beat you to it! Gentlemen, former Lieutenant King has picked a fine time to focus the world's attention. We're enduring quite enough criticism without a British officer – popularised by coverage of a football game – blasting his way out of hospital with the assistance of the IRA!'

'Steady on, Minister,' said Sir Ian, the police chief, 'shall we see what Inspector Mulraine has to say before we start making assumptions?'

'My dear fellow,' interrupted the minister, 'I'm in the dark, I'm merely quoting the Press' – extracting a stack of newspapers from his briefcase, smiling grimly. 'Perhaps you'd care to see a selection, gentlemen? Shall we begin with the *Mirror* – BRITS 1, BOGSIDE 1! The *Guardian* – BRITISH OFFICER PENALISED FOR OFFSIDE. And the following day, we have the *Star* – HEARTBREAK HERO KILLS TEENAGER, or would you prefer the *Telegraph* – DISGRACED OFFICER FUELS PLASTIC BULLETS ROW, or the *New York Times* – BRITISH ULSTER POLICY ROCKED BY OFFICER-HERO. And today's headlines, the *Sun* – IRA BOMBERS SNATCH BRIT HERO, and the *Express* – IRA KIDNAPS BRITISH OFFICER IN DEATH BLAST!'

Slapping the last newspaper down, he fixed his colleagues with a leaden gaze, apparently off-loading some of the anger he'd weathered in London.

'Where have they picked all this up from, I should like to know? Not from us I trust!'

'I can assure you,' said Sir Jeremy stiffly, 'that the Army did its utmost to hush all of it up. They've simply picked up the wrong impressions.'

'But you and I know, Sir Jeremy, it's impressions that count out here. As we keep saying, the first theatre of operations is the propaganda war. Now the impression of this rogue officer as some sort of campaigning hero must be redressed. I understood the fellow was a positive danger to his fellow officers, Sir Jeremy?'

'It should be said,' replied the Army commander carefully, 'that he *was* a superb, if controversial professional. Unfortunately he overstepped himself and finally cracked.'

'In any case,' pursued the minister vigorously, 'we permit this distorted image of the fellow to survive at our peril. There's nothing the IRA would like better than to put on display a captured British traitor – because let's make no bones about it, that's what he is! It's high time your press office and PR people pulled their fingers out. Why, for instance, has so little been said about him being unbalanced?'

'Because,' replied Sir Jeremy, 'we're not quite clear on that point. He was diagnosed as suffering from PTSD, post traumatic stress disorder, but was considered fit to face court martial.'

'Then I suggest, gentlemen, we put the dampers on his heroics and stress his subversive tendencies and mental instability. Now, without further delay . . .'

Frank Mulraine was summoned. The colourful thick-set Ulsterman breezed in and journeyed the length of the table to shake each man by the hand, ruffling the atmosphere and embarrassing his boss, the Chief Constable.

'I assigned Detective Inspector Mulraine to the case, Minister, because while to be frank, I haven't always applauded his style, his record of kills, so to speak, is second to none. Based with the Regional Crime Squad, he is leading the hunt for King, assisted by an élite team of young detectives.'

The Secretary of State regarded the detective critically.

'I'm anxious to hear your report, Inspector. Tell us the worst.'

'The worst, sir, was the slaughter of a young military policeman, roasted alive in a bolted cell.'

Unexpectedly flustered, 'Naturally, that was an appalling murder. But we were wondering how former Lieutenant King fits in. Are you in a position to tell us precisely how he escaped from the hospital?'

'Precisely, no. However – '

'I don't suppose he could have manufactured a bomb to facilitate his own escape?'

'Himself, you mean? Oh, unlikely – '

'But possible . . .'

'Hardly. It was a classic Doyle device, with a miniature ragdoll discovered nearby. What's more, the Provos claimed it.'

'Ragdoll? What are you talking about?'

'Mr Doyle leaves his little sign, like a visiting card.'

'Could Doyle have contacted King to plot a rescue?'

'In the hospital? Highly improbable – '

'But conceivable?'

'Anything's conceivable – '

'In which case, gentlemen, I don't see why the Press shouldn't know our hero is not only dangerously unstable, but conceivably involved in the murder of a Royal Military Policeman.'

'Now hold on a moment, sir,' smiled Frank Mulraine good humouredly, 'with respect, we're cavorting to conclusions!'

'We're doing nothing of the kind. Given that King threatened to murder his commanding officer and to testify against the Army, that he's undoubtedly deranged and appears to have been rescued by the IRA, is it unreasonable to speculate that we might be dealing with a treacherous accessory to murder?'

Words appeared to fail the normally garrulous detective.

'Well, Inspector?' persisted the Secretary of State.

'If you must know, Minister, I fear we're in danger of believing what we read in the papers.'

The minister reddened, the Chief Constable swallowed his discomfort, the Army commander barely suppressed a smile.

Mulraine shook his head patiently. 'Yer man did a bunk, gentlemen. Tests will confirm he pulled some old ruse to over-power the guard and was away shortly before Doyle's accomplice, disguised as a nurse, blew the wrong fellow into the next world – '

'Bit of a bloody coincidence, don't you think?' quizzed the minister.

'Life's full of coincidences.'

'How can we know, Inspector,' wondered Sir Ian, the police chief, 'that the guard wasn't already dead before the bomb? In other words, that King didn't kill him?'

'Quite possible, if tricky to prove. There wasn't a great deal left of the guard to examine.'

'Ah!' chimed the minister. 'Then it's still conceivable he murdered the guard, and conceivable the IRA lifted him.'

'If they lifted him, they would have kept him, not sent him by taxi to a convent.'

'So you're quite convinced he's at large?'

'Not only that, but – '

'Inspector, I hope the Chief Constable has impressed upon you the degree of importance attached to this case. He must be recaptured!'

'Forgive me, Minister,' said Mulraine genially, 'but I was under the impression you wanted to hear my report.'

'And I was under the impression you'd given it.'

'Well we seem to be getting our impressions in a twist, because I've been trying to tell you that you're looking at the only man in Christendom – save the Mother Superior and yer man himself – who knows where King is heading for . . .'

With a grand gesture, he unfolded two maps, one of Ireland, the other an enlarged photocopy of the map traced onto the holy mother's desk-blotter.

'The inscription "Brother Dominic" is the clue. Enquiries have uncovered a monastic community on this island – Inishtrahull, the most God-forsaken outrock in all of Ireland!'

Leaving their seats to cluster round him, his audience were agog, gazing at the little island cast adrift off Malin Head, the most northerly point in Ireland.

'By all accounts a wicked place for a picnic,' said Mulraine. 'There's no ferry, so God knows how King's going to manage it. Trouble is, all this area, and the island, belongs to the Republic, out of bounds and all that!'

'What about your men?' queried the police chief.

'Ach, they did a wee bit of discreet sightseeing and came home.'

'Keep me informed next time.' Turning to the minister, 'I'm afraid that's it, it's in the hands of the Garda now.'

The minister did a little excited pacing, finger to pursed lips.

'Sir Jeremy . . . couldn't we . . . find a way . . . of . . .'

The Army commander knew what he was getting at, but was damned if he was going to be the one to stick his neck out and suggest it.

'I mean . . . couldn't we simply dispatch the SAS?'

Frank Mulraine raised his eyes to Heaven. Please God not them.

The minister inhaled sharply. 'Well?'

Sir Jeremy reclaimed his seat, interlacing his fingers on the table. 'I'd have to have a word with the Defence Minister.' Leaning back, he lifted his gaze to the ornate ceiling. 'They'd need a few days to prepare. Then they'd have him out like a tooth.'

11

London

SAS Captain Douglas Lee was thrusting to the pitch of another orgasm when the phone rang. Letting it ring, he continued to ride the sumptuous buttocks wedged between his powerful thighs, kneading the plump rolling shoulders in his cruel hands, pounding harder and harder until finally unleashing a long agonised orgasm, shooting forth with all the pent-up tension of months of Ulster-abstinence, before collapsing over the long luxurious back of his Portuguese lover.

The languid blond sighed, as always, beneath him. By contrast to his soft pliant lover, Douglas Lee was lean and hard, raw-boned and narrow-hipped, a solid male shaft without a pinch of surplus flesh.

The record slid to the end and came on again automatically. Fucking to Wagner was the ultimate. But when the phone went insistently for the third time, Lee swore through his teeth and rolled off the tacky olive-skinned back.

'If that's one of those fucking posers you call friends, I guarantee they'll never ring again!'

He headed naked for the phone, London winking at him through the curtains. He snatched it up and knew the voice at once – the Boss. Could only be bad news. And knowing Lee, the Boss didn't bother with pleasantries or apologies. He put the boot straight in. Lee went white with fury. He knew there was no point in arguing. They wanted the best. He was the best. The best pay double. He'd barely started his leave, and it was already over.

'Jesus Christ all-fucking-mighty, Major – you're the limit!' Slamming down the receiver. At the other end the SAS chief would be splitting his sides laughing.

Sergio sat up, disappointed but philosophical. You could only take a human volcano like Douglas Lee in small doses. Lighting a cigarette he tossed the pack and lighter to Lee, who'd slumped into an armchair. The lighter caught Lee in the balls, he sat up as though electrified. Sergio fell back and laughed, flashing his beautiful eyes.

'Cheer up, you big baby.'

'I'm in no shape to go back.'

True by his own exacting standards. Known as Ironside by his men, Lee was a dedicated professional soldier. In war he drove himself and his men to the brink, but on leave, his interpretation of Rest and Recuperation was booze, sex and mayhem.

Since his divorce, Sergio had suited him well. The Portuguese computer analyst possessed an impressive body, salary, Ferrari and apartment on Cheyne Walk, looking out over the river to Battersea and Clapham beyond. Weekends with Sergio followed a routine of sex to Verdi, Wagner or Queen, expensive meals at fashionable landmarks and riotous behaviour in West End nightclubs, leaving trails of broken glass, sobbing women and badly beaten bouncers . . . the odd car chase with the police, scattering bollards in Piccadilly and stealing home to collapse into bed in hysterics.

He stood in the window smoking, watching a disco boat cruising upriver, couples crossing Battersea Bridge, shadows behind curtains in the houseboats moored below. He missed his children, had been looking forward to taking them out for the day. He'd have to phone and cancel. They wouldn't understand. *He* couldn't understand. He needed to force himself always to the edge, because life was so bloody futile, a remorseless one-way ticket to a dead-end. War and sex were the only escapes, both invariably leading nowhere, both taking an ever heavier toll on his waning stamina. At thirty-four he found he needed longer to recover from his wild vacations.

'I'm wrecked. They throw another special assignment at me and they don't know I'm wrecked. They must think I'm a fucking machine.'

'Poor Douglas . . .' Sergio came over and kissed him like an indulgent mamma. 'Come on, baby, let's not waste our last evening. We go out, OK? I know for a change a quiet little place . . .'

'A mortuary?' groaned Lee.

12

County Donegal, Eire

Somewhere on the most northerly peninsula in Ireland Marcus King stood high on clifftops, blinded by the sea, shading his eyes in search of Inishtrahull. He checked his map, discounting several ferocious but minor outcrops of rock. Only one sizeable island stood out. His heart sank.

He'd envisaged hiding and gathering himself somewhere green, forested and spoilt for beaches. But there it was, six miles out, a jagged mass of prehistoric rock crouching on the sea. A more desperate looking place he couldn't imagine.

He sat down beside his bicycle, watched the endless grey-green ocean rolling towards him, legions of white-capped waves riding in from the horizon, beating up and down the coast with the rumble of underground explosions.

The landscape over his shoulder was equally awesome, rugged and unpopulated, still and silent, as though waiting for something. For long hours he'd pedalled to the tune of bees and rusty spokes, a plaything for sun, wind and rain. Now and then a whitewashed farm in a sea of parcelled fields, a chasing dog, a placid donkey. Sometimes a gaggle of children, a band of gypsies, a car, and he'd quickly take another lane and hide. Now there was nothing, no roads or houses, a more beautiful and dismal place he'd never been.

Loneliness gnawed at him. He kept telling himself that every mile he pedalled further from Marcia and Jamie was accelerating the time when he'd be with them again. But a voice in his head jibed constantly: If you'd swallowed your bloody pride, you'd be out of the Army and home by now. Instinctively he hit back: If I slunk home like a whipped dog I'd be no damn use to anyone. But he wasn't hitting back so hard any more, and as he looked around, his head spoke with one voice.

What the fuck am I doing here?

He tried to work out what had brought him to this savagely beautiful God-forsaken spot. It seemed only the other day he was playing a laid-back game of squash with Charlie Winters, frustrated because they wouldn't promote him, but taking it, like most things, in his stride.

Then came Thorn Hill, Winters footless and ablaze in his arms, Robbie McLaren in a ditch with a bullet in his neck. After that everything went crazily wrong. They broke up the football game, stripped him of his modest rank. Then the night raids on Derry, the mindless thuggery in which he had excelled. And on the bloody Twelfth the bulldozing of the barricades, the loading of the baton guns, a clean hard plastic bullet leaving his gun, cleaving the cursed smoke-choked air, missing the man in red and striking someone further on. How the air stilled, everything clawing into slow-motion, like a nightmare from which somewhere in the unconscious mind you think you can escape. Only when he reached the body he was instantly admitted to the world of living nightmare, a girl with her skull smashed against a brick wall, her head spilling blood through his fingers, like some terrible game of his invention – you pull the trigger and run forty yards to catch the blood.

He was carrying the limp body, stunned and choked, when

Draycott broke the spell: Get your bloody arse up front, King. He lost sight of everything in that moment, scrambling up the Saracen to put a stop to Draycott's face, dragged down by men realising they were about to witness the murder of one officer by another. Then along came Kitson, gesticulating one minute, sagging to his knees the next with a look of bitter accusation.

Then they tried to gag him – no call to Marcia, no day or night, no news, sleep or privacy, strip search, threats and deals, and a wall of silence around the inquest. Like a cornered animal he had to choose – give in or break out.

He recalled the starlit crossroads where the cabbie told him he'd missed the inquest, the nerve-wracking night in the convent, and finally the previous dawn, the holy mother leading him with a flashlight to the shed, a sturdy old bike set aside and a change of clothes – trousers, collarless white shirt, tweed jacket, donated by the widow of a large local man. He was to change and leave his uniform for disposal. In the bike's basket were provisions and a tattered map. Go in peace, she'd said, blessing his big brown hands in hers. As he undressed chanting had filled the mist. *Monstra te esse matrem* . . . As he pedalled away, the nun who had first admitted him waved from a window.

Mid-morning had found him perspiring up a strangely familiar country road, drystone wall, ditch, cow trough – Thorn Hill. Such a picturesque spot. No ambush could have happened there. He stopped over the filled-in crater, where the Fox had leapt to heaven on a fountain of fire. In the field a solitary cow waded ankle deep in flowers. Laying down his bike, he went over and found the trough empty, its level controlled by a bullet hole low in the side.

He stood above the ditch where Robbie McLaren had lain stiff under a blanket, then climbed the hill to the ruined farm and sat down awhile, close to the place where the helicopter had nearly torn him in half, and where the red-haired sniper tried to shoot him. He'd found himself shaking, images of death and severed limbs merging with the reek of cordite and smouldering flesh. Sinking to his knees, he'd vomited into the grass. The hospital had been right, he was suffering symptoms related to severe trauma – nightmares, horrific daydreams, acute alertness, violent reactions, guilt feelings about what he'd done, guilty for being alive when others were dead. What made him so special?

In the distance he'd spotted packs of helicopters throbbing over

Derry and, taking up his bike, he'd got back on the road and pedalled furiously northward.

Now, as he sat on the clifftop remembering, the sea went dark before his eyes, the sun suddenly overtaken by clouds ambushing from behind Crockalough Mountain. Climbing on his bike he cycled hard along the headland, pursued by slanting rain. Briefly and fiercely sea and sky merged to settle ancient scores.

Carrying his bike on his back, Marcus climbed down a twisting track to a sliver of beach and sheltered in a secluded cove.

Sea and sky separated, clouds dispersed towards the horizon, the sun streamed out, setting rocks steaming, soothing the sea. Subsiding on the sand, he watched waves wash ever more calmly into his cove. Gulls cried, the sea turned turquoise. He ran his hands through the cool damp sand and, feeling a stinging in his wrist, saw the lingering teeth marks inflamed by sea salt. Bernie O'Rawe still had hold of him.

Jumping up, he tore off his jacket, kicked off his boots and plunged into the sea, lashing the freezing water until his blood raced. Then he stripped completely, leaving his clothes to tumble on the surf. Rolling on his back he closed his eyes and gave himself to the sun. He drifted, emptying his mind.

Rediscovering his swimming muscles, he herded his clothes to shore, spread them on rocks to dry and ran up and down the beach beating himself warm. Cleansed and exhausted, he lay down naked, and fell asleep.

The hours passed. He lay exposed on the sand, hostage to nightmares.

Cold woke him. Putting on his salt-stiff clothes, he began to panic. Dusk was creeping into the cove, cliffs closing in, sky darkening, sea growing dim. Where would he spend the night? Wasn't this the time to swallow his pride and give himself up at the first dwelling?

He pictured returning home humiliated, the C.O. and Draycott kicking his arse all the way back to North London, his pride buried with Bernie O'Rawe in Derry. If Jamie was getting hassled at school because of him, let the boy's suffering be for his father's bravery, not his cowardice. He didn't want to face Jamie in years to come on wobbly ground. He couldn't go home until somehow, somewhere, he'd made a stand for Bernie O'Rawe, and settled his score with the Army.

He felt better. Every time he rallied his thoughts he felt his pride pumping once more and felt good, knowing he wasn't beaten yet. He'd get to the island if he had to swim.

The sun rolled into the sea, night followed, deep and vast. He sat on the beach in the last of the sunset, while the lighthouse on Inishtrahull swept its cold eye across the sea.

Just then, as the beam clipped the water, it brushed a living thing. Marcus went rigid. Out in the darkness of the cove something was moving. One member of an outcrop of black rocks had broken free and disappeared. Without taking his eye off the water, he crept out of sight and lay down to watch. Long moments passed, straining his eyes. Whatever it was it had staying power underwater.

There! Surfacing closer to shore, a smooth curved back glimpsed in the fleeting afterglow of the lighthouse . . . and gone again. The sea lapped the beach, rolled over the rocks. His eyes leapt from sound to sound, anticipating.

Calmer, all his survival instincts awake, he crawled up onto a slippery boulder jutting over the water. For a few more minutes, nothing, only the rhythmic motion of the tide and the rasping breeze in the sea-holly.

Then he saw it clearly, twenty yards out, eyes like coins in the dark, whiskers catching the last embers of sunset – a solitary seal, hunting at its leisure.

He watched the seal dive and reappear, working its way along the coast. Marcus was alone again, thinking about Marcia worrying about him, wishing he could phone her, knowing that even if there was a coin box on the beach he couldn't use it, since the call would surely be intercepted.

The shadows of the night crept on. Huddled in an elbow of rock he dozed, or kept himself company with a murmured Bob Marley number. *Ambush in the night, they trying to conquer me . . . ambush in the night, all guns aiming at me . . . ambush in the night, they open fire on me . . .*

Eyelids drooping, he was sinking into deep sleep when something moved in the sand close by. His eyes leapt open, his hand reached automatically for the Browning pistol he no longer carried. His heart beat against the night-cooled ground and he waited for the eye of the lighthouse to cut the mist and illuminate his beach just long enough to catch sight of some tiny indeterminate creature rustling in the scrub, going about its business.

151

The cold bit deeper, and with it the loneliness. The darkness was darker than any he'd ever encountered. He thought of the street-lights back home which burned all night. He thought of Marcia lying awake wondering where he was, while he stared at the night sky in bleakest Donegal watching shoals of stars getting caught in cirrus nets.

Voices . . . on the sea breeze.

Marcus sat up and listened. Voices singing, faint at first, gradually louder, coming from out at sea. Round the headland swayed a light – a square eye – and the ghostly outline of a small craft. Accompanied by an eerie flute, boat and swaying eye parted the mist towards him.

He sat perfectly still. The boat, sail billowing, glided in. Two strapping young men vaulted into the water and heaved the craft onto the sand. Still quietly singing they unloaded their catch and busied themselves with the boat. The lantern cast a ring of light as far as Marcus's feet.

One of the fishermen ceased singing mid-phrase, looking directly in Marcus's direction. He addressed Marcus in Gaelic. Marcus smiled and shrugged. Encouraged, the man spoke in English, with a strong Donegal accent.

'Hello there!'

The second singer faltered. Who the hell was he talking to?

'Hi!' replied Marcus. 'Looks like a good catch you got there.' He thought of trying to disguise his Anglo-Caribbean accent, but knew he could no more pass for an Irishman than turn white.

'Not too bad at all,' agreed the weathered high-boned fisher-man. They gazed at Marcus, half seen in the shadows of the lamplight. Not only was he a total stranger on a lonely beach in the middle of the night, he was probably the first black man they had ever met. They returned to work, securing the boat in self-conscious silence. Marcus felt more than ever an intruder in a foreign land. Had they heard that a black British soldier was on the run?

'Don't stop singing for me, I was enjoying it.'

They stared up again tentatively. Finding their voices once more, they seemed to forget him as they began gathering drift-wood.

'Want a hand?' asked Marcus.

The two young men exchanged glances, and the one who did the talking replied, 'That'd be grand. Would you be feeling like eating with us?'

A fire was soon crackling, licking the flanks of a freshly caught herring, shooting sparks into the night. The air snapped, the herring sizzled. For a time they ate in silence, washing down the scalding flesh with coarse ale.

'I'm Pat Flanagan,' announced the talker. 'This is my younger brother Eamonn.'

Marcus reached over to offer a firm hand to both men, but didn't give a name. 'I'm trying to get to Inishtrahull.'

The brothers went 'Ahh!' in unison.

'Well there's the helicopter' – Eamonn broke his silence – 'takes supplies over.'

'Sure, it won't be going for another week,' Pat reminded him.

'I have to be there tomorrow,' said Marcus.

Wishing to be somewhere the next day seemed reasonable, but having to struck them as odd.

'I got to see the monk.'

Another 'ahh' from the brothers and they lapsed into silence.

'There was a monastery there in the sixth century,' said Pat after a while, 'till the Vikings put a stop to it. But they've reconstructed a good part of it.'

'What's it like, the island?' said Marcus.

'A mile long,' said Eamonn eagerly. 'Narrow at the neck, six hundred yards at its widest. Mostly Lewisiangneiss, oldest rock in Ireland. A lot of ruined houses, belonged to settlers fleeing from the famines long ago.'

'It's quiet now,' said Pat, sucking on a pipe, 'just the monks in summer, and the lighthouse fellers. Sometimes a farmer takes his sheep over to graze, or a yacht stops on its way over from Scotland. We best be away now. Mother will be sitting up worrying.' Getting to his feet, 'You're welcome to stop with us, if you like.'

Marcus wasn't sure he'd heard right. 'Pardon?'

'It's no hotel, but sure it'll be warm.'

'Be OK with your mother?'

'Ach, she'll be delighted!'

In the morning the sound was still calm. The small boat, assisted by a motor, hurdled the waves in slow motion, subsiding into deep swells, lifting over white crests.

153

Marcus held tight, watching the high-cliffed mainland slowly recede. Turning around, he faced the island, crouching in the open sea. Two hills, one at each end, created the effect of a two-headed monster joined by a jagged spine. Closing on the island, the brothers grew quiet, wary.

Spray doused their faces as they forged past the island into the deep Atlantic, wheeling round to come in on the current. As they approached, a seal surfaced as escort, bobbing to port and starboard, greyer than the sea, staring back at Marcus with guileless black eyes.

They rushed towards the daggered rockline, Marcus convinced they'd be dashed to bits. Then at the last moment a creek materialised through the cross-spray, drawing the boat into the open jaws of the island. With its sail becalmed, the boat was sucked gently towards a raised tongue of beach and a deserted jetty.

Young Eamonn climbed out and Pat handed up the bicycle.

'D'you want to keep the bike? I don't have any money.'

Marcus had left what money he had by the telephone in the Mother Superior's office.

'Get away with you!'

'What about – ?' Pointing to the heavy Aran sweater beneath his jacket.

'You'll need it.'

They accompanied him a short way up a dirt road until the island spread before them, bleak and treeless. Sheep occupied the central plain, goats bleated in the rocky hills, no sign of human activity.

'Prayer and chanting goes on all morning, and no talking!' explained Pat. 'You have to have one hell of an excuse to open your mouth to a neighbour. Things pick up later, and evenings there's good crack.'

'Crack?'

'Music and singing and letting the hair down a bit. Well, we best be off while the sound's in good humour.' Warm handshakes. 'Give us a shout when you want us to pick you up. They'll get a message to us.'

They'd gone, their heads dropping out of sight down to the port. Marcus looked about him. For all he could see he had the island to himself. Unless he was quick, in a few minutes the brothers would set sail and he'd be left to his fate. In years to come they'd find him, a modern-day Robinson Crusoe, white-bearded and covered in goatskins, wild-eyed and gibbering. Leaping on his bike he pedalled back along the dirt road. Flinging the bike down, he climbed a rocky knoll, scattering goats and gulls in his surge to the top. A small sail came into sight and he opened his lungs and threw his voice far and high.

'WAIT . . . COME BACK . . . PAT . . . PAT!'

His words were thrown back in his face by the wind and strewn across the island. As the boat turned the corner and out of sight the brothers were waving.

Gulls circled over Marcus's head, laughing. Turning his back on the sea, he scanned the island with a sinking heart. The dirt road led to the lighthouse on the western hill. A rough track wound its way up the opposite hill to the monastery, sheltering inside high-walled enclosures, dominating the plain.

Retrieving his bike he started towards the monastery on foot. On the way he paused to return the anguished gaze of a surreal rock-sculpture of Christ crucified, its tortured features more in keeping with Picasso than tradition.

The track steepened, he pushed up the last slope to the arched entrance and entered a broad cobbled compound crowded with curiously shaped stone dwellings huddled beneath the walls, watched over by a small stark chapel. Chanting issued from its windowless interior. People! The doorway was engraved with an inscription, Gaelic down one side, English down the other. Let us stop disputing on both sides – St Patrick.

A figure emerged, shielding his eyes to look across at Marcus, a tall willowy monk with bald pate and wisps of orange hair, nearly as tall as Marcus, about half as heavy. With simple gestures the monk indicated this wasn't the moment to speak and pointed Marcus towards the adjacent building, silently inviting him to take refreshment.

Marcus obeyed, a little afraid of the monk, whose mute gestures and vivid eyes carried more authority than any barking Army officer. Passing through an airy cloister, he entered a long one-roomed house, long tables and benches set for a meal with unvarnished plates and pewter tankards.

The house felt old, but its supporting beams were evidence of recent craftsmanship. A turf fire hummed in a vast fireplace, a row of copper kettles simmered on an ancient range. Marcus looked for tea or coffee but found only jars of desiccated leaves, and the milk, on closer inspection, was warm – straight from the goat. He made a pot of Inishtrahull Nettle and, removing from his head the woollen tam Eamonn had given him, settled on a stone seat inside the fireplace. After a time he heard sandalled footsteps, and rose to meet the tall willowy monk who had greeted him earlier, a man about ten years older than Marcus with burnished complexion and piercing blue eyes, who came directly and offered his hand.

'*Dia dhuit, a bhráthair, fáilte romhat.*'

'Sorry?' Marcus shrugged.

'Good day, welcome. Forgive me for whispering. We've another hour of silence to go. It's a thousand lashes if I'm caught!' he said with mock seriousness. 'How can I help you?'

'I'm looking for Brother Dominic.'

'You've found him.'

Marcus recalled his first sight of the name Brother Dominic on the holy mother's scrawled candle-lit map in the tower room of the convent and, looking now at the face of the real man, he felt a certain raw emotion.

The monk eyed him intently.

'I . . .' Marcus faltered, afraid to reveal who he was.

'Do you want to stay?'

'For a few days, if that's OK?'

'Come then . . .' touching Marcus's arm, leading him into the sunlight, 'how about a tour?'

Strolling through the cloisters, 'That was the chapter house, where we have our meetings. It trebles as refectory and calefactory.'

'Calefactory?'

'A warm house, somewhere where there's always a fire burning.'

He pointed out his own house, a corbelled stone dwelling shaped like an upturned boat, built by overlapping stones in the old way, sealed with mortar in the new.

'We're all monks from different orders – Franciscans, Carmelites and Dominicans, Cistercians, Carthusians and Benedictines. I'm their elected abbot – though I'm not really an abbot – so I get the fancy house! We come together every summer to rebuild this ancient monastery and to rekindle and experience the spirit and lifestyle of the founding fathers. It's also an eclectic experience, if you like, a pooling of different doctrines, a celebration of diversity.'

'It sounds a lot tougher – ' he was going to say than the Army – 'than anyone would have guessed.'

They ducked into an oblong building divided into workshops. 'We make and dye clothes here, and in here, the forge, we make jewellery to secure a supply of hard currency for our wee community. Replicas of eighth century Tara brooches sell like hotcakes!'

'So you're not trying to escape from the real world?' said Marcus cheerfully.

Stepping into a walled enclosure, where hardy vegetables flourished in beds of seaweed compost, Brother Dominic stooped to pluck a weed.

'There *is* no escape, my friend. Only the quest for isolation. Nor,' he said carefully, 'are there any solutions here. Only tasks.'

'Why the isolation, the hard life?'

The monk rose and fixed Marcus with his clear blue eyes.

'The need for penance drives us to remote and inhospitable places . . . does it not?'

Marcus blinked.

'I have to go now,' said the abbot. 'My house is yours, so is the island. We eat at seven.'

Marcus found himself walking alone round the island, already convinced of his need to escape from this place, afraid that running could become his life. He pictured his passport, 'Soldier' scratched out and replaced by 'Marcus King – Fugitive'.

At the eastern end of the island he stumbled upon the ancient graveyard creeping down into the sea, lichen-encrusted head-stones blasted by rain and salt, their broken stubs sheltering native plants, wild garlic and the downy nests of eider ducks, who squawked miserably when he came too close. As he picked his way among the graves, he imagined the weathered Gaelic inscriptions fading, to be replaced by fresh ones.

'Captain Charles Winters, 27, brave cavalier, led a convoy to disaster, Rest in Peace.'

'Private Robbie McLaren, terminated by a sniper after only eighteen years, Rest In Peace.'

'Bernadette O'Rawe, shot dead, aged 16, by a British soldier. . .'

Recalling the raid on Bernie's home, how she spat and fought, her face and body alive with hate and fury, he wondered what she would look like now, laid out in her coffin, inexorably decaying

. . . resting in peace? What became of her feelings, her rage, laughter, voice? Extinguished the instant the bullet struck her head? Could she really be alive in some promised heaven, or – Marcus gazed out to sea – was the afterlife merely lived out in the heads of the living? Holding his head in his hands, he yearned to drive Bernie out, expel everything – Army, Ireland, family. Throwing back his head he was half inclined to smash it against the nearest headstone and join the dead. Longing for oblivion, he began to stumble among the graves and squealing ducks to reach the sea, breaking invitingly in spume over rocks below. As he descended he slipped, boots skidding on bladderweed. Instinctively his arms sprang to his defence breaking the fall.

He lay on his back taking in the infinite blue sky and perpetual clouds. Dimly aware of pain, he lifted his left hand, split by barnacles, blood travelling freely down his wrist. Sitting up he soaked the wound in a rockpool, where fingernail crabs scurried to safety inside mussel shells. The pool, like Charlie Winters' cow trough, turned red. Withdrawing his hand he admired the clean cut.

The blood rose again, pumping unbidden from within, filling the shallow pool of his palm. He had no say in the matter.

Evening came, the island basking in sunshine. But the horizon was darkening with storm clouds, and a chill wind was already flinging spray up and down the island's north-facing coves. Lightheaded with hunger, Marcus wound his way back towards the monastery.

Entering the compound, he recoiled from the din coming from the chapter house – monks laughing, the clatter of crockery, musical instruments being tuned. Unable to face anyone, he turned away, an outcast. There had to be a way of leaving the island. He'd seen a collection of traditional rowing boats, curraghs, stacked above the port. He'd take one, he resolved guiltily, hurrying down the track, and chance his luck before the storm.

'Brother!' A voice from the monastery, like a West Indian friend calling in a soft Irish accent. Brother Dominic started down the track. Marcus didn't move. The tall spare monk stood before him, orange hair flying in strands about his tanned pate.

'Not quite ready for the limelight? Come, let's go to my house.'

Marcus allowed himself to be led gently, firmly by the arm.

'Your hand . . .' observed the monk. Marcus wasn't aware that he was still making a fist of his blood-stained hand. 'You've been in the wars' – stopping to open Marcus's hand – 'have you not?' he added meaningfully.

Their eyes met. Marcus didn't speak.

'We'd better patch you up.'

They regained the monastery and ducked inside the house that was built like an upturned boat. Inside was stark – charred fireplace, table and chair, two beds of straw, a bookcase and an illuminated manuscript.

'Sit down.' Brother Dominic crouched to light the fire. Marcus chose the chair and addressed the back of his host's head.

'You know about me, don't you?'

'You're big news, my friend. We listen to the radio. They're hunting you both sides of the border.'

'How did you know. . .?'

'It was you? You're not exactly inconspicuous! They're looking for a deserter from the British Army, six-foot-two and coloured' – looking over his shoulder – 'and with pain inscribed in his face.'

Marcus closed his eyes and breathed evenly, the energy beginning to course through him again, the juice rising like blood in the palm.

'I killed a girl.'

'That's not why they want you.'

'They didn't want me to testify.'

'You're wanted for desertion, attempted murder of a senior officer – '

'Draycott!' laughed Marcus.

'And for questioning about the murder of a Royal Military Policeman.'

The smile died on Marcus's face. He paled, his deep brown complexion shot with grey. He was sure he'd only knocked out the guard. Was this going to be another killing to bear for the rest of his life?

'How did you break out of the hospital?' said Dominic with the soft voice of an interrogator.

Marcus eyed him coldly, felt his hackles rising, the violence of self-defence. Rising to leave, 'I didn't come to this God-forsaken place to be interrogated.'

'Forgive me,' Dominic rose to meet him, 'I've not the slightest intention of handing you over to anyone. But I do need to ask you – did you know about the bomb?'

'What bomb? What the hell is this?'

Smiling with relief, 'There have been attempts to link you with a bomb planted by the IRA which burned a guard to death in your cell.'

'Christ . . .' Marcus subsided onto the chair, trying to visualise it. 'I put him to bed. He was breathing OK . . . Was it me they were after?'

'Evidently.'

'Revenge for Bernie O'Rawe,' guessed Marcus, shocked at the realisation that another man had died in his place. Leaning forward, he let his head lie in his hands. Another hand lighted on his shoulder.

'Have you any idea what you're going to do?'

'I want to get back to my wife and child. But first I want to find a way to make the Army pay for what they did to me, for what I did to the girl, for what we're doing to Northern Ireland.' Rising again, he began to pace the bare stone floor. 'Have they any idea where I am?'

'They haven't said so. Who brought you across?'

'The Flanagan brothers.'

'You're safe with them. The Irish are masters of the blind eye.'

13

Later that night, while Marcus was finally enjoying the company of the monks in the refectory, across the storm-tossed sound, a number of guests with a keen interest in him had checked into the only hotel on the headland.

Their conference over, maps were folded away and Dixie, Feeley and Annie went once more to look out of the window. Dixie swore in frustration. The night belonged to the elements, angry white waves storming the coast and exploding into the air around the little port.

A monastery on an island to the north, was what the nun had spluttered after Feeley pounced on her in the grounds of the convent. Enquiries suggested it had to be Inishtrahull. But how could they be sure the fugitive was there, and how were they going to reach the island in this weather?

They gazed out across the wild sea, the obliterated island betrayed only by the labouring beam of its lighthouse. Dixie wrestled with impatience.

'I'll fix a rota in the morning, so there's always one of us watching the port in case our man picks a lull in the weather to leave the island, or to slip over if he hasn't made it yet. We could have done with Michael. Why the hell did we leave him behind?'

'*You* left him behind,' Feeley reminded him, 'to prepare the farm for the fugitive.'

Leaving them to argue, Annie returned exultant to her room next door. Not only had Dixie leapt at her idea to kidnap Marcus King, but the IRA ruling council had embraced the inspired plot at a hastily convened meeting. Cock-a-hoop with pride, Annie did a little jig before slotting a cassette into a miniature tape-recorder and beginning her nightly programme of exercises. Ballet was her chosen medium, and for thirty minutes she performed stylistically and energetically to Tchaikovsky's *Romeo and Juliet*, there being nothing so taxing for the body as ballet.

In the next room, Eileen Feeley was in bed, waiting impatiently for Dixie to join her. But he sat resolutely by the window sewing one of his ragdolls. The bed was a double and Feeley wore a light jumper and nothing else. It was a long time since she'd had a man and Dixie was the only one she wanted. For six years they'd fought as comrades and sometimes had to sleep side by side, so it seemed only natural to consummate their special relationship. But he had remained as closed to her as a monk.

'Come on,' she said, smoothing back her sleek black hair. 'Tomorrow's a tough day, we need the sleep.'

'Good idea, get some sleep,' Dixie replied, stitching the hem on another tiny tricolour dress.

'You're the one who needs the sleep, you're wrecked! Look at you!'

She was right. Dark lines were carved under his eyes. But the ghosts of his bomb victims inhabited his nightmares nowadays and he dreaded sleep. He also wanted to put off getting into bed with Feeley.

'What's the matter?' said Feeley. 'I'm not good enough for you, is that it?'

No reply.

'Or is it you prefer that high-class piece of arse next door?'

'I prefer my wife.'

'Oh Jaysus . . .' Feeley lay back exasperated.

Dixie threw her a nervous glance. He hadn't had it for a long time either, not since he'd last made love with Mary one stolen night around Christmas, when he hoped she'd get pregnant. She didn't. His hit-and-run existence had certainly cooled his sexuality, but not extinguished it. He was well aware of Feeley's attractions. Men who knew her as Black Rose trembled with fear, but others who met her merely trembled with desire. If Dixie had any desire for her, it was securely locked in his subconscious. Marriage was sacred, and that was that. Annie was a different matter. She posed a serious threat to his sexual indifference to all women but Mary, partly because she sprang from a different social and cultural background and was therefore somehow other-worldly and out-side the normal rules, partly because she was so strangely and exotically attractive.

'I bet if *she* was warming this bed up, you'd be in it quick enough!' taunted Feeley.

'Bollocks,' he murmured guiltily.

The wind beat itself against the hotel; Annie's *Romeo and Juliet* penetrated the wall.

'For fuck sake come to bed,' said Feeley, 'I'm not going to eat you!'

Dixie glanced at her doubtfully and carried on sewing, until after a time there came the audible purr of Feeley feigning sleep, which didn't fool him for a moment. But then came another sound which arrested his needlework and made Feeley reach for the Colt .38 on the bedside table . . . voices on the stairs, male. The one that belonged to the proprietor they recognised, but the other was a hoarsely whispering Ulsterman, a deep gravelly bass.

In the next room Annie stopped her stretching and reached under the bedcover for her Armalite. Taking up a position behind the door, she listened to the men go past her room.

'How long would you give this unseasonable weather?' wondered the newly arrived Ulsterman.

'Ooh, I'd say we're in for a bit of a rough ride. The seasons please themselves here.' The sound of the room next to Annie's being opened. 'Goodnight, now.'

Annie listened to her neighbour whistling as he unpacked, and wondered who he was. Unaccountably troubled, she resumed her training.

While the last lights were going out in the hotel, across the night a small plane was approaching, its engines drowned by the gale, its pilot tracing circles, trying to pinpoint the target.

When finally the plane opened its belly, a human package tumbled out. Plummeting through rain and darkness towards the invisible earth, it burst suddenly into flower and sailed away on the wind.

Howling abuse at the Irish elements, SAS Captain Douglas Lee was swept blindly across wild Donegal towards the even wilder sea. Gritting his teeth, he laughed out loud. Through swirling darkness he glimpsed the foaming surf and knew it was going to be a close call.

Christ, a wall! Too late to miss it, he angled hard back, drew up his knees, landed briefly on top and sprang thirty feet into a boggy meadow. Boots sank, wind pulled, pitching him on his face. *Die, bastard, die!* he cried, subduing his parachute.

He slogged to the end of the field and almost fell into the sea. Waves exploded below and leapt over his head, drenching him in dissolving foam, reminding him of the ejaculations he was forgoing in London with Sergio. Bastards! There must have been other units they could have sent. This would have to be as bloody important as they said. But the thought of his castrated home leave made him boil. God help his men when he located them!

Nearby a soldier crouched behind a rock. Lance Corporal Tommy Baxter was twenty-one and keen, but tonight he felt mutinous. While the other two more senior members of the unit kipped comfy in their Gore-Tex bags, he was detailed to spend the night in the open in case someone stumbled by and discovered them, here in the unrelieved wilds in the middle of a bloody gale.

Sod this for a lark! He was still cursing when his breath was cut off from behind by a foreign hand. Flung to the ground, he found himself staring into a blackened face. That's it, it's all over –

'Who's a lucky boy?' breathed the face.

'Fuck me, sir – '

'Don't tempt me – '

'I took you for a Provo.'

163

Lying flat across young Baxter's body, impaled on his own erection, Lee hissed, 'Provos breakfast on squaddies' balls, so watch it next time!'

Releasing the soldier, Lee stalked away among the rocks, dimly making out two shapes on the ground, breathing imperceptibly inside their rain-proof cocoons. Creeping closer he crouched down and barked, 'STAND TO! STAND TO!'

As Lee counted, out they tumbled, two synchronised soldiers pitching into the wet, rolling dramatically, almost frightening each other to death before crouching rockstill with hearts bursting and sub-machine-guns poised to erupt in their hands. The wind howled, rain whipped the ground, the two SAS men remained coiled like petrified bog-faeries . . . until a familiar voice broke the spell.

'Evening, gentlemen!' The spectre of Lee surfaced. Sergeant Williams and Corporal Hurst stood up wearily. 'Good to see you so alert!'

Hurst muttered something unpleasant. Lee sprang down and thrust his face up close to Hurst's. He knew this corporal well, a vicious, beautifully built twenty-four-year-old killer.

'Did you say something, Corporal?'

'How nice it is to see you, sir!'

One of these days, vowed Hurst bitterly, one of these days!

14

There was scarcely any dawn over Inishtrahull the following morning, so persistent and impenetrable was the storm. Sitting just inside Dominic's house, Marcus watched the sea surging round the island, dashing itself against jagged bluffs, bursting brilliant white into the air and crashing down to deluge the rocks and vanish.

Dominic stood at his shoulder, frequently changing blades and applying fresh lather as he shaved Marcus's head.

'You're not going to change your mind, I hope!'

Marcus chuckled. 'You mean it won't stick back on?'

He felt the need for something dire, some symbolic act of penance. With some misgivings Dominic was obliging.

'My friend, it wasn't murder' – tufts of buoyant black hair fell at their feet – 'not even manslaughter . . . accidental homicide, if you like.'

'I joined the Army, knew the kind of things I'd be expected to do.'

'You tried not to do them, found and practised alternatives. They resented it and put a stop to you.'

'Tried to.'

'Yes. One should have some sympathy for them, don't you think, trying to put a stop to you.'

'I still feel' – he rooted amongst elusive feelings – 'responsible . . .'

'Racked by guilt?'

'Ashamed.'

'Is it the shame of failure that's tormenting you?'

'That too, but the girl's driving me nuts, she haunts me and always will unless . . .'

'Unless?' Dominic prompted.

'I'd like to put a baton gun to a famous head and threaten to pull the trigger unless they ban plastic bullets, at least temporarily, pending an inquiry.'

'There are better ways than that. Rest and pray and think.'

When the last obstinate stubble was cropped, Dominic massaged sweet oils into the tender scalp and stood back frowning. 'Feel any different?'

Marcus stood and, lifting his hands gingerly, ran his tremulous fingertips over his smooth gleaming mahogany head.

'A new man!'

Dominic smiled approvingly, noting a change in his guest, a brightness in the face, a mischievous light in the eyes.

Stepping into the gale, Marcus closed his eyes and offered his bare head to the rain.

Marcus wasn't the only one seeking absolution that night. Thirty miles inland Michael O'Cinneíde hadn't slept, both for missing Annie and for the gnawing of his conscience. Detailed by Dixie to mind the farm and prepare for the fugitive, he'd had time to think, too much time.

He was beginning to hate Dixie, suspecting the real reason for leaving him behind was so he could chance his luck with Annie.

As for Michael's tormented conscience, after three years in Dixie's bullet-happy, bomb-crazy outfit, he'd grown hardened to the sight of dead and injured comrades and enemies. He'd coped because there hadn't been an Annie McBride around to make him question it, and because the harvest of death had been relatively meagre. But Thorn Hill he'd seen on TV with Molly, fragments of men picked up off the road and plucked from the hedges and stuffed in plastic bags. Molly had watched in silence, never once glancing his way. But he knew she knew.

He ached to be free of the IRA, but the day he'd taken the oath was still branded on his memory.

I, Michael O'Cinneíde, do solemnly swear – This was the original 1923 Oath of Allegiance – *I will defend the Irish Republic against all enemies, foreign and domestic* – Dixie, a traditionalist, preferred it to the modern Declaration of Loyalty – *and shall not yield a voluntary support to any pretended government, authority or power* – in the blinking of an eye he was a bona fide member of the world's most ruthless long-suffering terrorist organisation – *I take this obligation freely, without any mental reservation* – and in no time was handling explosives – *So help me God.*

Now I'm a bloody expert, he reflected, slipping a jacket over his pyjamas and tiptoeing to the kitchen. My bombs have maimed and killed . . . sure to God, I wasn't meant for it . . . Without switching on a light, he took a beer from the fridge and sat at the kitchen table in the creeping glow of dawn.

Sweet Jaysus, for Christ's sake get me out of this!

When Molly appeared soon after, wrapped in her dressing-gown, she found Michael on his second beer, talking to his dog Pip.

'What you doing up?' she asked.

Smiling sheepishly, 'There's stacks of work to be done.'

At a glance Molly took in Michael's hollow tormented eyes. She loved him, if possible, more than a real son. It tortured her to see him like this. Filling a kettle, she decided to broach the forbidden subject.

'What's eating you, Michael?'

Man and dog looked up, startled by the force of Molly's whisper. 'We're grand!' he rallied, vigorously ruffling the Border collie's head. 'Sure we are, Pip!'

The wind moaned in the joints of the isolated farm, rain drummed on the windows. Molly, a sprightly sixty, stood obliquely behind Michael, grey hair pinned in a haphazard bun behind her head, sturdy back unbent by toil, eyes bright with battle.

'I remember Michael O'Cinneíde,' she said jauntily, 'broad as a barn door, tall as a tree, happy as a sandboy! Sure he had them clapping and stamping with his songs on a Friday night, and didn't he turn the head of every wee girl in the village? And didn't every farmer, Protestant and Catholic, from here to Derry, know they could call on him for a lift any time, day or night. Never a long face, always joking – what happened to him, Michael?'

'Will you stop, Mother, I'm grand – '

'Is it the magic that's wearing off?'

Michael couldn't speak. Nor was there any need. Molly knew him best, she'd do the talking for him.

'Or did the magic wear off long ago? Ach, you were young and headstrong. The soldiers kicked your wee dog to death and smashed your van. It was a good excuse to join up, but no reason – '

'I can't leave!' He looked at her beseechingly. 'Dixie and Feeley'd murder me!'

The air chilled with unmentionable names.

'We'll think of a way,' she said, laying her hands on his shoulders, her tone suggesting she'd done a lot of thinking already. 'Meantime, go and unburden yourself. It's six months since you darkened that church.'

'I don't trust Father D'Arcy.'

'Father Mahoney's on today. Sure, he's more Republican than all of us together. Remember how he led the prayers for the hunger strikers?'

Michael succumbed to Molly's strong kneading fingers.

In his eagerness he almost ran to the church. Arriving early, he was the first to kneel inside the secretive confessional. Confession started a few minutes late. Father D'Arcy had received a phonecall advising him that Father Mahoney had been taken ill, and requesting, with apologies for such late notice, that Father D'Arcy assume his colleague's duties for the evening. Not the most charitable of men at the best of times, Father Hugh D'Arcy arrived at the church in ill humour.

167

Michael's heart beat so fast and his breath came so thick he scarcely heard the priest step into the adjoining closet, and without a second glance at the obscure and pious profile of his confessor, began to unburden himself . . . not the usual regurgitated prattle, but a heart-rending deluge of remorse.

There was no need for Father D'Arcy to prompt. Michael poured forth. Indeed Father D'Arcy was too chilled to have uttered a word. Even when Michael was finally spent, the priest needed a moment to compose himself.

'Is there hope for me, Father?'

'There's always hope, my son,' said the priest with a semblance of calm, and stammered something about 'purpose of amendment'.

'Pardon, Father?'

'Not only must you resolve never again to sin in such a desperate fashion, but you must forthwith sever all links with that evil breed. Only on that condition can I give absolution.'

'I'll do my best, Father, but it's not easy.'

'Then I'm obliged to doubt that you're fully contrite.'

'But Jaysus, Father, I am! If only you knew – '

'My son, think it over. I'm always here.'

Michael didn't stay for Mass, but took himself home up the long hill exhausted. When Pip bounded along the lane to greet him, Michael absently ruffled her head and walked on. Molly was waiting, standing in from the rain.

'I have to sever all links at once,' he said as soon as he was in the door.

She sat him down, made him tell everything, then clasped his hands across the table.

'But are you ready to quit, Michael?'

'Yes! But – '

'No buts. You've done your bit for Ireland. I'll talk to him, make him see reason.'

'Dixie see reason? He's blind to reason. Everything has to be sacrificed, even his family, to "the cause".'

Molly shivered.

Later, Michael was lying awake in bed, wondering how the hell he was going to tell Molly that the farm had been earmarked for holding the captured fugitive, when he heard her door open. He thought she was going to the bathroom, but with a light knock on his door and a tentative 'Michael. . .?' she entered and sat down on the end of his bed, half her face lit by the hallway.

'What was that Father Mahoney said – You've to cut all links with that evil breed?'

He sat up. He saw what she was getting at and his mouth fell foolishly open.

'Are you sure it was Father Mahoney?'

A few miles away, Father D'Arcy slept well, his conscience at rest. It had been a shock. Moments after Michael O'Cinneíde left the confessional, Father D'Arcy, ignoring the patient queue of penitents, followed him out of the church and watched him labour up the hill.

It was all very well for Michael, offloading his guilt so lightly, but what, the priest had reflected, was he supposed to do with such a heinous confession? This wasn't the usual babbling beg-pardon for duties neglected or minor infringements of the person. Was it really sufficient that such a dire admission of multiple murder reached the confidential ears of the Lord? Didn't he, Father D'Arcy, have an overriding obligation to ensure it reached the ears of more worldly authorities as well?

Further debate had been superfluous. Before the massive figure of Michael O'Cinneíde was out of sight, the priest had made his decision.

The storms abated, and when dawn broke over Malin Head, Inishtrahull was visible again, basking out at sea like some prehistoric creature.

Feeley dressed sulkily. The whole night with Dixie and nothing more passionate than his obstinately turned back. Dixie ignored her mood. He was relishing the view from the window as he dressed, the first clear sight of the island, the subsiding sea. Feeley snorted.

'He probably took one look at the sea and changed his mind.'

Discreet enquiries, mainly by Annie, had uncovered no news or sightings of a six-foot-two-inch black man, but Dixie was confident.

'A feller with his nerve wouldn't be put off by anything. All we got to do is find a boat.'

So far, no one Annie had spoken to knew of anyone prepared to make the crossing.

Footsteps, quick and light, coming up the stairs. Feeley reached for a gun, Dixie recognised the steps.

'It's Annie.'

Feeley threw him a caustic look. Annie burst in.

'Just seen the Breakfast TV News – '

'Has her ladyship never heard of knocking?' said Feeley.

'IRA bombs in London! Bandsmen, horses, civilians blown to bits by nail bombs – and no fucking warning! Is that the kind of organisation I belong to?'   .

'Keep your voice down!' Dixie moved quickly to close the door.

'And you know what the big boys in Belfast put out? "Regret civilian casualties, but it was an act of war!" Well fuck that! No bloody warning. Most of those bandsmen and cavalrymen have never carried anything more lethal than a trombone!'

'Will you listen to her!' sneered Feeley. 'She should have joined the Salvation Army.'

'You should talk to them,' Annie appealed to Dixie, 'tell them this is no way for the movement to be going – '

'But it is, you soft bitch!' said Feeley. 'It's okay for the Brits to come over here shooting up the place, but she condemns us for going over there and giving it back.'

'Because they're barbarians, should we imitate them? Act of war, my arse!'

'You're being hysterical, woman,' said Dixie.

'Worse,' said Feeley, 'she's a fucking traitor.'

Annie flinched. The colour drained from her cheeks. Drawing herself up, she fixed Feeley with a murderous stare.

'Take it back.'

Feeley heard the menace in the younger woman's voice and laughed contemptuously. Weathering her gaze, she repeated, 'You're a traitor.'

Annie's eye strayed to the pistol lying cocked on the bedside table. Dixie intercepted the look and spoke low.

'We may despise her views, but she's no traitor. So take it back.'

'The bitch has you round her finger.'

'She may be squeamish, pig-headed and unreliable' – Dixie spoke with a certain bitterness – 'she may be weak-bellied, irresponsible and subversive, but she's brave, and I believe she'd give her life for Ireland. She's no traitor, take it back.'

'Never.'

A moment's pause. His voice slipped almost to a whisper. 'That was an order.'

Feeley flashed him a look of disbelief. The hands fell from her hips into fists. Flushed with rage and shame, she looked at him and shook her head slowly, more in supplication than defiance.

'Do I need to remind you about military discipline?' Dixie flared. 'She may be out of line – ' he rounded on Annie – 'and God knows you are, Annie McBride! Ever since the British Government allowed the hunger strikers to die rather than give an inch of justice, the hard-liners are back in business in Belfast. Moderation is *out*, Annie McBride, the British don't fucking understand it. Dead Catholics don't move them. And if it takes dead horses and trombone players in London to get them out of our country, then so be it!'

Scarred lungs rasping, Dixie stepped forward and faced Feeley hands on hips. He saw the pain in her face, her deep jealousy and bitter feeling of betrayal. He did not relent. 'I'm waiting.'

Feeley bowed her head. If eyes could burn there would have been scorch marks on the floor.

'She's no traitor' – there was a deadness in her voice – 'but near enough.'

Dixie released a heavy sigh and looked sharply at Annie.

'You're supposed to be on duty outside. Get to it!'

Along the passage, in the room next to Annie's, the mysterious guest, Detective Inspector Frank Mulraine, was waking to a vision. Brigid, the plump twenty-year-old maid, gently jogging him, leaning over him, mulberry nipples piercing her summer dress. Feigning confusion, he clasped her wrist, hoping she was as eager for a well-favoured forty-niner such as himself, as he was for a passable piece of anything. She wasn't. Patting his hand she repeated that Mr Lamb was awaiting the pleasure of his company at breakfast in the dining-room.

With a faintly reproving smile, Brigid departed, taking with her, he noted sadly, her strapping thighs, voluminous bottom, voluptuous breasts and her comely rustic face. Such a pity, he thought. If only life permitted a few more of one's sweeter fantasies. Instead of which he had breakfast to look forward to with that tiresome SAS Captain who operated ironically under the name of Lamb.

Dragging his bulk to the sink, he met his reflection in the mirror with distaste – dishevelled hoary hair, sagging eye-bags, whiskey eyes. Jaysus, you look like an old owl on the binge, God knows what you see in yourself!

He'd been on the go for thirty-six hours with scarcely time to draw breath. Posing as a Garda detective, he'd begun by telephoning Inishtrahull. The lighthouse keeper hadn't seen any six-foot-two-inch black men, and the monks, who didn't answer till afternoon, hadn't either. Then he'd done the coast roads from Malin to Glengad Head, making enquiries in isolated stores, at lonely crossroads and in every public house between, wetting his throat in each one – strictly in the line of duty.

'Tis no wonder you're wrecked!

But as he shaved, the humour left his face. His problem went deeper than ageing male vanity. The waning of looks and prowess was inevitable. What depressed him was the sensation of going psychologically to seed. It wasn't that his mental faculties were weakening, more that his appetite for success was waning. Exasperating as he was, his superiors invariably called him up for the big prestige cases. They were so used to him succeeding, their congratulations rang hollow. He felt like one of those wretched sows they keep confined in production-line crates, forever giving birth.

There was something impeccably pointless about his work. For every racket he busted, for every terrorist and kidnapper run to ground, another popped up behind his back; like toadstools in the rich seedbeds of Northern Ireland. If only accumulated successes were rewarded with early retirement, because the truth was he was becoming wonderfully lazy. In Barbara he had a fine indulgent wife; in Mark and David two healthily disruptive sons. None of them took the slightest interest in his work, nor ever complained about the risks and constraints endured by families of all Northern Ireland policemen.

His rare weekends at home were bliss. Breakfast and the papers in bed, an afternoon's fishing with the boys, a few endlessly drawn out jobs about the house, an evening meal with friends, a few whiskeys. That's the life. Instead of which, he reflected, as he straightened his tie and descended to breakfast, I'm chasing some unhinged island-hopping black man. Much worse was having to work with those uncouth gentlemen of the SAS. The thought made him long more than ever to kick over the traces.

Posing as a presentable English tourist, Captain Douglas Lee, complete with camera and Bord Fáilte guide books, waited down in the spacious dining-room, livid. What was keeping the bloody detective? His own men took four seconds to burst out of bed fully armed!

It had taken Frank Mulraine twenty minutes to freshen his image. The fine well-groomed head of hair, elegant suit and stylish tie weren't wasted. That delectable young woman was breakfasting alone again, and while Captain Lee was complaining about the outdated map of Inishtrahull, Mulraine's eye kept straying to admire the girl's brilliant raven hair and full body inside the thin black dress. Lee snorted his disapproval. Mulraine chuckled.

'What's up, Mr Lamb, have you not heard of mixing business with pleasure?'

'I keep them strictly apart.'

'Then you're a fine fellow,' said Mulraine jovially, 'but a terrible bore!'

'I take my work seriously, and I don't like working with cowboys.'

'Oh come now, sir – '

They spoke in lowered tones, though it would never have occurred to them that the IRA was in earshot, since they were convinced no one else could possibly know of Marcus King's whereabouts.

Leaning across the table, Lee hissed, 'The weather's delaying me, I've been given two days to get Mr K off the island, and we still don't know if the son-of-a-bitch is there! If your hunch about the island is wrong, my unit will be exposed for nothing. The maps you provided are bloody useless, so I'm going to have to fly across and film this morning, and all you can do is ponce about the seafront eyeing up the local crumpet . . .' Screwing up his serviette, he made to rise. Mulraine tried to detain him.

'If you'll just – '

'I'm warning you,' whispering hoarsely, 'I'll take it very person-ally if you fuck things up.'

The big Ulsterman flinched – those violent eyes!

'Before you go . . .'

'What?'

'I have some news for you.'

Mulraine lit himself a cigarette, Lee waited with ill-concealed irritability. It was the detective's turn to lean across and whisper.

'Between all the poncing and gallivanting I managed to find a moment to track down a couple of fellers who took yer man over in the week.'

'To the island?'

'I said he was going to Inishtrahull, and he's gone.'

The two men sat back and contemplated each other. Mulraine waved to Brigid and ordered more coffee.

'A fine wee lassie,' he observed, 'versatile, plays in any position.'

'What are you on about?'

'Brigid. Chambermaid, barmaid, receptionist, waitress!'

'What about Mr K?'

'Ah! I learned a good deal about him from their silences.'

'Whose silences?'

'The brothers Flanagan. When they twigged who and what I was, they became dumb as donkeys. He'd plainly made an impression. I had to read the riot act to get a word out of them. They were sufficiently intimidated to tell me when they took him across, nothing more.'

'You didn't arrest them?'

'What for? Anyway, this is the Republic, remember? I'm not supposed to be here. Nor, in case you'd forgotten, are you. But I left a detective and a bugging device on their house.'

'How long has he been on the island?'

'He's starting his third day.'

Lee tried to picture Mr Marcus King on the island, and anticipated their imminent first encounter with relish.

Mulraine dawdled over breakfast after Lee had gone, peeved with himself for allowing the SAS man to get under his skin. Dammit! Was there anything ever invented half so insufferable as a serious Englishman!

Not to worry, there was always the pleasant distraction of that enticing black rose at the far table, and he was about to ask if he might join her, when a lean, raw-boned fellow in dark glasses materialised from upstairs and joined her instead.

Dimly but unaccountably disturbed by the young couple, Mulraine brushed himself down, slipped an excessively generous tip under his serviette and left.

As he passed by on his way out to the waterfront, Feeley eyed him warily, twitching with vague suspicion, something more than routine vigilance. But just then Annie entered the hotel scarcely able to contain her excitement.

'Fixed up a boat?' said Dixie hopefully.

'Not yet . . .' Then whispering conspiratorially. 'But the man in the room next to me, just seen him on the front, snazzy suit, silver hair, maroon Vauxhall – remember, at the convent?'

Feeley looked round to where the two men had been sitting.

'Bloody knew it, if he's a cop the other shite was a Brit!'

Dixie rose abruptly, hoping to find no one at reception. But Brigid, sweeping the front steps, had seen him.

Slapping the counter. 'Anybody on this morning?'

Brigid arrived, blowing hair from her eyes and stepping smartly behind the counter.

'I am!'

'So you are! Must be these shades! I was wondering could I trouble you for some paper for the wee chapel?'

'Sure, I'm only after putting a new roll in this morning!'

'Well, you've a full house, and God knows what that fancy feller uses it for!'

While Brigid shrugged and took herself off, Dixie spun the register and picked out F. Mason at the foot of the guest list.

Mason? Dixie juggled with the name. 'That's not the feller we're thinking of . . .'

'Close,' said Feeley at his shoulder.

'I want to be sure.'

'How much surer can you get?'

'I'll check his room. You and McBride hold him up if he returns.'

Dixie climbed the stairs to the quiet landing and examined the lock on Mulraine's door. Then he delved in his pocket among a selection of pins and plastic and with the subtle touch of a craftsman contrived to divide the latch case from the keep. The lock gave, he eased open the door, entered and closed it softly behind him. The room was tidy and smelt of aftershave. Brigid had not yet made the bed, but the occupier of the room had evidently arranged it himself, not meticulously, but well enough to suggest an orderly man, or one anxious to leave a good impression.

If Dixie hoped to find revealing paperwork, log-books, diaries, he was disappointed. If Mr M was the man they suspected, he was

175

a careful professional. On the table lay an angler's newspaper, a book, *Game Fishing in Donegal*, a number of oranges and some loose change – sterling and Irish. Otherwise the room was tight-lipped.

On the point of giving up, Dixie's eye strayed to the wardrobe, a small key in the lock. Crossing the room he turned the key and parted the doors. Two suits were hanging up and a mackintosh. The suits, cleaned and pressed, had empty pockets revealing nothing. The mackintosh produced matches and sweet-papers and clipped to the inside pocket, perhaps overlooked by its owner, a silver ballpoint pen and miniature flashlight combined, sufficiently unusual for Dixie to unclip it and discover a name engraved on the side – Frank Mulraine.

Holy shit!

Dixie's first thought was that the renowned detective was after him, but since they had almost certainly seen him carrying out investigations at the convent, it seemed safe to conclude that Marcus King was his quarry, and that he was on the island.

He was uncharacteristically trembling as he quietly let himself out. If Feeley was right about the stranger at breakfast, then Mulraine was co-operating with the Brits, which in this area, out of bounds to the Brits, could only mean the SAS. Dixie hurried down to warn the others.

While various factions prepared to pluck him from the island, Marcus was sitting among the monks in the monastery's chapel, wrestling with his thoughts while his new brethren meditated, prayed and chanted.

He was growing calmer, the island didn't frighten him any more. He had walked all over it, imagining Jamie exploring with him. Now, as he pictured Jamie scrambling over the rocks, delighting in his discoveries, Marcus let out a chuckle. Several monks looked round. Marcus sheepishly mimed an apology.

A few more days and he would be ready to contact Pat and Eamonn, return to the mainland and strike back. But how? Dominic had counselled him against any course of action which might make his situation worse.

Haven't you atoned already?

Not enough.

Enough? How can you say that?

Enough to appease Bernie's ghost and wash her teeth-marks

from his wrist, enough to be able to take Marcia in his arms and say I'm home, I'm ready for a new life! Enough to feel OK about sporting civilian clothes and looking for a job, starting a business, picking up his music and forming a band? Or else he'd be forever looking over his shoulder saying, I should have done something more. Some debts can't be erased with a shaved head. Nor could he cheerfully overlook what the Army had done to him.

Whatever he settled on, the warning he'd given the C.O. and Draycott still held – I'm not finished yet! He'd hit back hard and then give himself up. His hands strayed once more to his head, fingers exploring his shaven skull, smooth and hard as a plastic bullet.

He was sitting rapt in thought, wishing by some miracle he had his saxophone with him, when he heard a distant sound which he couldn't fail to recognise and which set his heart pounding. Everyone appeared to hear it, but resumed worship as though they hadn't. Dominic looked round, Marcus motioned that he wanted to investigate, Dominic nodded and followed him out.

Emerging into daylight they saw a helicopter poised above the sea, banking hard around the lighthouse and hovering briefly over the western hill before beginning a slow sweep across the island.

Marcus took cover, Dominic stood in the open shielding his eyes. Marcus found he was shaking. The helicopter was a twin-engined Lynx, the kind that mistook him for the enemy on Thorn Hill, the British Army's favourite new flying machine. Could they have found him already?

Crouching in the shadow of the monastery wall, he saw to his relief that the helicopter bore civilian markings – VAN HOEVEN : DEE SEA PROSPECTORS. One of the crew was filming over the monastery and its surrounds, scattering goats and sheep, and driving gulls and eider ducks screeching into the air. The intruders made one more sweep along the north coast, and blustered away over the sea towards the mainland.

Marcus emerged. 'How often do you get them?'

Dominic was gazing after the receding machine, brows knitted with unease. 'Never happened before.'

Their eyes met, reading each other's thoughts.

Nursing a not unfamiliar hangover, Frank Mulraine walked along the waterfront, giving his pained head to the brisk sea breeze.

Shielding his eyes he watched the Lynx returning from Inishtrahull and disappear along the coast.

VAN HOEVEN indeed! It gave him scant satisfaction to see his detective work so crudely exploited. Was it because he was an Ulsterman that he felt protective about this harshly beautiful place? The British frequently employed the terms Ulster and Northern Ireland as if they were interchangeable. But the cold-blooded surgery of 1920 had not only partitioned Ireland, it had made a bloody mess of the ancient province of Ulster as well, cutting into Ulster's original nine counties in such a way that the six largely Protestant counties were sewn up into a new Northern Ireland, while the three mainly Catholic counties were discarded and given to the new Irish Free State.

Though not born at the time of Partition, Frank Mulraine felt queasy at the thought of his native Ulster being Irish in Donegal, British in Londonderry. Even dottier was the notion that Donegal, the most northerly county of all, was excluded from Northern Ireland and belonged to the South. And yet the British, who carried out the extraordinary operation in 1920, persisted in acting amazed at Ireland's difficulty in living with it, washing their hands of any responsibility for the daily haemorrhaging which had gone on ever since.

Mulraine had no illusions. It wasn't men such as himself or Captain Lee who could do any good. They could shoot and capture Provos till the cows came home and Ireland would go on bleeding.

The distant whirr and clatter of the Lynx faded. Mulraine shook his head and smiled. All it took was breakfast with an arrogant hothead like Captain Lee to bring out the Irish in a Protestant Ulsterman! Still, what the devil was he moaning about? Wasn't it preferable going after a poor bloody British officer who'd cracked, if cracked he had, than to have undertaken the job they'd lined up for him – hunting down Ragdoll Doyle?

Wandering back to the hotel, his seasoned eye strayed automatically to the vehicles in the car-park, observing details, probing for incongruities and generally disobeying his present wish to do nothing else but go up to his room and lie down. Too late! He'd spotted the non-local number plate of the blue Ford Escort, and couldn't help taking a closer look. It was a Derry city registration, belonging most likely to that slim gangster in the shades and his enticing black rose. Probably innocent, but slow-to-die instincts made him unlock his own car and activate the pye-phone concealed in the dashboard.

A mile away, Captain Lee was scanning the coastline through binoculars, while in the warm body of the Lynx, Welsh Sergeant Taffy Williams and Cockney Corporal Danny Hurst were replaying the video of the island and transposing landmarks to the map. Young Tommy Baxter was on stag and all four wore civilian clothing – jeans, T-shirts, hiking boots, nothing which might identify them as soldiers. The Lynx's pilot and navigator lounged in the grass.

Baxter kept himself to himself. He knew his place. But Williams and Hurst were still contesting theirs, as always, when the radio buzzed.

'Get it, Baxxy,' ordered Hurst.

Baxter complied, just quick enough to satisfy the bastard, slow enough for his own dignity.

'If it's me mother,' quipped Williams, 'I'm out!'

'Didn't know you had a mother!' said Hurst, amazed.

The big Welshman turned ugly. He didn't have a lot upstairs, but he was a brave, open man, easily hurt.

'I'll swing for you so hard one of these days, Hurst, *your* effing mother won't recognise you!'

Hurst grinned provocatively. After seducing girls and shooting Provos, bating Taffy Williams was his favourite sport. For all his bulk and bravado, Williams was afraid of the leaner, meaner, cheerfully sadistic Hurst.

'Answer that fucking radio, you morons!' barked Lee.

Hurst barged Baxter aside and answered it.

'It's Flash Paddy! Wants a low-down on a suspect vehicle.'

'Then get him one.'

Hurst used HF radio to contact central computer, then passed on to Mulraine that the sky-blue Ford Escort was partial to border-hopping but clean. Mulraine wasn't convinced.

'Paddy wants a bug on the jam-jar.'

Lee, absorbed in the futile drift of the sea, didn't hear.

'I said, Paddy wants a transmitter attached!'

'He wants one up his arse,' muttered Lee.

'Shall I tell him that, sir?'

Lee looked across at the beautifully carved face of Danny Hurst. Their eyes interlocked and wavered.

'Tell him you'll do it after dark.'

The Lynx departed, the hot afternoon wore on. Lee continued to watch the island and the sea through his binoculars, Baxter was out of sight guarding the little hollowed camp, Hurst was dozing in the grass, and Williams whistled as he prepared broth *à la* Donegal over a gas fire.

'When's D-Day, Boss?'

Lee took several minutes to reply. '02.30 hours.'

'What, tonight?'

'Tonight.'

Casually dressed and carrying a knapsack and fishing rod, Corporal Hurst loitered near the waterfront until the suspect Ford Escort returned to the hotel car-park from some undisclosed trip. A disgruntled couple got out, distinctly Irish, a lean character in shades and woolly cap and a woman with long black hair and beret. As he watched them enter the hotel, Hurst enjoyed a vivid fantasy of machine-gunning them all over the steps.

When night fell to within a foot of his face he approached the car, slid underneath and attached a tracking device comprising a die-cast box clamped to the underchassis with built-in magnets, all coated in black underseal.

Completing the job, he heard voices on the wind. A light swinging on the pier picked out a tall slender woman in a beret talking to a party of fishermen. As they gravitated towards the car-park, Hurst lay still, teeth clenched. He hated Ireland, down to the last lawless man and savage woman, not least because of what they'd done to Vince. The sound of their coarse accents made his hackles rise. They were, he noted, discussing the problem of reaching the island. From his greasy hideaway he watched the fishermen's boots dispersing to their cars, leaving the young woman to her own devices.

' 'Tis a pity you didn't catch us sooner,' one called back to her, 'we'd have got you across somehow.'

'Thanks, I'll get there.'

Her cultured Irish accent maddened him, an affront to his theory of savagery. The serenity and confidence in her husky feminine voice further roused his vengeful lust. The professional soldier in him generally held sway, but the urge to subjugate fellow humans and to defile women sometimes took possession of him. The fishermen drove away leaving the car-park quiet, and with his eyes Hurst pursued the woman slowly back to the waterfront, her long-legged silhouette sharply defined by the pier light. The soldier in Hurst was anxious to return to base, but with more than two hours to kill until the assault on the island, and with the rabid male in him on the loose, he found himself picking up her trail and slowly following her onto the front. There was nothing premeditated. Unlike his mentor Captain Lee, Danny Hurst was a weak man, impaired by childhood, drawn to excesses. A brutal father had schooled him in violence, an abused-abusing mother in the pleasures of inflicting humiliation. His older brother Vince, reared on the same irredeemable diet of scorn and thuggery, once actively shared his violent hostilities against the world, but an IRA bomb had sentenced the 25-year-old paratrooper to life in a wheelchair, and Danny, without quite knowing it, was trying to compensate by fulfilling the dictates of two warped natures, his brother's and his own.

'Was it the island you wanted?' Cap lowered over his eyes he spoke in a muffled voice, a garbled Irish accent.

She turned, eyes smarting in the wind and spray, focusing on him. 'Yes, as soon as possible.'

'Then it better be now, the weather's changing.'

Annie scarcely hesitated. Dixie would thank her after his failed mission with Feeley to find a willing ferryman.

'You can take us?'

'I can only fit one.'

'Tonight?'

'Now.'

'I'll be right back.'

'It'll cost you,' he called after her, eyes feasting on the tight arse of her jeans, the cut-away waist below the leather jacket as she ran, her wild hair. When she was gone he had time to remember his profession and return to his senses, but the pull of predatory lust was stronger. Possessed by his obsession he still had no plan, only a vague certainty that he could get away with anything, that his élite calling gave him immunity.

Annie hurried into the hotel and up the stairs and burst into the front room where Dixie was map-reading and Feeley undressing.

'For fuck sake, woman!'

'I've got a boat, he'll take me now, just me, before the weather changes.'

181

Dixie's face lit up, Feeley grimaced. 'What can she do on her own?'

'Locate King,' said Dixie, 'befriend him, stick with him, deliver him!' Clapping Annie on the shoulders, he bombarded her with instructions and strategies. 'He's all yours, we'll be waiting with a warm Irish welcome!'

Annie hurried to her room, changing into weather-proofs and bundling essentials into a rucksack. Casting a regretful eye over the Armalite she was obliged to leave behind, she felt for the comfort of the tiny Armalite charm she wore on a silver chain around her neck and departed.

Dixie was on the landing, waiting to present her with his pistol, pressing the Colt .38 Special into her hand. 'Just in case. Good luck!'

For a moment she thought he was going to embrace her, but his deep-sea eyes merely beheld her with something approaching reverence.

She found the man near where she'd left him. It was dark and blowy as they walked away from the port along the sands. There was no living thing in sight but the sea sweeping the shore. He put a casual arm round her.

'Thanks, I don't need it.'

'What's the matter, you don't like me?'

'This is business. I have to get to that island, you've offered to take me, I've agreed to pay. Kindly remove your arm.'

He did so, and they walked on.

Heading deeper into the night, they passed a number of beached boats before he selected one.

'That's mine.'

He took her arm down the beach, she barely tolerating it, still hoping he was nothing worse than a horny local pushing his luck, but growing more nervous with every moment at the sound of his curious accent and the aura of darkness emanating from him.

Suddenly she was off her feet, pitching through gravity, flying outside her control, borne to the ground by his vice-like hands, landing on her back with his entire body covering hers and his mouth engaging hers before she could draw breath. As she tried to wrench her head away, he drew back and a blade flashed through the air, no ordinary blade, but a twelve-inch bowie knife, paralysing her with fear as he brought it down towards her face and stabbed it into the sand beside her cheek, taking some of her hair down with it, making her cry out. He clapped a hot hand over her mouth.

'Be a good little whore now . . .'

He meant to retain the thin Irish disguise, but in his delirium an English accent slipped out. He could do what he liked with her, because he had her pinned beneath his hard loins and if she tried to move her head, her hair, pegged by the knife, held it back. If she tried to tear free, her face would be cut by the knife's obscene double-edged blade. To make it worse, the knife had made its mark inside the circumference of her chain, and the chain was biting into her neck.

Holding down her arms, he descended grinning and kissed her mouth at will, not with tenderness, but with an aggression which quickly turned to biting until she could taste the blood in her mouth.

Whimpering pathetically to deceive him, she counted on his needing at least one hand to proceed with the serious business of raping her. She was right. Tiring of abusing her mouth and neck, he tried to free one of his hands by wedging one of her arms under her body. She made it easy for him, and lay back so submissively terrified, that he discarded caution and followed his seething desire to her groin and the zip of her jeans.

She winced at the brutal invasion, his loveless violent hand grinding down between her legs, tearing at her underpants. She played helpless a moment longer, allowing his marauding hand to go deeper into the tight confines of her jeans.

Then without warning she struck back, wrenching free the arm crushed beneath her and lifting her hand to jab two stiffened fingers into his eyes.

He cried out in pain, brought both hands up to his face and reeled again as her two free fists swung together and caught him in both sides of the head.

Rolling off her into the sand, the astonishment and pain in his face quickly turned to maddened hate. Twisting round to come at her again, he didn't see the gun in her hand until it went off in his face.

The deafening report echoed away on the breeze.

'That one went over your head,' she said, 'the next one goes through it!'

Half-blinded by her fingers, he stood back from her, still and quiet. It was too dark to see his face, but she felt him thinking a way out. Switching the gun to her left hand, she struggled to free the knife and her hair from the sand. He ran, ducking and weaving towards the cover of rocks, and was gone.

The knife came free, her chain broke. A pair of headlights was approaching along the coast road from the direction of the hotel. Could someone have heard the shot? She gathered her rucksack, and the man's knapsack and fishing rod and crept among the rocks.

No need. She recognised the ailing grind of the Ford, heard a car door, saw Dixie's outline coming down the beach.

'Miss me already?' she called in a cracked voice.

Dixie stopped in his tracks. Annie stepped into the open, showed him the bowie knife, recounted the story.

Shaking his head. 'I had an uneasy feeling about it the minute you left.'

Back in the hotel they went through the man's knapsack. Apart from a few greasy tools, there was nothing to identify him. Only his accent, and the efficiency of the assault.

'SAS?' suspected Annie. Dixie nodded.

Annie took a shower, soothing her bruises, quiet as an animal that's sprung its trap and narrowly escaped.

Returning to her room, she heard Dixie going out to take the night watch. In the morning they'd have to go further afield to hire a boat. And all the time there was no way of knowing what that Detective Mulraine and company were up to.

Despite her tiredness, Annie did twenty minutes of rigorous ballet exercises. Then climbing into bed she examined the silver chain in her hand. It was irreparably broken, but the little silver Armalite, with the letters ARM engraved on the stock, was unscathed.

She took up her favourite book, one that inspired her whenever her spirits flagged – a dramatic biography of the romantic Irish aristocrat, Constance Markievicz, celebrated guerilla leader, sniper and forerunner of the IRA, who fought the British in 1916 and later became the first woman MP elected to Westminster: 'Countess Markievicz cut a striking figure in St Stephen's Green that Easter Week, leading her men against the encircling British, a plume of cock feathers springing from her black velour hat, a bullet-packed bandoleer strapped across her breast, her famous rifle hard against her shoulder . . .'

Book and chain slipped from Annie's hand and she fell asleep.

On the island that night, the deep walls of the chapter house trilled with flutes, uilleann pipes and Gaelic voices, a farewell concert to Brother Marcus, who was prematurely leaving. Dominic leaned closer to translate.

> There is a distant isle
> Around which sea-horses glisten
> A fair course against the white-swelling surge.
>
> And my house is small, not too small
> And always accessible, for women disguised as blackbirds
> To talk their words from its gable.

It was the wrong side of midnight, but tonight was exceptional. Tankards were refilled once more with Inishtrahull beetroot Claret, and a youthful Cistercian monk rose to propose a final toast.

'Brethren! To our illustrious fugitive . . . may he outwit his pursuers and find some awe-inspiring place to deliver his treatise on the abomination of plastic bullets to an enthralled world audience!'

A roar of approval, every man but Marcus on his feet.

'To Brother Marcus!'

The moon was high when the monks retired to their beehive huts, and Marcus went with Dominic to his house.

By the light of a turf fire Dominic applied a fresh dressing to Marcus's hand.

'See how quickly you heal?'

'But what about the soul, how long does that take?'

'Don't put a time on it. Live well and you'll heal. Kick up all the fuss you can about the plastic bullets, but don't overlook your family. Don't make them victims of your quest for Bernie O'Rawe.'

Marcus gazed into the fire, gripped by a dread of never setting eyes again on Marcia and Jamie.

The high speed inflatable dinghy pitched and plunged into a moderate wind. Lee lay flat, eyeing the island through an image-intensifying sight which lit its dark contours in an eerie light and magnified them.

Hurst steered, absorbing the brunt of the spray, sullen after the abortive sport with the bitch on the beach. Scarcely able to admit to himself what had happened, he hadn't dared tell the others that he strongly suspected he'd survived a close encounter with the IRA.

The sea was restless, unpredictable, delighting in lifting the dinghy clear of the water and pummelling it from underneath, then cunningly relenting, running smooth, lulling the concentration, undoing the grip, only to pounce again, mercilessly battering the hull.

Lee swore at Hurst. Hurst, choking on sea and salt, swore back. The running moon dashed from cloud to cloud. Through the image intensifiers, Inishtrahull floated in a pinkish glow. Scudding over the waves the dinghy steered clear of the daggered shores of the island and came at her from the north. Once inside the jaws of the creek, the sea released the dinghy and swept it unmolested up to the jetty.

In the pre-dawn stillness, they climbed ashore, peeled off their oilskins down to jeans and sweaters, deflated the dinghy and, carrying it soundlessly to higher ground, separated without a word.

Stalking across the plain, they climbed the rugged slopes and met at the entrance of the monastery. Moving in concert with the appearing and disappearing moon, they ghosted from one dwelling to the next.

It was Lee who came first to Dominic's house, sensing this was the place. Pistol drawn, he took time to engage the latch and freeze open the door a few inches. Moonlight followed his face around the edge of the door. Inside, embers glowed in a fireplace, a man slept on the floor in the far corner. Lee introduced himself a breath at a time, making certain the single-room dwelling was otherwise unoccupied. He inched closer to the sleeper, evidently a tall man, a coloured man, his black man's feet protruding from the straw and goatskins as if he were too big for his bed. Lee's pulse accelerated. In rare moments like this he forgot his quarrel with life, its miserly futility, its cheap narrow fare to the grave, and felt instead the richness of his own power, the rare privilege of his calling.

The sleeper lay on his front, black face to the wall, head covered in a seaman's tam, shoulders covered in a heavy Aran sweater. On the floor, heels together, stood the shin-high Army boots stolen from the Royal Military Policeman who perished in the hospital.

Lee gave the sleeper a shove in the shoulder with his foot. As the sleeper groaned and turned over, Lee seized him by the throat and pistol-whipped him back to deeper sleep. Binding his wrists and ankles, he dragged him outside and whistled. When Hurst materialised, they bundled their man over the cobbles and out of the compound, down the rocky track and over the plain to the high ground where their equipment was hidden, stopping on the way to call up the Lynx.

Within minutes they felt the vibrations of the helicopter hurtling over the sea towards them. Up went the winches over Inishtrahull, lifting the raiders and their prize into the belly of the Lynx. Below, in a haze of moonlit mist, hapless figures were scuttling from their huts and running across the island.

The sky looped, the island tumbled away, the captive was strapped in and doused with face slaps. The four SAS men grinned at each other, even Williams and Hurst relaxing their enmity in a lusty round of cheers and back-slapping.

Douglas Lee was experiencing an orgasmic sensation of triumph, another personal victory notched up, a defiant two-fingered gesture in the mocking face of life. He'd completed his mission, cleanly and discreetly executed. The six o'clock news from the BBC in London would open with the recapture of the runaway British officer somewhere in the borderlands of Ulster. Incursions in the Republic? Good Lord, no! VAN HOEVEN oil prospectors? Never heard of them! SAS involvement? No comment.

'Snap to it, let's be having you, King Kong!' laughed Danny Hurst, whipping off the captive's woollen tam to reveal twists of red hair and a bald white pate. Momentarily mystified, the captors' expressions turned to anger. Lee shone a flashlight in Dominic's face. Spitting on his fingers, he tried to scrape the colour from Dominic's cheeks, but the coarse brown dye held fast on his face and neck, hands and feet.

As the Lynx wheeled away from Inishtrahull four SAS-men stared dumbly at the blackened face of Brother Dominic. Lee had to shout over the din of the helicopter.

'Okay, Shitface, where is he?'

Dominic's eyes flickered, dazed with pain, hard and blue with secret triumph. The pistol held to his temple hurt also, but only superficially.

'Turn this fucking machine round!' Lee bawled at the pilot.

The world turned on its side.

Cocking the pistol in Dominic's ear, 'Where . . . is . . . he?'

'Flown.'

'When?'

'Last night.'

'How?'

The Lynx vibrated above the island. An angry black knot on the hill below shook fists, demanding the return of their brother.

'I'm warning you, Padre' – Lee slapped Dominic's face to left and right, and pressed the gun barrel hard into his kneecap – 'for the last time, where is he?'

'He left in the night, that's the truth, that's all I'm saying – now take my knee.'

'Put her down!' Lee bawled. 'Wait!' Too many fucking witnesses! 'Back to shore, sweep the coast!'

The Lynx throttled, banked away in a wide arc. Dominic stole a final look at his friends swarming over the hill.

Feeley heard the helicopter. Surfacing from sleep, she forced herself out of bed and looked out of the window. In the first dim flush of dawn she saw the waspish outline of the machine clipping the sea towards the island.

Dixie! Where the hell was he? He hadn't been to bed. Snatching field-glasses, she lost sight of the helicopter, but picked up something else, a small boat, barely half a mile out, coming straight for the pier.

Already dressed, she put on shoes and hurried down the dark stairs to the lobby, where she started at the discovery of a man in an armchair – Dixie! Asleep. Or half asleep.

'I heard it.' His voice was dead, defeated. She hated him when he was like this. She left him and stood in the hotel entrance, training her field-glasses on the sturdy old boat coming in, lights dimmed, watchful faces in the low cabin.

She stepped back into shadow and followed the boat with growing interest. 'Dixie,' she hissed.

'What?' came faintly from within.

'Get a load of this.'

He took his time, received the field-glasses and allowed his aim to be directed by Feeley. She zeroed on a small party of monks ascending the jetty.

Monks!

They were separating, two or three staying put, a solitary monk coming along the jetty, bag slung loosely over his back. Nearing the hotel, the lone monk turned and waved. The other three waved back and descended into their boat.

'Well. . .?' said Feeley.

Dixie remained riveted by the lone monk, who was tall, broad and, even in the hood, black!

'It's him.' He reached inside his jacket and started forward. Feeley seized his arm.

'You want to scare him off?'

Dixie withdrew into shadow. Feeley stepped into the uncertain moonlight and walked along the front tidying her hair.

'You OK, Brother?'

'A bit sea-sick.'

'You look like you could do with a warm,' she said, tender as a nun.

'Thank you, I must be on my way.'

'Why don't we give you a lift?'

He hesitated, wary of his luck. 'Where were you going?'

'Me and my husband were just checking out, heading home.'

Avoiding her eye: 'No, it's OK, I'm fine.'

He began to draw away, she moved closer. 'You're shaking, Brother. We'd like to help, can we drop you somewhere?'

He needed to get right away from the area, fast as possible. 'Are you going anywhere near a train station?'

'Sure, no problem.'

She took his arm lightly, impressed by her own display of seeming benevolence. As she conducted him towards the car-park he glanced at her. Reading his nervous look she smiled reassuringly.

Frank Mulraine was in bed in the hotel when his earpiece crackled and Captain Lee's voice assaulted him down the radio. King had escaped, Mulraine was to scour the coast road . . .

Mulraine, half out of bed, called his man on the Flanagans' house, warning him to expect the deserter at any moment. Then he started to dress, getting as far as trousers and braces before feeling the pressure on his bladder and hurrying from the room. The bleak fellow in the shades was swinging a stuffed suitcase down the stairs – at five in the morning? And coinciding with King's escape? Along the passage another door flew open emitting a tall redhead, who mumbled an apology and steered past him with a rucksack.

His drowsy brain reverberated with possibilities. He pressed on to the end-of-passage toilet, which afforded personal relief and a view of the car-park. Mother o' God! A monk in the back of the Escort, the beguiling black rose tucking him in. Who were these people? Suddenly he knew exactly who they were, marvelling at his failure not to have realised the young woman's identity and to have recognised the wanted-poster-face behind her feller's shades.

Hand froze on zip. Where had he left his gun? Cool it, Frank! The Escort's bugged.

He zipped himself up along the passage. No time to pack. He was struggling into his shirt when Brigid's voice startled him.

' 'Clare to God, this place must be on fire the way folks is leaving!'

'Emergency! I'm a cop, bill the police!' – shit, wrong country! 'I have to go after that crew – here!' He tossed her his car keys. 'See which way they go, then open up the maroon Vauxhall for me!'

'Hold on! How do I know – '

'Mother o' God!' – pressing a tenner into her hand – 'Do it now! I'll be back to settle, you've all my belongings and you never knew I was a cop, right?' He pushed her gently but resolutely out the door.

Marcus King sat monk-still in the back of the Ford, tired and queasy, but exhilarated by his smuggled return to the mainland. Like a hunted animal he was gambling on outfoxing his pursuers by turning and running among them.

Scarcely able to contain her feelings, Feeley got in behind the wheel and started the car. Annie climbed in beside her, amazed they'd caught their man so suddenly, unable to resist a glance over her shoulder, and a smile which wasn't entirely forced. The man she'd tried three times to kill returned her smile.

Dixie was getting in beside him with a cheery 'Morning, Brother!' when he spotted someone coming round the corner of the hotel. As he closed the door and the car shot away, he looked back and recognised the hotel maid walking quickly to the car-park, towards the detective's car, the Vauxhall he'd booby-trapped.

'Wait!' – fumbling for the window lever – 'Hold it!'

Feeley was climbing through the gears. 'What's up, forgot your toothbrush!'

'Stop! The Vauxhall's going to go up – '

The car sped away, Dixie leaning out, yelling into a sea breeze which snatched his words away.

'Keep clear of that car!'

Marcus tensed. Alarms went off in his sea-tossed brain, but as he started out of his seat, he came eye-to-eye with a pistol barrel.

The dawn exploded.

The car-park disappeared in a flash. Eyes streaming, lungs choking, Frank Mulraine charged into the smoke. The side of his car was gone, and the modest device had started a fire. Brigid lay on the tarmac, eyes open, horribly alive, hair singed back, dress smouldering, the breasts he'd so admired but never seen, exposed now and running in blood . . . and the arm she'd used to open the door lay severed several yards away.

He staggered to his knees, spilling his equipment on the ground. Screwing up his eyes, he was for a moment unable to endure the bloody joint where the arm should have been. Blindly he wrestled with his suit jacket, smothered her simmering dress, and carried her limp, wrapped body away from the fire to the nearest bed of moist grass. Through the roar of flames he heard the clatter of an approaching helicopter. It was imperative he spoke to Lee, but Lee was in first.

'Hello Starling, this is Magpie, what the hell's going on down there, over.'

Mulraine told him it was Doyle and Co in the Escort with the deserter, but first to land quick and get this badly injured girl to hospital . . .

'Take her by road,' argued Lee, peering down at Mulraine beside the burning car. 'I'm going after King, over.'

'Get down here, she'll bleed to death! Three of you can go after them by car, one of you can fly her to hospital, do you hear, over.'

'Take her yourself, we're going – out!'

'Now listen here! The car's bugged for Christ's sake – '

He was shouting at himself, the Lynx was wheeling away. The hotel's proprietors were on their knees, coats over nightclothes, comforting Brigid.

'Car keys quick!' snapped Mulraine, 'I'll take her.'

Already a mile away.

'There!'

Sure enough, all alone on the only ribbon of road in the mountainous reaches below, a blue Ford beetling flat out.

'Let's wipe them off the map!' said Danny Hurst.

'We want King alive,' Lee reminded them, exultant again, poised to reclaim his prize. 'We'll tail them covertly. All we need is a car. Eyes peeled!'

Marcus sat back petrified. The helicopter had offered brief hope. Now it was fading.

'Thank Christ!' said Feeley behind the wheel.

'They'll be back,' warned Dixie, still pointing a pistol at the prisoner.

'What happened in the car-park?' Annie wasn't posing an innocent question. Her voice was taut and vibrant with outrage.

'Shut it,' said Feeley, 'we got company.'

Annie, Armalite across her knees, looked round at Dixie. Dixie avoided her eye. Whatever he'd done, he wasn't singing about it.

'You bombed the car and got the girl?'

Now he faced her. 'I left a ragdoll round the aerial – '

'Will you two shut it!' said Feeley, trying to concentrate on the treacherous road.

'She wouldn't have known what it was,' explained Dixie, voice hollow, his countenance withdrawn behind the shades.

Feeley thumped the steering wheel. 'Not now!'

They fell silent, the Ford racing through the mountainous dawn landscape. Annie seethed. Feeley glanced at her and gave a snort of contempt, then glanced in her mirror at the prisoner.

'Does he know who we are?' No one spoke. Gloating, she addressed the Brit directly. 'Well, soldier?'

Annie couldn't help looking round at him. He was putting up a brave show, but the monk's hood made him look peculiarly vulnerable, and his eyes betrayed terror. He could guess who they were.

Leaving the Ford in their wake, the flying soldiers scoured the terrain ahead until a car came into sight, trundling down a furrowed track . . .

Through low clinging mist, the ageing farmer behind the wheel of his jalopy saw an apparition descend before him into his path. Having no brakes to speak of, he slammed the ancient Humber into reverse and jolted to a halt. Two figures, faces blackened, materialised through swirling dust and mist.

'Well hello there! A most unexpected sur– ' the farmer was saying as Hurst wrenched open his rusty door and dragged him out.

The helicopter lifted away again. The farmer stood where he'd been put, watching two men drive his car away. Dominic tried to stand where he'd been put, but his legs buckled. Focusing through a haze of pain, he saw the car carrying Marcus rounding a bend at speed. The old Humber was reversing into its path. Just too late. The Ford swerved and hurtled by. Dominic closed his eyes and prayed.

'Fucking move, you old bitch!' yelled Hurst behind the wheel, face contorted with blood-lust.

Lee, one hand on the broken door, watched the road ahead and the receiver perched on his lap. Its steady bleeps were remaining constant, telling him they were neither gaining nor losing on the Ford.

'Faster!'

'Won't go any bleeding faster!'

The Humber rattled and roared through the rocky, bleak and boundless landscape, the deceptively lonely road bending, dipping and concealing . . . SHEEP!

'JEEE-SUS!'

Hurst hit the brakes and horn and neither responded. Sheep goggled, continued to goggle and belatedly leapt.

'Bye-bye, Baa-baa!' he cheered, swerving after a decrepit ewe, catching her in the hip and tossing her in the air. He was still grinning when he caught sight of the look on Lee's face. Lee was staring at the receiver, wondering why it should suddenly be bleeping like mad. Could only mean . . .

'Pull up!'

'What?'

'Pull up!' – seizing his sub-machine-gun – 'AMBUSH!'

Hurst tried, but looked askance in horror. 'No fucking brakes!'

The Humber thundered over the brow and bounced onto the downhill. They saw the Ford immediately, abandoned at the foot of a corkscrew hill. To the left, also abandoned, stood the shell of a cottage. Otherwise the scene that met them was bare.

Lee braced himself for the hail of bullets, Hurst thrust the car into low gear and yanked up the handbrake, but nothing was going to stop the old banger now. The hairpin rushed towards them, the Humber careered off the road, demolishing the black-and-white barrier and sailing through thin mist. Plunging down a soft slope, it rolled over and over, skated on its roof and slid up a short ridge . . .

It fell back on its wheels and settled, glass tinkling on the bonnet. The engine spluttered and died.

Bruised and bloodied, they scrambled clear and threw themselves behind cover. The valley echoed, not with the menace of gunfire, but perfect stillness.

Bees worked the clover, unseen grasshoppers rustled, Douglas Lee got to his feet, breast exposed to enemy fire, a crazed grin on his face.

He's gone off his head, thought Hurst. Old Ironside's finally cracked!

But Lee was taking in the ruined cottage, tyre tracks emerging from a missing wall, leading to the road. 'Private garage for a getaway car!' he laughed bitterly, spitting a mouthful of blood into the grass.

Hurst rose slowly, glaring at Lee.

'They've lifted our man right under our noses . . . you've fucking ballsed it up, haven't you!'

Lee faced his corporal. Hurst saw the grey death-look in Lee's eyes, and shivered. Lee was coming towards him, the slow walk and vacant mask of an executioner.

'OK, I take it back' – backing away, hands spread for mercy – 'I said I was sorry . . . sir.'

Lee kept coming, an automaton. Hurst reached for his murderous bowie knife and with a shock remembered why it wasn't there – the bitch on the beach. Defenceless, he stumbled backwards and fell.

Lee was already airborne, Hurst rolled away, Lee missed and sprang again, catching his man by the leg. They wrestled violently, splashing and rolling down a steep incline, Lee spitting and dripping blood into the beautifully fashioned face of his corporal. At the foot of the slope, with Lee on top of him, Hurst panicked. Normally a match for any man, he couldn't hope to survive Lee in this mood. So as Lee pummelled him, Hurst reached for a slippery rock, twisted it out of the ground and swung it at Lee's head.

The SAS Captain rolled over and lay still.

A defiant smile went sour on Hurst's face. He thought he hadn't struck hard, but Lee wasn't moving. Jeee-sus, how was he going to explain this? I didn't hit him hard, honest . . . No, that wouldn't do. It was like this, the Provos jumped us, Lee and Doyle were . . .

Lee was dead still, no movement in his chest. Hurst crawled over, gripped Lee's shoulders, shook him desperately and bent down to try the kiss of life. Hands cupping Lee's face, he pressed his mouth to Lee's and tried without success to breathe life into him . . .

Jee-sus. . . As he hovered in despair over Lee's ashen face, the SAS Captain opened one bruised eye and grinned.

'Keep going, Corporal, I'm dying.'

15

The Holt Farm

Marcus regained consciousness. His head was pounding, shaved skull still reeling from a heavy blow, but when he tried to touch the back of his head where it hurt most, a chain jarred his wrist.

He was chained to the bare springs of a bedframe, shackled by his right wrist and left ankle. He was lying on his back in the dark. Judging by the sloping ceiling he was in an attic. Cool evening air entered through a skylight. He was naked, but for underpants.

He tested the chains, lightly first, then with all his might, pumping strength through his lungs from mind to muscle. Teeth set, skin running in sweat, he fought with dogged anticipation, flesh against iron. Flesh lost. He fell back on jagged springs, gulping air, gaping at the cobwebbed ceiling. Panic welled up, threatening to overwhelm and drown him. He'd never lacked courage, but this was different. He doubted his capacity to endure torture. For all his lofty principles, suddenly Bernie O'Rawe didn't matter, nor what the Army had done to him. Survival was everything now. To return home with his body and mind intact. To survive.

But the chains were unbearable, set in such a way that tempted him to try and rise, only to find he could half sit up, at a painful angle, for just a few tormenting moments. Reason made him lie still, but panic returned in waves. He writhed and whimpered, drowning in terror. Death, in these moments, would have been welcome.

A light came on, arresting his struggle, a bare bulb dangling from a beam above his head.

'The bastard's come to.' A woman's voice, the driver of the car. Almost certainly the notorious Black Rose.

'I'll follow you.' Male, the man with the gun and dark glasses. Ragdoll Doyle, the man who put the bomb under Charlie Winters.

He lay back. The woman was climbing the ladder, surfacing somewhere behind him, breathing closer. She was standing behind his head, looking down at him. She wasn't moving, but he could see her shape and obliquely her face.

Minutes passed. He felt her power, the force of her perverse pleasure. He felt his burning powerlessness and wanted to scream free of his chains. Pride kept him still.

Now she moved. At first he imagined she was undressing. Pushing back his head, he saw, upside down, that she was taking off her jeans and throwing them violently to the floor. Stepping up onto the bedframe from behind him, she turned round and stood over him, one foot planted on either side of his head.

'OK, soldier' – looking down at him with hateful eyes – 'how about some of your own back?'

He watched as she bent her knees and pulled down her underpants. Peering helplessly into her bushy vulva and anus, he tried to anticipate which indignity she had in store for him. As she squatted lower he turned his face in time to take the stream of warm sour piss on the cheek and temples instead of full in the face. Eyes and mouth tight shut, he absorbed the prolonged reeking deluge, marvelling at the force and capacity of her reserves. As the stream relented, she succeeded in summoning a few diminishing spurts. Then she stepped off and unashamedly adjusted herself behind him.

'Did you appreciate that, soldier? You been doing that to us for eight hundred fucking years!'

She departed, zipping up her jeans, switching out the light.

With the back of his free hand he wiped his face and waited. Nothing happened. Night was falling in the skylight. He became aware of farm sounds, and a dog barking. He tried to rally his spirits, recalling how they meant to break him in Army custody – and failed. Now the other army was trying, with different tactics, to achieve the same. And they would fail, he told himself over and over.

After a while he heard someone on the ladder, someone who breathed with a faint rasp. Footsteps across the boards behind him, alongside him, Doyle, hard eyes blinking in the darkness. And something else glowing. A gun. With a sudden movement Doyle lunged and pressed the mouth of the pistol to Marcus's skull.

'Say your prayers, soldier, you've got to three. One . . .'

Marcus went rigid, closed his eyes and thought of Marcia, her face when she heard the news . . .

'Two . . .'

His mother's face, his father trying to comfort her, blind for comfort himself.

'Three . . .'

'MARCIA!' he howled.

The empty gun went click.

Dixie blew on the barrel as though he'd fired it. Then he lifted something bulky as if to throw it.

Marcus braced himself, something flew through the air and landed on him – a coarse blanket.

'Don't misinterpret it. It's just that I want you alive.' The IRA man stood beneath the skylight, a Schmeisser sub-machine-gun strapped to his back, one side of his gaunt face dimly lit by the open trapdoor.

'We want our country back.' His voice was strangely soothing. 'We're sick of being a despised, intimidated minority in our own country, sick of begging jobs and houses off the Prods who control everything, sick of you bastards coming over to keep them in control and us under control . . .'

He came forward and pointed his hand at Marcus's head like a pistol. 'And you don't fool us with your soft-shit tactics, sapping the resistance of the people. All you've found is a better way of keeping us down, Lieutenant King!'

'I need to piss.'

Dixie kicked a basin under the bedframe and left Marcus to it.

Having delivered Brigid to hospital, Frank Mulraine returned, earlier that day, to find the hotel and car-park cordoned off by the Garda, and the area sealed by units of the Irish Army. His car lay where he'd left it, desecrated by fire and explosives. Garda officers seemed surprised that he'd returned to face them.

The questioning was polite and hesitant. Accustomed to nothing more alarming than the occasional IRA arms cache on a lonely beach, they seemed ill at ease dealing with the confused and appalling aftermath of an apparent IRA–SAS encounter on their normally tranquil beat. Mulraine put them at ease, pandering to their nervous professionalism, fostering the fragile bond between himself, a hard-bitten Protestant detective from the troubled North, and these mild-tempered Catholic counterparts from the rustic South.

But he knew that soon he must face serious questions from the heavyweights of both police forces. He'd been caught operating on the wrong side of the border. Captain Lee would have even more explaining to do. SAS squads had been caught by border patrols before, and promptly apologised for getting lost. But this was twenty-five miles inside the Republic. Hardly a map-reading error.

In the evening, as the sun descended through a red haze into the sea, the hotel's proprietors invited Mulraine to eat with them. Still badly shaken, they were grateful to him for putting Brigid's life before all else and rushing her to hospital. The first thing he'd told them was the good news. 'They assured me she's going to be grand!'

'Thanks be to God, and the arm?'

'Ah, the arm . . .' said Mulraine, placing his whiskey tenderly on the table and turning the glass in his stout fingers. 'She won't be using that any more.'

A long silence, broken by the husband. 'But how do you suppose, Inspector, that she came to be in the car-park at that hour?'

Mulraine stared into the slowly revolving void of the glass and spoke with difficulty. 'She was woken by the commotion of the hotel emptying itself of all its residents at five in the morning. She could have turned over, but up she got to stop the exodus. I explained who I was, sent her out before me to see which way they went and to speed me up by unlocking my car . . .' He lifted his gaze to meet theirs.

'Ach, sure it wasn't your fault,' said the man.

'Except I shouldn't have been here in the first place.'

'And it could have been *your* arm,' reasoned the woman sympathetically.

'And it should have been. I sent that child into a minefield.'

They all sat at a loss around the dining table.

'We'll eat as soon as Brother Dominic comes down,' rallied the woman. 'You'll feel ten times better after a good meal.'

'Wait,' said the man, 'I have something for you.'

The slight, twitchy proprietor with the goatee beard conducted Mulraine into an orderly little office at the back of house. 'I saved this for you, before the Gardaí went through the rooms.' He unlocked a drawer in his desk and turned round with a battered, fraying pocket-sized hardback book.

'It was in Miss Murray's room, least that's what she called herself.'

'The redhead?' Mulraine carried the book to the table lamp and put on his bold square reading glasses. *The Life and Trials of Constance Markievicz : Lives of Extraordinary Women Series.* He leafed through the well-worn, spine-split book, and pages came away in clumps. Towards the beginning of the book he found an unusual bookmark – a silver chain, broken, with a tiny silver rifle attached, an Armalite judging by its shape and the engraved letters ARM. Of course! The red-haired sniper the beleaguered cops had glimpsed in their sights on Thorn Hill before she shot dead one of the squaddies. And wasn't she the one who felled the officer – what was his name? Kitson – at Lieutenant King's feet?

Had she marked the beloved book with her name? That was the point. He returned to the inside front cover, and was immediately rewarded by the sight of a scribbled name and date. He held it closer to the light. Dingle, '76.

'Ah, shit! – Excuse me.'

'No use?'

199

'On the contrary, could be a vital wee find, a costly slip in their haste to get away. Only I thought we had her name, but it's Dingle in Kerry, a charming seaside spot, but hardly a woman's name. Imagine an IRA sniper called Dingle! And '76, wasn't it that scorcher of a summer? Could be her home town, but unlikely. Would you mind if I made a couple of calls?'

Mulraine called his office in Omagh and left instructions for his men to find out who sold such original and macabre jewellery as silver Armalites no bigger than a tie pin. Then he called his home, a sprawling bungalow in luxuriant country near Newtownstewart, County Tyrone. Barbara was philosophical as ever, she was going ahead with a small dinner party without him. The boys, she grudgingly conceded, missed him. She knew better than to ask where he was or what he was up to, though unusually she did tentatively broach the subject, almost as if she'd intuitively picked up that he was in trouble.

'I suppose it's an important case?' she said, betraying a twinge of anxiety. He grunted, neither yea or nay. 'I know! You'll tell me all when it's over. When will you be back, any idea?'

'No, but don't hold your breath.'

Brother Dominic was at table when Mulraine returned. He greeted the detective with cold blue eyes. He was still wearing Marcus King's clothing, though no one was aware of it, and his head was lightly bandaged.

Having been dumped on the cattle track by the SAS helicopter, he had been taken in by the bewildered farmer, and visited by a doctor. Robbed of his old car, the farmer had to ask a neighbour to drive Dominic back to the coast. Too late and too concussed to return to Inishtrahull, Dominic went to the hotel, where the proprietor, who knew him, offered him shelter on the house, provided he didn't mind the bed last occupied by the most wanted duet in Ireland.

Sure the room's been aired!

Dominic attributed his bandaged head to a fall while hill walking. He made no reference to Marcus King during the meal and appeared to be ignorant of all that had happened, even when they were interrupted by the BBC News from London. *'But tonight's main news comes from Donegal in the Republic of Ireland, where the Provisional IRA is claiming to have captured former*

200

Lieutenant Marcus King – the deserter at the centre of the plastic bullets row. A full-scale search is underway by units of the Irish Army and the Garda.

'Meanwhile Ministers in Dublin are expressing grave concern over reports that the RUC and the SAS have been conducting their own search inside the Republic, reports which have been strongly denied both by an RUC spokesman and by the Northern Ireland Office.

'The IRA also admitted responsibility for this morning's car bomb, which seriously injured a young woman, but which the IRA claim was intended for a senior RUC detective who tried to prevent the capture of Marcus King. The woman has not been named.'

Film crews had evidently taken a long time reaching the area. Mulraine's car was seen long gutted, and the cameras moved quickly to the small waterfront hotel where three of Ireland's most wanted terrorists had spent two nights.

'I'd like a word,' said Dominic in the middle of it all.

Mulraine was surprised. 'Will it not wait, Brother?'

'No.'

The hotel bar was congested with locals and not-so-locals, crowding the television set in deep silence. Dominic bought two whiskeys, and led the way up to his room.

Mulraine closed the door, uncharacteristically unnerved by the monk. Remaining standing, Dominic motioned the detective to sit. Mulraine pulled up a creaking chair and lit a cigarette. Dominic homed in.

'I think you know a lot more than you're pretending, Inspector.'

'Is that so? All right then, I think your hill walking tumble was a charming invention.

'I think you know where Marcus King was hiding and that you were working hand in glove with the British Army to lift him. But I haven't said anything yet, and no enquiries have been made on the island.'

'In other words,' said Mulraine, warming to the dialogue, 'the Garda don't know Marcus King was on the island, nor that a crude attempt was made to snatch him, because neither your brethren nor I have told them. Just as they don't know that you harboured a wanted man and facilitated his attempted escape by exchanging roles with him.'

They regarded each other evenly.

'Bear with me, Brother, if I'm a bit slow at the end of such an eventful day, but am I supposed to sense a pact in the offing?'

Dominic swallowed a good half of his whiskey with some discomfort, and then conjured a candle from his back pocket and asked Mulraine to light it. Dripping hot wax onto the table top Dominic secured the candle.

'Will you join me in prayer, Inspector?'

Mulraine blinked. 'I confess, Brother, 'tis a while since my hands were joined. I doubt the lines are still open, so to speak.'

'The lines are always open. And you should get a pretty clear one after what you did for the girl today.'

Putting down his drink, Dominic interlaced his fingers and closed his eyes. Mulraine, seated, hastily extinguished his cigarette and followed suit.

'Thank you, Lord, for Brother Frank's selfless fortitude today . . . for saving Brigid's life . . . We pray for Marcus King . . . that his captors will not see fit to send him to you prematurely . . . and that he be delivered from *all* his enemies' – Dominic briefly opened his eyes and looked pointedly at the detective – 'so that his true purpose and innocence may come to light . . . Amen.'

Dominic remained eyes closed. Mulraine studied the tall reedy monk, who evidently wished to turn a blind eye to the blundering SAS assault on Inishtrahull to save the island and his monastery from being overrun by the Irish authorities. But was another more intriguing motive emerging?

Dominic sat across the table from Mulraine with the burning candle between them. Mulraine lit another cigarette and let the sea breeze from the open windows waft away the smoke.

'Tell me, Brother, is he all there – in the head, I mean?'

'Oh yes.'

'They say he cracked.'

'They would like to think so.'

'You say he's sane as you or me?'

'More so.'

'You don't consider some of his recent conduct slightly mad?'

'No man is sane who does not know how to be insane on proper occasions.'

'Quite. So assuming his mind is fit, what of his motives, his purpose?'

'What should they be?'

202

'Bloody-mindedness, revenge, treachery?'

Dominic found a smile. Shaking his head, he said, 'He wants to clear his name, to restore his honour, to atone in some way for the death of the Derry girl, and to make the Army face up to what it's doing, with the misuse of plastic bullets in particular, and confrontation tactics in general.'

'A tall order for one man.'

'On his own, yes. But if he dies tonight, or tomorrow, let there be one voice in authority' – Dominic trained his hard blue gaze on the detective – 'who speaks up for him.'

Mulraine was rescued by footsteps and a knock on the door. The proprietor's goaty countenance appeared.

'Call for you, Inspector.'

Mulraine looked at his watch – twelve-twenty a.m.

'Excuse me, Brother. Can only be good news!'

Dominic went to the window. The lighthouse was reaching out across the sound, probing the dark coastline as though searching for someone.

Mulraine returned, tie loosened, suit creased, face stretched with tiredness, but with a lightness in his step.

'That's one hell of a hotline you've got there, Brother.' Meeting Dominic's calm gaze, he rummaged in his briefcase for a map. 'One of Ragdoll Doyle's outfit was moved to unburden himself to a priest. The priest was moved to alert the appropriate secular authorities.'

'Even terrorists have open lines to God.'

'Quite' – pinpointing an area on the map – 'so there's a strong possibility they've taken yer man to a farm about . . . here.'

'If he's there, I trust you won't be calling on the services of those brutes who wrenched me from the island, since he told me he intends to give himself up as soon as his mission is complete?'

'I've no say in it. They've dealt me a pack of wolfhounds and I'm to use them.'

'Don't pretend you've no influence.' Taking a step away from the window, the monk levelled with the detective, 'I'm expecting great things from you.'

The Holt Farm

Thirty miles away, Dixie Doyle was taking the nightwatch in the hayloft of Michael and Molly's border farm.

This should have been one of the great nights of his life. How many IRA units had ever captured a British officer, never mind a celebrated one, an embarrassing one, a thorn in the side of the British Army? The British Army was hunting him, along with the SAS, the RUC, the Irish Army and the Garda. Dixie was pleased that they hadn't killed him at Thorn Hill, the football game or during the Bogside battle. Kidnapping was evidently more potent than mere killing.

But Dixie's satisfaction was blighted by the inadvertent bombing of the girl at the hotel, coming as it did on top of his nightmares. The previous night, asleep in the hotel lobby, he'd dreamt of Dublin, sunny days in the park with Mary and Josie. Then he looked up and saw the bench opposite crowded with maimed and twisted soldiers, scorched, lack-limbed and alive, their faces untouched, gazing at him with unaccusing eyes. We're yours, they seemed to say, your retinue of the dead, doomed to follow you for the rest of your days.

And now the girl.

He was peering through the cracked wall of the hayloft across silent fields and trees along the border, caressing the long hard barrel of the American M6o machine-gun, wondering if he would ever be able to adjust to civilian life, when he heard someone enter the barn below. Drawing his pistol he watched Annie's untamed head ascend through the trapdoor. She swivelled to find him in the dark, her face weirdly lit from the barn below, wearing a look of fury.

He turned away, knowing why she'd come. There was a firing slit in each decaying wall, allowing the awesome machine-gun to be wheeled on an ancient tea-trolley to face the four winds. Dixie busied himself now, practising a manoeuvre from east to north.

'What was it supposed to achieve, the bomb in that car?'

'To keep the cop from pursuing us, and who the hell do you think you're talking to?'

'It stopped him all right, along with a young woman, about my age, who had fuck all to do with any of this. This is a day she won't easily forget, going round for the rest of her life with one arm, like a bloody war veteran. It'll do wonders for her love life!'

'Now you listen here,' Dixie erupted with a rage of his own, born of exhaustion and tension, 'I'm sick of you telling me what to do and feel. It was a bloody accident – '

'Bullshit! Bombs are always more or less indiscriminate!'

Dixie went to strike her, raised arm illuminated by the trapdoor. Annie thrust out her cheek to receive the blow. Dixie turned away.

'God give me patience.'

'God give you sense.'

Whirling round, 'I left a ragdoll swinging from his aerial. He'd have seen it and recognised it.'

'He'd have seen it and recognised it,' she echoed.

'Right!'

'And therefore not opened the door, not touched the car, not come after us.'

'You've got it!'

'Then why the bomb?'

'What?' It was a weak 'what?' Dixie appeared to shrink and turn in on himself, perhaps the realisation that the lost arm had been futile as well as tragic. He rallied hotly.

'How the hell was I to know she'd go to his car?'

'Exactly! That's why they're indiscriminate. You never know who'll pass at the wrong moment – '

'Jaysus, woman, we've been through this before! Non-combatants get caught in the crossfire, that's life! That's war! Mulraine was a prize target. Scores of our men are dead or behind bars because of him. I can't fight this war without explosives. Ragdolls don't scare unless they go bang!'

'Then maybe the war's better lost.'

Dixie drew himself up and stepped closer. 'Take care, Annie McBride' – A dark authority returned to his voice – 'or you'll pass the point where you're no use to me.'

She shivered, glimpsing for the first time behind the eyes and in the voice the man whose name had become synonymous with terror. She'd found the limit of her power over him. With one dangerous remark she'd strayed for a moment into that area where unspeakable acts were committed for the sake of the cause.

Turning to go, she paused at the top of the ladder.

'So what have you got in store for the prisoner?'

'You'll see.'

'Has consultation got caught in the crossfire as well?'

'Only with those I can no longer trust.'

She reeled inwardly. His words stung, quelling her offensive, slapping her back in her place. She felt young and foolish.

'You never did trust me, did you?'

'Get to bed. You're on at five.'

'And I'm not to be trusted to go near the prisoner, right?'

'You'll see him tomorrow, to do your part when I'm done with him.'

She climbed down through the warm animal smell of the barn and out into the sultry night. The fields around were pitch dark and very still. Not a breath of wind disturbed the trees on the skyline. For comfort she reached for the little Armalite around her neck, and remembered it was lost.

The night moved on. Marcus swayed between composure and panic, trying to shut Marcia and Jamie and his parents from his mind, their reactions when they heard the news of his disappearance. He prayed for sleep, but sleep, like everything else, seemed to have sided with his captors. Then he must have drifted, for they'd finally allowed a visit from Marcia – he was being escorted from his cell by four hulking military policemen, he could see Marcia through a glass door being politely frisked and her bag searched. She looked up, lighting up with joy and sorrow at the sight of him, her face saying, To hell with everything else, just get back to me!

He woke. It was intensely dark, the stars in the skylight covered by moon-grained cloud. Not a sound to be heard. He had no watch and was shivering under his coarse blanket. He may as well have been chained to a raft drifting on the sea. Feeling with his free hand for the crucifix round his neck, he filled his lungs and sang loudly. *Ambush in the night, they trying to conquer me . . . ambush in the night, all guns aiming at me . . . ambush in the night, they open fire on me . . .*

Michael woke to the sound of singing, and the prisoner rocking his bed and shaking the attic in time with the beat.

First light was filtering through the curtains. Dixie wanted him on watch at five, not crouching behind some bush or tree, but circulating on his tractor, keeping a look-out and making everything seem normal on the farm. And he was to set steel traps in the ground on likely approaches, not to catch hapless animals, but men.

At twenty to five he dressed in a rush, anxious to have a few moments alone with Molly, even if it was a pity to wake her. But when he gently knocked and looked in, she wasn't there. Her

206

bedclothes were thrown back, her nightie carelessly dropped on the floor. Fear gripped him. He scoured the room for signs that she had fled. She couldn't take it any more, her coat wasn't on the nail in the hall – she'd gone.

There was one place, he hoped desperately, as he ducked out of the house in his shirt sleeves, where she might just have . . .

He ran to the side of the house – Praise God! There she was, bending over in her vegetable patch, half lost in drizzling mist. As he approached he heard that she too was singing, very quietly, to herself. He hated her singing that song. Her own Dan, Michael's adopted father, was buried these five years and Molly was still amazed each morning when he wasn't there in the bed beside her.

'I remember a Friday in August, he'd been gone for a week and a day . . .'
She looked up, resenting the intrusion.

'You still have the sweet voice of a young girl, Mother.'

Normally glad to see him, she resumed her weeding, knees saturated, unkempt grey hair shot with drizzle.

'Oh his boat they never recovered, are you there, Dan, in Gweebarra Bay?'

'Are you OK, Mother?' He was afraid to approach her. He'd never seen her like this.

She dropped her trowel, wiped her muddy hands in drenched grass and came to him, standing beneath him, looking up, seizing him with bloodshot eyes.

'I had a wee word with your hero in the hayloft just now – '

'He's not my hero any more – '

'You're a bit late finding out. Look at you. Look at what you've got yourself sucked into. Bombings and killings outdoing each other for savagery. The IRA's not what it used to be. Dan remembered the time a British soldier went on the run and lost his mind and fell into the hands of the IRA. Didn't they take him to hospital and leave him at the back door! Not like this feller in the attic. I told your "friend" I'll have no torture nor bloodshed under my roof. I told him I want him and his gang out. O–U–T out!'

She was spitting anger. He wanted to touch her, comfort her, shut her up.

'Not so loud, Mother – '

'I'll be as loud as I like,' she shouted, 'on my own God-given farm!'

'OK, what did Dixie say?'

207

'Sure, he said, he didn't mind pulling out, but of course "your Michael would have to come with me!" '

'Bedamned, I said, my Michael's done enough for you and Ireland. I need him, the farm needs him, let him go! He laughed in my face. After the London bombings, which everybody saw on TV, new recruits would be hard to come by. You'd be needed a few more years. A few? Three or four, he said. Well, that's it! The more so after that wee girl losing her arm yesterday. I've made up my mind.'

She started towards the house.

'What d'you mean' – he stumbled after her – 'you've made up your mind?'

She kept going with a violent intent in her walk. He caught her by the shoulders – 'Mother!' he pleaded.

She saw him starting to shake and grew calm. Stretching to touch his face with trembling fingers, she said, 'Be prepared to dig two deep graves.'

He beheld her in horror. She saw what he was thinking.

'No, not you and me. You're going to cover those graves with your tractor, and you and me, Michael, are going to *live!*'

He was breathing heavily, excited, appalled.

'What about Annie?'

'She'll please herself.'

'Would you have her here, I mean . . . if she said yes to me.'

'She'd be welcome,' lied Molly, knowing intuitively that Annie was no use to him.

Michael swayed between hope and despair.

'Jaysus, Mother, the Provos would come asking questions – '

'They'd find nothing! We let the soldier go. You tell the Provos he escaped and you all went after him, only himself and herself never returned. I worked it all out in the cabbages.'

'You said no bloodshed, Mother.'

A faint smile crossed her lips.

'There won't be any.'

Watery sun was slanting through the skylight when Marcus heard the ladder creak. Angling back his head he saw upside-down a tray appear through the trapdoor, balancing buttered toast, soda bread and a steaming teapot.

It was followed by Doyle, dark glasses masking his unshaven

face, sub-machine-gun strapped to his back, a roll of newspapers falling out of his tweed jacket pocket and spilling over the floor.

'I trust you slept well sir,' said Dixie, drawing himself up like a porter delivering breakfast in a grand hotel. Producing a small key, he released the padlocks on the prisoner's chains. 'It's a grand morning, altogether. . .!' Stepping back and fanning out the newspapers with his toe: 'You've the pick of the papers, sir – yesterday's, I regret . . .'

Marcus began to sit up, warily. Dixie kicked an upturned crate against the wall and sat cradling the gun, his eyes raw and feverish in a strikingly gaunt and stubbled face.

'Eat. Walk. Keep to your side of the room,' he said. 'Make one false move and I'll take your head off.'

Pulling his blanket round his almost bare body, Marcus eased his feet onto the floor. Every glorious movement hurt, and he knew he'd do almost anything not to be chained again. Apart from water which a giant of a man had twice brought him, he'd taken nothing since sailing from Inishtrahull some thirty-six hours ago. He looked eagerly at the toast and bread, but when he came to lift a slice to his mouth, his appetite failed him, and he reached, hand trembling, for the teapot.

'They're searching for you, soldier. If they get too near, we'll have to shoot you.'

Marcus filled his mouth with tea, inhaled the vapour. The heat of the sun was on his back. It must have been noon.

'You're all the rage in London.'

Marcus's eyes strayed to the *Daily Mail* – IRA WINS RACE FOR RUNAWAY OFFICER. *The Sun* – IRA 'WE GOT MAD MARCUS!' *The Star* FINDERS KEEPERS! *The Guardian* – SECURITY FORCES DENY DUBLIN INCURSION CHARGES *Daily Express* EXCLUSIVE: 'TRAITOR KING JOINS IRA'

Dixie watched Marcus pause, teacup poised, over the *Express* story, citing unconfirmed reports that he had been identified in action as a member of Dixie Doyle's hell-raising Active Service Unit, and that the County Donegal car bomb was the second King had played a part in, the first occurring during the hospital breakout.

Marcus didn't dwell on this or any story. His situation was already incredible. The slaying of Bernie O'Rawe, his imprisonment and breakout, the convent, the ride north, Inishtrahull, his escape disguised as a monk, his capture by Doyle of all people, chained like a wild animal, and now his name in faraway headlines. He could only shake his head and laugh.

The reaction didn't appear to please Dixie.

'You want my autograph?' said Marcus.

Dixie watched his man closely, and something about the black Brit bothered him. Sitting there on the floor in his blanket he reminded Dixie of the IRA blanket men who'd slowly starved to death in the H-Blocks, wrapped in filthy blankets in cells smeared with their own excrement, waiting for the British Government to grant them prisoner of war status, waiting to die. In this case, reflected Dixie, the Brit was the blanket man, and the IRA man the jailor. The shaved skull, Dixie noted, contrasted strikingly with the flowing locks and beards of the hunger strikers.

'Why the skinhead, soldier?'

'Less wind resistance.'

They sat looking at each other, Marcus trying to penetrate the Provo's dark glasses. This was the man who'd slaughtered Charlie Winters and the Fox's crew. Thorn Hill returned to him as though it had happened yesterday.

'You're deep in shit, soldier, you know that? They think you were involved in the bomb that killed the guard at the hospital, they think you've got it in for the Army, they think you were involved in yesterday's bomb, they think you've joined me – so you may as well . . .'

'May as well what?'

'Join me.'

'What! You're looking at the man whose comrades you annihilated on Thorn Hill.'

'I'm looking at the man who wiped out Bernie O'Rawe.'

Flaring up, 'That was an accident!'

'Accident?' Getting to his feet. 'You bastards invaded the Bogside with guns and armoured cars and you call it an accident!'

'More of an accident than the girl you blew to bits yesterday.'

'She didn't get blown to bits and that was an accident and we said we were sorry.'

'Sorry!'

'People get hurt in war. You ought to know that, soldier.'

'But you people endanger life like it's cheap, like it was yours to give and take.'

'Don't fucking lecture me, soldier. My child is crippled because you bastards beat up my pregnant wife! I'm sick of your double standards. When one of ours is killed it's "Terrorist shot dead!" When one of yours is killed it's "Soldier murdered!" When an IRA bomb goes off prematurely killing British civilians, it's a callous bloody massacre by evil butchers. But when your boys shoot dead thirteen citizens of Derry, mostly in the back, on Bloody Sunday, they're publicly exonerated and their commanding officer gets a nice wee Order of the British fucking Empire in gratitude!'

He was standing over Marcus, gun pointed at his shaved skull.

'It's all square, soldier. You kill us, we kill you. Only difference is you're in my country, you're the aggressors, we've a right, a duty to fight back.'

'With bombs that blow the legs off bandsmen and passers-by in Regent's Park!' Getting to his feet he waved a tabloid newspaper at Dixie, jabbing a finger at a photograph of carnage and the headline, IRA DEATH TOLL RISES TO NINE; FIFTY INJURED.

'Is that the way you're going to unite Ireland?'

Dixie seized the paper from Marcus and brandished the Schmeisser in his face.

'I confess, Lieutenant,' he said with exaggerated patience, 'logic was never my best point, but tell me . . . how is it you fellers are heroes for butchering thousands of Argies over a poxy heap of islands on the other side of the world, but us, we're gutter-thugs for fighting for the right to live in our own country? You fellers got World War Two medals for bombing men, women and children to hell in Germany, but you cry bloody murder when you get a wee taste of it yourselves. And didn't the Brits applaud that wee bomb the Yanks dropped on Hiroshima, giving terrorism a whole new meaning? And didn't the Brits give the Yanks a standing ovation for nearly blasting and burning the population of Vietnam back to the Stone Age? If there's one thing you Brits have perfected it's hypocrisy!'

So saying, he screwed up the tabloid one-handed and flung it at Marcus's chest. Then taking a few steps back, he subsided, lungs rasping, onto the upturned crate, and leaned back against the wall.

'What in hell's name is the point of deserting the British Army if you're not going to join us?'

'Swap one bunch of thugs for another? You're talking to the wrong man, Doyle. I'm dead against everybody's brutality – my

211

army, your army, the Loyalists, the RUC. I don't want any of it.'

'Then you're a fucking idiot. Bloodshed,' Dixie quoted, 'is a cleansing and sanctifying thing, and the nation which regards it as the final horror has lost its manhood. There are a whole lot of things worse than bloodshed, like slavery for instance – Padraig Pearse, Irish revolutionary leader, 1913!'

'You can quote your dead heroes till you're blue in the face,' said Marcus 'You justify your atrocities by pointing the finger at ours.' Shaking his head and coldly smiling, 'British bombs are evil, Irish bombs are OK!'

'No, soldier. I never said Brit bombs were evil. I said we're not going to be lectured to on violence by a nation that specialises in violence. When your gallant Navy boys blew the *Belgrano* out of the water the other day, they sent more men to the bottom of the sea than we got in the whole of the IRA! The ship was sailing the other way. It was like shooting three hundred men in the back! And how many of the survivors went home to their wives and mothers without arms and legs. Bejaysus!' – he let out a roar of laughter – 'Is there anything stinks half as much as British righteousness!'

Dixie was enjoying himself, stretching out and crossing his legs.

'You Brits are a hoot! You wag your finger at apartheid in South Africa, but foster it in Ulster – communities divided, one encouraged to lord it over the other. In West Belfast where some of my less desirable comrades spring from, there's 80 per cent unemployment, some of the worst housing in Europe and squads of gun-toting British soldiers to make sure it stays that way! You comedians get froth in the mouth over abuse of human rights in the USSR, but it's OK in your back yard! Honest to God!'

When he'd stopped laughing, he removed his dark glasses and gazed expectantly at Marcus.

'Well, soldier, why not join us and get your own back?'

Marcus stretched his broad shoulders and long arms, and paced back and forth across the narrow confines of the attic, curiously unperturbed. The relief of this freedom, however brief, was to be relished. Also the argument had loosened him. There wasn't the same degree of hatred coming from Doyle. In arguing they were communicating. Doyle was no longer a faceless killer, just a killer.

'You want me to throw in my lot with you?' Marcus's turn to laugh. 'I didn't take on the boot-boys of the British Army so I could run away and join your bomb-happy brigade. Killing may sometimes be inevitable, but you people . . . OK, you've been provoked, but your ways of killing . . .' groping for the right words.

'God help the people of Ireland if ever you get your dream of unity. Killing becomes a habit. You won't be able to stop. Anyone who gets in your way . . .' Marcus slammed a fist into his palm to illustrate the fate of counter-revolutionaries. 'Your cause may be just in some ways – '

'In *some* ways?' scoffed Dixie.

Marcus shakily poured another cup of tea. 'My people in Britain are second-class citizens in our own country too. But I don't want to see black people in Britain taking to bombs. Once you start down that road there's no end but madness. That's what's happened to you people. You've gone mad.'

Dixie was on his feet again. 'There you go again with your bloody righteousness! We tried every other way. We marched in our thousands for civil rights, and you shot us! We went on hunger strikes and dirty protests and you let us die and rot! We elected Republicans to the British Parliament, but you wouldn't permit your hallowed benches to be contaminated by the arses of men of violence! We tried talking to you, offered time and again to negotiate, but by Heaven, no! We don't talk to terrorists!'

He came at Marcus again, Schmeisser ominously raised, driving him back against the wall.

'Don't you fucking see it doesn't matter what we do, bomb or ballot-box we're damned! The British are so fucking thick that the only way to make them listen to reason is by hitting them between the eyes, by outdoing them in brutality!'

'Well it hasn't worked, has it?' said Marcus, backed against the wall. 'Your one Ireland's no nearer now than it was when you started. Your bombs may have blown away limbs but they've hardened everybody's resistance' – Marcus's turn to point the finger and move off the wall. 'So British violence doesn't work, and yours doesn't work, but mine?' – towering over the IRA man – 'my way works!'

Dixie stopped him with the mouth of the gun.

'What the fuck are you talking about! You're on the run, you're my prisoner, you're nothing, I could snuff you out right now!'

'No, Mr-fucking-IRA-hero, you couldn't do that, because I'm worth too much to you alive! And why? Because my way works!

213

Look!' He brushed past Dixie and kicked up a storm of newspaper. 'All this shit in the papers! I'm front page news!'

They rounded on each other.

'Shoot me!' grinned Marcus, flinging wide his arms. 'Or better still put a bomb under me, another human sacrifice for Ireland!'

'Don't tempt me. After your tomfoolery in Derry, it'd be a pleasure!'

'There you go again. Killing for pleasure. You're off the wall, man!'

'Get back on that bed! Move!'

Dixie motioned Marcus with the barrel of the gun. Marcus shook his head and smiled again.

'I said get down, now!'

'Or what? You won't shoot me. You need me.'

'I don't need your knees, soldier!'

He aimed for Marcus's left knee. Marcus screwed up his face and braced himself. A brief burst of gunfire shattered the peace of the farm.

The others came running, crowding into the narrow hallway at the foot of the ladder.

'Get back to your posts!' ordered Dixie. 'Just Michael up here, nobody else.'

Black Rose objected.

'Michael!' repeated Dixie.

Michael climbed warily, wondering what grizzly task awaited him. When he surfaced in the attic, he saw the near-naked black soldier shaking where he stood, cordite drifting in falling sunlight, a rash of bullet holes in the wall where Dixie had fired to one side of the prisoner.

Dixie pointed to the chains and padlocks.

'Just chain his hands behind his back.'

Michael complied, making a show of treating the Brit roughly. As his hands were manacled behind him, Marcus experienced a surge of relief. Dixie read the look.

'My mistake. I should have granted you prisoner of war status from the outset. I'll see to it you're properly fed and watered, and you'll get your exercise after dark. Any questions?'

'Yeah. You're having me on, right?'

'About joining? I want you with us. Imagine it! British officer so disgusted with the Army, so abused, so blackened – '

'Blackened?' Marcus cocked a disapproving eyebrow.

'So smeared, he breaks out and joins the IRA! A black British officer in the IRA!'

'You haven't been listening to me. How could I join an army that singles out a Protestant for assassination, goes round to his home, smashes his way in and guns the man down in front of his wife and kids? No cause in this or any other world can make that OK.'

'A lot of those Loyalists are sectarian murderers!'

'So? You don't shoot them in front of their families, you don't shoot Adolf Hitler in front of his family. I wouldn't shoot you in front of your wife and kid. Would you shoot me in front of mine?'

Dixie weathered the storm, resenting the thought that his prisoner might have a wife and child as he did. Motioning Michael to leave, he faced Marcus once more. 'Just don't forget who first schooled us in terror. The British are charmingly civilised masters long as you're docile, but you soon learn the meaning of terror when you want your rights back.

'We've graduated, soldier, Doctors of Terror. You West Indians have learned to beat the masters at their own game of cricket, we've learned to match them at the other game they're so good at. Only you want us to play Queensberry Rules. Fuck that! There's a handful of us against the most sophisticated security forces in the world, plus loaded judges and a bent press. We make no apologies.'

Marcus was shaking his head. 'Down that road you end up excusing anything for the sake of the cause.'

'Down your road, soldier, you end up slaves.'

Dixie turned impatiently at the top of the ladder. 'Join us, King, for fuck sake. My commanders are waiting. You've twenty-four hours to make up your mind.'

'If I say no, have you got a ragdoll waiting for me?'

In the late afternoon, the fourth member of the gang visited the prisoner.

Marcus had passed the afternoon exercising as best he could while trying to think of a way out of his chains. The attic was hot under the July sun and his head pulsated with tension. Was Doyle really trying to persuade him to join, or was it a ploy? He no more trusted his current volatile IRA gaoler than the scheming C.O. who'd tried to buy him off in Army custody. He was convinced

Doyle would never allow him to go free. He'd seen too much, particularly the big man they called Michael. Doyle's cell was known to include a colossal masked man known as Doyle's Hulk, but no one had ever seen his face or knew his name . . . until now. The choice was stark – join the Provisional IRA, or die.

Or escape.

But how to rid himself of the chains that bit into his wrists? How to climb through that skylight without arms? How to fight his way out with hands behind his back?

He was pacing tirelessly when someone started up the ladder. First came a pair of long fine hands lifting a six-pack of Guinness, then a bundle of black clothes followed by a mass of red hair.

Marcus retreated, squatting down on his heels against a wall. Being down on her level, he met the young woman's nonchalant gaze as soon as her head surfaced through the trapdoor. No mask, no attempt at disguise. When she stood up she was tall and slender, and he knew her – the one who had tried to shoot him on Thorn Hill. She wore ankle books, black jeans, black T-shirt and short black leather jacket. Her face was long, pale and freckled, coloured above the cheeks and across the nose by sun and wind. Dense red curls burst around her head and over her shoulders. She wore a pistol thrust in her belt.

Breaking open two cans of beer, she set one down carefully on the floor as though approaching to feed an unpredictable animal, and inserted a long white straw. She carried the other can to the upturned crate and sat with her back to the wall. Raising her can she nodded a greeting and drank.

Light rain tapped on the skylight. He looked up.

'What time is it?'

'Six.'

'Where am I?'

'Somewhere in Ireland.'

'Which side of the border?'

'Border? The border's an illusion.'

She was deadpan and unblinking, relaxed as though she drank Guinness with a fresh captive every day. She was cool and distant, without Black Rose's seething hatred. Her accent was softer, she was younger, taller, thinner and calmer.

She drank and observed him, the man she had tried three times to kill. He was frightened, she could see that, but she wasn't disappointed. His eyes were steady, sensitive and angry, his full sensuous mouth hard-set and defiant. He was plainly uneasy sitting there in his underpants. As she persisted coolly looking at him, he tried not to show his discomfort. He had broad shoulders and fine strong hands. His powerful chest was smoothly carved and glistening with sweat. From where she sat, her nostrils picked up a strong animal odour coming from him. His magnificent skin reminded her of the rich dark surface of horse-chestnuts. His head was growing an even black stubble.

But the crucifix round his neck reminded her that she'd lost her own talisman, probably in the hotel, along with the biography of Countess Markievicz. Her hand went to her naked throat and she felt the loss keenly.

Marcus hesitated over the Guinness waiting on the dusty floor at his feet. To kneel and suck while she watched would be humiliating. Not to would look like a childish token of resistance. She sensed his dilemma.

'I'd undo you, soldier, but you've a terrible reputation.' Raising his head, he caught her mischievous look and looked away. Not wishing to appear to want to please her, he ignored the Guinness and began leafing through a newspaper, turning the pages with his feet.

'Would you have stayed on the island?'

The change of voice surprised him, like a genuinely interested question.

'Did you think you could remain free? And then what? Where were you running to?'

He lifted his eyes to hers and they vied silently with each other. Shaking her head gently she offered a smile of incomprehension.

'What were you going to do?'

He shrugged. 'Make peace with myself, get plastic bullets banned and have the British Army replaced by a neutral force.'

She frowned. Was he nuts or joking?

'All by yourself!'

'Why not?' Deadpan. 'Kidnap the Prime Minister, put a baton gun to her head and demand a review of the use of plastic bullets. Then invite the world to send its troops. Mozambique militia on the Springfield Road, Swiss Guards in the Bogside, Soviet commandos in Crossmaglen. Then I was going to go home and have a long bath.'

217

She laughed. He knelt forward and sucked hard and long on the straw. Breaking open another can, she set it before him. She lingered there, on her heels, looking at him.

'What were you really up to?'

'What's it to you? You're going to shoot me anyway.'

'Not if you join us.'

'I told Doyle, I didn't break from one bunch of thugs to join another.'

Clucking her tongue disapprovingly she stood.

'What kind of complacent crap is that! You're either with the oppressors or against them.'

He said nothing.

Someone on the ladder. Dixie surfaced with a sledgehammer. Annie stepped back.

'Is he with us or the Brits?' said Dixie, moving towards Marcus with the long heavy sledgehammer.

Marcus tensed, pressing back against the wall, turning his head away. Now they were really going to start. She'd just softened him up.

Dixie tossed Annie a small key.

'Get up!' said Annie.

He obeyed. She stood behind him freeing his chains, drawn and repelled by his male odour.

Freed, he faced away, rubbing his wrists, trying to decide whether or not to seize this desperate opportunity to try and escape.

'Turn around, soldier,' said Dixie, 'we've work to do.'

Marcus turned slowly. They had a sub-machine-gun and pistol trained on him. Dixie tapped the low north-facing wall with the sledgehammer.

'I want a hole beaten out big enough for a man to get through.' He heaved the sledgehammer across the attic. Marcus caught it, reflected a moment, considered the possibility that they were about to shoot him in the back and, taking a deep breath, swung the heavy tool. Recalling that the last time he had wielded a sledgehammer was to smash down Bernie O'Rawe's front door, he released the same vengeful energy now he'd applied then, assaulting the wall with a surge of pent-up violence, wondering what the hole might be for, enjoying a fantasy that he was pulverising his way to freedom.

Leaning out of the jagged hole, he caught the rain on his head and saw directly below him the sloping corrugated roof of a shed.

'Get back in,' growled Dixie.

Annie was untying a parcel of clothing – jeans, sweatshirt, combat jacket, beret and trainers, all in black and large fitting, and offset by two pairs of white underpants. Marcus regarded his latest uniform doubtfully.

'Black for night exercise,' explained Dixie, 'we don't want you seen.'

Annie fetched a basin of warm water, soap and towel. They stood around in silence while he washed. He washed with care, as though putting a high price on a body they were threatening to destroy. When it came to removing his underpants, he hesitated. Summoning his pride, he drew them down around his ankles and squatted over the steam, splashing himself, tenderly soaping his parts, remembering making love with Marcia in the kitchen, lifting her by the buttocks, lowering her onto him, fucking with no cap in, going for a baby.

Dixie sat on a crate, cradling the sub-machine-gun, averting his gaze, but watching his prisoner in the corner of his eye. Annie unashamedly watched, with a woman's eye and the curiosity of a child, neither repelled nor fascinated. When he had dried himself and finished dressing, they made him get on the bed and chained his ankle to the frame – which allowed him to sit up and read the papers, promising him a spell of night exercise later. Then they left him.

'What's the hole for?' he called after them.

No reply.

As dusk began to fall, Molly O'Cinneíde steeled herself for murder. She was in the kitchen preparing the evening meal. Dixie was there, marking details on a sketch map of the farm – approaches, man-traps, escape routes, Michael was on duty in the hayloft, and Annie had just relieved Feeley in the copse out back. Despite open windows, cooking smells filled the house.

Feeley marched in, hungry as ever, laying her rifle on the table. Molly was singing as she stirred a great pot of stew. '*I was left with your picture . . . A wain barely born . . . . Another wee one on the way . . .*'

'Well is it ready, or what?' demanded Feeley.

'Just coming!' chimed Molly.

Feeley was expecting a sharp retort, but Molly was singing again. *'I remember a Friday in August, Are you there Dan in Gweebarra Bay?'*

Feeley looked at Dixie. 'What's she so bloody cheerful about?'

Dixie wasn't listening. He'd spoken to Number One on the telephone. All they wanted was a snapshot of Marcus King in full IRA garb. Later, they'd offer the British Government an exchange – King for a selection of IRA prisoners of war, in a blaze of world publicity. Dixie would then be allowed an extended period of compassionate leave. His leave was going to stretch further than they imagined, reflected Dixie.

While a desperate act was about to be committed on the farm, in the wooded hills half a mile away a small band of men was materialising from the rain-soaked undergrowth, moving slowly forward without shape or sound.

Guided by the lighted windows of the farm, they crept through the trees and finally settled in hawthorn and bracken to watch through night-penetrating lenses. There was no certainty that the IRA gang and captured deserter were down there, but Father D'Arcy's testimony was given added weight by the physical description of the penitent.

Frank Mulraine's pack of detectives had made enquiries into Michael O'Cinneíde. At first sight he seemed a complete innocent, no known paramilitary connections, no Republican affiliations, no politics at all. But his late adopted father, Dan O'Cinneíde, had been a Sinn Fein man, and Michael had been involved in an incident with the Army in 1979, when a patrol had badly beaten him, smashed his van and killed his dog, apparently in retribution for the assassination of Lord Mountbatten and the slaughter of eighteen paratroopers at Warrenpoint. He was known to have been upset by the attitude of the RUC and was still, three years later, campaigning for compensation. Most telling of all was that that popular local character Michael O'Cinneíde just happened to match the proportions of Doyle's Hulk.

Michael O'Cinneíde prowled the hayloft, shifting the trolley-mounted machine-gun from one firing point to the next. He was more afraid tonight than ever in his life. He'd tried dissuading Molly from what she was about to do in the main house, but she was set on it.

He wanted what she wanted, a resumption of their hard and happy life on the farm. Why not call the confidential RUC number and grass on Dixie and Feeley? he'd argued. But he knew it was a doomed suggestion. If the RUC agreed to immunity from prosecution, it would mean Molly and Michael being smuggled into hiding, fresh identities, permanent exile, renunciation of home, roots, everything, and no guarantee that the long vengeful arm of the IRA wouldn't one day find them and bury them.

This was the only way, she said. Two evil ones buried that two blessed ones might live. If God had a heart he'd understand. There was a madness in her and Michael couldn't resist it.

Then at least let me help! he'd said unwillingly.

No, Michael, you haven't the stuff to live with it.

And you?

I have to, I'm a mother.

'Will you quit singing and serve up, woman!' said Feeley, cleaning her rifle on the table.

'Grub's up!' cried Molly, starting to ladle.

Feeley grimaced. The old woman's jauntiness was getting on her nerves. She preferred Molly's caustic tongue.

'Get some food over to Michael,' Dixie told Feeley.

'Why can't he wait till the Countess has hers?'

'He's been on guard several hours. Tell him to keep his concentration till I get over.'

Everyone was on edge. Their secluded situation seemed safe, but the enemy could be out there and you'd never know it.

Molly filled a deep dish. Adding an extra dollop she handed it over to Feeley. 'For Michael,' she said slyly.

'That's it, look after wee Michael!'

Feeley carried the steaming dish and a hunk of bread across the yard to the barn and up to Michael in the hayloft. Molly had warned him not to touch any of it.

When Feeley returned there was a bowl of stew by Dixie's arm, so far untouched while he studied his map.

'*I remember a Sat'day in summer, How the bells rang and uillean-pipes played . . .*' Molly glanced round when Feeley closed the door, and began ladling another dish of stew. '*How the whole world drank to our future . . .*' She handed Feeley the steaming dish with lowered eyes and, turning her back, picked up a broom and began sweeping the spotless floor. *'Are you there Dan in Gweebarra Bay?'*

'Will you shift yourself, Pip!' she said to Michael's dog, lying across the swept hearth, chin on paws, uneasily surveying the strangers.

'Aren't you eating?' said Feeley.

Molly made an impetuous but artless murderer. Where something quick and furtive was needed, she was unnatural and clumsy. Determination she had in abundance, but for sleight of execution she substituted faith. With God's blessing nothing could go wrong. Visible mistakes would pass undetected. But Feeley was twitching with suspicion.

'I said are you not eating?'

'Thanks, but I'll have mine later.'

'Later? It's eleven o'clock, for Christ's sake. Come and eat with us, there's plenty of room.'

'No, I'm grand, thanks – '

'Fill a bowl and get over here!'

The dog whimpered. Molly smiled gamely and returned to the stove. Dixie, still absorbed in his map, reached for his dish and spoon. Drained of all colour, Molly began hypnotically stirring the stew under Feeley's watchful gaze. Breaking off a hunk of bread, Dixie sank his spoon into the thick steaming stew and was lifting it to his mouth when Feeley clapped a hand on his wrist, upsetting the spoon, spilling stew down Dixie's front. 'What the – '

'I wouldn't, Dixie, if I was you.'

He saw the way Molly wavered under Feeley's gaze.

'Something the matter, young lady?' said Molly.

'We wouldn't like to start without you.'

'I've already eaten, thanks.'

'Don't touch yours,' Feeley ordered Dixie, picking up her own dish and starting across the room towards the dog.

'Why the hell not?'

'We haven't said grace.'

Molly went ashen.

'Here, Pip . . .' Feeley crouched, tempting the dog, sliding the dish towards it.

The dog alternately sniffed and growled.

'She's eaten,' said Molly.

'It needs to cool down. Meanwhile' – Feeley returned to the stove and ladled yet another serving – 'This one, old woman, is for you.'

Molly was on her feet, quivering.

Replacing the dish, Feeley came slowly, remorselessly towards her, suddenly seizing her by the back of the neck. 'You bloody old cow, what have you put in it?'

Thrusting Molly's head down to the table, Feeley scooped a spoonful of Dixie's stew and tried to force it into the woman's mouth.

A footfall on the far side of the door. Dixie reached for the sub-machine-gun, the door flew open, Michael stumbled in, pistol drawn. But for the dog's plaintive yelping, everything fell still.

'Drop it,' said Dixie quietly.

Michael took in the awful scene.

The back door opened, Annie stepped in from the rain. 'You lot can be heard in Timbuktu!'

'Tell us, Michael!' said Feeley, tightening her grip on Molly, 'what's this filthy old hag done to the stew?'

'Drop it,' repeated Dixie.

'Tell her to let go of my mother.'

'Do it,' said Dixie. Feeley started to object. 'Do it!'

Feeley thrust Molly violently away. Michael let fall his pistol and went and took Molly into his arms. For once they exchanged roles, Molly burying her face in Michael's body.

'Take the dish away from Pip,' she murmured.

'What the hell's going on?' Annie wanted to know.

'Shut it!' Feeley replied.

'Get back to your post,' said Dixie.

Annie drew herself up, Armalite across her breast. 'Am I part of this unit or what?'

'This bloody old witch tried to poison us!' said Feeley.

'Get out!' ordered Dixie. 'The hills could be crawling with Brits.'

Annie slowly backed out. Michael gently released Molly and removed the dish meant for Pip from the floor. Feeley kicked over the bin and rummaged until she found it. She held it up – a large screw-top jar, marked with a skull-and-crossbones and a crudely painted rodent.

'Rat poison!' A triumphant smile spread across her face.

The night crept on, an unmarked car turned off a dark road into an even darker lane, Frank Mulraine behind the unfamiliar wheel.

The car was likely to be his home for a time, so there were

blankets and basic food supplies in the back. On the edge of the woods he pulled over and doused his lights. Pouring himself a coffee from a flask, he rolled down the window and waited. Rain pattered on the leaves.

His head throbbed, he'd drunk too much at lunchtime after visiting the hospital again in the morning, where he was surprised to find Brother Dominic, still in fisherman's clothes, sitting holding Brigid's hand. A pretty picture, Brigid drugged and drifting, Dominic holding her hand, occasionally whispering. Mulraine would have liked to sit holding Brigid's other hand, only she didn't have another hand.

Adding a shot of brandy to his coffee he cursed himself for sending the girl out to his car. Looking out at the quiet woods and the dim outlines of hills, he wondered how it could be that this land was so beautiful, and so singled out for suffering.

A knock on the passenger door and Mulraine nearly jumped out of his skin. A blackened face with a sardonic grin pressed its nose to the window – Hurst, Captain Lee's man, a nasty piece of work who succeeded in making Lee seem almost pleasant. Mulraine put on a long mackintosh over his suit, hoisted an umbrella and followed Hurst into the wood. The wood was deep and still, but for the soft percussion of the rain.

Hurst stopped short at the sight of the elegant detective and his huge umbrella.

'Oi! This is a covert operation,' smiling patronisingly, 'we're not actually meant to be seen!'

'Heavens!' Mulraine pulled up. 'I had no idea.'

'You trying to be funny?'

'I'm reminding you that I was a case-hardened cop when you were a nappy-bound brat.'

'Then why not bleeding act like one?' He spat into a ditch and pressed on, Mulraine on his heels.

'What would strike you as more suspicious, Corporal, a copy-book sleuth stalking through the wood, or a tailored gentleman bowling along beneath an umbrella?'

Captain Douglas Lee lay on the edge of a wood surveying the farm through night-stripping sights, face cut from the previous day's car accident, back of his head throbbing where Hurst had struck him with the rock.

But his pride hurt most, a botched mission.

If sex was one of life's few authentic rewards, war was its great consolation. For a man with a blighted childhood, long alienated from his parents, divorced by his wife, robbed of his children and outcast for his sexuality, his life had been an assault course of rejections and humiliations. Only his sexual exploits and military prowess kept desperation from the door. His sexual exploits were his secret, but in war he was the celebrated Ironside, a legend within the narrow brotherhood of the SAS, a reputation he clung to.

The Boss had gone barmy, burning the phone lines with seething blasphemies, returned in equal measure by Lee, but wasted because he didn't need anyone telling him what he knew, rubbing salt into his wounds. He'd fucked it up, allowed Ragdoll Doyle to lift the prize, exposing the SAS on foreign soil. To make up for it, said the Boss, Lee was to get them both – Doyle as dead as he liked, Marcus King alive.

Lee didn't bother to look round when Mulraine arrived, folding his umbrella and spreading a plastic sheet under a bush.

'What time do you call this?' Lee whispered hoarsely.

It was late, Mulraine was tired, he longed to be at home with a good book and Barbara's buttocks snug against his. He longed for a cigarette. The last thing he wanted was this insufferable Englishman.

'You're twenty-four hours late!'

'I had to see a man about a helicopter.'

Lee lowered his binoculars and looked sideways at the detective.

'A man none too pleased about the assault on his monastery – '

'A man who pulled a cheap trick on us and harboured a fugitive.'

'In the best Irish tradition.'

'Bandits!'

'Don't be so sure, Captain. Have you not noticed there's been no mention of Inishtrahull in the news?'

Lee considered. Mulraine was right. The Boss hadn't mentioned the bungled assault. Now he knew why.

'You mean the monks said nothing?'

'Correct.'

'Why?'

'I made a bargain with the good man. No assault on the island took place . . . provided no harm comes to Marcus King.'

225

While Lee reflected, Mulraine recalled how at the hospital that morning Brother Dominic had scarcely acknowledged him until Mulraine rose to leave. 'Remember, Inspector, we're expecting great things from you.' It was an echo of the monk's last words in the hotel the night before, only 'we're' instead of 'I'm', as though speaking for the Almighty.

'I've orders to get the son-of-a-bitch out alive,' volunteered Lee.

'Glad to hear it. But are your men capable of that kind of subtlety?'

Their eyes met in the dark, Lee's dull with menace, Mulraine defiant. Lee gave a short laugh and returned to his binoculars. 'We're not even sure he's in there.'

'I'll have the equipment tomorrow.'

'Equipment?'

'I told you, the listening devices and pinhead cameras. Your men attach them to windows during the night, and we'll soon see – '

'Forget it. I want Mr King in the bag by then.'

The night wore on, Marcus waited for his promised exercise, a chance to breathe, maybe to escape. Instead there was a row downstairs, and the big man they called Michael was escorted to the attic and chained to the bedframe, head-to-toe beside Marcus. They chained both men by their ankles and one wrist, and went away leaving them in the dark.

Marcus questioned his unlikely bedfellow, but Michael lay back, staring blankly, unspeaking. Never said a word all night. They listened to the rain until it petered out. Time and again Marcus explored ways with his free hand of defeating the chains, but they were iron ship's chains with heavy duty padlocks.

He wandered from sleep to waking panic. In moments he was calm, watching the moon break free in the skylight, confident that somehow he would be back with Marcia and Jamie before long. Then, just as he thought he was over the worst, the terror would rise again. What had he escaped for from Army custody, from the convent, from the island – only to spend his last hours in a stifling attic before being shot? The panic came in waves, breaking over him, cutting his breathing, making him strain against the chains.

'Listen, man, between us we can get these things off!'

Nothing from Michael.

Marcus lay back. He recalled the last moments on Inishtrahull,

Dominic waving and calling from the windswept jetty, Bless you, may God be with you . . .

God!

Marcus tore the crucifix from his neck and hurled it across the room.

Morning came, bright and blustery. Marcus and Michael slept fitfully in the attic. Down in Michael's bedroom Annie slept fully dressed under a quilt, Armalite propped against the bedside table.

Dixie walked in without warning, jaded after a night on watch. He meant to wake Annie brusquely, asserting his position, but he stopped short of the bed and looked down at his curious comrade. Even in repose she wore a look of unpredictability, hair loosely restrained by a leather thong, lips closed and dry, eyelids still, conscience untroubled. As he exploited her unconscious state it occurred to him that it was more than anything her free spirit which attracted him, and needled him. She breathed freedom, or the pursuit of it, from every pore. A passionate individualist, she had no place in any army.

Her eyes were wide. 'Never seen a sleeping woman before?'

'You're late, it's after five, get some breakfast, I'll hang on in the loft.'

Instantly awake, she stood up in her boots. 'What dark fantasies were stirring in that chaste Republican mind of yours?'

Ducking the question, he moved to the window and parted the curtains, troubled by the quiet morning, the secretive surroundings, undulating fields and fathomless woods.

'You've picked a great time to chain Michael up,' said Annie, turning at the door, 'only three of us left to guard the place.'

A withering glance. 'He betrayed me.'

She switched tack. 'He could be out there with Pip playing the farmer and seeing if he can see anything.'

'Such as?'

'Signs of SAS.'

'If they're out there, you think they'll let us know? Didn't they teach you anything? They leave no signs, they even shit in plastic bags and carry it with them.' He looked out once more at the hooded hills.

'We pull out tonight.'

In the low-beamed passage Annie stepped over Michael's dog. Pip had ceased whining for her master, but maintained her vigil flat out at the foot of the attic ladder, chin propped on paws. Recalling her own adored dog, whom she hadn't seen in three years, she stopped to caress the animal, to comfort it and herself with soothing words. It remained inconsolable, eyes pools of misery, and she left it to its stubborn love, its fatal sense of belonging.

At the kitchen door she caught no sound or smell of breakfast cooking. Ducking beneath the lintel she found Molly at the table bent forward, eyes vacant, hands clasped around a glass of illicit poteen. The table was cluttered with unwashed crockery, all around were signs of a normally irreproachable kitchen falling into disarray. Her grey hair, usually gathered in a bun, fell loose and dishevelled, her bloodshot eyes sagged. She had become an old woman overnight.

Annie lay her rifle, wrapped in a coat, on the table.

'Shall I make it myself?' she said, harder than she meant.

Molly remained immobile for a moment more. Then she got up and moved, not towards the cooker but the door. Annie followed her into the yard. Hens clustered round Molly's scuffed shoes but she had nothing for them. The donkey and the cow came to meet her at the fence but she scarcely saw them, only turned this way and that, listening for a clue, like an ageing actress who's lost her wits, thought Annie, adrift on a once familiar stage. Molly reached up with her eyes; rays of diffused sunlight were probing the wooded hills, fields awash with summer flowers sparkled. She took in all her world in a slow panoramic gaze. Grass swayed, broken paths and fences spoke of relaxed neglect.

Annie stroked the donkey's smooth hard face.

'What's his name?'

She had to repeat the question before Molly would answer. 'De Valera.' She wouldn't look at Annie and spoke in a bitter monotone.

'Molly . . .'

'Don't speak to me,' Molly rounded on her.

'I'm really sorry – '

'You! You toyed with him, you led him on . . .' Annie shook her head. 'God love him, why did he have to fall into the hands of you and Doyle?'

'I'll do what I can for him – '

228

'I know your type.'

'I promise.'

The old woman, mouth open, was gazing at the ground. She'd forgotten Annie was there.

A shadow broke the line of the barn. Dixie whistled sharply, summoning Annie to her post.

The afternoon was fine, Molly was ordered to work outside to maintain an outward semblance of normality. Feeley covered the rear of the farm, Dixie and Annie manned the hayloft, Annie on the US Army surplus machine-gun, Dixie on the prowl.

'It serves no purpose.' She broke another silence.

'Don't start.'

'The Brits would probably get them anyway.'

'I said – '

'And you've no proof against Michael.'

'He confessed.'

'You beat him.'

'I didn't need to.'

'She was the one behind it, Michael could never organise a thing like that.'

Dixie spun round and aimed a rigid finger. 'I'm sick of you interfering, woman! You're a raw volunteer, stick to your job and hold your tongue!'

Annie flared. 'Never! As long as there's breath in me I'll speak out against oppression from whatever quarter!'

He was seething as he came towards her. 'Who the hell do you think you are, young lady!' He seized hold of her by the lapels of her leather jacket and pitched her in one violent movement into a heap of broken bales. 'You think you can stroll in and change decades of procedures born of war and privation . . .'

He took hold of her, shaking her, spitting and breathing into her face. 'She tried to murder us, for God's sake, and he was party to it, and they could both identify you, you fucking eejit! I'm fighting a war and we've traitors in our midst. I have to draw the line somewhere. Watch I don't draw the line around you as well!'

As he released her with a final violent thrust, she seized him by the neck, and pulling him back, assaulted his mouth with hers. His eyes bulged, he tried to wrench himself free, but she clung harder round his neck and by his hair. *'Get off!'* he managed to blurt as he freed his mouth, but she covered it again, kissing him with a violence and heat beyond his wildest fantasies of her. He tried to rise, but she tangled her impossibly long legs through his and thrust a hand between his buttocks. He freed his head and started to hit her in the face. As the blood burst from her lip and he began to escape, she lunged once more, sinking her teeth into the sinews of his neck and closing her jaws until he opened his mouth in pain. Then she closed his mouth once more with hers, sucking and kissing with remorseless passion, gripping him firmly round the head, tightening the knot of their legs.

His resistance, so strong and clumsy a moment ago, suddenly drained. She kissed him less frenziedly, smudging his face with her saliva. His eyes closed, she kissed them, stroked his hair, bit at the corners of his mouth, licked his lips, entered with her tongue. His body wakened heavily, mouth answering tremulously, hands holding on to her, groin coming to life, slowly hardening like something groping for the light. A shiver went through him and he lay still in her arms, nose and lips to the skin of her neck, hand resting on her breast, while she caressed his head.

He lay still until the tickling of her curls made him scratch. 'What self-respecting IRA woman has hair like you?'

'What self-respecting IRA commander,' she replied, mock-biting his stubbled cheek, 'lies in the hay with his troops?'

Lifting himself onto his elbows and looking into her laughing brown eyes, 'You're original all right, Annie McBride.'

'And you're a fool, Dixie Doyle. There's no need to be so bloody rigid.'

Just then, from across the farm, came the voice of Marcus King singing loudly in an extravagant Jamaican accent.

'One love, one heart, lez join togeddah and I'll feel ah'right . . .'

'Jaysus!' Dixie jumped up. 'Somebody shut him up!'

'Hey bruda, d'is aint no jive . . . dem outtah get me, dead or alive . . .'

They heard Marcus singing for a few more moments and then suddenly stop, silenced by Feeley no doubt.

Pressing his eye to a firing point in the wall, Dixie scanned the sleepy luxuriant countryside.

'They may be out there, listening and watching . . .'

She came and pulled him round. He leaned away, afraid of what she might do next. She gripped his arm.

'We're pulling out tonight, right? Taking the prisoner with us. . .?'

'We're too vulnerable here. We'll make a run for it in the car with

230

King around one a.m. If anything goes wrong, if any of us are caught in the attic, it's a clean jump through the wall onto mattresses in the shed below, where two motorbikes are waiting.'

'The shed has a roof, Mr Doyle!'

'*Had* a roof, Miss McBride.'

'Fine, then you'll consider sparing Molly and Michael?'

'Not a chance.'

Gripping him by both arms: 'But you can – '

Shaking her off: 'They're traitors!'

'They don't have to die!'

He shook her off again. 'Drop it, woman, and get back to your post.'

'Mercy is an expression of strength, Dixie.'

'Don't you ever give up?'

Marcus was singing again. *'One love, one heart, lez join togeddah and I'll feel ah'right . . .'*

'Christ, that bloody black bastard, I ought to shoot him now!'

'It's in your hands,' she persisted, 'you don't have to shoot them, you could –'

'They were happy enough to kill us. Jaysus, woman, haven't I enough fighting the Brits, the RUC and the UDA without covering my back as well?'

'Exile them! Drive them from the community to some remote place, but you've no right to kill them!'

'You and your romantic fantasies! Trying to plant your pretty middle-class morals on us primitives – '

'Well it is bloody primitive, shooting comrades in cold blood.'

'Comrades? Snakes and turncoats, more like!'

'They were desperate, Dixie. They just want to live and you wouldn't let them.'

'Do you think this is some club you join and leave when you feel like it?'

'That's what you're planning to do.'

'I've done twelve years – '

'He's done three, is that a death sentence?'

'I'm not a security risk. He is, he's weak, he's proved it. Traitors are more evil than anything. They wreak more terror and havoc than – '

'What, Molly and Michael?'

'Yes!'

'Then banish them, but don't kill them. You're not God, Dixie Doyle.'

'No, nor were you when you nutted those two British soldiers. Jaysus, woman, you wouldn't be so selective about life and death if you came from the Bogside or West Belfast, where killings, poverty and hopelessness are the air we breathe, where we ask our priests – Father, is it true there's life before death? Wise up, girl. You've joined the wrong gang, you with your manual for nicely brought up guerillas – Rules for paramilitary etiquette!' He mocked her accent.

A lump of flying spit hit him in the face.

'Fuck you,' she said, 'that was cheap.'

Wiping his cheek, livid again. 'So was that!' – pointing to where they'd tangled just then in the hay. 'Stupid me thinking you really wanted me, when all you were thinking about was Michael.'

'Michael's life, your body. You appeal to me, Dixie, but not in cold blood.'

They faced each other, Annie's breast heaving, Dixie's lungs wheezing.

'You ought never have joined,' he said, 'you don't fit.'

'I didn't join to fit the IRA but to change it!'

'Just like that?'

'Just like that.'

Shaking his head. 'Not overnight, girl. And not tonight. You cross me tonight and I'll put a stop to you, permanently.'

She saw the death-look in his eye.

The long day descended into evening. Seen from the wooded hills, the farm was a still-life, but for the scratching of chickens, the slow browsing of a cow and donkey, and the fitful barking of a dog.

On the edge of the wood Lee and his men lay still, watching and waiting. No cigarettes were smoked, no fire lit, no movement made, however small, which wasn't slow and in keeping with surroundings.

Lee's radio buzzed, the big Welshman Williams reporting a vehicle south of the wood. Lee turned serpent-slow and picked out the car through binoculars.

'Relax,' he reported back, 'it's only Flash Paddy.'

After a time, the man himself appeared, crawling through bracken in his long mackintosh.

'What kept you, Maigret?'

Mulraine ignored the sneer, though it deserved a sharp riposte, considering that Lee had got everything wrong so far and he had got everything right.

'I've got the bugging equipment.'

'Jolly good, Inspector.'

'I've left two of my men with it in the car.'

'Splendid.'

'Say the word and I'll acquaint your boys with how it works.'

'Very good, sir . . . only we shan't be needing it, we're going in tonight. All I need is tonight's weather. Rain would be fine, but I don't want a moon. What's your forecast?'

'A whole lot of unnecessary bloodshed.'

'Cut the crap, Mulraine.'

'No, you cut the shit, Mr Lee!' growled Mulraine incensed, 'I've had my bellyful of you and your bad manners. You're a lout, Mr Lee, and a bully to boot. What's more you're scarcely an improvement on those misbegotten madmen down there!'

Lee looked at the detective in amazement.

'No, Mr Lee, I'm not as wide of the mark as you suppose. To save a minute or two you left that young girl to bleed on the tarmac – '

'Yes! To save others bleeding by catching Doyle.'

'That's desperate cold logic, sir.'

'But true.'

'Heaven help us.'

'Will you two leave it out!' hissed Hurst from somewhere.

Lee made a supreme effort. 'Inspector, if we could get back to the moon for a moment – '

'Storms are forecast before midnight and I'm not expecting a moon. However I am expecting you to remember that my continuing silence over your little escapade on Inishtrahull depends on no harm coming to Lieutenant King.'

Lee inhaled lustily through his nose and reflected for a moment.

'Sounds remarkably like blackmail, Inspector.'

'Bless me, Captain, you're sharp this evening.'

Mulraine was right. Darkness filled the valley, wind shook the wood, lightning flickered in distant hills, and shadows crept forward like wolves to a fire.

Alone in the layloft, Annie licked her cut lip and savoured the bitter taste of defeat. Moving quietly from one firing point to the next, she peered out and felt the first harbingers of rain on her face. The loft was pitck dark, only the faintest light filtering across from the house. Outside was darker still, fields as close as a wall. Every now and then brief displays of lightning exposed the hills, catching trees in sharp relief against the sky, but without revealing any secrets. Who was out there? Were they coming? Were they far, or breathing down on the farm? Was that someone below, or the cow chewing hay?

As hordes of blood-lusting SAS men crawled through her imagination, she stayed close to the mobile machine-gun, caressing the heavy belts of NATO-issue 7.62 bullets which were poised to slice men in half with coloured tracer as far away as the woods.

Her mind kept wandering over to the house where Molly and Michael were facing the foregone conclusion of an improvised trial. Did they know that their last moments were running out like sand? What last thoughts did people have, waiting on death?

Annie wondered what her own last thoughts would be. A boy she once loved; her father, Eugene; or beloved Deirdre, the housekeeper; or herself, her life cut short at twenty-one? Perhaps she would dwell on the two British soldiers she killed, or else her stunning sense of failure – maximum effort, minimal achievement. If only she could have saved Michael. Maybe Dixie was right, she should never have joined.

Lightning flared over the hills, blitzing the woods and trailing far off thunder. Not for the first time that night, Annie considered storming the house to try and free a man she'd briefly loved.

Lying beside Michael, Marcus listened to the approaching thunder. Through the hole in the wall he watched the night flicker with lightning, and tormented by his chains he imagined calling down bolts of lightning to slash through them, leaping through the wall to freedom, running through the woods until he burst.

Voices below, footsteps. It was Marcus they came for first, freeing his wrists and immediately binding them together with a lightweight bicycle chain before unlocking his ankles. They were taking no chances, and his courage wavered. He thought they were taking him out for exercise. Dressed all in black, with a beret thrust over his head, they led him below. In the silent kitchen they surprised him by freeing his wrists. He acted indifferent, defeated, much as he had done in the hospital the night he faked the hanging. Though his limbs were stiff, his mind was sharp, his eyes alert, muscles coiled for an opportunity to spring.

He had hoped to be led outside for a night walk, and was anticipating possibilities when, instead, they stepped back, guns aimed at him.

'Decision time,' said Dixie, 'you with us or not?'

Marcus faltered. 'What's the rush? It's a big decision.'

'We're expecting company. What's it to be?'

Company? thought Marcus. What did Dixie mean? IRA chiefs? Police? SAS? Marcus didn't fancy any of them. He looked Dixie in the eye.

'I'm against the British Army, I'm against your army.'

'Marcus King's one-man-band,' smiled Dixie with grudging admiration.

'Get on with it!' snapped Feeley.

Dixie moved suddenly, seizing a rifle and flinging it at Marcus. Marcus caught it in front of his face – an Armalite. For a terrible moment he thought he was being thrown a desperate lifeline, a slim chance of defending himself while they gunned him down, but almost at once he was blinded by a succession of flashes as Black Rose took rapid photographs of him. Smiling gleefully, she came and seized back the rifle and made him turn round. He was bracing himself for execution when he felt himself toppling from behind by a judo thrust and flung to the floor. With Dixie standing over him, sub-machine-gun poised, Feeley bound Marcus's wrists in front with the bicycle chain and padlock.

They made him sit on the chair. While Feeley covered Marcus with a sub-machine gun, Dixie went to fetch Michael.

'We get our traitors too,' said Feeley.

Marcus looked. Michael entered, head bowed, hands chained. Despite his stoop, his dishevelled hair brushed the low ceiling. His expression was one of sadness and resignation. He looked around, perhaps expecting to see Molly. Seeing only Marcus, he dropped his gaze and allowed himself to be led quietly to stand against a wall, hung with a threadbare tricolour.

Marcus had scarcely a moment to wonder why they had photographed him. Now it was plain enough. They'd snapped him in black garb, beret and Armalite against an Irish flag. Looking round, he met Black Rose's gloating eye. They understood each other perfectly. He knew she could see he was desperately looking for a way out. But with the cradled sub-machine-gun levelled at his head, she knew he knew there wasn't one.

'Michael O'Cinnéide,' hurried Dixie, 'you stand accused of treachery, of plotting with your adopted mother – '

'Where is she?'

'Asleep. You want her to witness this?'

'You mean' – he brightened a little – 'you're not going to – '

'No.'

Michael swayed with relief. Then a terrible loneliness came over him.

While the thunderstorm seemed to circle the farm, unseen shapes crept nearer through the fields. And while Michael's trial was being hastened in the house, across the rainswept yard, up in the dark hayloft, Annie was creeping from wall to wall, peering out at the night, straining eyes and ears, trembling at the thought of whoever might be out there closing in. She moved with uncharacteristic heaviness, discouraged by her failure to save Michael and Molly, weighed down by a sense of powerlessness, despising herself and her efforts to stamp her mark on the world.

How she longed to do something great, something which would alter the complexion of the world. She was damned if she was going to be a nameless pebble, passed over by the sea. Nor did she want to be a pretty sandcastle, demolished by the first tide and completely erased by the next, not the faintest mark on the smooth sand to show she had existed. She wanted to be like a stake driven into the shore, parting the waves, switching, however slightly, the course of time.

Hearing Pip's whining drifting over from the house, her thoughts returned to Michael, living out his last moments. Poor foolish Michael. She checked her tears, reminding herself of the futility of her fantasies of storming the house and dying a traitor's death for friendship's sake. Even if she succeeded in freeing Michael and Molly, they would all be hunted until they dropped. Lightning zipped across the skyline, wind and thunder shook the loft. In her heart Annie said goodbye to Michael.

Michael stood blindfolded against the wall, Dixie faced him, pistol, with silencer attached, loose in his hand. Marcus sat, head bowed, covered by Feeley. Dixie spoke quietly.

'Is there anything you want to say, Michael?'

The condemned man lifted his head as if he'd thought this moment would never come. 'Some thoughts' – he fished in his back pocket, unfolded and waved a scrap of paper – 'while you were away. I want to read them out.'

Feeley rolled her eyes. 'Jaysus . . .'

Dixie looked at his watch. Well after midnight, almost time to make a run for it. He hurried over and removed the blindfold. 'Quick as you can.'

Not an able reader at the best of times, Michael stumbled over his own composition:

> Fuck the Taigs, fuck the Prods
> Fuck the guns and bombs and gods
> Fuck the Pope, fuck the Queen
> Fuck the Paisley's poison dream
> Fuck the priests who pray and prey
> Fuck the bloody IRA
> London lies, Dublin dodges
> Fuck the bloody Orange lodges
> Fuck our bastard cousin England
> Fuck that old bitch Mother Ireland . . .

Dixie looked stunned. Michael held his gaze, as though awaiting artistic judgement. Feeley sneered.

'Shoot the bastard.'

Dixie steeled himself, Marcus started to his feet.

'Jesus Christ, you're not going to shoot this man in cold blood!'

'Sit down!' Feeley raised the sub-machine-gun to Marcus's head. Sweat sprang up on Dixie's brow as he spoke.

'In the name of God and the dead generations' – embarking on his traditional oratory, Dixie slowly raised his pistol, mesmerising Michael where he stood – 'the Irish Republic is entitled to, and hereby claims, the allegiance of every Irishman and Irishwoman . . .'

That was as far as he got, before the window and surrounding wall erupted with a deafening explosion.

In the rain-lashed yard, Captain Lee and Corporal Hurst should have introduced a clutch of stun-grenades, but despite the blast and flying glass, Feeley emptied her magazine into the smoke, forcing the raiders to throw themselves flat in the mud.

The dog howled, muffled screaming came from the main bedroom, and in the kitchen the lights were blown out and bodies crawled and scrambled for cover, only to be flattened by the force of stun-grenades landing all around them in the dark. In the fleeting lull that followed, Marcus groped across the floor and collided with Michael, who was also trying blindly to get out. As Dixie crawled to reach his sub-machine-gun, two figures stepped into the smoking gap in the front wall and hosed the room with flying metal – scything table legs, disembowelling armchairs, cleaving cupboards, disintegrating crockery. The ruptured stove sagged, and Dixie, sheltering there, took a stray bullet in the foot. Scarcely aware he'd been hit, he loosed a return burst of fire and crashed through the back door, only to be blinded by the false daylight of exploding flares. Feeley was shouting at him from the shed and he made a run for it pursued by bullets fired by a gunner on the hill.

In the front yard, beneath the smoking wall of the house, Captain Lee radioed Sergeant Williams, who should have captured the barn by now. For reply, Lee received an anguished stream of Welsh obscenities. Taffy was caught in a fox trap.

'Who's a fucking moron!' hissed Lee, and spat into the mud. Turning to Hurst: 'Taffy's out of it, the barn's yours!'

Before Hurst could move, the upper storey of the barn shuddered with gunfire, someone in the loft letting free with a heavy machine-gun, its coloured tracer describing a concentrated arc across the roof of the house towards young Baxter's position on the rise at the back.

Up in the hayloft, Annie couldn't tell whether she'd hit anything on the dark slopes above the copse, but she'd certainly silenced a rival gunner. High with the terror of battle, she wheeled the gun-trolley away from the west wall and propelled it across to the south to fire at the raiders in the yard. She thought she saw them dimly through the smoke and squeezed the trigger. The gun jolted and jammed. She worked the bolt furiously, cursed and squeezed again. Nothing. A flash of lightning lit the yard, catching one of the raiders scurrying behind a wall, picking his way towards her. A chill went through her. In the sharp exposure of light, she felt a tremor of recognition – the knifeman on the beach.

Marcus was still dodging bullets in the house, belly-crawling over rubble to reach the passage, where he expected to be competing with Michael for the ladder to the attic, but he lost the big man and his yelping dog in the darkness and found himself scaling the ladder alone, stumbling each time his hands tried to reach further and faster than his shackles allowed, clinging and climbing again. Finding the attic flooded by the glow of flares, he crawled beneath the breach in the wall which he had sledge-hammered the day before, and peered out. Tracers of gunfire were streaming over the copse and dissolving into the hillside. Immediately below him, two people were quarrelling in the roofless shed.

'The bitch will never make it over!' Black Rose wanted to take both motorbikes.

'I told her there'd be a bike' – Doyle, staying loyal to the Red Sniper, climbed behind Black Rose.

While the others were making a bid for freedom, on the far side of the farm Annie was fighting for her life, throwing herself down as the walls of the hayloft rattled and jumped with gunfire from the raiders in the yard, bullets splintering wood, ricocheting through the air and sinking into beams over her head. Clutching her Armalite, she crawled into a tunnel of hay bales to reach the munitions hide. Plunging her hand into a box, she grabbed one, two Russian F1 grenades.

Below, at the barn's entrance, Hurst tossed a grenade of his own inside and followed up with a hail of bullets into the smoke. A cow was ripped apart, straw caught fire, Hurst fired at the open trapdoor and at the hayloft ladder, slicing it in two.

For reply, Annie lobbed a grenade down through the trapdoor. In the barn below, Hurst distinguished something on its way down, guessed what it was and bolted. The grenade failed to explode. Lying in the mud, Hurst looked round and grinned. The Provo in the loft was trapped.

The barn was catching fast, flames rushing through heaps of straw, pouncing on walls and uprights, eating quickly into the old decaying wood. The heat in the loft was rising, flames pushing up from below as Annie prayed for better luck with her second grenade, and hurled it not down the trapdoor, but across the loft to the far corner. She knew she was trapped, that the loft couldn't hold out for her much longer, that flames were poised to burst through and offer the entire barn in a fireball to the night sky.

Her aim once again was good, only this time the grenade fulfilled its purpose, exploding in the far corner with a deafening bang.

239

Annie couldn't tell, through the smoke, whether her plan had worked, but she scrambled choking and coughing towards the fire which had broken out, praying that the grenade had fractured the fragile wall, a fire-escape to the night, a leap through darkness to the silage heap below.

Moments earlier, Captain Lee had been working his way through the eerie darkened house, everything still but for the drift of gunsmoke and the whimpering of a dog. In the passage, he glimpsed a ladder to the attic, but first the bedroom from where the whimpering was coming. Kicking open Molly's door he stepped back, fired a burst of bullets and dived in after them, rolling across the floor and crouching to fire again. The echoes died, replaced at once by a motorbike in full flight at the rear of the house, and the staccato rattle of Baxter firing from the rise and striking the tree tops.

Lee spun round and ran through the house into the yard. Fire lit the sky, Hurst firing exultantly into the burning loft. He looked round at the sound of the motorbike, seemingly surprised that anyone in the house had survived, never mind ridden away. As Lee shouted orders at him, they both heard a second motorbike revving up, and ran to intercept it.

Half a rainswept mile away, Feeley and Dixie slewed to a muddy halt in a strip of woodland.

'You're hearing things, woman!'

'Am I?'

A motorbike was coming after them, its high-pitched engine getting louder. They sat rooted on the bike, wondering who it was, Dixie hoping Annie had somehow reached the shed and that it was her. Feeley guessed his thoughts.

'Forget it, Dixie, they'll have got her in the hayloft.'

Dixie shuddered. 'Michael then?'

'What, leave his mammy? It's the fucking darkie.'

Wheeling the bike off the track, they took up firing positions in the trees. Closer and closer they heard him coming, charging towards them with no headlight or any glimmer to betray him. Dixie drew his pistol, Feeley slammed a fresh magazine into her sub-machine-gun. She'd pissed in his face, she'd photographed him, now she was going to kill him. The engine grew louder still, they tensed and strained their eyes along the rain-lashed track, and though the rattling motor reverberated all around them through

240

the trees, no bike materialised and its roar passed and faded down another track.

Dixie uttered a stifled curse and tottered. Feeley stooped to examine his foot. A flash of lightning revealed his blood on her hands, blood all over his boot.

'The camera. . ?' he said desperately. 'Did you get the camera?'

She smiled a defiant rain-sodden smile, and slapped a saddle bag.

'Thank Christ,' he groaned, 'let's go.'

By faith and lightning the phantom rider careered through the wood, rain whipping his face, stones flying up off the track, his chains restricting him to the use of one hand and an awkward twisted posture, testing his strength and balance. Time and again, he lost it, righting himself with his feet on the track, or lost it completely and slid off. Mercifully the bike, lying on its side in the mud, kept running. He picked it up and rode on.

Hardly daring to believe what was happening, he was still trying to calculate in which direction he was going when a blaze of lightning lit the night and revealed no track ahead, only a rugged slippery slope down which he plunged, clinging grimly, bouncing, feeling himself falling and finally pitching into a cascading stream at the bottom. The bike sank between his legs and he waded waist deep to the far bank, crawled out and melted into darkness.

Turning off the main road which marked the border, Frank Mulraine drove cautiously along the lane to the farm. Although the burning barn and reverberating gunfire would shortly attract the Garda to this remote spot, he hoped to have a few minutes to himself and escape detection.

For fear of encountering any of Doyle's troop, he placed a sign saying DOCTOR prominently in the windscreen and hoped to God he wouldn't be called upon to attend to anyone. Stopping short of the farm, he got out. The barn was spitting and roaring like an immense blazing matchbox, a donkey was kicking up a terrible din, otherwise all was quiet.

Feeling in his raincoat pocket for the comfort of his pistol, he raised his umbrella and walked into the yard. Giving the barn, its heat and falling timber, a wide berth, he proceeded round the house, shining his flashlight through windows like a village bobby. Whistling loudly, he entered the darkened dwelling, automatically shaking his umbrella.

'Anybody home?'

The torch beam wandered back and forth through the grotesque landscape of destruction. Gunsmoke and dust drifted aimlessly in the beam, which found no one dead or alive until suddenly it illuminated a pair of red eyes on the floor. Mulraine moved towards the dark shape lying on its side and bent down. A dog, opened up with bullets, its white fur stained with blood, its face transfixed with terror.

'God love him,' murmured Mulraine. 'Her . . .' he corrected himself.

A curious sound reached him just then from somewhere in the house, like the anguish of one bereaved. He rose and tracked the soft keening to a bedroom, where he was moved to knock on the open door before entering. His beam travelled over a hastily abandoned bed and probed the far corner, where two people were huddled half in and half out of a wardrobe.

Mulraine tried the bedside lamp. It worked, spreading a low coloured light. Michael O'Cinneíde was cradling his mother, rocking her and stroking her bleeding head. He too appeared to be hit and, judging by the bullet holes in the wardrobe's open door, the two of them must have been hiding inside, close and secure in the illusion of safety and darkness.

Michael saw Mulraine, but his presence had no meaning and he continued rocking and softly wailing. Even when Mulraine came close and looked to see that Molly O'Cinneíde was truly dead, Michael continued as if he and Molly were the only two people in existence.

'FREEZE!'

Mulraine started with fright, Michael barely blinked. Mulraine turned slowly, expecting the Garda. Young Baxter, one of Captain Lee's men, was crouching dramatically, rifle poised.

'That you, Inspector?'

'For God's sake,' said Mulraine shortly.

'Sorry.'

'Where is everybody?'

'Number One and Number Three fucked off after King.'

'What!'

'He escaped, sir.'

'Again?'

'So did at least two of theirs.'

Mulraine made a snap decision. 'Help me get these two people to my car.'

Michael, without a word, insisted on carrying Molly himself. Out in the yard, big Sergeant Williams, limping badly from his encounter with a fox trap, was escorting the party to the car when a host of whirring blue lights materialised soundlessly along the main road.

'It looks like it'll have to be the back way through the wood, gentlemen,' said Mulraine.

16

Dawn found Marcus crossing trackless country swept by rain and circling thunder. Behind him he heard the distant tireless throbbing of helicopters searching border country. Shivering in saturated all black second-skin clothing, he trudged south at his best pace with two obsessions in mind – not to get caught again, and how to rid himself of his chains.

Mid-morning the storms rolled on; the sun burst free time and again through dispersing clouds, heating his back. His obsessions remained constant and conflicting. To remain free he needed to steer clear of people; to rid himself of his chains, he would need to stalk some isolated community and find something like a circular saw.

He walked rapidly, sometimes breaking into a run, his lungs and legs jubilant with freedom, his eyes alert for danger and opportunity. After the first few miles he hardly ever looked over his shoulder. He'd come too far, too fast, he believed, for anyone to follow. He was too imbued with his own good fortune to worry about the distinctive shoe prints he deposited on every muddy track he crossed.

Jogging over the crown of a hill he saw smoking caravans in a lay-by on a deserted road winding interminably north and south. He sat down in a hollow and watched. There were two traditional silver caravans and five modern, and an assortment of jalopies to pull them. Fire smoke billowed, fluttering clothes dried in the breeze, dogs and children fought and played.

He was quickly spotted as he descended the hill and walked along the road. An army of children gathered with sticks and stones on the far side of the road, taunting, threatening, frightened and fascinated by the big brown man, his badly cut face, shaved head and lacerated black clothes.

Marcus walked with hands interlocked, chains concealed inside the sleeves of his combat jacket. A stone flew, bouncing in the road in front of him, more a test than an attack. Ignoring it, he went a little further and sat down on the grass verge, reducing the threat he posed, much as he used to do in Derry when he stopped people in the street, rifle shouldered.

They watched, conferring, stones turning in sweaty hands.

'I won't eat you,' he called, half smiling, 'I've had breakfast.'

The children exchanged looks. The alien had spoken, reassuring some, scaring others. A boy stepped into the road, lean, sharp-eyed and wind-burned. Taking a swing at the stone with his stick, he looked up and met Marcus's startling grin. 'What's your name? I'm Ammi,' he said, taking care to give his Jamaican name.

The boy mumbled a name and the children ventured into the road, jostling closer and closer until they made a watchful semi-circle.

'What you doing, mister?' He pronounced it 'mithtah'.

For reply Marcus withdrew his hands and chains. The children sprang back in alarm.

'Some bad men caught me and put these on me' – holding up the chains to the sun – 'I ran away. Can you help me get them off?'

The crowd thought and acted as one. Some ran ahead, others walked with him, barely able to contain their excitement. Why had men caught him? What were they like? Did they hurt him? How had he got away?

Women watched from caravan doorways, silent men gathered in loose knots. Marcus was escorted before them like a captured king. A man about Marcus's age stepped up and looked him directly in the face. He was swarthy and weathered, with coal-black brows and hair.

Marcus held out his wrists. 'Can you get these off for me?'

The man looked at the chains and padlock, then at Marcus's face, nastily cut by flying glass. Marcus saw dark glances exchanged, heard one or two muffled remarks, which could have been another language. It was plain some of them knew who he must be. There were aerials on several caravans. They would have followed his story on television, a black British soldier on the run in their own back yard – and here he was, standing before them.

Dogs sniffed nervously at his legs, a few women approached. Away in the distance helicopters could be heard. The man saw Marcus listening. Meeting Marcus's eye again, he gave an almost imperceptible nod. Otherwise his face remained immobile and inscrutable as he motioned Marcus to follow him.

London

The high street supermarket was crowded and hot. Marcia held fast to her composure, shuffling forward in the long checkout queue with her loaded basket, trying to be patient with Jamie, who was daily more restless and edgy. He was pestering her again about sweets. However many she allowed him, his craving was never satisfied.

'Quit bellyaching! Enough's enough.'

A woman in the congested queue sympathised. Marcia would normally have reciprocated, but people irritated her now. She wanted no contact with anyone. For all she knew her man was being tortured at that very moment by the IRA. Or he was lying stripped and murdered, waiting to be found. Every time the phone rang she nearly jumped out of her skin.

Everything upset her. She was repelled by the shabby lifeless people around her, the glaring ordinariness of their preoccupations. The inane piped music, the squeak of warped trolleys, the maddening bleeping of the tills – there was no escaping any of it. When Jamie, idly spinning, knocked a bottle of vinegar to the floor, where it smashed and reeked in an ever spreading pool, Marcia's nerves snapped. Abandoning her full basket, she screamed at him, shaming him and humiliating herself in front of scores of gaping shoppers and staff, dragging him wailing from the store.

There were no taxis in sight, the bus queues were daunting. She dragged him into a side road and slapped his legs until he became hysterical and her hand stung. Jamie shrank from her, terrified, against a wall. People turned to stare. She felt herself swaying on

245

the edge of madness. The street teetered as though she were on a ship, traffic and people blurred. With tremendous effort she pulled herself back from the brink.

She moved towards Jamie, he flinched and bared his teeth. 'I'm sorry, sweetheart,' she begged, trying to comfort him, trying to envelop him in her arms.

A man asked cautiously, 'You OK?'

'Get me a taxi . . .'

On the way home she told him the truth. She'd kept him off school so kids wouldn't ask about his daddy. Daddy had been captured by the enemy. He was a prisoner and might never come home. She said she was sorry for being so horrible. Would he like to go stay with his grandparents? Jamie said nothing, only looked out of the window.

On the way up to the flat, she heard the phone ringing. It wasn't her nature to chase phones, but lately it was standard practice, and she dashed up the stairs, fumbled with her key, burst indoors and reached the phone just as it stopped ringing. She screwed up her eyes and groaned. Jamie crept in. She found a smile.

'Never knew your mummy was an Olympic runner, huh?'

'When can I go to Grandma's?'

His words caught her in the belly like a knife. She had hoped he'd decline the suggestion. People were being good to her, like her parents, with whom she normally didn't get on, and Marcus's parents, who were suffering terribly in their quiet way. Friends who might have looked the other way were rallying to her, none more than Donna and Elroy, with whom Marcus had quarrelled so bitterly. But Jamie was everything to her at this time. The thought of him going was unbearable. She went to the bathroom and swallowed one of her new pills. 'I'll call Grandma in a minute. Pour yourself some juice.'

She was getting to know their voices at Regimental Headquarters. Initially they'd been pleasant, if unhelpful. Now they tartly reminded her that she would be informed at once of any developments. Controlling her temper, she replaced the receiver and switched on the radio for the midday news. And this time she didn't try and prevent Jamie from hearing. It was still only five to twelve.

'I'll ring Grandma for you now,' she said brightly, dreading the prospect of being alone, the long hours between phonecalls and news bulletins. Jamie's face puckered up and his lip quivered.

246

'What's wrong now?'

'I don't want to go,' he reproached her.

'You said you did.'

'No you did.'

'Sweetheart . . .' He allowed himself to be cuddled. The news came on. The tenth victim of Tuesday's double IRA bomb, a bandsman, had died; the IRA 'regretted civilian casualties', but argued the bombings had been a 'legitimate act of war'. Thousands of refugees were fleeing Beirut, Israeli air-raids had been launched against Lebanon . . .

'And finally, we're just receiving unconfirmed reports from our Belfast studio that former Lieutenant Marcus King, the deserter thought to have been captured by the IRA, is now believed to have escaped, and to be on the run once again somewhere in County Donegal. If these reports turn out to be true, both the security forces in Northern Ireland and the police and Army in the Republic will be anxious to recapture him . . .'

Jamie was gaping at his mother, as if to confirm his own ears. Clapping a hand over her mouth as though to contain a scream, she stretched out a hand to him.

While Marcia was on her knees in her kitchen in North London, in the wilds of Donegal her husband's pursuers were laboriously tracking him, two men in black, muddied, bruised and jaded from the night's combat and hunt, surfacing in a strip of bog at the back of a gipsy encampment.

Dogs barked savagely and children crept away as Douglas Lee and Danny Hurst vaulted a fence, sub-machine-guns over their shoulders, stern intent in their eyes. They knew they weren't supposed to be in Donegal, that the diplomatic consequences could be serious if they were caught and positively identified by the Garda. But that would be nothing as compared to the wrath of their own bosses if they failed to bag their man after the night's fiasco.

'Morning!' piped Lee, striding boldly into the midst of the caravans. 'Or is it afternoon?'

The men who gathered didn't call off the dogs, which snarled and harried the strangers. Lee ignored them, Hurst intermittently flung out an accurate but tactless boot.

'We're looking for a deserter, a lunatic,' announced Lee. 'Hard to miss him, over six feet and chocolate coloured.'

No one moved or spoke. The SAS men made a show of eyeing up the caravans.

'We know he came this way, be a shame to have to call in the Army.'

The barefaced threat appeared for a moment to work. Men looked at each other and started to move. But it became apparent at once that they were merely returning to their normal business.

Lee and Hurst went quickly through each caravan. No one spoke to them and they might as well not have been there.

Afterwards, as they departed to a ragged chorus of abuse from some of the children, Lee said to Hurst, 'It's obvious he was here from their reaction. Maybe they fed him and delayed him.' His tracks wouldn't be hard to pick up again.

Buoyed by the liberation of his hands, Marcus made rapid progress across country, until exhaustion set in and he surrendered to the call of an isolated barn. The barn was high and wide, neatly stacked with bales of hay from floor to roof. Climbing to a high perch, he threw himself down and closed his eyes, intending to rest up for a couple of hours and move on.

He slept twice as long. Waking suddenly, wondering for a moment where he was – London, Derry, custody, convent, Inishtrahull, the attic – he peered out through a split in the warm wall and saw the sun already on the slide. He tensed, calculating the time to be already about four o'clock. He cursed himself and moved quickly.

Where the crossbeams met the flat roof, there was a gap big enough to squeeze through and climb out of the corrugated lid of the barn. Belly-crawling to the edge of the roof, he scanned the boundless landscape, both to decide where to go next, and for signs of danger. He lay still, concentrating his energy in his eyes, knowing the SAS were trained to be invisible. He lay there for some time, wishing he had a map, wondering where to aim for.

Then he saw them.

Coarse grass swayed evenly, back and forth in the breeze. But about fifty yards away, steam was faintly visible rising in two places, some thirty yards apart, where the sun was beating down on two damp bodies. His eyes detected no more steam in any direction.

His heart sank, drumming weakly against the hot roof.

Recapture would be unendurable. He was unarmed and tired. Surrender and get it over with, a voice told him.

But if these were the men who had attacked the farm, they would be even more tired. He recalled his martial arts training: Use and return your enemy's strength . . . counter superior weaponry with cunning.

'FREEZE!' he called, without showing his face. The word drifted over swaying bog into the hills. 'Stand up, the pair of you, weapons high!'

A moment's pause for reflection, vapour continuing to rise in the same places.

'Don't be an ass,' replied Lee, 'you can't hit us both at once.'

'Then show your faces and stop skulking in the grass!'

Two figures in black, with rain-streaked blackened faces, surfaced, aiming the latest unanswerable German Heckler submachine-guns at the roof.

'Why aren't you bastards chasing Doyle?'

'We want you, you fucking lunatic.'

'Two of you, armed to the teeth. No wonder you're so bloody cocky.'

The SAS men exchanged glances. They didn't like the implication.

'Without all the heavy metal, you bastards are a joke.'

Lee had to smile. 'Do you know something, Lieutenant? I've a funny feeling you're unarmed.'

Marcus's heart lurched again . . . and rallied.

'Is that why they sent you?' he bellowed. 'Shouldn't be too difficult, just up your street, an unarmed man, a bullet in the back . . . I had kids in my platoon with more balls than you!'

Hurst seethed, Lee smiled appreciatively.

'He's not getting away with that,' vowed Hurst.

'That's the spirit!' Marcus rose and opened himself into an outspread star on the roof. 'Be a man and shoot me!'

'Black bastard!' Hurst spat into the grass and strode towards the barn.

'Wait!' said Lee.

Hurst spun round. 'You're not going to let him – '

Lee lifted his gaze to the magnificent creature spreadeagled against the blue sky. 'Cut the crap, Mr King, you're coming home.'

249

Dropping his pose, Marcus shielded his eyes and pitched his challenge. 'Hand to hand combat, one at a time.'

Lee shook his head and smiled. The cheek of the man!

He recalled Marcus King's file – thirty years old, decorated for bravery, and some sort of kung fu merchant. He might conceivably be a match for Hurst, who had to be one of the most ruthless finishers of men. But against himself, in bare combat. . .? No, my beautiful black friend, I'm afraid you've picked the wrong man.

'Come on, chief,' pleaded Hurst, desperate to prove himself after the incident with the IRA girl on the beach, 'leave him to me!'

Lee felt a spasm of excitement, half hoping Hurst would lose so he could unleash himself against the arrogant black renegade, impose his iron will, force a submission from those full Caribbean lips. The thrill of combat began to pump through him. He nodded to Hurst.

Hurst brandished a fist and shouted exultantly, 'You're on, King Kong!'

The barn doors flew apart, framing Lee and Hurst, weapons poised, against a brilliant sky.

By contrast, the interior of the barn was subdued. In the centre of an arena walled in by towers of hay, stood Marcus King, stock-still, stripped to the waist, unshaven, bullet-headed, a picture of awesome simplicity. They met his gaze full on, his eyes hard and shining with the lonely defiance of the fugitive.

The SAS men entered and laid down their guns. Without ado Danny Hurst threw off his combat tunic and stepped up to face the lunatic, fists opening and closing, eyes hungry.

Marcus read the cruelty in the eyes and the power behind them. He knew he must win early, or face the Captain exhausted and stripped of his secrets.

Hurst spat into his palms and moved closer.

Marcus remained rooted, bare chest breathing easily, arms deceptively loose by his sides. The quicker you beat this man . . .

'OK, King Coon,' sneered Hurst, 'let's see what you're made of!'

Marcus responded by humbly bowing in the time-honoured Oriental fashion.

'You don't fucking impress me – ' Hurst was saying as Marcus's foot swung high and wide of Hurst's guard and struck him like a hammer blow on the side of the head, knocking him headlong into the hay-wall and senseless to the ground.

Marcus bowed to the insensible body and lifted his gaze to meet Lee. The SAS Captain nodded reflectively.

'You bastard,' he breathed, peeling off his tunic and T-shirt, revealing a long, lean, muscular torso, rising on a vigorous neck to a finely moulded face. Keeping his grey fathomless eyes on Marcus, he stepped into the vacant space, assessing his adversary's splendid chest and shoulders, before fixing on his cut face, probing for signs of weakness, remorselessly staring at the black man's eyes, knowing he possessed the power to break a man's spirit before moving in to smash the body.

Marcus stared back, defying those hollow grey eyes. This was no common brawler sharpened by the SAS. All Marcus's instincts told him he was faced with a professional killer – streamlined, lean to the point of dissipation, a ruthless life-quencher. Marcus was taller and heavier, but he was like a large powerful animal threatened by what at first sight seemed a lesser one, only to catch the scent of something infinitely more dangerous than anything he'd ever met, a creature for whom size meant nothing, a predator designed to extinguish the lives of others.

Marcus kept pace with those pitiless eyes, but his flesh broke out in cold sweat. Fear, like slow ice, seeped into his veins, threatening to paralyse him.

They circled carefully, Lee trying to break his man with his will. He found Marcus beautiful; not the smooth good looks of Danny Hurst, but with the primitive majesty of Africa. There were all manner of things he would rather have been doing to this black prince's body than destroying it, but he knew not to be distracted, for he was a little afraid of Marcus King, whose hidden weapons and evident depth of intelligence were more formidable than all of Hurst's barefaced violence. This wouldn't be like incapacitating two or three bruisers guarding a Mayfair nightclub. Lee was like a snake closing in on something balanced, patient and powerful. One telling blow either way could settle it.

To break the mesmerising spell, Marcus leapt unexpectedly into a more formal 'horse stance', legs well apart, fists upturned and tucked into the waist, a dramatic posture which was simultaneously menacing and defensive.

Lee tensed and leaned back, and relaxed again, looselimbed, torso firm, eyes dull and morbid, shoulders down to indicate that an attack might be coming – or not – at any moment.

Opting for the initiative once again, Marcus broke the deadlock with another gambit popular in ancient China. He bowed respectfully as before. Thus his head was lowered for a tantalising moment, and Lee, snapping at the apparent sacrificial lunacy, delivered a swift circular kick, echoing the one which had so sweetly eliminated Hurst. Quick as it was, Marcus had played for it, and eluded the flying boot by dropping his whole body below it, leaving Lee's leg parting thin air, and his groin glaringly exposed. One accurate punch would have terminated proceedings, but Marcus was out of practice and missed.

Lee sprang clear and faced up, eyes blazing. Brushing straw from his tacky flesh, he came at Marcus hands unsheathed. Marcus retreated carefully, knowing he'd lost his chance, aware that Lee was driving him backwards towards the prostrate body of Hurst. As expected, the instant Marcus glanced round to avoid the human obstacle, Lee struck.

Feigning a bid for the groin, he delivered a favourite combination of blows, inflicted by fists and elbows, to the face and belly, culminating in the decisive kick to the groin.

Marcus parried them all but the last. As the boot arrived for the finish, the best he could do was raise a knee in time to deflect the kick to the ribs. He doubled up in pain. The next few seconds were crucial. He needed breath to recover. Lee knew it. Caution fell from him like a cloak. As Marcus fell back, Lee charged after him, besieging him from all angles, flaying, lunging, kicking, while Marcus, driven against the hay-wall, fended off blows like a cornered swordsman, holding out in desperate hope of an error.

It came, a combination repeated once too often, enabling Marcus to drop below it. Again his counter-punch lacked precision, but it unbalanced Lee, and Marcus broke free towards the open doors of the barn.

With a predator's obsession Lee turned and gave chase, devouring the distance between himself and the injured man.

As he fled, Marcus presented his unguarded back like a running wound to a shark. The bait was irresistible. Sensing Lee bearing down on him, Marcus stopped suddenly, inclined forward, raised one knee, and delivered a driving back-kick, catching Lee in full flight in the shoulder, dislocating it. Lee crash-landed, gripping his shoulder as though afraid to lose it. Marcus kept his feet, but held himself doubled up, as though trying not to spill his entrails. Lee raised his head, a look of stunned resignation in his eyes. Then, almost imperceptibly, Lee was distracted by something over Marcus's shoulder. Marcus looked round. Hurst, dazed but on his feet, was backing towards the guns in the far corner. Marcus sprang up and began a dash calculated to reach them first. Too late. Hurst found his strength and lunged, seizing the nearest weapon and whirling round.

Marcus was gone, a flutter of hay in his wake where he'd plunged through a crack in the hay-wall. They heard him scurrying for cover, and then heard him no more.

The barn was still, and growing dark, the vaulted roof receding, the hay-wall seeming to sway like skyscrapers. Brandishing the sub-machine-gun, Hurst scoured the sheer towers of hay, seething with anger, his burned pride crying out for retribution. Lee got up painfully.

'Game's up!' he shouted, filling the barn. 'Get your black arse out here . . . or face the consequences.'

A massive silence answered. Hurst, incapable of containing himself any longer, thrust the gun into the hay-wall like a dagger and loosed a rapid burst of fire.

'Cut that out!' said Lee. 'We'll take him alive.'

But, deaf and blind to reason and repercussion, Hurst strutted back and forth firing into the hay, stopping to listen and firing again. Livid, Lee bawled across the barn.

'You heard me, Corporal . . .' Dragging his useless shoulder, Lee gravitated towards him. 'Fire one more round and I'll fucking brain you!'

Hurst looked slowly round, eyes crazed with shame and rage, while high above them, among the vaulted rafters, a bale drifted free, leaned over the edge and plummeted, then a second bale, and another, parcel after parcel of compressed meadow, a summer landslide crashing all around them. As they dodged and danced, they caught a glimpse of Marcus scrambling over the soaring roofscape of hay in search of an exit. Hurst let out a shout of delight, raising his gun one-handed to bring down his enemy in a rising torrent of fire.

He never pulled the trigger. Even before Lee could stop him, both their attentions were wrested away by the outline of a woman looking down the sights of a rifle in the open doorway.

Annie fired, the force and accuracy of the bullet whipping the gun from Hurst's grasp as neatly as the work of invisible hands, plucking the weapon and tossing it away. Hurst stood rooted, awestruck, fear transfixing the smooth features of his face.

Annie stood framed in the doorway, sun in her hair, a murderous sparkle in her eyes. Squinting along the barrel of her Armalite, she aimed first at one man, then at the other.

'Your next move, either of you, is your last.'

Her voice was so full of assurance and lethal expectancy that neither man breathed.

'Soldier, get down here!' she called up to Marcus. 'Get some string from these bales and tie up these terrorists!'

Marcus peered down, wary of traps and trickery.

'What are you waiting for?' Annie shouted. 'I'm on my own.' Still he doubted. 'Doyle's a million miles away! Do you want it in writing?'

As Marcus began his uncertain descent, Lee and Hurst were subtly shifting, conspiratorial glances passing between them, beginning almost imperceptibly to make some unspoken move, inwardly coiling themselves in readiness to spring. But Annie watched with a hunter's withering concentration, and before either man could execute an idea, she fired twice in rapid succession, the bullets singeing the air past the cheek of each man, arresting them both.

'Up against the hay, the pair of you, legs spread!' The SAS men obeyed. Annie stood staring at Hurst's back, her rifle trained on him. Wasn't this the man? She moved closer, round to the side for a better look at his face. The certainty of recognition revived a spasm of revulsion, recalling those violent hands, merciless eyes, the attempt to violate her. He leaned forward against the hay-wall, aware of her, avoiding her, until the tension made him glance sideways and meet her eye, only to look away again with a snort of shameless resignation, almost a schoolboy's smirk. 'Wider!' she snapped. They parted their legs further and her eye went to Hurst, to the loose seat of his trousers, picturing the vulnerable scrotum and penis lurking inside, tools of the rapist.

'Did you think I wouldn't remember what you tried to do to me on that beach?'

Marcus hovered, scrutinising Annie, eyeing the open door.

'Relax!' Annie told him. 'There's just you and me, and these two glorious specimens of manhood.' She returned to them, their backs turned, hands flat against the hay-wall.

'Did you take me for a defenceless Irish girl, ripe for rape? Thought you could terrorise me like the worst kind of prowling pervert.'

'Liar!' blurted Hurst.

'What!'

'You're bloody lying!'

Lee threw him a sidelong glance. 'What's she on about?'

'She was fucking begging for it!'

'That's why you needed a knife,' sneered Annie.

'Bollocks! I never had a knife.'

'What's this then?' Annie delivered the bowie knife with venom, the blade shading Hurst's ear like a bat's wing, embedding itself in the hay-wall before his eyes. For a moment he gazed longingly at the tempting weapon. Then he felt the electrifying sock of Annie's foot between his legs, the up-thrusting kick driven in hard from behind, wringing the breath from his body, drawing from his lips a strangled gasp, causing him to sag to his knees, hands grasping himself in muted agony.

'Tie them up,' Annie ordered Marcus.

Marcus freed the knife from the hay and began cutting lengths of string.

'What are you doing?' said Lee, icily calm.

'Doing what I'm told.'

'You out of your mind? Between us three, we can overpower her.'

Ignoring Lee, Marcus grabbed hold of Hurst, forced him face down on the ground, bound his hands behind his back, wrenched off his boots and tied his ankles.

'You're a Brit,' said Lee through his teeth, 'she's a Provo, or hadn't you noticed?'

For reply Marcus seized hold of Lee by the back of his jacket and flung him brutally to the ground.

'You *are* crazy,' hissed Lee, holding his dislocated shoulder, 'they were right.'

While Marcus held him down and tied him, Lee reasoned in lowered tones.

'Use your head, man, she's IRA, it won't look good – '

Marcus seized him by the lapels and shook him.

'She's foe and you're friend, is that it? Then why you fucking chasing me everywhere? You got nothing better to do? Who sent you?'

255

'Orders, for Christ's sake, only you wouldn't understand that any more.'

'To do what?'

'To take you back, what else?'

'Then why was he shooting at me?' Teeth bared, Marcus held Lee by the throat, raging into his face. 'It's you who's fucking crazy. I've committed no crime. All I did was stand up for what I believe, and now I've got you bastards hunting me like a wild animal – '

'And illegally crossing the border,' Annie pitched in. 'Gunmen and sexual delinquents spreading mayhem in the Irish Republic!'

Marcus tied Lee's hands, removed his boots and socks and bound his feet. 'You better keep out of my sight, because if I catch you bastards again, I'll kill you, you understand?'

Lee shook his head regretfully. 'You're really asking for trouble.'

Marcus could only laugh. 'Seems to me I get trouble whether I ask for it or not.'

When Marcus had tied the men together back-to-back, Annie told him to go through their pockets. He duly plundered a rich supply of Sterling, Irish money and an assortment of maps, before turning his attention to the SAS men's unclaimed sub-machine-guns, and met Annie's eye. She motioned him to recover them. Lee watched in muted horror as Marcus collected the guns. Afraid of nothing in life except failure, he was trembling.

Hurst was slumped forward, cursing under his breath, pale with pain. Lee made one more bid to save the situation.

'King! There's no hope for you if you do this . . . I'm offering you safe conduct, be reasonable!'

'Reasonable!' Marcus roared with laughter, as he struggled into his T-shirt and turned to face Lee. 'I was a good officer, they stripped me of my rank. I warned them plastic bullets would kill someone, they made me use them, and *I* went and killed someone, everything I'd worked for smashed like that girl's head. I wanted to make up for her, they locked me up like a madman. I break out to attend the inquest, they send you bastards after me . . . and you want me to be reasonable!'

Marcus was shaking, aiming a finger at Lee. 'You tell your masters to get off my back. Tell them I'm going to pay for what I done, and they're going to pay for what they done.'

'Wait!' cried Annie as Marcus departed with the guns.

Lee called after her in a voice morbid with certainty. 'You're dead, woman.'

She was laughing as she gathered up the soldiers' boots and socks and ran out, but the prophecy sent a compelling chill through her. Shielding her eyes, she looked for Marcus.

'Where are you?' she shouted, her voice resounding over the trackless grassland. 'I could have killed you!' Heart hammering, she ran forward searching for him.

He reappeared on the ridge, tall and vigilant against the late afternoon sky. Resisting the urge to run, she went to him, but so intent was he in scanning the landscape that he scarcely seemed to notice her. With one gun-barrel he was absently massaging his ribcage through his torn T-shirt. Relief and pain jostled in his cut face.

'You're hurt,' she said roughly.

'I'm free!'

'Are you? Where will you find food tonight? Are you going to stroll into a village store? And tomorrow? And the next day? Where are you going to go? A black man sticks out in Ireland like a prick in a nunnery.'

He regarded her dubiously. 'What do you want?'

'You don't trust me.'

He gave a derisive laugh.

'You need me,' she asserted.

'That so?'

'You won't get anywhere without me.'

'I had no idea.'

'Sarcasm doesn't become you.'

Alert and suspicious, he continued to scan the landscape as they argued.

'I thank you, sister, for what you just done, but I am a British soldier – '

'Were!'

'I say I am. But you' – he turned to face her – 'are a member of the Provisional IRA, an organisation which bombs innocent people and has wiped out comrades of mine. I don't know what the hell I'm doing standing here talking to you.'

'You bastards don't shoot and incarcerate innocent people? That's priceless coming from you. Are sixteen-year-old stone-throwers fair game. . .?' Marcus visibly paled. 'Do the dead and

257

wounded count for less when they're Irish? God you've a nerve. Look at your feet!' Marcus looked down. 'Is that West Indian or English soil you're standing on? No, soldier, you're walking over my country, so what am I doing standing here talking to you?'

'I'm still waiting to find out.'

'Let's get away from here first.' She motioned him to follow her, but he stayed put.

'If you're still entertaining that shit about me joining – '

'You left the Army, I've left the IRA. That do you?'

'Why?' He was sceptical.

'The bombing made me sick. Remember Thorn Hill. . .?'

'I think I can, just about – '

'I told Doyle to stuff his bombs, I'd have nothing to do them. Things were never the same between us after that.'

He regarded her speculatively, a strange creature, long and lithe and armed with dark, inescapable eyes.

'Maybe we could do business together,' she said. 'How about a consultation over dinner in the hills?'

His eyes plumbed the depths of her face. She went on: '*If* you can squeeze me into your busy diary.'

Swinging the SAS men's boots, she set off towards the hills.

Ditching the boots and guns, they tracked south until they came upon a village. Leaving Marcus to mind the Armalite and nurse his cracked ribs in a hollow, Annie tied her hair back as best she could and descended into the village to buy provisions.

Rain was threatening and dusk falling when she returned, half expecting Marcus to be gone. But he was lying where she'd left him, head pillowed on a mossed-over rock.

'We won't starve tonight,' she said, offering a hand-up. He hesitated before allowing her to help him up.

'Embarrassed?'

'No.'

'Is it because I'm supposed to be the enemy?' She squared up to him, arms akimbo. He looked away, not relishing another argument. 'Or maybe you don't like being rescued by a woman, a woman a lot younger than you.'

'I'm just glad to be free,' he said evenly, 'and I want to stay free, aligned to nobody, used by nobody.'

She wanted to strike out at him, swear at him, but she saw the physical pain in his eyes, and the smudges which were bloodstains on his lacerated black clothing, and the cuts on his face from flying glass. Marshalling her sympathies for all he must have been through, she turned away, pointing towards higher ground. He let out a doubtful sigh and followed. The first drops of rain brushed their cheeks as they picked their way along barely discernible paths into the hills, Annie looking over her shoulder now and then, making sure he was still there. In the distance an abandoned dwelling leaned in stark relief against the sunset. When they reached it, they found only the meagre ruins of a very old chapel, overrun with rabbits, yellow pimpernel and ivy. Bleeting sheep bolted as they entered.

Annie motioned Marcus to a bed of grass, warmed and flattened by sheep. With no roof to the ruins, she dragged a rusting sheet of corrugated iron and secured it with rocks over the corner where Marcus lay. Without a word she spread the food on a flat stone, basic fare from a general store – bread, cheese, cold meats, tired fruit, orange juice. They ate for a time in silence, Annie glancing at Marcus in the fading light.

'When was the last time you ate?'

'Some gipsies fed me.'

'Travellers.'

'What?'

'Travellers,' she corrected, 'is what they're called. Those kids were pleased as Punch about helping you off with your chains.'

He cocked an eyebrow. 'How do you know about that?'

Taking a swig of juice, she smacked her lips and wiped her mouth. 'You made quite an impression. The camp was a hive of nerves when I appeared, cowed by those two SAS gangsters, but when they saw the Armalite, and that I was going to rescue you, everybody cheered up and the kids were eager to show me which way the SAS had gone after you.'

'So Doyle didn't send you?'

'Doyle and I weren't even speaking. If ever he catches up with me . . .' She whistled through her teeth to convey the dire consequences.

The rain fell, tapping on the corrugated shelter. A chill breeze found gaps in the ruins. Annie sat facing him in the open, arms wrapped round her knees, getting wet and cold.

'You shaved your head?'

'A monk did.'

'Why?'

He fumbled a reply, loath to answer.

'A statement of remorse?' she said.

He looked away, drawn to the encroaching night in the jagged outline of the doorway. Delayed shock had claimed him. He'd felt neither nerves nor fear in the barn, only a blind will to survive. Now he was trembling, revisited by a plague of violent images – Charlie's bloodbath at Thorn Hill, Bernie O'Rawe's battered skull, the girl blown up in the car-park. A glut of horrors, and now a narrow escape with his own life in the barn. He bowed his head, closed his eyes.

Rain fell on Annie's head and shoulders, drops in her hair catching embers of sunset.

'In the attic,' she reminded him, 'you joked about kidnapping someone, getting the Army pulled out, plastic bullets banned. What did you mean?'

'Why?'

'I told you. On your own you're up Shit Creek. But together . . .'

He laughed unkindly.

'What's so damned funny?'

'Wasn't it you killed one of my men, Robbie McLaren, on Thorn Hill? Christ Almighty' – he could only shake his head and smile – 'I'll manage just fine on my own, lady.'

'Lady?' With a snort of derision, she walked out, hands thrust in her leather jacket, Armalite over her shoulder. She did not return. He got to his feet and went out. All around him the receding landscape was sinking in a tide of darkness. He'd never imagined night could be so still, deep-dark and infinite. Had she really gone? An awful sense of isolation crept over him, and anger at his nameless rescuer for abandoning him, anger at himself for provoking her. The rain had almost ceased, the breeze was crackling in the gorse. Somewhere in an unseen valley, a dog faintly barked. Far across the darkness a pair of headlights worked the gloom. With a sharp pang of regret, he returned to the sanctuary. Lying down in his sheltered corner, he thought of Marcia, Jamie, his mother and father. Did Jamie know his Daddy was in trouble? Did they point him out at school – the traitor's little boy? How was Marcia, who was never panicked by anything, coping with this one?

He thought about the Red Sniper, feeling foolish for overreacting. He'd thrown away an opportunity to double the size of his army. Given the chance, Robbie McLaren would have taken satisfaction in shooting her dead. As for bragging that he could manage his mission alone, she'd already proved him wrong in the barn. Perhaps she was right, without support he was doomed. With the damp and the cold creeping over him, he closed his eyes and drifted into sleep.

His dreams were crowded with suppressed images – a late-night party in London, black friends mingling with white comrades, all scornful of him, embarrassed by him. Worst of all, Marcia, dismayed and let down, openly voicing her disillusion, even turning for comfort to another man, a man bearing a bone-chilling resemblance to Major Draycott. Suddenly he was wide awake, listening to the sound of someone approaching the sanctuary. His heart stopped, gripped by the spectre of recapture. He strained his ears, trying to persuade himself it was only sheep clipping rocks. But the steps grew louder. He sat up, groping on the ground, selecting a rock. The steps kept coming, closer and closer without arriving. Pressing himself against the broken wall beside the entrance, he raised the rock in his fist and prepared to strike.

A leather jacket gleamed dully under the watery moonlight. She entered bearing an armful of branches and sticks, setting them down on the ground. 'You're hurt, you should be in bed,' she said, brusque as a ward sister.

Juggling his rock: 'What time is it?'

'About midnight,' she said, and was gone like a breath of wind.

'Where you going?' He watched her go, wading through the long grass, a creature of the night melting into darkness. He stood shivering in the entrance, bewildered. Time passed, he was about to lie down when he saw an apparition, the moon-glow of the sniper's face returning, something heavy on her shoulder.

She brushed past him balancing a bale of straw. 'Lie down,' she ordered, still the ward sister. He lay down. Breaking open the bale, she tossed handfuls of straw over him and spread them evenly.

'Get some sleep, or you won't be any use to anyone.'

Armalite in hand she settled down outside the sanctuary, somewhere in the wilderness to keep the night-watch.

His dreams reclaimed him, drawing him into feverish sleep. When next he woke it was in the misty half-light of dawn. His curious companion was rearranging his straw covers, shaken loose in the night. Lying still, he could see her bending over him, hands and sleeves coated in droplets of dew or mist. Then she retired to the opposite corner of the sanctuary, and crouched down, arms wrapped around herself, suppressing a shiver.

He began to sit up, surprised at the resistance of his damaged ribs.

'What are you doing?' she said.

'You lie down,' he said, rising stiffly, 'I'll take over.'

'Save the heroics, get some sleep.'

He shook his head, brooking no argument, motioning her to pass him the rifle. She tossed it over.

'I should have got you bandages for your ribs in the village, and plasters for those cuts.'

'You don't bandage ribs,' he said, 'they heal of their own accord.'

'Like the spirit,' she suggested meaningfully.

He went out, disturbed by her words, because they echoed Dominic's reassurances on the island. Live right and the soul will heal in time. Wading through dense mist in ever widening circles around the sanctuary, he wondered at the awesome rifle in his hand, the one she had used to fire at him on Thorn Hill, and to shoot dead Robbie McLaren and Kitson? He kept going, probing the mist-shrouded landscape, trying to plan his next move, aware that he would need to be restored to full mental and physical fitness before he tackled anything.

Annie stood in the entrance with her thumbs to her lips and whistled. He didn't reply, there was no sign of him. She whistled again and waited. Behind her she had a fire going, fresh flames crackling, smoke billowing, fusing with mist. She whistled more insistently, and when he didn't materialise, she added a note of anguish, and finally rage. Nothing stirred out there. The man she'd rescued was gone, and her eyes stung. Together, she was convinced, they could have surprised the world and set it on a new course. Standing alone in the grey void, she was struck by the absurdity of her position, an IRA deserter unarmed and dispossessed of purpose. Fists and face clenched, she cursed aloud. 'The mean-minded, contemptible, low-down – '

She started at the sound of some unnatural disturbance behind her. Slowly she turned her head. He was leaning over the sanctuary wall, sober expression betrayed by a mocking light in his eyes.

' – bastard!' she finished with satisfaction. The smell of over-done bacon swelled his nostrils. 'Breakfast's burnt and I hope your ribs fall out!'

Water was boiling in an old can when he came round to the entrance. She blocked his way, looking at him intently, as if debating whether to admit him or not. His face was tired, stubbled and swollen with cuts, but he was alive again, his grave expression lit with humour.

'Password?' she demanded.

He scratched his cheek, an educated guess: 'Traveller.'

'No.'

'Coffee and bacon?'

'Certainly not!'

'British Army . . . open up!'

'Fuck off.'

He held fast to her withering gaze. A serious game demanded a serious answer. 'Deserters . . .' he said with quiet assurance.

'Close enough,' she conceded, taking him firmly by the arm and conducting him to the straw bed, where she made him sit down. Dipping a handkerchief in the boiling water, she began to swab his face, taking care over the open cuts.

'You realise your face is full of glass! You must have picked up half a window.'

Blood and grime came away on the handkerchief, which she rinsed time and again, scalding her fingers. Leaning back against a wall, he took involuntary pleasure in her close proximity – the concentration on her lips and in her flared nostrils, her constel-lations of freckles, the firm line of her eyebrows . . .

'Keep still!' Steadying his chin, she started on another cut, while he absorbed the smoky odour of her hair, the pale soft down on her upper lip, the force of her large hazel eyes challenging his each time they met. She glanced at him reproachfully.

'I hope you realise you'd be dead if it wasn't for me.'

'I wouldn't dare deny it.'

'Not to mention walking round with an infected face.'

'My debts pile up.'

'And I'll be the one who has to find you some respectable clothes.'

'A British officer is ever mindful of his image.'

'Forget your image. You blew that with the shaved head.'

'And what happened to your hair?' He lifted a hand to her head, carefully selecting several singed curls for inspection.

'I jumped through a fire.'

'You make a habit of jumping through fires?'

'The barn on the farm, eejit, I was trapped by your illustrious compatriots.'

'Anything else you want to blame me for while you're at it?' She glanced up, noting the sudden edge to his voice. 'Invading your country, killing your people, fighting under the same flag as the SAS . . .'

'Yes. Being too pig-headed to seize the opportunity of a lifetime.' Moving abruptly away, she produced the bowie knife which Corporal Hurst had assailed her with on the beach, and introduced its long blade to the flames of the fire.

'I hope you can take pain,' she said dispassionately.

She came at him with the white-hot knife, waved it in the moist air until it cooled and started on his face, delving into his flesh for slivers of glass which had eluded her.

'What's your name?' he asked through gritted teeth.

'Mind your own business and keep still.'

'You don't trust me with your name?'

'I'll start trusting you when you start trusting me.'

He flinched as she gouged out a splinter of glass and offered it to him on the tip of her finger.

'What happened to Michael?' A note of concern rang in her brisk question. 'Did Dixie . . .' She faltered, in loyalty to her former commander.

'Execute him?' supplied Marcus. 'No, the SAS arrived in the nick of time.'

'Did he get away?'

'I don't know.'

For a time, after she'd swabbed his face again, they compared experiences of the night the farm was raided.

'When I jumped from the burning barn, my first thought was not to escape but to get the bastards who'd tried to burn me to death. But as I went after them, tracking them like my father taught me as a girl to track wild animals, I realised that they in turn were tracking someone, and I wondered if it was you.'

264

'You tracked them so you could hassle me?'

'And I'm only going to ask you once more. After that you can go to hell. Take your shirt off.'

'Pardon?'

'Your shirt, off with it!'

He began to remove his jacket, smarting with the reaction of his ribs as he raised his arms. So she helped him out of his jacket and off with his T-shirt. Squatting back on his heels, his torso caught the golden light of the fire. Kneeling up in front of him, she ran her hands slowly over his burnished skin, testing its texture and heat, feeling it tremble slightly, alive to her touch. Eyes closing, she guided her fingertips over his skin from one small wound to the next, lingering on each abrasion, as if to heal it by the communion of touch. For a trance-like moment they knelt in the dawn-lit ruin, her hands resting on his body.

Then she took the knife to him, mainly his upper chest where slivers of glass were embedded in his firm flesh. These she dug out carefully, and washed the open cuts while threads of blood trickled down his body. Finally she drenched the boiled handkerchief in antiseptic solution, dabbed his cuts until his flesh burned and then caught him off guard.

'So what's it to be?'

Lulled by her touch, distracted by the antiseptic, it took a moment to realise what she was getting at.

'You want to join forces,' he recalled.

'And you?' she said, allowing him to struggle on with his clothes without her help.

'What did you have in mind?'

'You tell me first what you planned to do solo.'

He spread his hands in a gesture of modesty. 'A press conference – '

'Press conference!' she snorted.

'With TV cameras to reach the widest audience.'

She gave him a look which more or less said he was the biggest fool in the world and rose to scour the waking landscape through field-glasses. 'Even if they don't grab you beforehand, the power will still be in their hands. They'll decide which bit to show and whether you'll get one or two minutes squeezed between the World Cup and the new Royal baby. No sir!' – her face lit up with subversive inspiration – 'I'm thinking of something that will have the world on the edge of its seat!'

265

'What?' He scarcely wanted to hear.

The plan she proceeded to outline was so straightforward and appalling, so daring and on such a grand scale, that he could only gaze at her unblinking, wishing she was fantasising, knowing she wasn't. What most alarmed and intrigued him was that she had designed the plan to be carried out by him in partnership with her. But, stunned as he was, he opted to confound her by assuming a look of disappointment, a note of disdain. 'Is that it?'

'What do you mean, is that it?'

'I was expecting something ambitious, dramatic . . .'

Momentarily thrown, afraid she'd deluded herself, she quickly found her fury. 'Do you have to try, or are you naturally simple? Are you too dim-witted to see the sensation we'd cause, the blind panic down the corridors of power?'

Behind the frown, she saw he was laughing.

'Bastard,' she said, kicking a stray stone in his direction. She leaned in the doorway, hands thrust into her jacket pockets. 'What do you really think?'

'If it went wrong I could spend the rest of my life behind bars.'

'It won't go wrong.'

As the day passed and the fugitives conspired in the Donegal hills, Frank Mulraine flew south by helicopter from Derry. Descending over the Gothic-style spires and dusk-lit rivers of Omagh, he felt profoundly dejected by Marcus King's apparent treachery. Captain Lee and Corporal Hurst, whom he had interviewed at Strand Road RUC station in Derry, stated that they had tracked King together with the Red Sniper fifteen miles to an isolated barn. On closing in to apprehend them, Lee and Hurst were ambushed by a waiting IRA unit firing from the roof, while King and the sniper fired from inside the barn, forcing Lee and Hurst to withdraw, sustaining injuries taking avoiding action from exploding grenades, though not before firing back and wounding at least two Provos.

Mulraine sensed that he'd been treated to a mixed charade of bluff and truth, but it was plain from Lee and Hurst's cheerfully menacing expressions that he was expected to play the game. He was disinclined, though he didn't tell them so. Now he was faced with the problem of deciding which part of their story was distorted. Their description of the Red Sniper closely matched that provided by the proprietor of the hotel, suggesting a strong degree of truth in their account of tracking King and the IRA woman together. Yet Brother Dominic had spoken highly of Marcus King, rejecting insinuations of treachery. King was on the side of the angels and it was Mulraine's duty to protect him. Was Dominic naïve, too easily taken in? Or had circumstances forced King to throw in his lot with the IRA?

Mulraine subsided in his office, in the heavily fortified police station. A woman police constable landed yet another memorandum on his congested desk.

'That's right,' he protested, 'keep them coming!'

'Serves you right, sir, for neglecting us!'

She brought coffee, sandwiches, aspirin, a clean tumbler for his whiskey and a selection of newspapers featuring 'The Traitor' as starkly as a wanted poster on the front pages. Clad all in black, down to Provo-style beret, Marcus King was flourishing an Armalite two-handed, a tricolour flag for background. Not all the papers were convinced, some speculating that he might have been coerced. Despite mounting evidence, Mulraine resolved to keep an open mind as long as possible.

Loosening his tie, he poured a whiskey, lit a cigarette and skimmed through a stack of interrogation reports and confessions, including one signed by Michael O'Cinneíde, all ending with the standard rider, 'This statement is true. I made it of my own free will.' The next report that came to hand erased the satisfaction from his face. It amounted to an indictment from Doctor Nye, Senior Medical Officer at the station, accusing Mulraine's men of back-sliding into the kind of appalling practices which Amnesty International had uncovered, and which were supposed to have been eradicated by, amongst other measures, closed-circuit television. Attached to Doctor Nye's report was a letter of resignation.

Mulraine swore wearily. Tired, edgy and at sea with the Marcus King case, running on a poisonous mixture of alcohol, nicotine, catnaps and coffee, he was in the wrong humour for a crisis. Doctor Nye was a respected professional. The publicity would be appalling. To make matters worse, Michael O'Cinneíde should never have been interrogated at all. Mulraine had lifted him, however marginally, from the Irish side of the meandering border.

Summoning the two detectives against whom the most serious

accusations of torture had been made, Mulraine was rehearsing the encounter when the phone went: the red one – could only be one man. Lighting a fresh cigarette from its predecessor, he took a deep breath and answered with a jocund tone.

'Good evening!'

'That you, Inspector?' – The man himself, sitting on the right hand of God, the Chief Constable.

' 'Tis indeed, Sir Ian, I've been meaning – '

'Where on earth have you been? London's going mad, the traitor's picture is circulating the globe and I've been leaving messages all day!'

'Well it's all a bit of a pantomime, what with one thing and – '

'Where is King now, have you the slightest idea?'

'I've every port and airport sealed, so I'd say he's still in the country.'

'Oh that's a great help! Inspector, are you aware that not only has the deserter escaped again, but that in spite of our strenuous denials, Dublin is accusing us of deliberate incursions and shooting inside the Republic?'

'There was always that risk, Sir Ian.'

'I take it that you believed at the time that you knew where you were, if you take my meaning?'

'I knew exactly where I was – on the unmentionable side of the border.'

'Good God, Inspector, I trust that won't appear in your report? I'm fighting a rearguard action explaining your antics. It's vital you acted in good faith, believing the entire farm to have been in Ulster.' Mulraine wavered. 'Well?' snapped the Police Chief. 'I trust I may count on your co-operation?'

'To be sure, the border wiggles about a good deal in that region. A slight miscalculation can be – and was – fatal.'

'Exactly. It's a bad job and you're doing your best . . .' Mulraine knew his boss too well to be deceived by the switch to a more conciliatory tone, 'but let me be candid, Inspector. If this rascal isn't apprehended soon, someone will have to swing.' It was said lightly, almost jovially, a friendly warning, in deadly earnest.

'Keep up the good work, Inspector. Good night!'

Mulraine replaced the receiver without a word. So we're down to thinly veiled threats, he reflected, as there came a knock on the door, and two men entered hesitantly. Laurel and Hardy, he privately called them – Detective Sergeant Hewitt, a hearty ox of a man, and Detective Sergeant Fairley, a morose featherweight.

'Take a seat, gentlemen,' invited Mulraine dully, undone by the phonecall.

Hewitt set down a manila folder on Mulraine's desk. Something silver slid out and showed itself – a chain and charm. 'Good news, Chief! The boys have discovered the rat who makes these miniature Armalites, a Mr O'Duffy of Armagh.'

Mulraine swivelled the envelope and noted the jeweller's boldly printed address. A possible lead to identifying the Red Sniper. But he said nothing, muzzling his customary eagerness to praise. He merely looked up and met the wary gazes of his detectives. Hewitt a heavily-built, aggressively genial cop, sat perched on the edge of his chair, knee bouncing with nervous energy, face considerably older looking than his thirty-odd years, a permanent band of perspiration round his receding forehead. Mulraine had always worked well with Hewitt, but Fairley, blond and waspish, with a silent angular face and crisp moustache, made no attempt to hide his low opinion of Mulraine.

'Not a bad bunch of confessions!' suggested Hewitt affably. 'Another pack of bloody Provos nailed! Membership of the IRA, possession of explosives, hijacking, arson, murder, nose-picking – you name it, we got them!'

Mulraine lit another throat-parching cigarette and allowed a stressful pause to permeate the room.

'Did you read Doctor Nye's report, gentlemen?'

Hewitt glanced at Fairley, who remained inscrutable. It was plain to Mulraine by their loaded silence that they had read the report. Hewitt confirmed it.

'He's still recovering from a breakdown. His marriage is on the rocks. It may have affected his judgement.'

'That was unworthy of you,' said Mulraine. 'Doctor Nye is an impeccable professional.' He found the report and put on his glasses.

'These diagrams show abrasions, bruising, haemotomae and injuries to the tympanic membrane . . .' Mulraine looked calmly over the rims of his glasses at his men opposite, and continued in an even tone. 'Deprivation of sleep, nine-hour interrogations, hoodings, dorsi-flexing and the additional side-show of Michael O'Cinneíde – his dying mother's blood fresh on his clothing –

made to stand all night with his underpants on his head, beaten on parts of the body which don't bruise readily, genitals struck with a rolled-up newspaper each time the pants fell from his head . . .'

Silence.

Mulraine removed his glasses. 'But what does it achieve, gentlemen? Did you discover the names of Doyle's sidekicks, Black Rose and the redhead? No. Or Doyle's, or Marcus King's whereabouts? No. Did you make the world a safer place for the people of Ulster, or for ourselves in the RUC – ?'

'Aye, we did,' said Fairley darkly, breaking his silence. 'Every one of these vicious murdering bastards we send down is one less out there to ambush us, or plant a bomb under our cars!'

'No, Sergeant. Whatever you or I believe they deserve, every man we send down in this fashion' – slapping the report with the back of his hand – 'gives birth to another. Each time we break a man in here or Castlereagh, there's another waiting to pick up where he left off. A vicious cycle, reprisals begetting reprisals. How many of these confessions are admissible, and how many signed because they couldn't take any more? Out there in the community they're watching what we do, and what they see doesn't make them feel like turning against the IRA. No, gentlemen, we're making the world more dangerous for ourselves.'

Detective Sergeant Fairley rose abruptly. 'I'll tell you straight, sir. Some of the men don't care for your attitude. We don't like being told to go soft on terrorists who are shooting and bombing us at will. Most of us have seen mates maimed or killed, and you're expecting us to mind our manners! Now if you'll excuse me . . .' He made to leave.

'I do not excuse you, Sergeant,' growled Mulraine, and motioned the detective to return to his seat. 'Do you suppose I haven't lost my share of friends and colleagues? The longer you're in the job the more your heart becomes a graveyard . . . and the more heartless you become.'

Rising, he went to the blocked up reinforced window and hit it with the flat of his fist.

'The proof of folly, gentlemen. No light, no air. Why? Because this isn't a police station any more, it's a fortress. We're not policing communities any more, we're engaged in desperate civil war with them. You've seen the statistics. The harder we come down on the Nationalist community, the more of our men get killed. The harder the prison service comes down on Republican prisoners, the more of their members get killed. In which year did the British Army lose most men? '72, the year of Bloody Sunday. The harder we are, the harder we fall. When are we going to learn that simple formula?'

Unpredictably and untypically, Mulraine brought his fist down on his desk like a hammer, and told the men they could leave. 'And gentlemen?'

The detectives, one subdued, one glowering, turned at the door.

'I have a duty to preserve the good name of the force and to safeguard the lives of my men. However understandable your conduct may be, you are sullying the force and endangering lives. Think on it!'

Mulraine slumped in his chair. He privately predicted he would be outrageously misquoted and bitterly resented. Brooding at his desk, smoking and drinking, weary of mindless interrogators, cursing the insufferable Chief Constable, dreading reunion with the odious SAS, disillusioned with inglorious Marcus King, he cut a wretched, isolated figure as the night grew late.

He woke to find himself at his desk. The first light of a new day couldn't penetrate the sightless window, but his watch said six a.m. He needed no mirror to be shocked by the state of himself, and he was cradling his head when the phone went off in his ear. Please God, not yer man again!

The sound of Joe Twomey's voice instantly lifted him. Twomey, a Catholic counterpart in the Garda with whom he enjoyed a reciprocal back-scratching arrangement, had been appointed to track Marcus King on his side of the border. After interviewing Messrs Lee and Hurst in Derry the previous day, Mulraine had taken the risk of contacting Twomey.

'Didn't expect to catch you so early, Frank.'

'Making an early start, Joe.'

'How would you like some news?'

'Depends what it is.' Groping for a cigarette.

'Try this for size. We located the barn where Marcus King and assorted Provos ambushed, machine-gunned and rained grenades on your SAS associates . . . only they're leading you up the garden. There was no ambush, no bullets fired from the roof or anywhere outside the barn, and no grenades discharged. We

271

found evidence inside the barn of three rounds fired by an Armalite and about forty by Hecklers, German guns used by the SAS. No blood anywhere. The mystery thickens when we discover, in a ditch a few minutes away, the said Hecklers and two pairs of lightweight boots and socks, belonging, I suspect, to the SAS men. Interesting, don't you think?'

'Exceedingly.'

'We're working on it, but I confess, Frank, I'm flummoxed!'

'Quite so. Keep me posted. I owe you a Bushmills.'

'Make it a Jameson!'

'Ach, is there no culture in the South?'

Mulraine immediately put through a call to the border checkpoint where Lee and Hurst claimed to have gone after their adventure, and asked to speak to the officer in charge.

'Major Lomax here,' said Mulraine in his best Oxford English, 'just checking up on two gallivanting officers of mine . . .'

The officer in charge confirmed that Lee and Hurst had indeed materialised the previous day.

'Thank you, Lieutenant . . . Oh one more thing, did you notice anything unusual about their footwear?'

A pause. 'Yes, as a matter of fact. They didn't have any.'

'And how was this explained?'

'Lost them in a river, I think.'

'Splendid. Good-day.'

Mulraine sat back and closed his eyes. Why would Lee and Hurst abandon their boots and firearms and proceed to the border unarmed in bare feet? The answer which leapt to mind was too astonishing and too obvious. He would have to come back to it.

Plucking a fresh suit, shirt and tie from a hanger on the filing cabinet, he peeled off the polythene cover and went off to wash, shave and change, emerging a new man.

Down a harshly lit flight of steps he came to the cells and had himself admitted, without a guard, to Michael O'Cinneíde's cell. The cell was hot and airless, and reeked of the prisoner. Michael lay on his bed facing the scarred wall. The surrounding space was entirely empty, void, nothing with which a man could do himself in, save smashing his skull.

'Hello . . . ?' Too soft. The prisoner couldn't have heard. 'Mr O'Cinneíde?'

The big man came to life in a panic, sitting bolt upright, eyes flickering with terror. With one arm in a sling, his free hand groped for the safety of the corner.

'Remember me? Detective Inspector Mulraine. I found you in a wardrobe.'

Michael remembered and the fear began to drain from his swollen face.

'Your neighbours are cleaning up and the donkey's none the worse. I need to ask you some questions . . .'

He offered a cigarette to Michael, who declined with a hasty shake of the head. Mulraine lit up.

'It's about Marcus King – '

'I've a right to attend. . .!' Michael interrupted angrily.

'To attend what?'

'My mother's funeral!'

'Ah, yes.'

'God rot them!'

'You asked permission?'

'They laughed in my face, called me a bastard and her a whore.'

'And you want very much to be there?'

'I've a right, she's my mother!'

'I'll do what I can – '

'I don't care what they say!'

'It won't be easy. They won't like it for security reasons, but I'll do my best' – Michael was stilled – 'if you'll help me.'

'Swear?'

'Swear. Did Marcus King join the IRA?'

Michael shook his head. Mulraine held up a newspaper with the damning photograph on the front.

'Dixie's trick . . . King refused to join, the rifle was empty.'

'What's it doing in his hands?'

'I wasn't there, but they were going to chuck it at him.'

That explained the way King was holding the Armalite.

'Who was going to chuck it?'

'Dixie or Black Rose.'

'Her real name?'

Michael blinked and said nothing.

'Michael, I'm going to have to go to the very top to get you to that funeral. I need something from you. I want the name of one of the two women at least.'

'Eileen Feeley.'

'The redhead?'

'No! Black Rose – the bloody bitch!'

'Tell me about the redhead.' Michael clammed up. 'Why should she have teamed up with Marcus King?' Michael looked up, Mulraine thought he detected jealousy. 'You liked her?'

'Where is she?'

'I'm looking for her.'

'She's not like them!' Michael blurted. 'She fought cat and dog with Dixie and Feeley. She was against the bombs, like yer man – '

'King?'

'She wanted to clean up the IRA, she wanted to change us, she changed me, she made me think . . .' He was on his feet, swaying, making his points with clumsy gestures of his free arm. 'She's no terrorist!'

'What was she doing in the IRA?'

'What else is there to join? Nobody else is going to shift the Brits. But she wouldn't toe the line. Feeley wanted her shot, Dixie chained her up . . .'

'They appear to be in tandem at the moment, King and the redhead. What d'you make of that, Michael?'

Michael fell silent, eyeing Mulraine. At once sceptical, he sat down on the bed and became reflective, then troubled.

'You tried to kill Doyle . . .' Mulraine changing tack.

'Molly tried. He wouldn't let me go.'

'But you knew about it?'

'Yes. I wanted out. I was sick of it too.'

Mulraine pulled a scrap of paper from his pocket.

'What do you know about this? "Fuck the Taigs, Fuck the Prods, fuck the guns and bombs and Gods – " '

'Fuck the Pope, fuck the Queen,' continued Michael, 'Fuck the Paisley's poison dream – '

'OK, where does it originate?'

'I wrote it. I did my bit. But Dixie had to have more. He'd no right to take over the farm. It was Molly's home, our life. I wanted to go back to it, but Dixie wouldn't let me, and now . . .'

And now there was no Molly to return to. Michael closed his eyes, swayed. 'They got Pip too . . .'

Touching his arm, Mulraine led him back to the bed, where he resumed the position in which Mulraine had found him, curled up facing the wall.

17

Hiding in the hills, moving only at night, Annie and Marcus were thrown together for long periods. A volatile collaboration, highly inflammable.

Annie was an instinctive and aggressive leader and seized the role from Marcus at the outset. Or tried to. She had an unconscious need to contest the leadership. She was fearless and boundlessly self-confident. Being nine years younger than her new comrade didn't matter a jot. She'd rescued him from the SAS. She'd fought in the most feared active service unit in the province. She was convinced she could outshoot, outrun and outwit any soldier in the British Army.

Her self-confidence fed itself, and was finally her weakness. In order to cover the trauma of her childhood and youth, in order to protect her raw emotions, she had cultivated the thickest of skins, carved her sense of purpose from the hardest rock and assumed the darkest role she could bear to wear. But beneath the cloak, behind the resolve, crouching within her, was a dazed child ducking the next blow.

This did not prevent her, here and now, from setting her sights on taking Marcus home. Home was a country house in Rostrevor, a small picturesque town on the far side of Northern Ireland, in the south-eastern corner of the province. Home would be somewhere to hide and gather strength, a place from which to launch their joint assault on Dublin. And her father, if he didn't slam the door in her face, or call the police, had money, contacts and a pilot's licence. Annie had not told Marcus that she had quarrelled with her father and hadn't been home since. That was three years ago. It was even possible that her father, who had often spoken longingly of death, had finally done something about it.

Optimistic to the point of recklessness, Annie did not seriously consider the possibility that Papa would show her the door, turn her over to the law, or refuse to offer his services. She knew he adored her deep down, and that behind the successful civilised film-maker was a romantic revolutionary. All she had to do was stir the memory of his love, and awaken the rebel. Always assuming he was alive.

As time passed in the undisturbed hills, Marcus recovered his strength. His cracked ribs pained him, but he became quick and alert again, no longer the tame tiger Annie had taken him for. She discovered, to her annoyance and relief, that he was as single-minded as she was. He was as stubborn as she was determined. She couldn't move him. Time and again she turned away, exasperated by what she called his quaint sensibilities, his high-mindedness. She accused him of all the moral fussiness which Dixie and Feeley had found in her. He was attracted to the scale and drama of her vision, but stood firm against any plans which might lead to bloodshed. Pooh-poohing his cautiousness, Annie envisaged a deed in Dublin so grand and so spectacular that it would be worth having lived and died for. It would be the pinnacle of her life, a performance to erase all failures. Death would be but a stunned curtain-call.

Marcus agreed to the deed. But Annie was forced to compromise on the method. In their conflicting personalities and separate quests, there was just sufficient common spirit and purpose to fashion an awe-inspiring alliance.

Leaving Marcus to chew his nerves in the hills, Annie crossed the border into Northern Ireland under cover of darkness and crept into Strabane, a market town on the gravelly banks of the River Mourne, lying in the shadow of the Sperrin Mountains. Annie had heard only two details about Strabane: it had reputedly the highest unemployment of any town in Europe, and its RUC barracks had once been bombed from the air by the IRA in a hijacked helicopter.

Her interest in the town was confined to the range of department stores she hoped it would provide. She wanted to find some sort of disguise for Marcus – dark glasses, hooded anorak, skin lightener. The thought of bleaching his skin repelled her even more than it did him.

The town woke slowly. Scratching her insect bites she sauntered through the centre, locating a chemist and modest department store, neither open yet. An RUC patrol appeared, two Landrovers bristling with armed men cutting across the light traffic. Turning her back, she gazed into a shop window, monitoring the reflected progress of the patrol. The first Landrover cruised by, the second slowed, and she felt policemen's eyes like lasers in her back. She remained still, a loaded pistol in her shoulder-bag, her hair pinned up inside her beret, hands thrust in the pockets of her short leather jacket. The patrol moved on.

She looked about, indifferent to the scattering of citizens abroad in the first rays of morning. Her eyes scanned one street after another – a betting shop, newsagent, repair garage, church hall advertising its gym for young boxers, a funeral parlour, chip shop, café. She strolled along the street and entered the café, crowded with rough men at failing tables, faces lined with drink and toil, shoulders down, voices low.

Gravitating to the only unoccupied table, she sat down, her back to the wall, skimming faces, mechanically absorbing the details of the room through the smoke and steam which held up the flaking ceiling – worn tiles, strip lighting, plastic ads for Tango, Pepsi, 7– Up, a sign saying DO NOT ASK FOR CREDIT, and on every table a salt and pepper cellar, vinegar bottle and charred aluminium ashtray.

An aproned teenage girl came to take her order. Annie opted for a full cooked breakfast and sat back again. The room began to fall quiet, voices and crockery stilled, until by the time her meal arrived, only the radio was imperviously predicting the weather. She was very hungry, and began to eat, her senses attentive to the smell, taste and texture of hot food. And a chipped mug of glorious tea.

At first she mistook the excessive interest in her for sexual appetite. But when the place became hushed as a church, she looked up and met rows of hard gazes, all asking a single unspoken question. Word had reached the farthest table, a question mark on every face. Eyes were shifting back and forth between a picture on the front pages of their newspapers and Annie's face and dress. Each time she intercepted their gazes they averted their eyes, only to return to her bolder than before.

She ate regardless, her appetite ruined, the food flavourless and slippery in her mouth. Forcing it down with gulps of tea, she hurried without seeming to, ignoring the men and their murmurings, but watching the windows and door for the framed figures of armed police, or the bark of an Army loudhailer.

A man by the window broke the hush. 'Here they come . . .'

She heard him. Incapable of telling whether he was broadcasting a fraternal warning or merely testing her, she obstinately finished her meal before slapping enough stolen SAS money on the table to cover the bill, and headed for the door. Men twisted in their chairs, all eyes following her. Opening the door, she peered out. A pair of RUC Landrovers had one end of the street blocked, officers checking pedestrians and motorists wishing to pass. Turning to the men in the café, she spread a winsome smile.

'Raise your mugs, gentlemen . . . to a united Ireland!'

She walked up the street away from the road-block, only to find, as she came to the other end of the street, that this too was covered, albeit more casually, by a solitary parked vehicle and four officers, two in the vehicle and two in the street.

Reaching inside her shoulder-bag, her hand emerged holding a scarf, with something hard and heavy concealed within its silken folds. The officers in the street were holding a relaxed conversation, but without once looking at each other, their eyes scanning the thin crowds.

She came closer, walking confidently, mind fixed on getting safely past and out of the town as quickly as possible, no lingering, no purchases. She felt herself enter their line of vision, and added a lighter note to her step. She felt the eyes of both officers attach themselves to her. Holding her breath, she braced herself but kept walking, past them now, well past, safe, almost safe . . .

'One moment, Miss. . .!'

She felt the pull of his harsh Ulster voice. There were other young women about but she felt the cut of that voice like a whip. Making as though she hadn't heard, she strolled innocently on.

'Hold it, Miss. . .!' She heard heavy footsteps breaking into a run. 'Stop right there!'

She kept walking, heart drumming in step with her will. As the footfalls bore down on her, she broke into a run, calling over her shoulder as she went. 'Can't stop, I've a bus to catch!'

'Never mind your bus' – the chase was on – 'halt or we fire!'

The full seriousness of her situation struck her. She didn't need to look round to know that the two constables were at that moment on the point of shooting her.

She spun round, caught them midway through the act of lifting their rifles, and fired.

Three shots in quick succession . . .

The scene developed before her eyes like a run of rapid photographs – the first policeman clutching his left thigh and dropping his rifle, his colleague also receiving a round in the left thigh and performing an identical routine, as though part of a double act. Behind them, a third oficer, stepping from the Landrover, suddenly seized his shoulder and reeled backwards, different routine, same shock fusing with agony on his face.

Annie ran, the screams of horrified passers-by reverberating in her ears. She turned the first corner and went herself like a bullet, bolting as never before, creating a keen wind resistance as she sprinted down one street after another, pausing suddenly at the sound of sirens breaking over the town behind her. Before she could take another step, she saw a posse of police running down a side street towards her, scattering people and shouting as they hunted for her.

Taking the next turning, she walked rapidly, fighting back unfamiliar pangs of fear, scouring the route ahead for an escape. Sirens grew more strident, coverging from all directions. Pressing on, she caught sight of a church and rushed towards its open doors.

It was a Catholic church, rich in carvings, studded with mosaics, dim down the ambulatories, bright where the sun broke in streams through the east window. A false sense of peace filled her eyes and ears. The deeper she went, the fainter the sirens sank in the distance. Here was a cool sanctuary, adrift from the world, deceptively safe, so blissfully detached that people who'd arrived early for Mass seemed not to hear the rise and fall of the approaching hunt. Waiting for the priest to arrive, they moved quietly about the church, or sat with their thoughts, or kneeled with their rosaries.

Annie picked her way among the shadows to the rear of the church, seeking a back way out. Venturing into the priests' private quarters she came to the sacristy, where a nun was arranging flowers in a vase.

'Forgive me, Sister . . .' Locking the door, Annie turned to the nun, gun in hand.

Landrovers slewed to a halt in the street, armed police spilled out. A heated argument was in progress, a woman vowing that the fugitive had gone into the church, a man swearing she hadn't. The man was promptly arrested. Policemen rushed to cover the rear of the church, three others entered cautiously at the front, sub-machine-guns discreet but ready, and fanned out to choose their own cover, searching the outlines, faces and dress of the scattered worshippers, who even now would not be distracted from their quiet wanderings.

One officer advanced up each ambulatory, a sergeant progressed carefully up the aisle, a nun appeared, placing flowers on the altar, genuflecting and kneeling to pray.

'Sister. . .?' whispered the sergeant. He waited, hovering, hoping she wouldn't be long. 'Sister, pardon me for interrupting . . .'

The nun rose, turned, focused blearily through thick lenses on the darkly clad officer, hugely inflated by his flak jacket, and gasped. 'Holy heart o' Jesus, will you put that thing away!'

'I'm sorry, Sister,' said the sergeant, retracting the awful sub-machine-gun, 'but we believe a terrorist may have come in just now. I was wondering did you see a tall redhead in a beret and leather jacket?'

'Here's Father O'Driscoll now,' replied the nun, nodding past his shoulder.

The sergeant turned to meet the disconcerted priest. As the two men conferred, the nun tripped along the aisle and slipped out through the front doors into the sunshine. Wearing a grey veil and habit, thick glasses on her face and trainers on her feet, she attracted little interest as she walked by the policemen moving onlookers away, and proceeded along the street, which more police were already cordoning off. A helicopter throbbed above the church, sirens wailed, soldiers began to arrive from several directions, running past her, faces drawn with excitement and tension.

Back in the church, confessionals, antechambers and chapels had been searched. Only the sacristy and vestry remained. The priest was ushered out of danger, the sergeant tried the door-handle and jumped to one side. The door swung open. An elderly nun was sitting upright on a chair. Dressed only in a plain slip, she was modestly covered by a priest's vestment. Gazing steadfastly ahead, she was murmuring to herself: '. . . ninety-three, ninety-four, ninety-five . . .'

The sergeant and his men entered gingerly.

'Are you all right, Sister?'

The nun finished counting and sighed. 'She made me promise to count to a hundred before raising the alarm, in return for not hurting me or locking me in.' Then in response to the officers' dumb stares she added, 'One must keep one's promises.'

'Sergeant!' A constable had just uncovered a pile of clothes – jeans, leather jacket, scarf and beret.

The nun doubled back through the town and reached a main street, walking quickly, drawing scant attention despite the flabby ill-fitting habit, the long bare legs which it failed to cover, and the incongruous trainers. Tucking stray locks of red hair inside her veil, peering over the rims of her impenetrable lenses, she combed the street for the best way out of town.

Sirens were coming after her. By now they would know they were hunting a grey nun. She had minutes, or less, to find an escape. She thought about jumping on a bus or hijacking a car, but road-blocks would be in place. She started to run, eyes working feverishly now, scouring doorways, alleys, rooftops . . .

Across the street a coffinless hearse was squeezing into a funeral parlour's forecourt. Leaving the engine running, the driver threw his cap on the seat and hurried into the office.

The nun crossed the street. The driver could be seen in the office, back turned, smoking a cigarette. Without further deliberation, she opened the driver's door and climbed behind the wheel. Slapping the driver's stiff cap over the veil on her head, she reversed the heavy black limousine into the street. As she pulled away, she saw the driver in the office window, chatting, smoking, fanning his face with a newspaper.

Traffic was light but unpredictable, motorists distracted by the sirens. To get past them, Annie opened up the throttle, switched on her headlights and recklessly overtook every vehicle in her path, forcing oncoming traffic to yield. Teeth clenched, she drove with gusto, taking desperate risks . . . until the traffic began to accumulate, slowing and swelling, grinding gradually to a halt, a long queue to the inevitable road-block at the edge of the town. Trapped. There had to be another way out.

Thrusting the hearse into gear, she reared out into the path of oncoming traffic and roared off down a narrow side street, swinging the limousine through a maze of grim terraces, emerging

281

suddenly on a disused cobbled road that cut through a stretch of wasteland, where packs of dogs gave chase and knots of children, thinking it must be something official, hurled stones at the passing hearse. Annie ducked. A stone missed her window but cracked the one behind her. Stones clattered off the chassis to cheers from the children.

The terraces ended abruptly like broken ribs. Ahead stood a wire fence, running seemingly for ever to left and right, blocking the way to rising countryside and a vast sweep of hills. Swerving along the fence, Annie drove over the hard jagged ground until she came to a gate. When she leapt out to open it, she found it padlocked. The first of the trailing band of children to arrive stood in amazement at the sight of a tall nun in a cap reaching into the folds of her habit, taking aim with a gun and shooting the padlock off the gate. Throwing the gate wide, she ran back to the car, calling after the fleeing children.

'Hey! Don't go!' A few of them stopped and looked round. 'Do me a favour, and close it after me!'

Plunging the car into lush fields on the far side, she saw in her mirror the children dutifully closing the gate. Sounding the horn in thanks, she concentrated on the wild open ranges ahead, trying to find her bearings.

As sirens wailed over the outspread town behind her, she climbed through clipped meadow, where families stopped their hay-making to watch the hearse rush by. Sweeping serenely through farmyards, panicking chickens, causing old men to raise their caps, the limousine soared into the hills.

Swerving onto a signposted road, Annie swung south and then east, anxious to cross back into the Republic without meeting a checkpoint and without being trapped by one of the many rivers around the town.

Tyres slashed and sagging, the hearse limped up to a quiet petrol station. A little earlier Annie had passed a lonely Orange Lodge, its Union Jack limp in the breezeless morning air, reminding her that she was still in British County Tyrone. But here, opposite the garage, stood a roadside shrine, a timeless reposeful Virgin Mary, reassuring the hectic modern traveller that he – or she – was safely back in the arms of the Republic.

By the limousine's clock it was twenty to eleven. She'd warned

Marcus to come down from the hills at eleven, and to expect her in a stolen car. If she wasn't there by eleven, he was liable to throw off the rough cover of nature and expose himself to great danger for nothing. She wasn't sure where she was, but she calculated he was at least five miles away and all she had was a disabled hearse.

Irish security forces might have been alerted by now, and the hearse would betray her if she simply abandoned it on the road. Still just out of sight of the garage's office, she reversed the wobbly vehicle as far as the rusty iron gate of a hedged field. Parking the limousine tight behind the hedge inside the field, she refastened the gate and ran back along the road, walking sedately across the garage forecourt, too late to prevent a delivery van from pulling out onto the road and driving away.

Adjusting her hair beneath the veil, she entered the office.

'Morning, Sister.' A young man smiled at her, his eyes more than politely interested in her youthful face. He stopped chewing and turned down the volume on his transistor radio. 'What can I be doing for you?'

'I'm lost, so I am.'

'Lost!'

'And I'm very late!' she smiled. 'Quick, if you please – a map!'

'Right away!'

He selected and spread a map, leaning over the counter to interpret the map and enjoy a closer look at this breathtaking young lady of the cloth. As she followed his effusive but protracted efforts to pinpoint the garage, her eyes strayed past his nose to the sleek red Mercedes swinging off the road into the garage, and to the portly well-heeled gentleman who climbed out.

The young man continued whispering sweet directions in her ear, the Mercedes owner filled up and strode towards the office, and a happy-go-lucky radio DJ broke transmission to announce:

'An item of local news has just landed before me . . . and it's not so good . . . Three members of the RUC shot and wounded this morning in the centre of Strabane, apparently by a terrorist disguised as a nun and thought to be Dixie Ragdoll Doyle's mysterious redhead. . .'

'Thanks,' said Annie, straightening to leave, 'you're very good.'

'Not at all, any time!' said the young admirer, his smile wavering as he began to register what his ears were picking up from the radio.

Her expression changed, a shadow crossed her face, she held him in a penetrating gaze.

'You never saw me, right?' She winked, stepping back from the door to allow the Mercedes owner to barge in.

Armalite wrapped in sacking, Marcus sprang from the hills, emerging on a minor road near the riverside village of Killygordon at a minute to eleven by Annie's watch.

He felt good. His cracked ribs pained him, but he felt sharp and hopeful. In partnership with Annie, there was a good chance of pulling off an all-purging act of atonement, sufficiently non-violent – if nothing went wrong – to avoid bloodshed and consequent imprisonment, but dramatic enough to bury the ghost of Bernie O'Rawe and settle his score with the Army.

Standing between himself and an act as daring as any British soldier had ever contemplated was a perilous journey to Annie's home, an unscheduled flight to Dublin, and finally the execution of the operation. He was reflecting how, if all went to plan, he would still almost certainly face a spell in gaol, when he noticed the approach of a car, coming at high speed, flashing in the sun, almost a mirage on the bend. Glancing at his watch – one minute past eleven – he turned his back and concentrated on the river. The car beeped and screeched to a searing halt. His heart thundered, a door opened.

'Get in, dreamer!'

A red Mercedes, a nun leaning across, an ironic grin on her face.

Armagh City

In the tumbling streets beneath the medieval carved heads of the Protestant cathedral, Frank Mulraine discovered a narrow door-way, and checked the number against the piece of paper in his hand.

The door jingled as he entered the dim dusty jeweller's and waited for someone to appear. The door squeaked shut, removing the town. Mulraine stood patiently, taking in the well-trodden floor, the murky cobwebbed ceiling, the lustreless wares in gloomy display cases – pendants and lockets, brooches and bracelets, cufflinks and pocket watches.

An old dog, worn and scraggy, appeared from behind the ancient counter, shuffled a few steps and lay down to scratch and lick himself. Mulraine recalled the Border collie he'd found dead in the smoke-filled bullet-ridden farm, and the call he'd put through just now to the Chief Constable, requesting permission for Michael O'Cinneíde to attend his mother's funeral. Permission refused. Mulraine was wondering how he was going to deliver the news to the tormented man, when the jeweller appeared through a threadbare curtain and limped behind the counter, a wizened old man in a tired pin-striped suit. Peering speculatively over the rims of his half-moon spectacles, he said wistfully, 'I suppose this one could go down as a reasonably agreeable morning.'

'Quite so, but a touch close for me.'

'So long as we're not cold.'

Pausing to nod politely, Mulraine hit the point. 'I wonder if you can help me?'

'Let's hope so.'

'I'm trying to trace a young relation of mine, who may have visited your shop. I was wondering if you might remember a striking young woman, five-foot-nine or ten and slender, rangy you might say, with a long face and a shock of red hair – hard to miss.'

The jeweller pursed his lips and shook his head.

'A lot of people have come through that door, and to be frank I wouldn't remember her if she'd appeared in all her glory.'

Undeterred, Mulraine produced a manila envelope and slid the broken chain and Armalite charm into his palm.

'This is what she would have purchased.'

The jeweller grunted an accord. But taking a close look at the miniature Armalite, he shook his head once more.

'Do you sell many?'

'One or two.'

'A week, a year?'

'A month.'

'But you're positive you wouldn't remember. . .?'

'No.'

'Perhaps you keep a record of purchases?'

The old man cleared his throat and pushed a well-thumbed ledger across the counter. 'It'll say something like chain-and-Arm.'

Donning his glasses, Mulraine leafed through the book. The chain-and-Arms had been yielding £13 for more than three years, but nothing else was recorded, only the date and method of payment.

'You don't often raise your prices,' he observed.

'I forget.'

Mulraine removed his glasses and, smiling philosophically, produced a printed card with his name, address and telephone number.

'I wonder if you would be so kind, not withstanding the matter of a handsome reward, to contact me should the young lady return in search of a replacement?'

'What would her name be?'

Caught off guard, Mulraine flushed. He hadn't a clue, that was the point. Quickly recovering, he said, 'She goes under various names. Joan of Arc, I dare say!'

As he opened the door, he turned. 'One more thing, Mr O'Duffy, could I buy one of these over the counter?'

'No. You give me your initials and return in ten days.'

'You send off for them?'

'I make them myself and I take my own time.'

'You don't keep them in stock? A customer would have to return to collect?'

'Naturally, since I can't predict the names they go by.'

Mulraine stepped back inside the shop. 'I don't think I follow.'

'The inscription' – the old man consulted the card on the counter – 'Mr Mulraine, represents the wearer's initials. Your charm would be inscribed "FM".'

Mulraine felt an unexpected rush of anticipation. 'Then this one's an exception?'

'A coincidence,' corrected the jeweller. 'A–R–M form your young lady's initials, do they not? Or the initials of her latest persona.'

Mulraine gazed at the charm in his palm. 'Of course. How silly of me. Good day.'

He stood, momentarily dazed, in the street. How foolish he'd been to assume blindly that ARM stood, unimaginatively, impersonally and pointlessly, for Armalite. Instead he carried in his fist the first letter of the Red Sniper's Christian name, middle name and surname. His men would simply have to check the births of females born with those initials between the years of roughly 1957 and 1962. If Joe Twomey would carry out identical checks on the other side of the border . . .

Crossing town to rejoin his helicopter, Mulraine entertained a

few inspired guesses. Anne Rosaleen McKenna. . .? Agnes
Roxanna Moloney. . .? Angela Rowena McLaughlin. . .?

18

In a safe house deep in Donegal, in an upstairs room with a long
range view of the turquoise sea, Dixie Doyle set down his crutches
and lay down, hands behind head, to listen to the latest radio
news.

'Fuck the news,' said Feeley, standing in the window, elbow in
hand, smoking a cigarette. 'We've got work to do, new recruits to
find. We've got to get that foot back to life and go after McBride and
the Brit.'

The SAS bullet had permanently damaged Dixie's foot. The
doctor who'd secretly attended him and removed the bullet had
admitted as much. 'Bollocks!' had been Feeley's diagnosis, the
doctor simply couldn't conceive of Dixie's willpower.

*'The headlines. Three RUC officers were shot and wounded in Strabane
this morning by the so-called Red Sniper. She subsequently evaded a joint
Army–RUC net, apparently disguised as a nun. The hunt continues both
sides of the border for escaped Army deserter Marcus King, thought until
this morning's incident to be on the run in tandem with the Red Sniper . . .
the hunt also continues for Dixie Doyle and Black Rose, named last night
by the RUC as Eileen Feeley of Beechwood Avenue, Creggan, Derry. It is
the first time a name has been attached to the notorious raven-haired
terrorist . . .'*

Feeley turned from the window and glowered at the radio.

*'In the Donegal village of Johnstown, security preparations are underway
for the funeral tomorrow of Molly O'Cinneíde, mother of captured terrorist
Michael O'Cinneíde. Molly O'Cinneíde was shot dead on Wednesday night
during a controversial SAS assault on her border farm . . .'*

'The slippery bastard!' fumed Feeley, referring to Michael. 'I
knew the minute they got him he'd never keep his mouth shut.'
Flinging her cigarette out of the window, she let a smile transform
her face: 'Now we'll be pasted up together – Wanted! Ten
thousand pound reward for Dixie Doyle and Eileen Feeley!'

He returned her smile.

'We'll be back in business in no time, Dixie!'

He let out a wry laugh. He was thinking of Annie as a gun-toting nun. Original all right! How he'd hated her for running out on him and running off with that black Brit.

But now, as he lay back blinded by the spectacular pain from his foot, he could almost find it in his heart to forgive her, and though he longed more than anything to reach Mary and Josie in Dublin, a part of him wanted to be out there with Annie McBride, raising merry hell through Tyrone and Londonderry. To his surprise and shame he found himself missing Annie McBride with the pangs of a smitten youth.

Inspired, he swung his feet to the floor, grabbed his crutches and hobbled carefully back and forth across the room, finally pausing for breath.

'Getting there,' applauded Feeley, restlessly lighting another cigarette, hawkishly watching Dixie, trying to read his mind, gauge his condition. Despite the wounded foot and the gaunt face made haggard by his refusal to take painkillers, he still cut a grand figure in the window, raw-boned and keen-eyed against the summer sky.

'Where do you say we'll start?' she asked eagerly.

'What?'

'Tracking down those wormy bastards.'

'Damn them, forget them, they're doomed.'

Scandalised: 'Forget them?'

'I've no time for Annie McBride, and as for Mr King, our job was to get him and we got him, snatched the bastard from the invincible SAS, fooled half the world that he'd joined us. That'll do. I've had my fill of Marcus King, and anyway – '

'We're not letting McBride get away with this,' vowed Feeley, 'somebody's got to go after her.'

'Somebody, yes. But I'm going to Dublin to see my family and recuperate – '

'They're the last people you need now.'

'I've been away fighting twelve years,' he said, setting off once more on his crutches, dragging his shattered foot like a ball and chain. 'I need a break.'

'You need me to get you back in shape.'

'A long break.'

'They'll only sap your will.'

'I'm going home.'

'How long for?' She tried to sound casual.

He didn't reply. Instead he flung one of his crutches away. 'Got to learn to walk without these . . .' and set his sights on crossing the room with only one stick.

Grinding her cigarette under her heel, she made to come to his aid.

'Stay where you are!' Finding his balance, he eased himself off the wall and started across the room, steering a course between the bed and the breakfast table, face taut with suppressed pain. There was even a glint of triumph in his eye, up till the moment that a bolt of pain snatched away his breath, making him stagger and lose himself, propelling him drunkenly into the low table, where he crashed to the floor under an avalanche of crusts and crockery.

Out in the fields crows gathered, filling the summer air with their malevolent cries.

An hour earlier, only a few miles away, Annie McBride was collecting Marcus from the roadside.

'From sharpshooter to nun,' he admired, climbing into the car, 'that's quite a transformation, sister!'

'Sister' he playfully pronounced in a broad Jamaican accent. She smiled mysteriously, imbued with her own power.

'Like the car?'

'I like the car. Where did you get it, or shouldn't I ask?'

As she began to tell him, he found himself sitting on a newspaper, the *Cavan Leader*, belonging to the Mercedes' real owner. He became grave at the sight of himself on the front, in black IRA uniform brandishing an Armalite, beside an artist's impression of Annie in a short leather jacket, curls bursting from under her beret. The sketch traced her long nose and face, dark brows and full mouth, and captured in the eyes her fearless spirit. Under the headline RED SNIPER AND BLACK FUGITIVE TEAM UP was an account of how the SAS allegedly tracked the unlikely twosome across the border into Donegal, before they escaped, probably into the hills.

'We're famous already!' Annie declared.

'Famous?' Marcus's humour failed him. 'Everyone wants to believe I've gone over to your lot.'

'My lot!' Annie protested. 'They're not my lot any more, I'm on my own.'

'This kind of shit,' said Marcus, slapping the paper, 'isn't going to help us in Dublin.'

'Don't worry,' Annie laughed, 'there's worse to come!'

The worse she was predicting came from the car radio as Annie steered the Mercedes through the narrow heights of the Barnesmore Gap in the shadow of the Blue Stack Mountains. The midday news reported the shooting of three policemen in Strabane that morning by the Red Sniper.

'Don't look at me like that!' said Annie with an angry laugh. 'It was self-defence. I shot to wound, I could have killed them, they'd have killed me.'

They drove for a time in silence, Annie seething, feeling Marcus's reservations, his heavy brooding. Skirting Donegal town, they were coming out of the mountains, descending to the coastal plain, when Annie suddenly slammed on the brakes, throwing Marcus forward, jarring his ribs.

'Get out!' she said.

He looked at her, amazed.

'I said get out!'

He spread his arms and shrugged, as if to say, What did I do?

'Listen, mister, you're either with me or against me. We're either up to our necks together, or we're not' – eyes blazing – 'You think this is a picnic for me? You think it's easier deserting from the British Army than the IRA? Have you any idea what they'd do to me if they caught me? *You're* OK. Any murders you've committed are considered legitimate. You even get medals! I've shot dead two soldiers of an occupying army and I've had it, soldier. I've got nowhere to go. After we pull our stunt in Dublin, what happens to me, huh?'

'You make it sound like a game, you make it all sound like a game.'

'How else am I going to get through this? You think I'm made of mortar? I could have got pumped with bullets this morning and this is your attitude! I was threatened with guns and protected myself, and all you can do is pull a long face. I was caught in Strabane by police and soldiers, and shot my way out without killing anyone. What should I have done? Knocked them down with my tits? Get out!'

Lowering his eyes, he found the door handle. 'I'm sorry,' he said quietly, and slowly got out, closing the door after him. He thought he ought to have some luggage, a knapsack – something. But he stood in the road with nothing but the clothes on his body, and watched the Mercedes roar away, gathering speed through the gears, disappearing round the bend.

Dust settled, and the stillness of the valley. He stood for a time dazed on the deserted pass. Then he climbed a heathery slope, startling a pair of ducks which erupted in his face before lifting over the glen and climbing to the refuge of one of the many brooding mountain lakes. He sat down.

He closed his eyes. Soft drizzle, warmed by sunlight, played on his bullet head. His fingers found the growing stubble, pushing forth to find the light, covering his guilt. He thought of Bernie O'Rawe, barely able to recapture her face. He thought of his quarrel with the Army, their attempts to gag him, to have him certified. He recalled the breakout, the Landrover drive in search of a newspaper, the weird night in the convent, the journey north via the ghostlands of Thorn Hill, the crossing to Inishtrahull, Dominic's clear blue eyes. With a spasm of horror he remembered the car-park kidnapping and how they had chained him in the attic, the terrifying moments after Black Rose photographed him, when he thought they were going to shoot him in cold blood. Then to be saved by the night-splitting assault on the farm, and to break free once more, leaping from the attic into the raging storm, fleeing through the woods on a slithering motorbike, trying to steer with his hands still in chains, struggling to stay with the bike as it plummeted down a blind bank to a stream. He recalled his trek over wild boglands and heathery moors, his encounter with the gipsies – travellers as Annie called them – then the vicious hand-to-hand combat in the gloomy barn, and finally his timely deliverance, courtesy of the Red Sniper!

And all to end up on his arse in the gorse, dressed in black tatters, unwashed and unshaven, gazing out over Donegal Bay and no plan in sight.

As the rain washed his head, he heard a car, its compelling roar carrying through the valley. He listened to it coming and prayed it was her, returning up the hill she'd gone down. It sounded like the same car. His mind conjured its shape and colour, and he found himself scrambling down the hillside, willing it to be her, wondering what he would do, after this rush of hope, if it wasn't.

A red Mercedes shot into view, soaring up the hill, slowing, the driver looking for him, perhaps surprised he wasn't there. He cupped his hands and shouted, his voice lifting over the valley. The car carried on, climbing and out of sight.

He reached the road, heart beating hard, convinced she'd be back, drawn to the exact spot where she'd left him. He waited, staring at the place where she'd melted into the hillside, listening to the silence that hung like heat on the road.

She came slowly, window rolled down, looking not ahead but up at the lush and rugged slopes. When she saw him, there was a moment's trance-like recognition, before she must have flattened the accelerator in fury, making the car leap down the hill towards him. He put out his thumb and smiled like a polite hitcher.

Screeching to a halt, she got out, slamming the door, and came round the bonnet of the car, arms folded, glaring at him with the tears standing up in her eyes. He read the hard mask, the vulnerable expression. Unswervingly returning her gaze, he slowly offered his hand.

'I'm with you.'

It was eighty miles, as the crow flies, to Annie's home in the east. But crossing Northern Ireland would have been too dangerous and they opted to work their way round through the Republic, keeping to obscure roads, trebling the distance.

But before they could begin to go east, they were forced south and west by the encroaching border, driving them towards the Atlantic where they met a test of nerves at Ballyshannon, a steeply clinging town on the River Erne. On the right-hand side the sea, on the left-hand side the border, ahead the river. The only way forward was through the town and over the bridge.

'A road-block on the bridge and it's all over,' observed Marcus.

'Bar the shooting,' said Annie.

He looked at her sharply.

'Joke,' she said, cocking her eye at him. 'All the same, we better stick you in the boot.'

They pulled off the road on the outskirts of town. Annie removed her veil and told him to take off his T-shirt.

'What for?'

Frowning, motioning him to hurry: 'Give!'

He pulled the torn sweaty garment over his head and she made herself a scarf with it.

'What happened to your crucifix?' she wondered, taking in the bare valley of his chest bone. His hand went uneasily to the space.

'Tore it off in the attic.'

'A fugitive's despair! Lord, why hast thou forsaken me? I aimed for that crucifix on Thorn Hill. You're quick for a big man. How do I look?'

Reaching over, he tucked several unruly locks of flaming hair inside the makeshift scarf.

'Did you know I had three cracks at you?' she said as he worked on her. He shook his head and glanced evenly into her eyes. 'Dixie never told you?' She let out a laugh. 'You didn't know you were top of the hit list?'

'Me! Why me?'

'Christ, you're naïve.'

'Because I was winning – '

' – the hearts and minds of the community!' she chimed.

'Three times?'

'The football game, remember?'

'You were there?'

'I had you fixed in my sights, but the armour arrived in the nick of time.'

Marcus smiled. Major Draycott and the C.O. had inadvertently saved his life that day.

'And the third time?'

'Oh, come on!'

He laughed and shook his head. 'How should I know?'

'During the battle, after you handed over the body, didn't an officer fall dead at your feet?'

'And you were aiming for me! You're supposed to be a crackshot!'

'I changed my mind, eejit! I had the sights slipped over your head like a necklace. But when it came to the sticking point . . .' She lowered her eyes.

'You had a soft spot for me?' He threw back his head and roared with laughter, only to be shocked by a violent slap on his breast. Blowing on her scorched hand, she said 'Come on!' and got out of the car. Finding the right key, she opened the boot. 'This would all be a lot simpler if you weren't black, you realise that!'

'I didn't have a lot of say in it,' he replied, climbing in. 'If I'd known, I'd have asked God to make me reversible.'

'You believe in God?'

She held the boot open, he drew in his limbs.

'Yeah.'

'What God?'

'God knows!'

'If it's a man in the sky watching us masturbate, you can keep him.'

'Who said it was a man?'

'I should hope not!'

'No woman either, sister!'

'Don't be so sure.'

'More like a feeling.'

'Like orgasm?'

Marcus reflected, and rain ducked under the boot and jewelled his bare arms and shoulders.

'Yeah. If it's a good feeling, it's God.'

'Bullshit. I can feel good kicking some people I know up the arse. Call that God!'

'No. A good feeling has to be a right feeling.'

'A right good feeling!' she scorned. 'Get down!' Her hand landed on his shoulder, pressing him down so she could slam the boot.

'Hey! I don't want it closed!'

'What do you mean, you don't want it closed!'

'What I said, I want to breathe!'

The rain was kind, stippling the windows of the car, making it harder to see in. Annie drove calmly through the town, the nun's habit a respectable dress, Marcus's T-shirt covering her famous hair. Under her thigh lay her pistol, down by her side lurked the unfolded loaded Armalite. She was not prepared to be taken alive.

In the event the town was disappointingly quiet, cyclists taking shelter, off-duty soldiers heading for the bars, drifts of American tourists lingering in sensible weatherproofs on the bridge, not a cop in sight, the whole place lulled by the onshore breeze, oblivious to the troubled border.

Marcus held on, peering out of the boot, watching one town recede and the next arrive – Bundoran, a crowded seaside resort, crawling with traffic. Once again there was no incident, no Gardaí forcing him from the boot at the point of a gun, no public humiliation, a shirtless black fugitive herded through the town.

The car picked up speed, leaving behind civilisation at play. But even with the restricted view from the boot, Marcus knew Annie had taken the wrong turning. He began thumping with his foot. She should have gone south in order to swing east through the mountains. She was heading on south-westward down the coast. He beat the inside of the car, but it was some time before Annie pulled off the road.

He was angry as he put on his T-shirt, but the anger was wasted. Annie was strangely withdrawn. She asked him to drive and she climbed into the passenger seat with the map spread over her knees. Of course she knew they were going the wrong way.

'Now we're here, there's something I've always wanted to see.'

'What?'

'You'll see.'

'For Christ's sake!'

'You'll laugh, or say it's too risky. Just drive.'

He sat back behind the wheel, arms folded.

'Let's go!' she said.

Grinning at her. 'Either we're in this glorious shit together, or not.'

'All right, all right, I'll tell you as we go.'

Thrusting into gear, he bounced the car back onto the road. 'You drive a hard bargain, sister.'

She made it sound like a pilgrimage. It was a drive of some twenty miles, with dazzling views across Sligo Bay to the Ox Mountains.

'I want to see where Countess Markievicz grew up.'

'Who?'

'Don't tell me you never heard of her! If you're coming over to police us at the point of a gun, you should at least have a working knowledge of Irish history.'

'I wouldn't mind a working knowledge of Caribbean history. All I got at school was the glorious British Empire, countries saved from ignorance by civilised England. Blacks were natives, Irish were savages.'

'What's new? They still think like that.'

A signpost for Lissadell House directed them down a leafy lane to an imposing house in the classic style set in woods and farmland overlooking the sea. A number of cars were parked, a group of people were being led on a guided tour. Marcus drew up well short. Getting out they circled the house at a distance, lingering in a dense grove, viewing through field-glasses.

'She was a beautiful young woman, a star of London and Dublin society, got presented to Queen Victoria at Buckingham Palace . . . But the starvation in the countryside at the turn of the century upset her, and the terrible poverty in Dublin . . .'

Annie spoke with a faraway intensity, as though she'd been there and seen it herself. 'One day she threw off the shackles of her prescribed destiny . . . betraying her class and dismaying her family, she rolled up her sleeves and gave the rest of her life to the oppressed, to women's rights and Irish freedom. She was the first woman elected to Westminster, but refused to take her seat in a foreign parliament and attended the illegal Irish one, the *Dáil*, on the run! She spent much of her later years on the run or in prisons like Aylesbury and Holloway. She was forty-eight when she fought the British as a guerilla leader in the 1916 rising in the streets of Dublin. After the surrender, she wept in Kilmainham Jail as she listened to the firing squads shooting her comrades in the yard, cursing because as a woman she didn't have the right to join them. The British, in their infinite stupidity, murdered fifteen leaders of an unpopular rebellion, turning them into national heroes. Last to be shot was her friend, the statesman-like James Connolly. He couldn't stand because his foot had been shattered by a bullet. They propped him in a chair, he blessed them, and they shot him . . .'

Marcus looked at her. Even now, more than half a century after the event, this twenty-one-year-old had tears of rage in her eyes. He was beginning to understand her.

'The year she died, aged fifty-nine, she was still humping bags of fuel to the freezing poor of Dublin's tenements. She died on a public ward. She insisted. The funeral was one of the greatest the city had ever seen, tens of thousands lining the streets, rich and poor. De Valera delivered the oration – Ireland's first Prime Minister, but you wouldn't know that. He called her a champion of right, a soldier of Ireland . . .'

She gazed reverently at the house. 'Wouldn't it be great to meet her ghost now, coming through the trees!'

*

When Frank Mulraine left the jewellers in Armagh, toying with the initials A.R.M., trying to guess the Red Sniper's name, he returned to his helicopter in time to receive promising news. Amidst all the excitement of reported sightings of the Red Sniper and the black traitor, the most improbable rumour of all seemed to have been confirmed. A missing hearse had been found hidden in a field, and an irate businessman from County Cavan was insisting that his Mercedes had been stolen from a nearby petrol station by a woman dressed as a nun, a description flatly contradicted by the garage attendant.

Rushed by unmarked car to a helicopter landing site, Mulraine studied his maps and the facts as he knew them: 8.45 a.m. A.R.M. shoots three cops in Strabane, seeks refuge in Catholic church . . . 9.05, she commandeers hearse disguised as nun . . . 10.45, she materialises across the border, apparently thieving a Mercedes at a filling station . . . Overwhelmed by a deluge of hoaxes and sightings, the Gardaí don't follow up the incident and find the hearse until 1.40 p.m., by which time three hours are lost, and the audacious nun-with-the-gun could have covered considerable distances.

Before taking off for Donegal, he circulated details of the Mercedes to police forces both sides of the border, but stressing that the occupant or occupants – could Marcus King still be with her? – should be detained if possible, and not wantonly killed. He would inevitably encounter resentment. It was, he realised, a gross impertinence to expect RUC officers to show restraint towards an enemy which sought to blow them to pieces at every opportunity. Furthermore, he was liable to be reprimanded for overreaching himself. He had no brief to hunt the Red Sniper. He was meant to be catching Marcus King.

It was just that he was still clinging to the hunch and hope that they were still together, despite A.R.M.'s solo performance. Forensic evidence supplied by his Southern Irish counterpart Joe Twomey suggested that both were involved in the encounter with Captain Lee and Corporal Hurst in the isolated barn in Donegal.

As he left behind the lush pastures of north Armagh and flew north and west across the sparsely populated moors and hills of Tyrone, Frank Mulraine was far from despondent, even surprised by his unflagging energy, the rediscovery of an exhilaration he hadn't felt for years. He remained convinced that Marcus King was no traitor. He had Brother Dominic's word on that, and Michael O'Cinneíde's evidence. The more he thought about the deranged and disgraced British officer whom he was hunting, the more he found himself sharing with him some elusive yearning for atonement – Marcus King for the O'Rawe girl, himself for young Brigid, and perhaps for other unresolved sins in his relentless career.

He'd had time to digest the known facts about the shoot-out in the barn, and to absorb Joe Twomey's latest findings, and, surprisingly, his first instinctive interpretation, extravagant as it was, had not so far been discredited. Lee and Hurst had blatantly lied; they had never lost their boots in a river. Someone had dumped their boots, socks and guns in a ditch, and Mulraine was looking forward, not without trepidation, to confronting the SAS men again when he rejoined them. Meanwhile the tantalising fantasy endured: Lee and Hurst being overpowered by Marcus King and the enigmatic A.R.M. – operating together.

After all, he reflected, looking down at the undulating river-bright landscape of Tyrone, such an unholy alliance was not without logic. According to Michael O'Cinneíde's passionate eulogy, his former comrade was sufficiently appalled by its use of bombs to turn against the IRA, an attitude not unlike Marcus King's response to Army brutality. O'Cinneíde could have been making it up, but Mulraine didn't think so.

He was becoming intrigued by the Red Sniper. What kind of terrorist eschewed the use of bombs? What kind of young woman had the skill and nerve to evade capture by stopping three armed pursuers, almost certainly shooting to wound, with three single bullets, before extricating herself from a church-trap disguised as a nun?

Soon, with luck, her identity would be uncovered from records of births of females now in their early twenties. As his helicopter hurtled towards a rendezvous with Joe Twomey at a petrol station in Donegal, Frank Mulraine found himself idly speculating once more about the young woman inspired by Countess Markievicz – Annabel Rosemary McCafferty. . .? April Rita Malone. . .?

Selecting lesser roads and sharing the wheel, Marcus and Annie set out across the sleepy secretive county of Leitrim, the Mercedes dwarfed by craggy mountains, driven wide by summer lakes, impeded by potholes and hairpin bends.

On through watery County Cavan, half forgotten in the lakeland mazes beneath the border, and into sheltered rolling Monaghan, where the fuel gauge began to fade dramatically.

'We need a petrol station quick,' said Annie.

The afternoon grew longer, the roads quieter, no garage in sight. The plan was to reach Carlingford Lough and steal a passage over the water to her home which lay in Northern Ireland on the far side of the lough. The alternative they didn't want to contemplate: crossing the border into Armagh and working their way all the way round the lough and Newry Canal through perilous Army-infested country.

The petrol gauge keeled over. They were running on luck, obliged now to risk the dangers of a town. Approaching Castleblaney from the north, the car began to jerk and splutter up a gentle incline, Annie bouncing in the driving seat, urging it on at least to the summit. Lurching and choking, the Mercedes staggered over the hill and gave up.

They free-wheeled as far as a sprawling fun-fair on the outskirts of town. There was no parking space left on the bustling road, and the car sailed to a halt well short of the improvised car-park roped off in an adjoining field. Holiday traffic began to build up behind them, unable to pass in the crush of people and vehicles.

'Shit,' said Annie coolly.

Marcus broke out in cold sweat in the heat of the car.

'I must be the only black face for a hundred miles.'

'People are too busy enjoying themselves,' said Annie optimistically, looking around for inspiration.

'And the place isn't exactly overcrowded with young redheads dressed as nuns,' added Marcus, abruptly getting out of the car. 'You steer, I'll push!'

'Where we going?'

Marcus indicated the car-park and, fighting the resistance of his injured ribs, heaved his weight at the back of the car, attracting a good deal of unwelcome interest from a mixed gang of teenagers.

'You posers got any muscles?' grinned Marcus.

They exchanged glances, and descended on the car in a pack, whooping and laughing as they propelled it along the road and bumped it into a space in the car-park. Walking behind, Marcus gave them a grateful thumbs up with both hands. Panting and laughing, the gang loitered, intrigued.

In the car, Annie found a roll of insulating tape in the glove compartment and fashioned a belt for her waist, transforming the nun's habit into a simple dress. There wasn't much she could do for the moment with her conspicuous hair, but a pair of sunglasses afforded some illusion of anonymity.

Still the youngsters lingered, fascinated by Marcus and the young woman emerging from the car.

'Push off!' said Marcus good-humouredly. 'Don't you recognise a honeymoon couple when you see one?'

They drifted away. Annie appeared at his side, slipping her arm through his.

'You never told me,' she said huskily, 'that we were married.'

'Thought I'd keep it a surprise.'

She slipped him the pistol and map, and carried the folded Armalite wrapped in sacking in her free hand. Arm in arm they headed for the fair.

The smell of fast-food reached them on the breeze. Annie's nose twitched. 'I'm starving! I'll eat this sack if we don't find some food soon.'

'You'll have to wait, sister.'

'I'll eat you if I have to!'

They quickly glanced at each other.

'Think I'd taste all right?'

Her hand wandered, feeling the flesh and muscle of his back. 'Cooked right, and with ketchup.'

The fair throbbed, huge generators guarded by chained dogs pounding a summer beat, strident music resounding in waves, chart hits competing aggressively with country-and-western. The fair engulfed them, no one seeming to know or care who they were. Annie guided Marcus towards a hot food stall, Marcus steered her away.

'Confucius say – car fuel first: belly fuel later!'

The first youngsters they approached refused. But they quickly found two boys of about twelve who agreed to go into town for petrol.

'I want a big can, OK?' He put money into their hands and offered to double it on their return. 'Say your daddy and mummy broke down.'

The boys ran off.

300

'Smooth operator,' conceded Annie, 'only you never told me we had two sons as well.'

'You don't recall giving birth to them?' said Marcus in mock dismay.

'I don't recall us fucking either,' said Annie, retracting her arm and going off to buy food.

Marcus sat on the ground in the shadow of the mobile amusement arcade and observed the charged atmosphere of the bumper car arena, the broad sweep of the Ferris wheel, the nonchalant or frightened faces on the swirling Rocket-Plane and in the madly revolving carriage chairs. He watched the stallholders touting passers-by with easy prizes – shooting galleries, dart boards, coconut ranges, all looking so simple, and each tempting trial of skill a trap, erasing the bravado from victims' faces. He took in the raucous banter and professional swagger of the hard young men running the prestige attractions. And he watched, as ever, for danger.

Annie whistled. He followed her towards the lure of the shooting gallery, and as they tore into synthetically seasoned burgers, Annie observed a throng of brash young men pitting their skill against a succession of rusty crouching soldiers dragged across a paint-chipped battlefield.

'Five down, five pounds,' announced the hard-bitten stallholder wearily, a woman of thirty or forty whose seasoned eyes strayed as she handed over seven rifle pellets to each upstart. 'Six down, bottle of whiskey. . . All seven, made in heaven, top prize!'

Annie threw a glance at the top prize, a huge teddy bear, bright pink, hanging in a dusty cellophane bag. Annie passed her sack and sunglasses to Marcus and, still chewing, paid her one Irish pound and selected a rifle, eyeing it distastefully.

'No, sister,' murmured Marcus, 'don't ask her if you can use your own.'

Annie had noticed how often the flat tin soldiers were hit without going down. A pellet in the torso was not sufficient. It had to hit the tiny head. Receiving her supply of seven pellets, she took her time to begin with, attracting interest as her first shot flattened a target . . . and her second.

Marcus remained loosely alert, willing the boys to return with the petrol, monitoring the milling crowds for danger, watching those closer at hand, outstaring anyone who looked too hard at him. He heard the murmurs of admiration in the crowd pressing in now behind Annie. He looked round. As the soldiers came round on their perpetual circuit, all were down but one, and she was taking aim once more.

'The whiskey's hers already,' said a man.

The final pellet cracked the air, pinged on the target.

'Bejaysus, so's the bear!'

Applause broke out. The stallholder woke from her reverie and seemed dazed as she cut the bear down.

'I'll have it out of the bag,' said Annie. The woman complied. Annie received the great gaudy toy in her arms, and coming towards Marcus, publicly presented it to him.

A chill seemed to pass through the crowd. They looked at her and they looked at him. The whispers died on their lips. They fell silent, unable to take their eyes off the charismatic couple. Marcus took Annie by the arm and led her away, just in time to see the boys arriving, each carrying a modest-sized can. Tucking the bear under his arm, Marcus took the boys aside and paid them, while Annie unscrewed each can to make sure of its contents. Burdened by cans, bear, concealed Armalite and the intense interest of the gathering crowd, they hurried away, past the parked caravans and roaring generators and across the road to the car-park . . . only to catch sight of an official car, a still blue light on its roof, GARDA SIOCHANA emblazoned on its side, and two uniformed policemen examining the red Mercedes.

'Shit . . .' said Annie.

They backed away, back towards the road.

'And another,' said Marcus.

'Where?'

'Don't look . . . approaching from the right.'

They merged with the ebb and flow of people crossing the road, Marcus shrinking, trying to lose height, casually swinging the bear . . .

'They've see us,' he said.

Carried back into the fairground on the leisurely tide of humanity, they deposited the petrol cans and lengthened their stride. Halfway across the ground they glanced back.

'Shit!' said Annie. The two Gardaí from the second car were calmly but intently following, craning their necks. 'Why do you have to be so tall?'

'You're not exactly a midget yourself,' Marcus replied, nodding towards the fringe of caravans as a possible way out. Picking their way across, they drifted free of the crowds and entered the quiet lanes of parked caravans, where round the first corner a dog leapt to its feet, snarling and snapping, straining on its rope in a frenzied effort to reach the intruders.

They doubled back, heard their pursuers calling to arriving colleagues, and hurried on, squeezing between caravans to re-emerge in the fairground scarcely twenty yards from the nearest policemen. Ducking unseen behind a run of stalls, they worked their way around the ground, winning for themselves a moment or two to scan the view over the heads of the crowd, some of whom were inadvertently assisting the Gardaí by pursuing the fugitives in curious throngs, changing direction whenever one of their number spotted them.

As the sound of approaching sirens rent the late afternoon air, Annie squeezed Marcus's arm and nodded towards the ghost train, an unspoken question in her face. He reflected a moment, chilled by the sirens.

'Long as you hold my hand.' They dropped their shoulders and hurried to the entrance to join the brief queue. Annie counted out the last of the SAS money, Marcus ducking and craning to watch a posse of armed detectives closing in, taking care not to panic the crowds, moving with the even step of routine, but with dark intent in their eyes, and nervous tension in hands which stuck to their shouldered guns.

The queue dwindled, Marcus felt for his crucifix and found it gone. Annie bought two tickets, and climbed with Marcus into car number nine, which was immediately shunted into the darkened tunnel and halted, waiting for the remaining three cars to be filled.

They filled quickly, the operator preparing to set the ghost train in motion, only to be stopped by two plain-clothed, flat-capped detectives. Unslinging their alarming UZI sub-machine-guns, they insisted on having the last three cars emptied of their paid passengers.

While the unarmed uniformed Gardaí ushered back the growing crowds, the two detectives explained to the operator precisely how the operation would work. The man anxiously smoothed his hair and massaged his neck. There were eight carloads of innocent passengers waiting in dark tunnels, wondering at the delay. 'OK,'

303

he said, thrusting down the starting lever, 'please God, nobody gets hurt.'

The fair petered out, one by one its noisy extravaganzas grinding to a halt. Fairground operators assisted the overstretched Gardaí to clear a broad space before the entrance to the ghost train, moving the public further back and providing passage for carloads of armed police arriving with a flourish of squealing tyres, slewing to a halt at all angles.

An eerie silence merged with the rapidly fading light, disturbed only by the rumble of the train and the thin wailing of unseen ghosts in the tunnels. Four and a half minutes passed, the crowd grew tense, the first car trundled into view, occupants dazzled by the sunset, shocked by the sight of men with guns rising to meet them. One after another, unsuspecting passengers were seized and ushered firmly to safety. Car number seven rattled into the light, the young couple aboard manhandled with unintended roughness. The eighth car appeared, detectives leaping to ambush a father and two children, passing them bodily to safety, before flattening themselves against the walls around the exit.

The crowd held its breath. Almost at once the fugitives' car rolled from the tunnel and broke into view. But the sea of faces and phalanx of telescopic sights which rose to meet it zeroed in not on the wanted couple, but on a solitary bear, plump, pink and unaccompanied, sitting up grandly, a complacent smile on its face.

It needed the strength of a man possessed to claw, wrench and heave forth a wriggling-space beneath the structure. Aflame with a horror of recapture, Marcus wrestled frenziedly in the almost dark, the noise he and Annie made covered by the clatter and howls of the ghost train. He worked so fast and feverishly that he and Annie broke free several moments before detectives could find their way round in the fading dusk to cover the rear.

Annie and Marcus scurried from shadow to shadow. A broad lough lay between them and the Northern Ireland border a few miles away. Around the lough stood dense forest through which they ran, Annie galloping Armalite in hand through the trees, Marcus clutching his freshly strained ribs, scarcely keeping up, Annie pausing now and then to let him catch up, laughing aloud with the helpless thrill of freedom, infecting Marcus with her hilarity, reducing him to painful doubled-up laughter. As night closed in, they caught their breath in a raised glade, and looked back to the sirens and whirring blue lights infesting the lakeside town. Pressing on, they picked their way through the ever darkening forest.

'That was quite a performance back in the ghost train, soldier,' Annie grudgingly applauded.

'I'd have chewed through steel,' said Marcus.

The moon lifted over a backdrop of copper beeches, spreading its silky light through the forest, trailing shadows as it rose. But for the distant throb of helicopters, the night was still, their softly padding steps magnified through the trees.

They crossed the border around midnight, forging into the notorious bandit country of South Armagh, a region of harsh beauty ferociously contested by the IRA and British Army. They followed the moon for several miles, proceeding gingerly, alert to the danger of stumbling into an enemy patrol, IRA or British, crouching in the darkness. They kept going until dawn began to clear the night from their path. The moon faded, a blanket of mist lay on the land, gathering in glens, covering the slopes of mountains to the east. Mute with fatigue, they sank to the twigged and spongy ground on the edge of a scrap of woodland, surrounded by moors bathed in moonlight.

'Get some sleep,' said Marcus, 'I'll keep watch.'

She didn't argue. He took the Armalite and settled back, propped against a tree. Arms wrapped around herself, Annie curled up on a bed of damp dead leaves, a forlorn shape on the ground.

'Come here,' he said. She lifted her head, he patted his lap. She came like a dog, too tired to be grateful, snuggled into the crook of his outstretched leg and laid her head on his ample thigh. She was asleep almost at once, only half aware of his fingertips lightly, absently, stroking her head.

19

Rostrevor, County Down

Two a.m. A sturdy ageing house stood out in elegant relief against the night sky, alone in hills above the silent town and moonlit lough.

'Christ, it's a palace,' murmured Marcus.

Vaulting a harmless fence, they made their way across a seemingly endless garden towards the home Annie hadn't seen in three years. Meandering paths led them through silent groves, over flowering banks, past the glint of concealed ponds emitting uneasy duck-talk as they went by. Away from the house, between shrubs, Marcus glimpsed the moon floating on the surface of a swimming-pool.

Annie had gone very quiet. Marcus voiced his nerves.

'You sure your parents are going to go for this?'

'There's only Papa to worry about,' Annie whispered. Something in her dispassionate tone made him lengthen his stride and touch her arm.

'What about your mother?'

'She's dead.'

A lawn gone to meadow ran up to the house. Annie stood in contemplation, remembering scenes, times of pain and innocence.

'You spoke of her,' he whispered, 'as if she were alive.'

'She died in a flying accident. Papa taught her how to fly. It was her first solo. He blamed himself, never got over it.'

'You didn't see it?'

'He pushed her too hard. No, I was only five, I didn't even know . . .' Her voice became bitter. 'He sent me away. I wasn't allowed home for a year.'

'Why didn't you tell me?'

She didn't reply. Her face, hollowed by moonlight, had drawn in on itself. Instinctively Marcus tiptoed on the noisy gravel, but Annie walked straight up to the crumbling portico and rang the bell.

As they waited, Marcus became conscious of their physical state, bedraggled as a pair of down-and-outs. Annie's bare legs were cut and muddied, her shabby dress torn, hair wild and matted, face smeared with camouflaging mud, looking as if she wanted to emulate her partner.

'Clean your face,' he said.

She spat on her hands and pawed her cheeks. 'I can't see, for Christ's sake!' She tilted her face for him. 'Spit! I'm dry.'

He took hold of her hand to spit on it.

'On your hands!' she said, grabbing his hands and thrusting them up to his face.

He spat on his hands and was cleaning her face when two lanterns came on, throwing pools of light around the entrance. A first floor window opened, a woman leaned out.

'Who's there?'

Annie stepped boldly into the light. 'Hi, Deirdre.'

The window closed. After a few minutes a chain was released, the door opened, a woman stepping back to admit them clasping her dressing-gown to her throat. She was a handsome woman of about sixty, no more than five feet tall, but gaining from her upright posture. Hair tousled and skin furrowed by her pillow, she looked more anxious than startled by Annie's appearance, and more surprised than alarmed by her black middle-of-the-night companion. When she spoke, it was in a tone both chastising and gentle, and in an accent which was melodic and distinctly Belfast.

'What on earth have you been up to, child?'

Securing the door, Deirdre turned and faltered. For a moment the two women gazed at one another. Then Annie made the move, crossing the space between them, enfolding Deirdre in her long arms, hugging her, gently rocking her, rocking herself.

'Deirdre's been with us since I was born,' she explained to Marcus, still holding the older woman. 'In fact I raised her!'

Deirdre gently freed herself. 'I shouldn't be speaking to you at all. Running off like that, two letters in three years, and never an address so I could write back. Can you imagine the frustration . . .'

More than frustration, observed Marcus. Annie and her father's housekeeper must have been very close once, Deirdre a surrogate mother. But now she was looking strangely from Annie to Marcus, and to the sacking which concealed something in Marcus's hand. Realisation and disbelief jostled in Deirdre's face, as if something she'd feared was unfolding before her eyes.

'Go to bed,' said Annie tersely, 'we'll talk in the morning . . .'

Footsteps above made them all look up to the gallery over-hanging the stairs. A man leaned over the balustrade, face grimly lit from below.

'What's going on?' he growled, a deep American voice.

For a moment no one could reply.

'I said, what's – '

'It's me, Papa . . .'

The house froze.

The face withdrew. Heavy footfalls proceeded around the gallery. Deirdre looked fearfully from Annie to Marcus.

'Good night,' she murmured, and started up the stairs.

'Deirdre. . .?' Annie called girlishly. Deirdre paused, half turned. 'Where's Sheeba?'

Deirdre lowered her eyes and appeared to take a deep breath. 'She had to be put down.'

Marcus looked at Annie, saw the shock undo her, the tears springing to her eyes.

'She was old, child . . .'

Annie turned away, walked off along the hall, leaving Marcus in the firing line at the foot of the stairs. The heavy steps descended, passing Deirdre on her way up. Marcus lifted his gaze to meet the man, an immensely tall and broad man with a full head of ash-grey hair and a masterful face, vigorously marked by passions and anger. A glance at Annie receding down the hall, and he focused on the tall black stranger.

The stranger offered his hand. 'Marcus King. Sorry about barging in at this hour.'

The voice was sincere. Mr McBride accepted the hand, shook it distractedly and went after Annie.

Aware of being watched, Marcus looked up and met Deirdre's frightened gaze. He gave a wry apologetic smile. She found a hesitant smile and hurried away to bed. Marcus followed Mr McBride to the kitchen, where Annie was raiding the larder, setting food on the long pine table.

'You could have called to say you were coming,' said her father, hands deep in the pockets of an old silk dressing-gown, 'instead of rolling up at two in the morning.'

Despite the deep commanding voice, he seemed curiously vulnerable in his bare feet and loose dressing-gown.

'And how the hell did you get yourself into such a state? The pair of you' – he glanced at Marcus, taking him in with a sweep of his hand – 'look like a couple of . . .'

It dawned.

As though to shake off the crazy idea, he looked rapidly from Annie to Marcus and back again. The truth bit deeper, and he looked slowly and directly at each of them, first Marcus, who returned his searching gaze unswervingly, finally settling on his daughter, who stared vacantly back at him. Her voice was equally bland.

'Papa, this is Marcus. Marcus, my father, Eugene.'

She proceeded to cut the bread, a fresh loaf, and in her state of tension and distraction kept going until she had sliced the loaf end to end.

Eugene's attention was drawn to the lump of sacking Marcus had smuggled onto a shelf. He set a course across the room towards it, eyeing Marcus, both men watching each other, almost the same height and build, Eugene fractionally shorter with the stooping of age, and somewhat heavier, a man in his mid-fifties who had always identified himself with selected heavyweights of American culture – Errol Flynn, Hemingway, William Holden. If he was afraid of Marcus he didn't show it. Marcus didn't move and Eugene McBride kept a straight line, brushing Marcus by and reaching for the sacking. Feeling its weight, he carried it to the table, swept Annie's foodstuffs out of the way and unfolded the sacking, exposing the folded butt, barrel and telescopic sights of a rifle.

'Jesus . . .'

He seemed to age before their eyes, shoulders sagging, feet digging in as though to prevent himself subsiding. He leaned heavily on the table, his back lifting and falling with his breathing. He remained so for some moments before standing back and throwing violent looks at the fugitives in his kitchen. Unable to endure his silence, Annie appealed to him. 'For God's sake, Papa, you raised me on Republicanism, on the noble cause of freeing Ireland . . .'

He stared at her in deepening disbelief. She begged him to understand, confidently laughing. 'Remember that old song you used to sing me about the British always causing trouble – *Everywhere the British go, it's Bang! Bang!* Papa, you ought to be proud . . .'

'Proud?' – Quietly at first – 'Proud? That what you think? My daughter a terrorist and I'm supposed – '

'I'm not a terrorist, Papa.'

'I've raised a goddamn terrorist and I'm supposed to – '

'I told you, I'm not a terrorist!' She came round the table, appealing to him. 'Papa . . .'

He shrank from her. She drew herself up. 'I share their cause but not their methods. I took on the British Army with that rifle and nothing more. I fought the bombs tooth and nail, just like Marcus fought Army brutality tooth and nail. We're here to make amends, Papa. We're going to make a stand against the bombs and the plastic bullets. I've quit the Provos and he's quit the Army. We're not the biggest armed force that ever set out to conquer Ireland, but we're not afraid to give it a try.'

She was tall and proud and shaking. Marcus wanted to clap, but remained still, arms folded. Eugene succumbed to a chair dumb-struck. Annie spoke to him gently. 'Papa. . .?' He seemed to require an inordinate effort to raise his eyes and look his daughter in the face.

'Remember, Papa, how you used to tell me about the great rebels of the world – George Washington, James Connolly, Martin Luther King, the Countess? Papa, we visited her house the other day. You and I were always going to go together, remember?'

They both looked away, arrested by a darker meaning recalled in the words 'We were always going to go together.'

'Dammit, Annie, those people were meant to inspire you, not incite you to . . .' He swallowed his words.

'To what?' Annie flared again.

'What about those cops in Strabane?'

'Oh for God's sake,' she said indignantly. 'I shot to wound when I could have killed. Who taught me to shoot like that, huh?'

He was on his feet, livid again. 'I told you to go make your own life, I never said get the hell out for three years and never tell me where you are! Postcards from here and goddamn there, waxing lyrical about breathtaking Antrim and mystical Donegal. Three goddamn years, Annie, not knowing when I was ever going to see you again. Me and Deirdre looking at each other near Christmas and saying, "Any minute now she'll walk right in through that door!" And what do we get? A goddamn Christmas card on New Year's Eve!'

It was Annie's turn to subside, relieved and dimly happy onto a chair.

'Maybe I better . . .' said Marcus, motioning that he was thinking of making himself scarce.

'You stay right there!' ordered Mr McBride. 'I want to know how the hell my daughter ended up with you.'

Annie started to laugh.

'What's so goddamn funny?'

'Papa, relax!'

'Relax?'

'You think he seduced me? No way! *I* saved *his* life. Not that he's ever thanked me for it. And I suggested that me plus him together was better than him and me solo. He none too graciously agreed, and now we've got the SAS, the RUC, the IRA and the Garda falling over each other trying to find us, loyally supported by the bumsucking media, all trying to brand us as savage terrorist and traitor. We need your help, Papa. We're counting on you.'

'That so? Well thanks for letting me know. And exactly what did you have in mind by a "last stand"?'

Annie caught Marcus's eye, handing him the initiative. Marcus offered Annie's father a cool, hard smile.

'Mr McBride you may not like the idea, you may not be willing to help us. That's your decision – '

'Too right it is.'

'But we have to be sure, before we give anything away, that you're not going to try and block us.'

'That's great. I don't have the right to act in my daughter's best interests!'

'No, Papa, you don't. I'm twenty-one, I'm not your little girl any more.'

'And if I refuse to give any guarantee?'

'We leave first thing,' said Annie.

Her father glowered at her. 'So how long were you fixing on staying?'

'A few days. Marcus needs to rest his injuries. We need you or Deirdre to buy some things for us.'

'We'll talk in the morning,' said Eugene, rising abruptly and heading for the door.

'Papa, Marcus needs some clothes.'

'Don't forget the lights.'

Marcus showered, then dried himself before a long mirror, tracing the lines of his healing ribs, protruding through weight loss. He frowned at himself, cheeks pushing forth a young beard, bullet head patiently covering itself with new hair.

'Bathroom's yours,' he called through to Annie's room. No reply. 'What about one of us keeping watch?'

'No need.' Her voice was flat, empty.

He didn't argue. They were both exhausted, and they were confident they'd arrived undetected. 'Good night,' he called. No reply. Retiring to the guest room, he lingered at the window, taking in the stark shapes of oak and beech, the scattered lights of the town below and the moonlit lough, which he knew to be patrolled by the Special Boat Service, waterborne equivalent of the SAS. Then, crawling naked under a duvet reminding him of home, he lay thinking of Marcia and Jamie.

He was finally falling asleep when he heard soft steps. In the light from open curtains he saw the old-style door knob turn and the door quietly open. He held his breath. It was Annie in loose pyjamas, Armalite in hand. Closing the door she came round the bed, out of his eyeline. He heard her prop the rifle carefully against the wall, then felt her climb into the spacious bed with him, turning her back to him, her spine and buttocks flush with his. With a drawn-out nasal sigh she fell still. Almost at once he heard her sleeping.

Now and then his eyes sprang wide in the night, mind doggedly alert to sounds. Annie slept on, warm against his back.

Newtownstewart, County Tyrone

While the couple he was hunting were sharing a bed in Rostrevor, Frank Mulraine's first night at home in weeks was broken by a four o'clock phonecall which he was too exhausted to hear. Since the fugitives' escape from the fairground, the trail had gone cold and the Chief Constable had vented his rage on the Commissioner of the Garda and on Mulraine, lashing out blindly for a scapegoat. Mulraine had simply removed himself from the field of fire, stealing home for a quiet weekend, hoping that the initials A.R.M. would work their magic while he slept.

Groping for the bedside light and telephone, Barbara grunted in reply to the caller, 'It's four in the morning and I don't want to wake him.'

'Believe me, Mrs Mulraine, this is something the Inspector's been waiting for, day or night. I honestly wouldn't call, only – '

'All right, all right . . .'

She had to take Frank by his shoulders and shake him before passing over the receiver. What he heard brought him rapidly to his senses. Fumbling for pad and pencil, he covered a page in his own scrawled shorthand.

'Good man. Now get my chopper over here at the double.'

Replacing the receiver, he offered Barbara an apologetic smile and rose to dress, pausing before the open wardrobe, trying to anticipate what the day would bring before selecting a suit.

'You'll want some breakfast,' said Barbara flatly.

'Nah, don't bother.'

'What will you have?'

'Whatever's going . . . have we got a map of the province handy?'

The map would seem to confirm what he scarcely dared hope. The Red Sniper was going home, *with* Marcus King.

Dawn crept through bullet-proof windows and into the kitchen. Barbara, in her dressing-gown, poured Frank more coffee.

'Am I permitted to know what startling news woke you when I couldn't?'

'Another woman, I'm afraid,' confessed Mulraine, donning his glasses to peer at the scrawl on his notepad. 'One Annie Roberta McBride, of Springfield Mount, Rostrevor!'

'Eat up, here comes your taxi.'

The pulsation of a helicopter broke the stillness. As she helped him with his coat and absently returned his embrace, she was surprised by the strangeness and force of his hug. Locked in his arms, she looked into his face. His eyes were puffy, his skin tired. In two weeks he'd aged two years and looked every bit of his fifty years. She studied him at arm's length.

'You're worried about this one, aren't you?'

'Me worried? Come on!'

'Deeper water than usual.'

Smiling wryly. 'Dammit, at my age, don't we need a bit of deep water now and then to remind us we're alive!'

Floodlights rained down, saplings reeled, the house rattled, the helicopter sank into the field. Barbara brushed Frank's cheek with hers.

'Mind you don't get out of your depth.'

Marcus woke to a strange house, strange bed and to an unfamiliar back against his. Annie was not as soft and smooth as Marcia.

Sunlight shone obliquely through the open curtains. He looked over the sea of Annie's curls at the bedside clock. Twenty past eight. Annie slept soundly, not a flicker of an eyelid. Marcus toyed with fantasy, fingers delighting in playing in those wild curls, hands exploring the curve of her thighs and buttocks, his mouth waking her with a slow kiss. He imagined her responding with mild alarm and, realising who it was, yielding to him – though not without some wisecrack – and sliding beneath him.

Agitated, he slid out of bed, opened the French windows and leaned out over the balcony. Clean cool summer air caressed his body. The blue-green lough was already alive with sails, and across the far shore he could see the hills of the Irish Republic, from where they'd come the previous day.

Having no clothes, he wrapped a towel round his loins before slipping out into the gallery. All was still. The house, almost a mansion, had seen its best years. It was sliding into shabbily dignified old age – cracked cornices, chipped paint, fading pictures, endlessly trailing plants crowding windows and crawling over ceilings. He found himself looking up at Annie's mother, Eleanor McBride, hanging in full prominence overseeing the house, a slim slip of a woman in dated evening dress on a moonlit terrace. She lacked Annie's height, but like her daughter she had a long angular face, sylph-like waist and flaming hair.

Leaning over the balustrade, he heard the faint tones of a radio, and someone working in the kitchen. He wondered what Marcia would make of such a house, admiring the size of the high-ceilinged rooms, the long lush views from so many windows. He withdrew and ran a bath, and while it filled he wandered into Annie's bedroom. The bed had been abruptly abandoned, and he wondered whether it was this room she'd felt the need to escape from in the night, more than any desire to sleep with him.

It was a disquieting room, painted in dark suffocating purple, assailed by violent pop-art, relieved by Cuban revolutionary posters. On the mantelpiece were photographs of her father and mother, in love and laughing; of her father more recently, mouth smiling for the camera, eyes ringed with torment. There were snaps of Deirdre, a trim woman holding a little girl by the hand; Annie as a child, wide-eyed, angelic. There was one shot of her aged about seventeen, astride a motorbike, hair severely cropped, mouth and eyes set hard.

He climbed aching into the bath. The tub was deeper and more solid than any he'd ever seen. He fitted it well, and was soaking in sweet salts when a rapid knock came on the door and Annie walked straight in, wide awake but expressionless. One glance at him and, lowering the toilet seat and her pyjama bottoms, she sat down to piss. Averting his eyes, Marcus splashed his face and hummed a Bob Marley number, all the while recalling the time that Black Rose had visited him in the attic, straddled his head and pissed in his face. Remembering the shackles, he shivered.

As Annie lifted her pyjamas and pulled the chain, there came a knock on her bedroom door. When she went out and opened it there was no one there, only two covered breakfast trays on the carpet, and footsteps hurrying down the stairs. Running to lean over the balustrade, she watched Deirdre's grey head bobbing out of sight.

They took breakfast by the pool, Marcus in a pair of Eugene's shorts and a towelling robe, Annie in a simple dress over a swimsuit, her bare arms and legs multi-freckled in the sun. A hotplate kept the coffee warm.

They ate in silence, waiting for a gardener, a middle-aged man in overalls and a straw hat, to finish dead-heading nearby roses and move out of hearing.

'How did your parents meet?'

'Papa was in Belfast making a documentary in '58. But deprivation and discrimination in Nationalist areas wasn't all he discovered. He was invited to a party and met an Irish actress called Eleanor Devenney. Love at first sight.'

'And you followed soon after?'

'My first mistake.'

Marcus refilled her coffee and kept a wary eye on the roving gardener. 'Were you close to your mother?'

'How do I know? I was five when she died . . . Actually we fought like cats.'

'You were sent away.'

315

'To my grandparents.'

'How did you get on?'

'What do you think? Cooped up with an old couple who handled me like a doll. I was dying to go home, didn't even know Mama was dead. Papa would take me out, but even as a child I knew he wasn't all there, he wasn't there at all. More and more I tried to take Mama's place, and never could.'

'You didn't see Deirdre?'

'She took me out. I used to beg her to take me home. It was left to her to explain about the accident.'

'When did they let you home?'

'About a year after. Don't you listen?'

'Were you OK then?'

'Wasn't the same. The house was deathly quiet. No laughter, no joy. Papa half crazy, high as a kite one day, doomstruck the next. He'd take me fishing, hunting, tracking, sailing, he'd read to me late into the night, jogging me awake so he wouldn't be alone. I was his son and daughter and companion, he was my mama and papa and teacher. We live to serve, he taught me, not to acquire wealth and heap glory on ourselves, to serve the world and die cleanly, unashamed of our humble contribution. Death was to be welcomed like a fairy godmother. One day, he'd say, as we swung together in a hammock under the stars . . . over there!' – she sat up and pointed out a pair of wild cherry trees – 'one day we'd go together, and fly hand in hand through the universe, just me and him, looking down at everyone going about their business. What about Deirdre? – I'd say, and Sheeba? They can come too if they want, he'd say.'

Her voice dropped to an absent whisper.

'He used to get very low sometimes . . . he wanted badly to die and would send me away . . . I was afraid he'd forget and go without me . . .'

Her voice tailed off. She seemed abruptly to return to the present. Stepping out of her dress, she walked to the pool's edge and dived in, describing a perfect arc and barely disturbing the water.

Marcus got up, removed his robe and dived in. He swam carefully, attentive to his injured ribs.

Annie swam mostly underwater, seeming perfectly at ease doing two widths without surfacing. Marcus swam over and above her, free-styling fluently and leisurely in the clear cold water, length after length, back and forth, smooth head parting the water, powerful arms sweeping the water behind him, long vigorous legs propelling him with even splashes.

Surfacing, he saw Annie sitting on the cracked edge of the pool, dangling her feet. In her face he read an invitation to join her. As he swam to her, she held out her closed hands.

'Look what I've got!'

Hauling himself out, he sat beside her, conscious of how thin she was in her clinging swimsuit.

'Look!' She opened her hand a fraction. A thumb-sized frog peered out. 'It was flapping around in the water.' Holding it gently, she stroked its head with the tip of her little finger.

'My boy would love to see that.'

The smile turned to surprise on her face. She looked at him afresh, then released the creature into the overgrown grass.

'You must miss them,' she said coldly.

Before Marcus could reply, he became aware of someone behind them – the gardener.

'Good morning, forgive me . . .'

Looking round, they saw he had a gun in his hand.

'Detective Inspector Frank Mulraine, Regional Crime Squad. Don't be alarmed. This is not an arrest, only an interview.' Gesturing with the gun, he invited them to return to their breakfast table, calmly selecting for himself a poolside chair, placing it where he could keep an eye on the house, and sat down. Removing a pair of clear-lensed glasses which he'd worn for disguise, he crossed his legs and watched the fugitives' reaction from under the brim of his straw hat.

They remained rooted, feet dangling in the water, speechless.

'How silly of me!' said Mulraine, indicating the Ruger pistol in his lap. 'There!' he declared, pocketing the gun and, standing to strip off his overalls, revealing a sombre suit and tie. Resuming his seat, he lit himself a cigarette, apparently enjoying the view, covering his nerves in a display of confidence.

Annie and Marcus rose as one, scanning the trees and slopes, the road, the half-built neighbouring property for signs of lurking police or soldiers. But the still summer's morning betrayed nothing. Pigeons cooed, a dog barked somewhere, distant sails stood motionless on the lough. They looked at Mulraine again,

317

receiving from the detective a little smile which seemed to say, You see, we're all alone.

'I would only ask you, should someone appear, not to reveal my identity . . . much as I have not disclosed to the good gentlemen of the SAS your whereabouts . . . not yet.'

'Who else knows?' said Marcus, hackles up, hating the smug policeman.

'Ah, but he's quick!' said Mulraine appreciatively. 'But sadly I must disappoint you. I'm not the only man who knows you're here, and you have only as much grace here as I grant you.'

Seething, Annie made a show of nonchalance, lightly towelling her hair, offering it to the sun.

'How did you find us?' she said, indifferent as a seasoned truant.

'Please sit down,' invited Mulraine.

Annie and Marcus exchanged doubtful glances.

'It's your precious time you're throwing away,' said Mulraine, drawing with apparent ease on his cigarette. 'I can only hold back the SAS dogs so long, before my own position is compromised.'

'What the hell do you want?' snapped Marcus.

'I want you to understand that I am the key to the success or failure of your mission.'

Marcus stared at the cop, exchanged another searching look with Annie and, putting on his towelling robe, opted to resume his seat at the breakfast table, pouring himself a fresh glass of juice and drinking it down. Annie followed suit, taking her time, guarding her dignity.

'What do you know about a mission? And why,' scoffed Marcus, 'would a cop be interested in its success or failure?'

'Spare the astonishment, Lieutenant. You're hardly a man who operates by the book yourself. Nor you, Miss McBride.'

Annie was appalled at the ease with which he came out with her name. Marcus, so cold towards the cop, involuntarily melted slightly on being addressed as Lieutenant.

'Aside from walking a tightrope, I've been on the road since dawn to offer you two a lifeline' – Mulraine's humour was beginning to wear thin. 'A coffee would go down very nicely!'

Again Marcus and Annie silently conferred. With a gesture of impatience, Marcus wiped out a cup, snatched the pot from the hotplate and poured the dregs of the coffee, sardonically holding up the cup and saucer as if to say, Where would Sir care to have it?

Mulraine picked up his chair and surprised them once more by joining them at table, placing himself across from them.

'I made the acquaintance,' said Mulraine, sugaring his coffee, 'of a certain Brother Dominic . . .'

Marcus was stilled. Mulraine met his eye.

'Far from giving me the impression of a deranged and bitterly vengeful soldier, he persuaded me that you had a mission of atonement to carry out, and would give yourself up after. I also spoke with Michael O'Cinneíde . . .'

Annie looked narrowly at him. 'What have you done to him?'

'I understand from him – '

'Michael was going to be shot by Doyle, for God's sake! He wanted out, he was never cut out for the IRA. He tried his damndest to get out of it. God keep him from you bastards!'

'I know about his confession,' said Mulraine, 'and the conspiracy to poison Doyle and Black Rose. I am his only hope and will speak for him when the time comes.'

Annie could only stare at him.

Mulraine drained his coffee and lit another cigarette, a tremble in his fingers. 'I believe you also quarrelled with Doyle?'

'So?'

Mulraine stood abruptly, composure shattered, visibly furious. 'If you two want to play the bloody fool, that's your funeral! This place will shortly be stormed. You can still get away. With luck you'll survive, for a time. But I'll be after you, and when your luck runs dry, or your ingenuity fails you, I'll be there, to scoop you both up from some God-forsaken bloody pavement . . . and it'll be too late to recall, in your dying breath, how a simple-minded cop came to parley with you and you refused!'

Turning on his heel, Mulraine grabbed his belongings and started off in the direction of the fence from where he'd come. Annie remained rooted. Marcus went after him, seizing him by the arm. Mulraine brushed him off, and they faced up, glowering. 'You're the one who's fooling with us!' charged Marcus. 'How the hell do we know what you're playing at? We've survived by the skin of our teeth this far, and we've got every bloody cop and squaddie in the country hunting us. It's going to take more than a handful of cryptic clues from some smarmy cop to get us to listen.'

Annie was seated regally at the table, disdainful, mistrustful, when they returned. Mulraine motioned Marcus to sit, and himself

319

remained on his feet, removing his hat to run a handkerchief across his brow.

Marcus sprawled on a chair. 'OK, let's have it.'

Mulraine, clearly in difficulties, gazed into the distance.

'I gave Brother Dominic my word – no, never mind that – '

'Your word? About what?'

'The fact is, I'm loath to hunt to ground a soldier whose crime appears to have been the courage to stand up against Army brutality. I'm not enthralled by the idea of seeing you scapegoated and sacrificed by our soulless masters.'

'You got religion or something all of a sudden?' sneered Annie. 'What is this? Since when does a top-dog detective go soft on the man he's after? He's bullshitting,' she told Marcus, 'setting us up!'

'Is that a fact, young lady?' Mulraine rounded on her. 'And your good self, since when does a celebrated IRA fighter mutiny over the use of bombs?'

'Who told you that?'

'O Cinneíde, who else? And team up with a British Army fugitive? Stretching the imagination a bit, wouldn't you say? And while we're on it, since when does a British soldier risk his neck and break out of custody in order to attend the inquest of a girl he accidentally shot? If I've gone soft in the head, I'm in pretty good company! Do you two think you've a monopoly on atonement? I've my own atoning to do – a young woman whose arm was blown off because of my stupidity. And furthermore' – he fixed them both with a glowering smile – 'if you two imagine you've cornered the integrity market, I'll remind you that this is also *my* country that's being bombed by the Provos, battered and bullied by the Army and poisoned by RUC torture. Who are you to deny me my sense of fair play and decency, and my convictions about sensitive policing? Damn your insolence!'

'What did you have in mind?' asked Marcus quietly.

Mulraine exhaled and took a seat, just as a figure appeared shading her eyes on the far side of the flowering lawn.

'That's all I need,' he groaned.

'We'll be right in!' called Annie.

Deirdre, evidently uneasy about the third party by the pool, withdrew.

'I need to know your plans and movements,' said Mulraine bluntly.

320

Annie laughed derisively.

'Then what?' said Marcus.

'I might, so to speak, be willing to give you my unofficial blessing, in other words to facilitate your – '

'You'd allow us to do it, you mean?'

'I mean I wouldn't obstruct you.'

'I get it,' said Annie, 'he grabs us when it's over and steals his slice of the glory.'

'And why not?' said Marcus. 'Jesus, if he lets us do what we plan, he's welcome.'

'Try me,' said Mulraine.

Marcus searched Mulraine's face for tricks or treachery.

'OK, this is what we had in mind – '

'You crazy?' said Annie.

'It's a chance we have to take.'

'Don't kid yourself. He wants our plan, so he can grab us *before* we do it!'

'What's the alternative? You want to let the SAS have another crack at us?'

Elbows propped on the table, chin on joined hands, Annie fixed her large brown eyes on Mulraine. 'He won't go for it.'

A full minute passed. Mulraine, at first patient, made to rise. Marcus stilled him with a raised hand and addressed Annie. 'If we confide in him, he may say no. If we don't, it's definitely no.' Annie folded her arms and looked away. 'OK?'

Annie remained tight-lipped. With a fateful sigh Marcus turned to the detective and delivered a rough sketch of their plan. Mulraine, recovering his humour, laughed good-naturedly. When he saw Marcus was serious, his face fell. Apart from murmuring 'Holy Mother . . .' it was his turn to find himself speechless, dividing his unblinking gaze between the fugitives.

'The pair of you are demented' – he rose abruptly – 'stark raving mad!' They regarded him evenly, apparently unmoved. 'What the hell do you imagine you'd achieve, save an eternity behind bars or early graves?'

Annie gave a contemptuous snort and looked away.

'There are,' said Mulraine, 'more temperate ways of making the same point.'

'I don't intend to kill anybody,' said Marcus.

'Oh splendid!' Mulraine looked curiously from one fugitive to

321

the other. Why had King said '*I* don't intend?' He shook his head in disbelief. 'If you're bent on such a desperate course don't expect any favours from me.'

'Who wants them?' said Annie.

Gathering his hat and overalls, he cast them a final reproachful look, turned on his heel and walked away. Again Marcus was inclined to go after him, but there was no need. Mulraine didn't go far. Slowing, he took himself for a walk around the pool's edge, pausing now and again to contemplate the little waves made by insects struggling on the surface, and to gaze through slowly cohering clouds reflected in the water. Removing his hat, he ran a heavy hand through his hair and took deep breaths as if the morning had become oppressively close. Then, returning, he resumed his seat, propping his head in his hand, closing his eyes and massaging his brow.

Marcus studied the cop, who wore the look of a convict contemplating escape. Or a bull, he thought, who's backed himself into a tight corner.

Mulrain looked up. 'I urge you seriously to consider a compromise . . .' They regarded him stealthily. 'It seems to me the depths of irresponsibility to embark on such a mission, leading almost certainly to widespread bloodshed, not to mention suicide.'

'Got a better idea, spit it out,' said Annie.

'If I were able to guarantee your safe conduct to a major press conference – '

'Terrific! Don't you think we've thought of that?'

Mulraine faltered. 'You didn't see any merit – '

'None!'

But Mulraine thought he intercepted a restraining glance fired at King by McBride.

'Listen, mister' – Annie on her feet beating the table – 'we're controlling this, it's our invention, we make the rules, we don't want two minutes on TV or two inches in *The Times*, we haven't come this far to arrive with a sigh, we're going to explode all over the media, we're going to take Dublin and Westminster by the ears and crack their heads together, we're going to take the great British public by the scruff of the neck and rub its nose in its own shit, we're going to stop traffic in the streets and send ministers running for cover, we're going to expose the Army and shame the Provos,

322

we're going to seize power, mister, and hold it' – she smiled triumphantly – 'for as long as it takes.'

She held the detective in the grip of her gaze until he looked away, glancing at Marcus King to test his reaction. But Marcus, chewing a blade of grass, remained inscrutable. Annie dropped back in her chair flushed, resolute and happy.

'The pair of you will stand out a mile in Dublin!' He made a throwaway gesture. 'Anyway, you better move fast. I can delay the hounds another hour' – consulting his watch – 'maybe two.'

Marcus shook his head. 'We can't go yet.'

'Ah yes, of course . . .' It was all falling into place. 'Miss McBride will have to speak to her father . . .'

Annie blanched, Mulraine rose to leave.

'He may not be willing to fly you. I can't help you there. Once the SAS are in place, you're on your own.'

'You could hold them back till dawn,' said Annie brazenly.

'If I were you, I'd be gone before that. I can't answer for what may happen in the early hours. But if you do get out and reach Dublin, leave a message for me' – he thought for a moment – 'at the Belvedere Hotel, where I'll book in under the name Frank Mason. Your continuing liberty depends on me.'

With a courteous nod, and a final look at once assured and sceptical, Frank Mulraine departed, wending his way round the flower-beds.

'Bastard,' fumed Annie, 'who the hell does he think he is?'

'He's the man whose job it is to put us away,' replied Marcus pensively, 'and what's he doing? Protecting us. He tracked us down, sister, he could have been basking in the limelight. I broke ranks with the Army, you did the same with the Provos, but this guy . . .' nodding in the direction Mulraine had taken. Words failed him.

She laughed at him. 'You're so naïve, Marcus, so pitifully naïve.'

They returned the trays to the kitchen.

'Deirdre, you don't know what a treat that was.'

Deirdre turned and looked up wistfully at Annie. 'How are you, child?' It was a genuine heart-filled question from the woman who'd joined the household in 1961, a widow from the Ardoyne, one of the war-scarred Catholic enclaves of Belfast.

'I'm grand, Deirdre, really grand.' Annie took her by the shoulders and smiled beseechingly down into her face. 'I'm alive, not merely living. I'm doing something, I'm shaping history, I'm bedevilling the British, tormenting the IRA. Ireland can't ignore this particular child! Don't you think Papa's just a little bit proud?'

Deirdre removed Annie's hands and clasped them tightly together. 'I want you to promise me something.'

'You will do some shopping for us? It's absolutely vital.'

'Not as vital as this.'

'What?'

'I want you to promise me that as long as you remain' – Deirdre stumbled over ominous thoughts – 'that whatever happens you will not treat us, your father and me, so lightly again, that you'll stay in constant touch, as far as possible.'

Annie took back her hands, eyes swimming, mouth set. She stood a moment bewildered and defiant as a child, and Marcus looked away, across the meadow-lawn towards the belt of forest which the SAS might already be invading.

'I have to see Papa,' said Annie.

'He's expecting you, both of you. There's a tracksuit on the landing for your . . . friend.'

Eugene McBride was waiting in his wood panelled studio, a long open-plan room with views of the lough at one end and the mountains at the other behind his mammoth desk. A stag's head, complete with mighty antlers, presided over one wall, variously guarded by an array of mounted rifles, old and new. The wall facing was paved with framed awards for documentaries he'd made all over the world. An archway led to the bedroom Eugene had once shared with Annie's mother – the shrine, Annie dubbed it caustically, cleaned and aired but otherwise untouched since the day Eleanor McBride had died in a mangled light aircraft. Photographs of the lovely young woman adorned the studio.

When they entered, Eugene rose from his desk without emotion, sporting jeans, denim shirt and a black silk scarf. Annie, wearing a plain red dress and optimistic smile, went directly to him. 'Good morning, Papa,' respectfully and affectionately kissing him.

'Morning.' He conceded his cheek, nothing more. Distant and businesslike, he motioned his visitors to take a seat. Annie obeyed, visibly hurt. Marcus, dressed in the borrowed black tracksuit, joined her on the leather sofa, observing the discipline Eugene had invested in that dour greeting, and the cost in pain fleetingly glimpsed in his face.

'OK, let's hear it. What have you two got planned?'

'You still look good, Papa,' said Annie tenderly. 'Pretty good for a man of, what, fifty-six, who's come through so much.'

He acknowledged her sentiments with a gruff nod. It seemed to Marcus that she'd spoken from the heart, but that he had made a point of taking it as calculated flattery. Watching the battle of their eyes, her imploring gaze tinged with adulation, his doubting resistance, Marcus felt the father's hold over the daughter, and the daughter's power over the father. He could see how they must always have fought and loved, and always would.

'Still hunting, Papa?'

'No.' He seemed offended, and spoke impatiently. 'So what's this last stand going to be?'

Marcus expected Annie to confer with him at this point, but with a brisk change of manner, she divulged a skeletal outline of the plan. She spoke in a matter-of-fact tone, as though justifying a holiday she intended to take with a boyfriend. Unsure whether she was being serious or provocative, Eugene resorted to a humourless chuckle and a reply which betrayed nothing.

'Yeah, that's exactly the kind of crazy thing you'd dream up.'

'Only it's no dream. We're going to do it.'

Staring dumbly at her. 'You're going to . . .' Another sceptical laugh. 'What do you mean – take over?'

'Gunpoint,' said Annie.

Lost for a response, he stepped back and perched on the edge of his remote desk, toying with a cigar cutter. Finally he shook his head and spoke dazedly. 'You can't do this . . .'

'We can, Papa, and we're going to.'

'You got to be out of your mind.'

'Anywhere else would be too difficult. Even if we found a way to London, security's much tighter.'

'What's it for, for Christ's sake?' he flared.

'I just told you, to shame the IRA into laying down their bombs – '

'Don't be ridiculous, they don't give a shit!'

'Then into questioning their use of bombs. And to expose the British Army.'

325

'Did you put her up to this?' He rounded on Marcus. 'Haven't you done enough already? Why did you have to involve Annie?'

'Just because you ruled Mama,' cut in Annie, 'doesn't mean he rules me. Nobody rules me. It was my idea.'

'Goddamn you . . .' Eugene slid off the desk and came forward with an angry stoop, like a boxer hurt below the belt, jabbing a warning finger. 'How dare you speak of my wife like that. How dare you speak of her at all . . .'

'That's right' – Annie trembled – 'you always had more time for the dead than the living.'

For a moment he was still, stunned by the invisible blow. Then he came at her half crazed, bent on seizing her by the wrist and ejecting her from his studio, from the house, from his world. Annie, undaunted, braced herself, but before Eugene could reach her, Marcus was on his feet, challenging without blocking, making no aggressive move other than to shake his head slowly, warning Annie's father off. Eugene faltered. Not one to be physically intimidated, he would have thrown the first punch without ado, too maddened to consider Marcus's advantage in age and training. Had Marcus overtly threatened him, there would have been no stopping the American, but Marcus was calm, uncritical. Without taking his eyes off Eugene, he said, 'I think you should apologise, Annie.'

Annie laughed derisively. 'Me apologise!'

'You're wounding each other, but you struck first.'

'Me apologise, after living most of my life in that woman's ghostly shadow!'

'We're talking about now,' reasoned Marcus, 'today, not what happened in the past.'

'I get it, the past doesn't count. I should concentrate on today. Never mind a lifetime's indignities.' She leapt up and stormed off, turning at the door: 'I suppose the same goes for the Irish question. History's of no consequence. Forget eight hundred years of oppression, nothing that's brought us to this moment is of any importance. Now is all. Bullshit! Thanks, soldier, for taking the oppressor's side' – she glared at Marcus – 'even when the SAS at this very moment are probably closing in on us.'

Finally she levelled her withering gaze at Eugene.

'You're going to help us, Papa . . . or you're not my father.'

'Where you going – ?' Marcus started towards her.

'Stay where you are!'

'It'd be suicide to go anywhere now in broad daylight.'

'I'm leaving tonight, after dark. I'll carry this thing through on my own if I have to. You can please yourself.'

Annie slammed the door. Eugene turned away, pacing back and forth, gesticulating.

'What the hell's she talking about, living in her mother's ghostly shadow – Jesus! Dammit, hasn't a man the right to mourn? And before you tell me no man in his right mind mourns for sixteen years, let me tell you you know nothing. There's no time limit on grief. Some never mourn, some never stop. Doesn't mean I neglected Annie. OK, I was away a lot, but back home no father ever spent more time with his daughter, heaped more love on her. And now she wants to blame her craziness on me – no way!'

'Forgive me,' said Marcus, 'but you sent her away when your wife died. She's never got over that. To this day you refer to Mrs McBride in front of Annie as "my wife" – '

'She was . . . *is* my wife, for Christ's sake!'

'And Annie's mother.'

Eugene subjected Marcus to a silent scrutiny. Marcus wavered momentarily and stood firm. 'We haven't long,' he said quietly.

'They'll put Annie away for a long time,' Eugene warned.

'They'll do that anyway. She's killed two soldiers, wounded three cops.'

Eugene looked away. 'Not the kind of accomplishments you anticipate from your own flesh and blood.'

'There's a war on, Mr McBride; she volunteered.'

'Yes, and look what she joined. A terrorist organisation.'

'It was the only available army. She tried to improve it. She's still trying. Your daughter's no terrorist.'

'Of course, these people are freedom fighters. If I say it often enough, maybe I'll believe it.'

'Just don't take too long about it.' Marcus felt his temper slipping. 'We've been warned the SAS could raid tonight.'

'What here? This house? I don't believe this!'

'So Deirdre will also need to be evacuated.'

'Christ, you've thought of everything.'

He retreated to the bay window, looked out across his estate, hands restless in his pockets, in his hair, round the back of his neck, over the contours of his clean-shaven face. Marcus, watching him, had the feeling that he'd spent too much time alone, cut off from the world.

'What do you want of me?' Eugene barked the question, but Marcus thought he detected a change in mood.

'To accept your daughter. Even better, to appreciate her.'

'Practically, dammit! What do you want me to *do*?'

'We need some things bought, hair dye, false beard, a few other things. May mean a trip to Belfast, today – '

'What else?'

'We need you to use your contacts in Dublin to get us three passes – '

'Three passes? You expect me to go in with you!'

'No. There may be a third party.'

'Jeesus. Is that it?'

'We need you to fly us to Dublin tonight.'

He shook his head and laughed in disbelief. 'After nearly three years, she arrives out of the blue, only to fly away again.' There was a sharp undertone of sadness to his anger. Subsiding into the chair behind his desk, he swivelled to face the window, his back to Marcus, talking almost to himself. 'First my wife, then my daughter. God knows where or when I'll see her again. A gaol. A mortuary.'

Night closed around the house, shrouding the sloping garden and surrounding woods. One hundred and fifty yards along the descending approach road, the shell of an evolving villa filled with moonlight, and emptied again each time the sky clouded over.

Building progress on the half-completed property had been poor that day, the workforce only arriving at noon, and consisting not of brickies and masons, but professionals of an entirely different persuasion. Appropriately dressed in mud-caked boots and overalls, they'd given a passable imitation of a gang of labourers late into the evening. But when finally they downed tools and drove away, it wasn't to go home; rather they scattered into the darkness to take up positions in the grounds around the McBride residence.

Captain Douglas Lee had the darkened villa to himself, pacing the hard floors in a vain attempt to burn his feverish energy, praying to a godless heaven that Marcus King was either installed in the McBrides' mansion, as Mulraine suggested, or arriving any day. There was a limit to the number of setbacks his spirit could take. Three times he'd missed his man – on Inishtrahull, then at the farm, finally in humiliating circumstances in the barn. The Boss had gone berserk again on the phone, drawing on a rich repertoire of expletives. The SAS's mythical status and inviolable reputation, normally safe in Lee's hands, was taking a beating. Worse still, his self-esteem was under fire, when it was only his infallible prowess and unflagging virility which kept him on an even keel. He lived on success. He had a horror of failure. It woke him in the long nights, its laughter rattling the windows. He'd lie awake in a cold sweat, with only the burning lights of his exploits to keep the spectre at bay. Now failure was pressing in again, closer than ever, and Lee trembled, afraid, not of death, but chilled by the vast mirrored pointlessness of life. He thought of Sergio, his long-suffering Portuguese lover. How long before Sergio threw up his hands and said enough!, walking out on him as Lee's wife had done, as everyone had always done, leaving him alone, exposed.

Oblivious to the pain in his shoulder, which was still heavily strapped from the driving back-kick received from Marcus King in the barn, he crouched down and made radio contact across the deepening night with Sergeant Williams, the big Welshman who was still limping from the fox trap he had stumbled into when they raided the farm, instructing him to pick three of the six men at his disposal and prepare to move in and attach the transmitters and pinhead cameras to the appointed windows of the mansion.

In return, Williams had nothing to report. The house was quiet, only human outlines discernible now and then through drawn curtains. Earlier in the day, they'd seen the housekeeper, Deirdre McDonough, drive off in her Peugeot, to be tailed all the way to Belfast, where she visited a chemist, a theatrical costume agency and a toy shop. She made another appearance at seven p.m. to cut a generous bunch of garden flowers. Eugene McBride had been spied in his studio, but there had been no sign of the fugitives.

The faint purr of a car drew Lee's attention. After an interval there came footsteps, preceded by the odour of cigarette smoke.

'Put it out,' growled Lee.

A stocky figure filled the doorway.

'What are you doing here?' said Lee. 'I don't need you.'

With a last drag on his cigarette, Mulraine stubbed it out and stepped into the empty concrete room.

'Jaysus, you're sparkling company, Captain.'

'I think you've slipped up this time, Inspector.' Their hoarse whispers permeated the house.

'Is that what you think?' Mulraine managed to sound supremely relaxed.

'I don't think they're in there, and I'm unconvinced they're coming.'

'Did I say they were?'

'If not, what the fuck are we doing here?'

'I believe this is where they were heading.'

'Don't tell me you've changed your mind.'

'No reason to.'

'Unless,' cut in Danny Hurst, a disembodied voice in the darkness, 'they've been and bleeding gone!'

'What do you want?' hissed Lee.

'I heard the car.'

'Get back to your post.'

'What if they have bleeding gone? We're sitting here like soft dicks.'

'He wouldn't move on that quickly,' reasoned Lee. 'He was hurt, he'd want to rest up.'

Lee grimaced in the darkness, cursing himself, praying Mulraine hadn't noticed the gaffe, sensing Hurst glaring, a who's-a-fucking-idiot? expression on his face.

Mulraine allowed the tension to thicken before speaking.

'You never mentioned Lieutenant King being hurt, Captain.'

'Wishful thinking.'

The moon sailed free, pouring through gaping windows, scuttling men into shadows.

'It's not too late to alter your story, gentlemen.'

'Stick to your job, Mulraine,' warned Lee, 'we'll stick to ours.'

'That's precisely what I'm doing.' Mulraine, shaking, would not be intimidated. 'Therefore, I repeat, would you care to make some minor alterations to your statements?'

Hurst filled the pause with a cheerful note of menace.

'I'd be happy to arrange some minor alterations for you, Inspector.'

'Thank you, Corporal,' said Lee, 'that'll do.'

Mulraine hesitated, partly from fear, also because his own professional conduct was proving even more irregular than theirs, if only they knew it.

'The boots you mislaid in a river, gentlemen, were discovered by Gardaí in a ditch, along with your socks and guns . . .' No response. Mulraine waded deeper. 'You graphically described to me a gun battle outside the barn. It never took place. You reported being on the receiving end of a torrent of grenades. No grenades were discharged. All the action took place, in reality, inside the barn, where I believe you came unstuck, your lives spared by the two desperadoes we're hunting. Instead of veiled threats, gentlemen, I suggest you play your cards very carefully from now on.'

Silence prevailed.

Hurst went away. Dying for a cigarette, Mulraine subsided onto a plank-bench, wondering what chance Marcus King and Annie McBride had of escaping, what chance he himself had, if they did escape, of keeping track of them and arresting them at the finale, and what chance he had of keeping secret his shady involvement, of fooling his superiors into believing he'd merely hunted them to ground. With a shiver he wondered what Barbara and the boys would think visiting him in a Dublin gaol. Of course they'd stand by him. Or would they? With his pay stopped, Barbara might have to sell up. Would she remarry while he languished in gaol, tormented by the drifting aroma of Dublin's breweries?

Lee was radioing Sergeant Williams. 'You're on, Taf, move in.'

'Already?' blurted Mulraine, dismayed. 'It's only eleven.'

'Your spying equipment's going in.'

'Not yet! It's barely dark. You'll alert them.'

'I thought you were sticking to your job, Inspector?'

Mulraine groped his way downstairs, out of the doorless back door and into the nettled wilderness of the back garden. Lighting a cigarette, he subsided against the wall of the house. The surveillance equipment would locate the fugitives, the house would be stormed. If they were taken alive, they'd be bound to give him away, or was there a chance they would omit to mention his poolside intervention? Nausea gripped him.

Suddenly, the stillness was broken by a sound he couldn't immediately identify, a low rumbling noise, like a gigantic clock being wound, an oddly familiar sound inducing a moment's home-sickness – a garage door lifting. The deep throated roar of an engine took possession of the night.

Hurrying upstairs, he burst into the front room, panting for air. 'What's going on?'

Lee was standing in the window, training night-scanning binoculars on the mansion, jumping to one side as a pair of headlights were flung across the darkness, a vehicle surging forth and drawing up with a rasping of gravel in front of the portico.

'It's the American,' said Lee almost to himself, teeth on edge, his whole body taut with anticipation, 'in evening dress under a sweeping coat, standing in the drive, sniffing the night . . .'

'Is he alone?'

'Seems to be. No one else in the Range Rover, at least no one in sight . . . Here comes someone, emerging from the front door, a woman . . . suitcase, umbrella and a bouquet . . .'

'How old?'

'He's opening the passenger door – '

'How old is she?'

'Middle-aged.'

'Deirdre McDonough, the housekeeper.'

'He's coming round, getting in . . . where the fuck are they off to at this time of night?'

'They live it up round here,' stumbled Mulraine.

'We better tail them.' Lee began activating the two-way radio.

'I'll do it,' volunteered Mulraine, groping his way out.

'You'll want back-up,' said Lee.

'Why deplete your forces? I'll keep you posted.'

Lee ran after him, calling down the stairs. 'Stop and question him.'

'I'll tail him for a while,' Mulraine called up.

'No! Stop him, grill him, search the car! You hear me?'

Mulraine took his time down the road to his car, parked on the verge beneath the trees. He could hear the Range Rover approaching, its headlights probing the darkness as it turned out of the gates of the estate. By the time Mulraine had ducked into his car, the Range Rover was sweeping by down the hill. He started the engine, depressed the clutch, engaged the gears and eased onto the road. The radio crackled, Lee's metallic voice filled the car.

'What are you fucking playing at? He's getting away, you were supposed to stop him . . .'

Mulraine picked up speed, rolled down his window, and slapped a whirring blue light on the roof. The Range Rover had taken the mountain road north, exactly the direction Mulraine would have expected. Eugene McBride was steadily increasing his speed, and Mulraine had no alternative but to sound the siren and flash his lights. The effect was instantaneous, the Range Rover losing speed, allowing Mulraine to overtake and motion the driver to pull over. Dwarfed by mountains and looming forest, Mulraine stepped into the road, cold blue light revolving in his face. Flashlight in hand, he walked towards the Range Rover, his steps ringing in the echoing stillness. The driver rolled down his window.

'Good evening, sir, madam,' said Mulraine genially, stooping to look in. 'Detective Inspector Frank Mulraine, Regional Crime Squad!'

'Good evening to you, sir!' replied Eugene McBride, with strained authority and humour, voice steady, but eyes puffy with drink or tears or both. 'Looks like I got a speeding ticket coming to me.'

'You were doing a hell of a lick all right. Where were you heading?'

'Just visiting friends, and I'm kind of late, so if you'll – '

'And where would that be, sir?'

Eugene hesitated.

'Killyleagh,' supplied Deirdre helpfully.

'On the lough,' recalled Mulraine, 'very nice.'

'At the castle, as a matter of fact,' said Eugene.

'Sure that'll be grand. It is Eugene McBride, is it not?' The American didn't deny it. 'I was wondering had you seen your daughter lately?'

Eugene blanched. 'No, she's away.'

'And where would that be?'

'She's an independent young lady, Inspector,' Deirdre explained. 'She's not in trouble, we hope?'

'Let's say . . .' Mulraine faltered at the sound and sight of a car, something in the speed it was doing giving him the uneasy feeling that it might be . . .

The car slowed abruptly. To overtake, willed Mulraine. But instead it continued to decelerate, pulling up sharply behind the Range Rover. Front doors opened slowly, two familiar figures stepped into the blue revolving glare. Mulraine cursed silently and broke into a sweat.

'Be so good as to contact your local RUC station if she shows up,' he said steadily.

'Of course,' said Eugene. 'Now if you don't mind – '

'I'll just take a look in the back.'

'Will that really be necessary. . .?' The tall American had one foot in the road as Mulraine took a stroll round the rear of the vehicle, playing the flashlight through the interior, down behind the high-backed seats where a tarpaulin was spread loosely over something bulky and motionless, all cluttered with a jumble of articles – tool kits, golf clubs, weatherproof jackets and boots . . .

Mulraine heard Captain Lee and Corporal Hurst take several steps closer. Mastering his nerves, he briskly tried the rear door of the Range Rover. It was locked. He felt the eyes of the SAS men on his back.

'We better have this open,' he called.

'Look, I'm late as it is, Inspector,' argued Eugene.

'Let's have it open right away then.'

Mulraine stood hunched in the road, the SAS at his back, mountains bearing down to left and right, darkness ahead and behind, and the harsh blue light on his car beating its silent rhythm.

Eugene removed the keys from the ignition, the engine ceased, he came slowly, face tense in the headlights of the third car, and stopped a moment to shield his eyes and take in the SAS men. Corporal Hurst stood rooted in the road, sub-machine-gun cocked in his hands, face in shadow, hiding a broad sneer. Captain Lee eyed Eugene coldly, head high, legs struck provocatively apart, hands behind back. Eugene turned and unlocked the rear door of the Range Rover. Lifting it open to its full extent, he walked away, wiping his hands, stopping at the far side of the road to stand and gaze up into moonlit gullies and forested bluffs.

Mulraine began a brisk energetic inspection of the interior of the vehicle, shifting bags and tools, ruffling garments, vigorously patting the tarpaulin with shaking hands. Then with a deep breath he grunted his satisfaction and stepped back to close the door. But even as he raised his arm and gripped the rim, he was aware of steps behind him, and as he began to slam the door he experienced the iron resistance of another hand.

'Just a moment,' said Lee in his clear precise English, his cold eyes boring into Mulraine's, before concentrating on the palpably tense bulk beneath the tarpaulin.

'Don't get carried away, Captain,' said Mulraine.

Oblivious, Lee drew his pistol and began carefully evacuating the rear of the vehicle, item by item into the road.

'I've been through the lot,' said Mulraine, 'we're holding the gentleman up.'

The space was clear, only the tarpaulin to be lifted. Lee waited for Hurst, sub-machine-gun primed, to step closer. Drawing away, Mulraine found himself standing beside Eugene McBride, seeking the sheer distraction of the mountainside. Exchanging telling glances with Hurst, Lee took a slow breath, reached for the edge of the tarpaulin and, with a violent jerk, whipped it back and leapt aside to safety. Hurst squeezed the trigger to the very point of contact and held fast, poised to fire. Mulraine held his breath, unwilling to look. Seconds passed.

He dared to look. Lee, shoulders sagging, was examining a bulky tent, unravelling lengths of canvas, discovering stacks of poles, bunches of pegs. With a gesture of impatience he came away and snatched the flashlight from Mulraine's hand. Dropping to the ground, he peered beneath the vehicle. Finally he stood up, teeth clenched, glowering at the mountains.

'Damn you,' said Eugene. 'One of these days you people are going to realise this isn't your country.'

Lee gave a laugh and tossed the flashlight back to Mulraine. 'You can keep it.'

With the departure of the soldiers and the detective, Eugene and Deirdre drove on. After less than half a mile, they came to a bridge and pulled up. Windows rolled down, they listened to the awful darkness, and to the river rushing beneath, and watched the moon alternately exposing the mountains, and restoring them to silhouettes.

Suddenly two figures, a man and a woman, appeared. Eugene got out, his daughter coming towards him, once his princess, now a sniper, a lapsed terrorist, an outlaw hellbent on a desperate mission.

'Christ, Papa, we thought you weren't coming!' He opened the rear of the vehicle. 'What kept you?'

He looked away, unable to speak.

An hour later the Range Rover approached the airfield perched at the northern tip of Strangford Lough. As an established member of the Ulster Flying Club, Eugene had no difficulty gaining late-night access to his plane.

Smuggled into the hangar, Marcus and Annie were met by no ordinary flying machine. Eugene's plane was a venerable maverick among the modern aircraft and gliders inhabiting and visiting the airfield – a chrome-plated P–51 Mustang American World War Two fighter, lovingly preserved, a charismatic presence crouching expectantly on its front wheels.

The hangar's doors slid wide, the Mustang rolled forward and nosed into the moonlight. The night was still for a few moments longer. Then the single four-bladed propeller began to turn in jerks, the engine coughed and spluttered and emitted a whining roar across the lough.

Annie and Deirdre embraced, a brief fusion of strangers, each protecting herself from the barbs of the other's love. Annie even looked a stranger, hair dyed jet-black, face grim with resolve. Deirdre smiled gamely, but she too was mentally removing herself in preparation for the drive to her daughter in Ballynahinch, where with a cock-and-bull story still to be invented, she would ask to spend a few nights. Only in the last moment, when they broke apart, and physical space rushed like a dark tide between them, did cracks appear in their defences, their eyes filming over, blinding them.

'God be with you, child,' murmured Deirdre.

Marcus came forward to offer his hand, but Deirdre was walking away. Annie, roused as though from a trance, vaulted onto a wing and climbed into the cockpit. Marcus followed, agile for one who now looked so much older, his freshly shaven cheeks covered with a neat silvery beard, eyebrows flecked to match, and his cropped head chalky grey.

The Mustang taxied over the airfield, alone in the widespread night, coming to rest at the end of an illuminated runway, lights receding and converging like candles into obscurity. Annie and Marcus crouched squashed together behind the pilot's seat. Eugene sat slack at the controls, constellations of tiny lights at his fingertips, communicating in snatches with a flight controller.

'Perfect flying weather, Mr McBride.'

'Thanks for fixing it for me!'

Muffled laughter. 'Ach, no trouble!'

Behind the bravura and humour, Annie was relieved to hear the pain in her father's voice, confirming feelings for her which he rarely acknowledged and she scarcely believed. His heart a void, his brain on automatic pilot, he would deposit his daughter and her accomplice in some far-flung corner of an airfield in the South, with his suitcases in their hands and his money in their pockets. Then he would find himself a lonely hotel room for a few days, leaving his home, presided over by his wife's spirit, to its fate.

'You're cleared for take-off, Mr McBride . . . enjoy your trip.'

Annie caught her breath, cockpit lights playing eerily on her distraught face. 'Papa?' she shouted above the engines. 'Papa, will you be all right?' Her face crumpled before Marcus's eyes, revealing fears and emotions which he hadn't seen in her before. After a pause Eugene replied over his shoulder, 'Of course I'll be all right.' Suddenly animated. 'And when it's all over, you and me are going to have some good times together!'

Annie clapped a hand over her mouth, choking.

Marcus touched her shoulder. 'You can still change your mind, drop me down South and return with your father.'

She closed her eyes for a moment, and seemed to waver, fighting some private perpetual battle.

'Papa!' she cried, throwing her arms about her father's neck, 'Let's go!'

Submitting to her will, Eugene took the controls and released the plane. Its guttural roar filled the night, it jolted forward, wings reaching for the runway lights, making a game of passing them back, slowly at first, quicker now, tail lifting off the tarmac, wind rushing over the wings, bursting off the canopy, speed doubling and redoubling, engine finding a higher strain, wheels pitching free, nose rising, the ground falling away, runway lights tumbling like flames into the sea, the whole plane soaring over the tilting lough, up and up over shore-lights and scattered settlements.

Annie slumped forward. Marcus hesitated, starkly aware of how little he knew her. The dramatic transformation from red to jet-black reinforced his sense of partnering a total stranger. Head bowed, she was inaudibly crying as the plane levelled off, her slight shoulders heaving, her whole body trembling. Taking her head against his shoulder, he held her.

337

20

By ten o'clock the following morning, a second emergency meeting was underway in the ministerial conference room attended once more by the same three men – the Northern Ireland Secretary representing the British Government, Sir Ian McNab the Chief Constable, and the Army commander Sir Jeremy Pemberton-Billing. And once again the top policeman and soldier were both impeccably turned out down to their last gleaming button, and suitably restrained to the point of studied indifference, while the politician looked jaded, sallow and flustered.

'I spoke with the PM an hour ago,' said the minister, still reeling from the call. 'Needless to say she is not amused. She finds it incredible, and frankly, gentlemen, I share her astonishment, that a soldier who's as coloured as . . . they come, cannot be found by the combined security forces. I warned you what would happen if we didn't catch him quickly. We now have the European Parliament passing a resolution calling for the banning of plastic bullets in Northern Ireland and throughout the EEC. Naturally we won't take the slightest bit of notice, but we really cannot tolerate this wild goose chase focusing world attention on us. The lunatic must be caught!'

'I understand he's about to be,' announced Sir Ian. 'Inspector Mulraine tells me – '

'I thought he was supposed to be here,' interrupted the minister.

'He's not the most punctual sleuth in the province,' conceded the portly Chief Constable, 'but he believes he has the deserter and the Red Sniper under surveillance in a house in Rostrevor.'

The minister brightened, patting the polished table.

'Touch wood! Only this time,' he threw a reproving look at Sir Jeremy, the Army commander, 'let's hope we don't let him wriggle out.'

A timely knock on the door.

Mulraine was admitted. They noticed the change. The last two weeks had taken their toll on the flamboyant Ulsterman. Gone was the gay suit and reckless entrance. He was soberly dressed in a dark suit, tie loosened at the neck, rebellious silver hair over his collar. He looked haggard and humourless as he carefully laid his sturdy briefcase on the table.

There was a general murmur of good-mornings as the minister invited the detective to take a seat at the far end of the table. It seemed a long time ago that the minister had hurried to Mulraine's side to peer at a sketch map marked with a God-forsaken island called Inishtrahull.

'I understand we finally have some promising news,' declared the minister.

Mulraine clicked his tongue judiciously and shook his head, as though reprimanding the minister for his haste.

'If you're referring to the house in Rostrevor, the good gentlemen of the SAS stormed it this morning and found no one.'

The room sagged, Mulraine's audience groaning as one.

'Then you were wrong,' said the minister with satisfaction.

More infuriating tongue-clicking. 'No, I believe that forensic evidence will establish that they were there, but slipped through our fingers – '

'I don't believe it!' blurted the minister, believing only too well.

'It's not as bad as it sounds – '

'It sounds bad, Inspector,' rumbled Sir Ian, Mulraine's boss.

'The trail is not cold, I have an idea what they're up to, and I have a proposal to make . . .'

He paused, looking round for indulgence to proceed.

'If it's more powers you want,' said the minister, 'how much more power can a policeman have?'

'Considerably more, Minister. I request permission formally to offer the fugitives safe conduct to a major press conference, where they would be allowed to state their case before being taken into custody . . .'

The three men stared at him incredulously.

'I have reason to believe they are planning something far more alarming than a press conference, and that I could deflect them from their desperate purpose and draw this sorry saga to an honourable conclusion.'

He set his broad hands on the table, resting his case. Silence fell, disturbed only by birds outside the window. Sir Ian looked embarrassed, Sir Jeremy bemused, the minister dumbfounded.

'Are you actually suggesting an amnesty for an extremely dangerous traitor and his terrorist accomplice?'

'No, on the contrary, Lieutenant King – '

'He's no longer a lieutenant,' Sir Jeremy reminded him bluntly.

' – isn't looking for a pardon. He is prepared to give himself up and stand trial. Nor do I consider him to be dangerous or treacherous. The man has been misjudged. Handled intelligently, he could be brought quietly to trial.'

'Not dangerous! Not a traitor! What do you call teaming up with the IRA?'

'With respect, Minister, there's no evidence – '

'No evidence! He just happened to be two minutes away from the bomb in the hospital and the one in the car-park at Malin Head. He just happened to find himself in IRA uniform flourishing an Armalite!'

'Not a scrap of evidence, Minister, we'd be laughed out of court.'

'Really! I suppose it was pure coincidence that he fled across Donegal in the company of a notorious woman terrorist, sheer accident that he became involved in a murderous attack on members of the SAS!'

'I take it then you haven't read my report?'

'About an IRA sniper who's a little squeamish about bombs, but has no qualms about attempting to murder three policemen in Strabane!'

'I don't believe there was any attempt to murder – '

'You hold very generous beliefs, Inspector.'

'And my report, you'll recall, expressed serious doubts about the SAS version of events at the isolated barn.'

The Army commander came to life. 'Are you calling into question the testimony of Captain Lee and his men?'

'They have a reputation to defend.'

'That wasn't my question.'

From his briefcase Mulraine produced a folder. 'The Garda's report – '

'You've shown us the Garda's report. It's your conclusion I'm interested in.'

'My conclusion, Sir Jeremy, is that Captain Lee is a liar.'

The word hung irresistibly in the air.

'I think Inspector Mulraine may be tired,' suggested the disconcerted police chief.

The Army commander appealed to the minister at the head of the table.

'Captain Lee has a record second to none. I resent these insinuations, which depend entirely on the initial impressions of a Garda detective. This is doing our cause no good whatsoever!'

The minister had grown strangely calm, sitting back, legs crossed, finger to his pursed lips.

'For myself,' said Mulraine in a voice beginning to shake, 'I would prefer to give credence to investigations carried out by a Garda officer whom I know personally to be highly qualified, than to accept the word of Dixie Doyle that Marcus King joined the IRA.'

Feeling trapped in his end-of-table seat, Mulraine stood up, and began taking a few short paces back and forth, hands in trouser pockets.

'I'm sorry, gentlemen, if the apparent truth does not accord with your perceptions, but the fact is that all my enquiries leave me in no doubt that I am hunting a brave and honourable soldier, whose only wish is to set the record straight and atone for the death of the O'Rawe girl.'

'A monk you interviewed,' recalled Sir Jeremy with a barely concealed smirk on his immobile face, 'made a considerable impression on you, Inspector.'

'Yes. Brother Dominic went so far as to write saying that he would be willing to attest to the goodness and sanity of Marcus King at any subsequent trial.'

'So the word of a Gaelic monk,' marvelled the Secretary of State, 'counts for more than the diagnoses and judgements of doctors, psychiatrists and senior Army officers?'

'Indeed, sir. But I wouldn't expect an Englishman to understand that.'

The minister reddened, too piqued to counter. Sir Ian shook his head in dismay. Sir Jeremy gazed steadfastly ahead. Frank Mulraine remained on his feet, holding himself up. The ground seemed far away and out of focus. He felt strangely detached from himself, a sympathetic witness to his own professional undoing. Afraid he was going to pass out, he clung to a mental picture of home – Barbara, the boys, muddy motorbikes, thick carpets, carpet slippers, burnt bacon . . .

'It seems to me to be a great shame,' said the minister coolly, 'that after all the faith we've invested in you, you should lack the necessary commitment to bringing this troublesome soldier to justice . . .'

In preparation for departing, Mulraine lifted his briefcase down onto his seat and replied, 'And it seems to me an even greater shame that you haven't been listening, gentlemen. It is precisely to justice that I am trying to bring this troublesome soldier.'

The Chief Constable was on his feet. 'You've said quite enough, Inspector.'

'I think you'd better wait outside,' said the minister.

'I am trying to give you a true picture, gentlemen,' lamented Mulraine.

'Damn your true picture,' said the minister, 'I've more important things to consider.'

Mulraine lowered his head. 'We are throwing away a great opportunity . . .'

'That's no longer your concern,' snapped Sir Ian, 'I am removing you from the case as from this minute!'

Lowering his eyes, Mulraine absorbed the shock. Then without a word, he turned on his heels and walked out, softly closing the door behind him.

'I apologise, gentlemen,' said the Chief Constable resuming his seat, 'I take full responsibility for appointing a man whose loyalty has turned out to be wanting.'

'Never mind, Sir Ian. All that concerns us now is that you replace him quickly and find the traitor. Press releases should make it quite clear that he is on the run with an IRA terrorist, probably planning some appalling outrage. And gentlemen, he must be stopped. I shall leave it up to you to interpret that duty as you see fit.'

As the other two men thoughtfully nodded, there came a knock on the door. Without waiting for a reply, Mulraine walked in. The room tensed. Mulraine looked at no one, merely collected his briefcase from his chair and walked out again.

'Something he said earlier worries me,' confessed Sir Jeremy lowering his voice.

'Yes,' agreed Sir Ian, 'he thought he knew what King and the woman were up to . . .'

'And that they're planning something more dramatic than a press conference,' recalled the minister.

Sir Ian and Sir Jeremy looked at each other. Sir Ian rose to his feet and lowered his voice.

342

'I think we had better keep the good detective in sight, don't you, Sir Jeremy?'

The Army commander rose to meet him. 'A pleasant change for Captain Lee.'

'If you'll excuse us, Minister.'

21

Dublin

A sultry afternoon, a wayward detective stepping from the Belfast – Dublin train, face set with resolve, furrowed with worry. To a compassionate observer he cuts a lonely figure, a once flamboyant professional dispensing nervous glances before picking a taxi. But the two men who have followed him from Belfast have no charity to spare.

Dressed as smart young executives, shielded by dark glasses, the two Englishman – one drawn, lean and dark-haired, the other blond and conventionally handsome – board the next taxi and tail the disgraced detective from Connolly Station across the north face of the oppressively warm city, hopeful that he will inadvertently lead them to the fugitives. This time the orders are stark and simple. No concessions, no variations. Only that the deed will be untraceable. Captured IRA weapons will be used. And the dark-haired Englishman carries in his pocket a small item which will point the finger at one man – Dixie Doyle.

This time, there will be no mistakes.

The taxi turns into a narrow graceless street and pulls up on a corner. Mulraine pays, steps cautiously out and mounts the hotel steps, half hoping that there will be no messages, the fugitives pursuing their wild scheme without him, even dying in the attempt.

But the youthful short-sleeved receptionist beams.

'A Miss Murray phoned. She'll call again.'

For a moment he's thrown. Then in the cramped lift he remembers: Murray, the name she used at the hotel in Donegal. Locking himself in his hotel room, he lights a cigarette and pulls up a chair to the telephone. Any minute Miss Murray will ring, sealing his fate? But first, a call he dreads to make. Sick with nerves, he dials. The phone rings a hundred miles away. With a shock he feels the absence of well-being and safeness associated with home. It's as if his home port is out of reach, maybe even closed to him.

Barbara answers, voice neither bright nor dull, and unchanging when she hears it's him. With another jolt he sees that their marriage is like her voice, complacent, incapable of surprises – perhaps until now. They talk about the boys, the hot weather, the garden. He waits for her unfailing ear to pick up that something is wrong, and for her to draw it out of him.

He replaces the receiver. The call is over. She detected nothing, he divulged nothing. Dazed, he stands up, gazing at a blank wall. He has changed, no longer the man he was. His old life, like a shoreline, is receding, never to be reclaimed. He is speculating on what future there may be, if any, for himself and Barbara, when the phone rings, making him start. Barbara! She sensed it after all, nothing has changed, she'll persuade him to change his mind and let the fugitives stew. Lifting the receiver, he hears a voice that is less familiar, younger, vibrant.

'Frank Mason?'

'Miss Murray.'

'Stephen's Green, 6 p.m., bridge over lake.' Click.

5.30 p.m.

On the south side of the city two outlaws are on the move, driving east through Dolphin's Barn in a fast car with Donegal number plates. Eileen Feeley glances tensely at her passenger.

'OK, you'll need secret surgery, but once you've mended, the Brits won't know what hit them!'

Dixie smiles, but only because she refuses to see that he's burned out and badly needs a rest. British soldiers sleep in forts, endure relatively brief tours. Dixie's lived and fought on the run for twelve long years. His family has suffered. He wants to live, to have another child.

Feeley pulls up a hundred yards from the address.

'Thanks.' He starts to get out.

'Dixie . . .' She grips his arm.

He meets her artless gaze, knowing he may never see her again,

344

his constant comrade. The only milk of human kindness she possesses has always been reserved for him. And he never wanted it.

'You'll be in touch' – she won't let go – 'the minute you get back?'

'You ought to be leading a unit of your own.'

'We're brilliant together!' she flares, eyes hard and pleading.

'Sure . . .' Squeezing her hand.

He gets out, dragging his case from the back, and starts to cross the wide busy road, lined with pleasant terraces set back over gardens. He only needs a walking stick now, moving with scarcely a limp, resolutely covering his constant pain. He wears a trim tan suit, white open-necked shirt, gleaming shoes. His overlong hair is sleekly combed back, he looks relaxed, debonair, happy. Feeley is shocked, and as she pulls away from the kerb, she feels bitter pangs of jealousy, and can only hope that Mary and Josie are away, so he will be stranded, dependent on her.

As Feeley rejoins the traffic and Dixie crosses the road, two disbelieving men come to life in the shadows of the cigarette factory opposite. Nameless, faceless, they've been waiting a long time for this moment. Dispatched three weeks earlier by Loyalist leader Teddy Paxton, but unable to find their man, they've pursued the rumour that Mary Doyle has fled to her sister's in Dublin. Now here's the man himself.

Lifting the gate, Dixie takes the sunlit garden path to a front door crowned with a fanlight window. With a twist of disappointment he finds no names, only numbers on the bellboard. He tries several bells. While he waits, doubts beset him. Mary will have followed news reports of him bombing a hospital, killing a guard instead of Marcus King, bombing a car-park and maiming a hotel maid instead of Mulraine, and of his catching and losing King. She may fear he's gone back on his word to quit the war and join her.

The big front door opens, a tenant on his way out. Exchanging awkward nods, Dixie finds himself in a cool entrance hall, rooting through stray mail on the table. Several letters for Mary's sister, Kathleen Donaghy, Flat 3. Discovering bedsits 1 and 2 on the ground floor, he starts up the stairs, aided by the banister. With luck the uncollected mail means Kathleen's away, and that Mary and Josie are alone. He reaches a door marked 3, leans against it, listening. No sound. Out shopping? He knocks, heart pounding. And again. 'Mary. . .?'

345

Across the landing a door opens fractionally, a suspicious eye. Dixie outstares it, the door closes softly. 'Mary. . .?'

Heart sinking, he resolves to wait.

Briefcase in hand, Frank Mulraine paces the humped bridge in St Stephen's Green, a park rich in shrubs and trees forming a great square in the heart of the city. He consults his watch repeatedly. 5.57, 5.59, 6.02 . . . Now it's 6.09 on a humid evening, his untypically sombre suit suffocating him, shirt clinging to flesh, gnats tormenting him. Lighting another cigarette, coughing mechanically, he scours the flocks of casual Dubliners drifting through the park, his eyesight playing tricks, conjuring six-foot black men and statuesque redheads at every turn. He is filled with an aching sense of isolation, at once invigorating and terrifying. He imagines himself entirely alone and alienated in this Southern city, unaware of being watched, hawkishly and discreetly, from across the lake. Two more men – one slim and boyish, one bull-large and limping – have joined the pair who followed Mulraine from Belfast. The original team is complete, and as they observe the restless detective, they share the feeling that their grit and sweat and relentless tenacity is about to be rewarded.

A long-limbed, loose-tracksuited jogger mounts the bridge and leans over the parapet, close to Mulraine. He barely notices. It's not until he meets the runner's reflection in the water that he turns slowly to face her. Her profusion of hair is jet-black and restrained by a headband, but the slightly imperious expression is the one she reserved for him by the poolside in Rostrevor.

'Where is he?' Mulraine demands.

'Patience!' she replies, mocking him. With a jerk of the head she bids him follow. She jogs lightly, drawing away, leading him to a lakeside pavilion, its sides open to the air. He hesitates on the threshold, as though resisting his fate. Just then his attention is drawn to a man coming round the lake. The path abounds with people, but the tall black priest stands out, broad frame filling a layman's dove-grey suit, dog-collar snow-white about his deep-brown neck. He has cropped grey hair, trim grey beard, and broad spectacles. The imposing figure strolls towards him, taking his ease with ample dignity, punctuating his strides with a rolled umbrella propelled like a walking stick. Mulraine is enthralled, but the young jogger observes the priest critically as he joins her in the

346

pavilion with a polite nod. 'You're not stooping, you're too straight. There's still too much spring in your step.'

Reassured, Mulraine joins them, picks a bench and opens a paper. African and West Indian priests are a not uncommon sight in Dublin, and with practice Marcus may pass for a man of sixty.

'I take it you're both still hell-bent on this plan?'

Annie laughs derisively. 'If you've turned up to put us off – '

'What did you expect?'

'Forget it. How's Michael?'

'Michael?'

'Jesus, he's forgot him already. You promised – '

'I'll speak for him at his trial.'

'If you're not brought to trial first.'

'Precisely.' They vie with smiles. 'Now listen here. The press is agog with rumour, you're celebrities, the scene is perfectly set for a spectacular press conference.' Mulraine spreads his hands to illustrate the magnitude of the coming event. 'Journalists descending on Dublin like bees to rare blossom, TV pictures beamed across the world, your denunciations of bombs and baton rounds broadcast like far-flung seed – '

'On stony ground,' Annie cut in scornfully, 'snatches of Marcus, snatches of me, cut to size, shaped to fit. "And she was wearing" – she mimics an animated reporter – "and I could have sworn they were holding hands," bla-bla-bla!'

Marcus is silent, troubled. A press conference has always seemed the most prudent option. But then again . . .

'Now if you'll excuse us,' says Annie grandly.

'I'm not done yet.'

'We've wasted enough time.'

'Keep your voice down, sister,' says Marcus.

'They're out to smear you with lies,' warns Mulraine heatedly, 'brand you, vilify and crucify you – '

'And you' – Annie publicly introduces him with a sweeping theatrical gesture – 'are going to save us!'

She's on her way out, Marcus rises to follow.

'One moment, I've brought you something.' They falter, Annie's anxious to be gone. Mulraine lifts his briefcase onto his knees, plays with the locking catch, activating a tape-recorder built into the false bottom. He glances about as his own voice, muffled but distinct, escapes through concealed speakers. *The trail is not*

347

cold, *I have an idea what they're up to, and I have a proposal to make . . .'*

'If it's more power you want' – this voice is clipped, English, censorious – 'how much more power can a policeman have?'

'Who's that?' Marcus, intrigued.

'Who do you think?'

'I request permission formally to offer the fugitives safe conduct to a major press conference, where they would be allowed to state their case before being taken into custody . . .'

Marcus and Annie exchange glances. Gazing at the talking briefcase they resume their seats.

'I seem to recall,' Mulraine smiles grimly, 'that at this point they looked at me as if I'd just laid my member on the ministerial table.'

'I have reason to believe they are planning something far more alarming than a press conference, and that I could deflect them from their desperate purpose and draw this sorry saga to an honourable – '

'You didn't tell them?' blurts Annie.

Mulraine shakes his head, and for a further ten minutes they hear him trying to defend them against the intransigence of the top three men in Northern Ireland. They hear the Northern Ireland Secretary unbending in his determination to condemn them, the Army commander scandalised by Mulraine calling into question the integrity of Captain Lee and his men, the police chief embarrassed by Mulraine's performance.

'I'm sorry, gentlemen, if the apparent truth does not accord with your perceptions, but the fact is that all my enquiries leave me in no doubt that I am hunting a brave and honourable soldier whose only wish is to set the record straight and atone for the death of the O'Rawe girl . . .'

'A monk you interviewed' – the Army Commander's tone is patronising – 'made a considerable impression on you, Inspector.'

'Yes. Brother Dominic went so far as to write saying that he would be willing to attest to the goodness and sanity of Marcus King at any subsequent trial . . .'

Marcus is moved. Dominic's voice and spirit, if not his face, return to him. And the windswept beauty and desolation of the island.

'So the word of a Gaelic monk' – the minister from London sounds amused – 'counts for more than the diagnoses and judgements of doctors, psychiatrists and senior Army officers?'

'Indeed, sir. But I wouldn't expect an Englishman to understand that . . .'

Annie guffaws. Mulraine meets her eye, and feels for the first time her grudging admiration.

'At this point I'm shaking in my boots.'

'It seems to me to be a great shame' – the minister is controlled, icy – 'that after all the faith we've invested in you, you should lack the necessary commitment to bring this troublesome soldier to justice . . .'

'Listen! The interference, that's me transferring the briefcase to my chair as I'm about to leave.'

'And it seems to me an even greater shame that you haven't been listening, gentlemen. It is precisely to justice that I am trying to bring this troublesome soldier . . .'

'You've said quite enough, Inspector' – the Police Chief.

'I think you'd better wait outside' – the minister.

'I am trying to give you a true picture, gentlemen . . .'

'Damn your true picture' – the minister in like a knife – 'I've more important things to consider . . .'

'Bastard!' Annie shows her teeth.

Marcus whistles through his.

'We are throwing away a great opportunity . . .'

'That's no longer your concern' – the Police Chief is livid – 'I am removing you from this case as from this minute!'

They look at Mulraine in amazement.

'I've just walked out,' Mulraine refers them back to the tape. 'I apologise, gentlemen. I take full responsibility for appointing a man whose loyalty has turned out to be wanting . . .'

'My loyalty to my job has never been wanting,' objects Mulraine.

Annie and Marcus look puzzled.

'You just said you left,' says Marcus.

'Yes, but the briefcase' – 'Never mind, Sir Ian. All that concerns us now is that you replace him quickly and find the traitor' – 'is still on the chair.' 'Press releases should make it quite clear that he is on the run with an IRA terrorist, probably planning some appalling outrage. And gentlemen, he must be stopped. I shall leave it up to you to interpret that duty as you see fit . . .'

Annie swears obscenely, Marcus pales behind his beard and hangs his head. 'I don't believe it . . . the men at the top more guilty than the ones they're hunting.'

Annie catches Mulraine's eye: 'Will you listen to him. He's so naïve it's like travelling with a kid.'

'Unfortunately I felt I must return at this point for my case . . .' The knock on the door is audible, the case being removed, the door closed, and presently the recorder switched off. 'Whatever else they plot we don't hear.'

'You left it on purpose,' says Annie, shaking her head approvingly.

He basks in her light. 'I hope you see now it's my fight too. So long as I kept bringing them the heads of gangsters and terrorists, my masters were content. But the day I dare protest the innocence of one man – '

'Yes but you chose their sacrificial lamb,' observes Annie.

'You even offered to bring me in,' Marcus notes.

'And like a good sheriff I shall. It's imperative if the pair of you are not to be damned that I come in with you and make the arrest at the end.'

A look from Marcus quells Annie. 'He's our witness, the only proof of our intentions.'

For the next few minutes Mulraine reveals what he knows about the security arrangements they're liable to encounter.

Marcus is getting nervous. They arrange for Mulraine to pick them up the following day by taxi at two p.m. Annie and Mulraine can't agree on where. Marcus assumes a priestly air.

'Better make it a church.'

Mulraine unfolds a map, selects a nearby church. All rise to leave. Peering over the rims of his false glasses, Marcus exchanges a conspiratorial nod with Mulraine before stepping out along the lake. On her way out, Annie glances over her shoulder and warms the detective with a smile.

They disperse. But the men watching from across the water are only interested now in the black priest walking leisurely around the lake and in the loose-limbed jogger who throws him a look as she passes. The men, well spread, begin to move as one. They are relaxed, and will be for a few more hours, while there is daylight. But when night falls . . .

6.40 p.m.

Waiting demoralises him. He arrived an hour ago full of hope.
Now, wondering where Mary and Josie could be, he leaves his
suitcase outside their door, goes down to the garden and looks up
at their window. The curtains are closed. Panic seizes him, draws
tight around his neck. Why the drawn curtains? Innocent explana-
tions spring to mind, but it's horrific ones which assail him.
Trembling uncontrollably, he reminds himself that he has faced
this panic before and always found them safe. With fresh heart he
returns indoors, climbing the stairs one at a time, testing the door
with his shoulder. Solid. Delving in his jacket pocket, he chooses
from a selection of tools, scraps of wire, strips of plastic, addressing
the task of separating the latch case from the keep. The lock yields,
the door gives. He enters softly, the room dim and silent as a crypt.
Hearing neighbours stirring on the landing, he draws the door
closed after him, moves to switch on a light – freezes. On the far
side of the room, on top of a double bed, two figures lie. He leans
transfixed on his walking stick, remaining so for some moments.

Manoeuvring to the window, he parts the curtains fractionally,
permitting a band of light to enter. He follows it to the bed. They lie
on their sides, perfectly still, facing inward, Josie's left hand held
awkwardly in Mary's right, Josie curiously restful, eyes closed, as
though Mary had found a simple way (with the pillow?) of
returning her to Heaven.

Dixie sits on the bed. Mary's departure has evidently been
harder. She looks ghastly, once so pretty. On the bedside table, an
empty gin bottle and a crowd of pill bottles. No note. Reaching, he
tries to join hands with them. But their rubber-cool fingers unite
against him. He sits up. All is settled. He need no longer be torn
between cause and family, belonging now to neither. Mary
needn't struggle any longer, and Josie, the butt of British soldiers'
jokes, is Doyle's idiot no more.

Voices from the landing rouse him. Somewhere in his mind
sirens wail. Capture. Extradition. A gleeful welcome from his
enemies. Time to be gone.

He can't move. His wife and child, he'll never see them again,
never hear them, never touch Mary, never another child.

Someone's knocking, investigating. He goes to close Mary's
eyes, his hand casting a shadow over her face, his fingertips

closing her eyelids for ever. He bows his head, shuts his own eyes. Tears come, springing from the depths of his soul.

Standing, he starts to make the sign of the cross, but his hand loses its way. Stepping back he takes a final look at his family, burning the picture in his mind. He turns to the door. Outside he's met by a consortium of fearful, neighbourly expressions. He looks them in the eye, closing the door firmly behind him. They shrink from him, he starts down the stairs. 'Your case!' someone calls. He's gone.

Out in the bright evening he falters this way and that at the garden gate. A police car is approaching at speed from the direction of Dolphin's Barn. Swinging his walking stick, he moves off in the opposite direction, taking the first corner past a grocer's store, over a hump-backed bridge and down to the canal, slowing to a blind measured tread, in and out of sun and shade along the towpath, oblivious to his surroundings, to his pain, to his assassins gaining from behind. He walks stiff and farsighted as a sleep-walker. A courting couple make way, a dog-walker draws in his pet, a boy fishing follows his progress over one shoulder and then the other. Dixie walks, sightless.

The assassins are young, denimed, pitiless, come to do what the Police and Army in the North have failed to do. Days of lurking in the Catholic capital have made them edgy. Generations of fear and hatred gleam in their eyes, the promise of folklore fame breaks the discipline of their step as they close on him.

At that moment some inner ear hears or senses the danger. But far from being spurred into action, he turns obediently to meet it. The sun hitting the water dazes him. Through the swirling dust step two figures walking quickly. Two shots ring out, crashing over the still water, startling a pair of mallards flapping into the haze, causing strollers to freeze, dogs to yelp and Dixie to break his fall against a tree. Somewhere in the darkroom of his mind, he pictures the two merciful bullet-holes, culverts delivering his lifeblood to the roots of the tree. But he's still on his feet, clawing the coarse bark of the tree, listening to the rapid arrival of feet along the towpath, a familiar voice.

'Move, you stupid bastard.'

Unscathed, he permits Feeley to seize hold of him and hustle him up the grassy bank towards the waiting car. A sidelong glance and the canal comes back into focus, complete with petrified passers-by and two bodies on the towpath, one still, the other belly-crawling in a blind attempt at escape.

Feeley flings open the passenger door and bundles Dixie in. Running to the driver's side, she dives behind the wheel, slams the car into gear and takes it away at high speed.

9.00 p.m.

A sturdy redbrick hotel on the riverfront, sash windows thrown open to the sunset. In Annie's room on the third floor, Marcus sits at a small table reading through a stack of newspapers. Though he experiences the reports like thorns in the flesh, he tries hard to remain detached, resolutely amused, keeping at bay his sense of rage and personal injury.

Annie sits on the carpet, back against a wall, maps and diagrams spread before her, pencilling in the stages of the plan where they may be most vulnerable, pausing now and then to test Marcus's mood, anxious to prevent him brooding, trying to keep his spirits up.

'The more shit they print about us the better. All they're doing is focusing world attention in time for tomorrow.'

But Marcus's anger boils over. Seizing a sheet of newspaper he scrunched it in his fist and shakes it as though it's an editor he has by the throat. 'Why do they have to start on my family?'

A lean dark Englishman loiters down in the lobby, lingering over a long iced drink, leafing through a rack of tourist brochures. Outwardly relaxed in dark glasses and a cool cotton suit, he blends effortlessly with guests flowing in and out of the bars and restaurant. Sporting a pink carnation, he appears to have strayed from the hundred-strong wedding party occupying one of the bars. Calm hands and quiet eyes betray none of his burning impatience.

Out on the waterfront and at the back of the hotel, his men kill time, waiting, watching.

Three floors up Annie calls him over, he joins her on the carpet. They go over the plan again, trying to anticipate pitfalls.

'How the hell are we supposed to anticipate when we don't know where they hide their security troops?'

She objects to imagined or implied criticism in his tone.

'What do you want me do, ring them up and ask?'

They argue frequently and briefly. Annie is for holding out until all their demands are met. Marcus is for a more flexible approach.

'I won't be satisfied with grand gestures,' she vows.

'You'd rather die in a glorious shoot-out.'

'Yes!'

'Count me out.'

Like wilful horses harnessed to a single chariot they drag each other back and forth, trying to dictate direction. Neither holds sway, rather they pull, by virtue of equal strength, together.

He goes back to the papers, slaps the face of one tabloid with the back of his hand. 'Who says we don't have a free press? They tell all the lies they like. They haven't two facts to rub together but they're free to judge and sentence me like lynch mobs!' Others trade in lurid fantasies, fashioning images of him training IRA units, setting ambushes to avenge himself on the SAS. One jubilant headline reads 'MY TRAITOR HUBBY'S IRA MISTRESS! Pretty Marcia King says she's sick to death of her randy husband's antics. His treacherous flirtation with the IRA is shocking enough, but she's even more livid over rumours that he is carrying on a steamy on-the-run love affair with the IRA's wild redhaired terrorist . . .' An Army photo of him is juxtaposed with an Annie McBride look-alike, eyeing her hungrily. A more sober paper reveals that a TV documentary *Crusader or Traitor* featuring interviews with members of his family, unidentified soldiers from his battalion and a community of monks who sheltered him on a remote island, has been seized by the police on orders from the Home Secretary.

'Let's go out!' Annie pipes up.

He looks at her doubtfully.

'Our last night of freedom,' she smiles tantalisingly, 'candle-lit dinner, last glass of wine!'

With a dry laugh he leaves the table and stands in the window. The sky over the city is turning purple, a curtain holding back the night.

'Tomorrow we'll give them something to write about.'

Leaning out into the cooling evening he takes in the long view of the sun-stained river, frayed Georgian façades, spires and sea-green domes, gulls wheeling over ancient bridges. A wry smile. He recalls the afternoon of the football game in the Bogside, summoned to the C.O.'s stuffy office, stripped of his rank, sent packing like a birched schoolboy, seen off by the C.O.'s vindictive little eyes and the Major's inflated look of satisfaction. 'They thought they could squash me' – he turns to meet Annie's gaze – 'but I warned them.'

'I feel cooped up. Let's go out!'

'You crazy?'

'Christ, you've come through hell since then, and you're worried about a night on the town?'

She wears a red silk sleeveless dress, medium-heeled shoes, long looping earrings and her first strokes of make-up in more than twelve months. She strikes a coquettish pose before the mirror, catches Marcus's eye. They laugh, he stands beside her, slips an arm about her narrow waist. He has on the second of two suits donated by Eugene, a classic beige cotton suit with fine gold stripe, matching silk shirt, black tie and soft cream Italian shoes. They gaze at the picture they make.

'Not bad,' she says, 'for a British soldier.'

'Not bad for a terrorist.'

His cheeks have had a couple of hours rest. Before venturing out, he applies spirit gum, fits his flawless beard and sprays a little more grey in his hair. She brings no jacket, longing for the night-breeze on her skin. She carries a slim leather shoulder bag, into which, with a mock-sinister grin, she drops a loaded pistol, the Colt .38 Special she used against the RUC in Strabane.

Playing the gallant officer, he draws himself up and offers her his arm. With exaggerated dignity and a modest flutter of the eyelids, she comes to him.

They step into the dusk, the sky dying down over the roofs on the opposite quay, the heat of the day still rising underfoot, the breeze off the river playing, as promised, on their skin. On Capel Street Bridge they lean over the parapet and look upstream towards the city centre, domes and glass edifices adrift on the water, receding into night.

They head for the lights along the north bank, Annie so light on his arm, Marcus hardly feels her. Lit softly by lanterns, an arched pedestrian footbridge returns them to the south bank, where Annie takes a fancy to an Italian restaurant on Dame Street.

'No.' Marcus recoils from the close intimacy of the place, where idle eyes may peel away their disguises. 'Somewhere big and busy.'

355

When they pause, their hunters follow suit, watching the evening thicken around them. They keep their distance, two of them enclosed inside a black BMW, the other two on foot, one on either pavement, waiting only for the moment when witnesses are few, when they will exchange suit jackets for leather, tourist cameras for machine pistols.

Drawn like moths to candlelight, the fugitives enter a restaurant off Grafton Street, the spacious venue swelled by tourists from the country and abroad, vibrant with running conversation and flushed faces. Business is brisk, Marcus moves swiftly to claim a window table. With a cavalier gesture he draws back a chair for Annie. She responds with a gracious smile. Taking his seat opposite, he gives the street a routine look, and among the drift of unremarkable details, his eye touches on a cruising BMW turning the corner out of sight.

'We're on holiday, brother,' she reminds him.

A waiter leaves a menu, Annie seizes his arm before he can escape. 'We'll kick off right away with a bottle of ice-cool champagne.'

Marcus clucks his tongue reprovingly. 'What was it Doyle used to say?'

'No sex or drink on the eve of an op!' She grins provocatively. 'We make our own rules in this outfit.'

'You mean you do. Major McBride and Private King.'

'You're lucky to be in my army at all.'

Champagne gushes, white foam, clear gold. They touch glasses, catch each other over level rims, candleflame in the eyes. Her eyes shine through jet-black curls. His skin glows, her skin glows, face and hands and neck, freckled pink, deep brown.

At quarter to midnight they emerge, Annie clasping a bottle of red wine to her bosom as though to warm it, uncorked and untouched, intended for their return to the hotel. They have already mixed wine and champagne with their meal. Their heads are light and their limbs are heavy. Struck by the dark intensity of the night, Marcus tries to get his bearings. Catching his mood, Annie looks around, heart pounding. But they're in Dublin on a balmy night and no one knows they are here. Squeezing the bottle of wine into her bag, she grabs his hand and takes off along the street, running together like children, catching their breath when they turn the corner. It's quieter here, crowds thinning, streets dimmer. She feels the tightness in his hand. He's on edge, like a raw recruit in the back streets of Derry.

'Why don't we make love tonight?'

Her tone is so spirited and innocent that he can only laugh. She laughs with him, but he has hurt her and it shows.

'Make love?' He tries to compensate, 'I wouldn't remember how!'

Hands on his shoulders, she looks up into his stealthy eyes. 'Want to be reminded?'

'We've steered clear of it this far, sister.'

Eyes bright with mischief. 'You afraid of me?'

'Throw me to the SAS any day.'

Joining her hands behind his neck, her breath warm on his face: 'Our Marcus is not afraid to take on terrorists, armies, governments, but to leap through the flames of desire . . .'

Desire rushes him, he draws her in, her thinly clothed body lashed to his. 'Sister, I don't think you really want to make love.'

'No. Anyway, you'd regret it.'

'Right. As they say, before marriage keep two eyes open; after marriage shut one. And anyway, we got lines to learn tonight.'

'What for?' Her fingers find his face, straying almost regretfully over his skin. 'It'll come naturally tomorrow' – tracing his nose, his eyebrows – 'we just need to stay calm, united . . .' There's fire in her eyes again, the fire of battle, her power joined with his. Then she softens. 'But I don't want to sleep alone tonight.'

'OK.' As he goes to plant a kiss on her forehead, he sees the sidelights of a car creeping through her hair – a night-black BMW. His lips freeze on her skin. The low-lit street is almost deserted, a young couple turning the corner, litter ruffled by the breeze, a weaving drunk, the scene unravelling as faithfully as a million city nights. Only this scene is all wrong, the BMW approaching soundlessly, a man in dark glasses and leather jacket advancing on either pavement, synchronised.

Unaware, Annie begins to pull away. He clings to her, watching the even hand of death unfold. A few moments remain – with luck. She looks at him questioningly.

'Annie, we're in trouble . . .' She stops breathing, arrested by the chill of his voice. 'Two men on foot and a black BMW. Anything behind me?'

Fused together, pulses beating. 'No.'

She waits, suspended in his arms, relying on his eyes. The car has pulled into the centre of the road. The two men, bone-tense and coldly familiar, lengthen their stride. Marcus sees exactly what is about to happen.

'Get ready to run to your right.'

Brief pause: 'Which way's that? I was never very good with left and right.'

Tugging on her right arm, be brushes her neck with his lips, watching the moment arriving . . .

'Any second . . .'

The car's headlights open up, blazing.

'NOW!'

Seizing the scant advantage of surprise, they bolt from the blinding light, turn the first corner and run for their lives, Annie kicking off her shoes in full flight, Marcus tearing at his tie, jacket flapping behind him, glancing back to catch sight of the two leather-coated gunmen turning the corner, racing teeth-bared down the middle of the road. After a rapid succession of short streets, Annie finds herself leading the way into a broad extended road, part-cobbled, part derelict, without end or alley in sight, a street from a nightmare, a shooting gallery. To the right loom bleak flats, to the left a long-running wall, intermittently crowned with jagged glass. The flats are the clear choice, if only their labyrinths of passageways will lose them. But as they wheel right towards the low-lit entrance, a pair of headlights materialises in a gully dividing the complex. Their hunters have done their groundwork.

'The wall!' Marcus cries, switching direction, making for a buckled section where the glass is thin on top, surprised to find himself leaping alone. Annie hears him, but doesn't immediately follow. In one movement she thrusts a hand into her bag, drops behind a parked vehicle and takes aim first at the chasing gunmen, then the BMW in the flats. Too late to check, Marcus launches himself at the wall, hears the loud confident report of Annie's pistol, a windscreen shattering, a car swerving and almost at once a muffled salvo in reply. If he could he would twist in mid-air to look, but as a burst of bullets rakes the wall, he's vaulting over, flying into darkness, breaking his fall in a wasteland car-park. He has barely landed when the staccato rumble ceases and he hears a pursuer scrambling over the wall behind him. With a stab of relief he recognises Annie dropping into shadow.

358

He's poised to run on, but she calls him sharply, indistinctly. He reaches her, she's handing him the gun with strange intensity. Does she mean it's his turn? He catches the gun, she slumps back against the wall, fixing him with a lopsided stare, calling to him with her eyes, clutching her belly to keep it from spilling, her dress bullet-riddled, her lacerated legs running blood. How did she manage the wall? He tries to speak, but words stick in his throat. He tries to lift her, she thrusts him off. Life-juices draining fast, she clasps his wrists, parts her lips. Transfixed, he watches her delve deep to summon back the strength to make two words. They come almost soundlessly, underlined by the force of her eyes – 'Do it!' Until now she's held on with supernatural strength, but once the words are out he feels the painful grip on his wrists diminish. She's sinking further down the wall. He seizes her arms, her shoulders. There's a moment when her eyes are fixed on him, drumming home the message, and in the next they've filmed over, gazing at him from beyond. There's a moment when she's alive in his hands, and another when she's gone, and he experiences the transition like a knife in the belly, twisted. Lifting her head, her hair, her warm flesh in his hands, he searches her empty eyes and slack mouth for some remaining flicker of life. Seizing her in his arms he envelops her violently. Her skull flops on its limp neck. As though in answer he throws back his head and stifles a shrieking howl. He cannot leave her, and he is compelled to. He wants to remain until they tear her from him, and he needs to run.

Faint murmurs and muffled treads come from the far side of the wall. He senses her thrusting him off, he reels against the wall, scraps of her dress coming away in his hands, his suit smeared with her blood, splashed by wine pumping from her punctured bag. Commanding his raging tears to silence, he reaches for a good-sized stone, lobs it high over the wall, hears men scuttle in dread of a grenade, and takes flight across the car-park half-blinded by emotion. This exposed ground stretches endlessly. Doubling for the shelter of a lorry abandoned for the night, he feels Annie's executioners scaling the wall, finding her, seeing him. Cursing the paleness of his suit, he throws himself beneath the lorry, muted shots winging by, piercing rubber and metal. They're using silencers, they mean it to be clean and quiet. Spurred by the heat of the bullets, masked by the body of the truck, he strikes out for the darkest corner of the car-park, twisting and weaving towards the far wall, feeling his back stripped in the executioners' sights, hurling himself at a high impermanent wooden structure and vaulting over, his outline caught briefly in flight above the wall. Shots ring out, he drops like a stone, lands catlike in a deserted back street and runs, beckoned by the glare of a main road.

He reaches it and looks back. No sign of them. Comforted and unnerved by street lights, he walks quickly, drawn to fellow pedestrians – human shields. Catching sight of a taxi, he draws himself up and waves. It rushes by, occupied.

The sound of sirens breaks his step, wailing across the city. A scene leaps to mind, flat-capped Gardaí scaling the car-park wall, prodding Annie, floodlighting her, smothering her in a blanket. Detectives, photographers, onlookers desecrating the lonely spot.

Sirens rise and fall, shaking him from harrowing reverie. Quickening his pace, he waves at passing cabs, glancing repeatedly over his shoulder. Suddenly he feels a car bearing down on him from behind, rearing towards him, mounting the kerb and bumping down again. Too late to run, he remains rooted, ready for doors to fly open and guns to blaze, tearing him from Marcia and Jamie for ever. The moment passes, traffic, people, voices. The driver is peering at him, sounding his horn, the vehicle sways into focus – a taxi. Marcus ducks into the back.

'Where to?'

'Drive.'

Alarmed, the slight ageless cabby drags his cab into the traffic-stream. Braced for the cab to be torn apart by bullets, Marcus reaches inside his jacket, dons his newly cracked spectacles and sits back composed to die.

The city sweeps by to left and right, rain scattering from an unseen sky, windscreen wipers beating steadily, the cabby glancing repeatedly at his passenger in the mirror.

Where to, Marcus wonders. God knows. He daren't return to the hotel, he's in a foreign city and he's low on money. The cabby's clearly nervous, beads of sweat on his pate, reminding Marcus of his own bloody appearance. The cabby takes courage, lowers the volume on his radio.

'Visiting Dublin?'

Marcus meets his eye. 'You got any docks in this city?'

'Docks?'

'Docks, ships.'

'Sure, we're right on the sea here.'

'Take me, fast as you can.'

The cabby brakes sharply, pitches the cab into a screeching U-turn and swings east, parrying the sparse night traffic and taking in Stephen's Green on its way to the river. In the dark, Marcus doesn't immediately recognise the park. Then it strikes him to the quick, the imposing entrance and overhanging trees, and some-where on the glinting ornamental lake a pavilion open to the breeze, silver-haired Mulraine and his talking briefcase, and Annie in headband and baggy tracksuit, all limbs and no hips, only a few hours ago.

The cabby reaches out of his window to adjust his radio aerial. Reception clears, traditional music gives way for news headlines – anger in Eire over rises in the cost of petrol and alcohol; a mysterious shooting on Dublin's Grand Canal – one man dead, one seriously wounded; riots in the Toxteth district of Liverpool; Israeli warplanes and gunboats bombarding Palestinian positions in West Beirut and, just in, another fatal shooting in Dublin, a woman gunned down in a city centre car-park, the Garda purportedly hunting an IRA gang . . .

'Would you listen to that!' The cabby animated, hoping to draw Marcus out: 'Desperate! They ought to confine the Troubles to where they belong – up North.' And almost in the same breath: 'You been in an accident?'

Marcus doesn't reply, he's sitting forward, they're crossing the Liffey on the furthest-flung bridge, the smell of the sea in the rain-flecked air, the deep groan of a ship rebounding over the water. They're entering a cobbled netherworld of railway arches, abandoned container lorries, dormant warehouses, darkened pubs with slits of light hinting at illicit drinkers. The sky opens out over great stretches of water, gigantic cranes brooding over the motionless hulks of trawlers and freighters.

'Where do you want?'

'Slow down, keep going.'

Window rolled down, he looks out, noting their home ports: Belfast, Birkenhead, Le Havre, Quimper, Piraeus, Leningrad.

'OK.' The cabby pulls up, Marcus steps out onto the quayside, walks a few steps along the edge, disturbing a gull which lifts from its perch, wings spread in slow motion as he passes, treading air and softly settling again. Marcus stands at the end of a wharf sniffing the salt breeze, the dark open sea, a clear run to England, or to France and then to England, or to Greece and back through Europe to England, Marcia and Jamie, Mum and Dad, Elroy and Donna and all the gang, home-smells, old haunts – illusion. There's a nagging weight in his pocket, a pistol still warm from firing, sticky with Annie's blood. Do it, she said, her wide insistent eyes still fixed on him, her hands still burning his wrists, just as Bernie O'Rawe's teeth still mark one wrist. He tosses the gun in the air, watches it tumble into the water. A soft splash, a little white plume far below, quickly smothered.

He takes in the vast stillness of the port, relieved by the winking passage of a small boat, the hollow ring of repairs going on in a ship, the slow beams of a string of lighthouses near and far, and with uncharacteristic heaviness, turns back towards the taxi. The cabby's standing in the drizzle, worried. As he reaches him, he sees over his head a car approaching at a crawl, sidelights burning, its outline becoming familiar, and finally betrayed even at a distance by its flawed windscreen. Marcus stands stock still, gripped not by fear, but an overwhelming weariness, a deep and terrible anger. His jaws tighten, his blood turns cold. Paying off the cabby, he scans the deserted quays, empty streets, silent warehouses and idle ships, and steps back under the towering steel legs of a crane, watching the taxi turn round and drive away into the path of the oncoming BMW, which swerves without warning to block the taxi's escape, doors opening while the car's still in motion, the cab surrounded. As Marcus breaks cover and walks rapidly away along the quay, he can hear the hapless cabby being dragged from his cab.

Marcus has picked his ship, a rusting freighter rising in sombre relief against the sky. It seems deserted, decklights illuminating great spaces on several levels. From the gangway he looks back and sees their business with the cabby is over, dark shapes fanning out along the quay, the BMW cutting its lights and creeping forward. Picking his way round to the starboard side of the ship he looks across the open port to the scattered lights on the far side. Recalling Annie's underwater prowess in the pool in Rostrevor, he considers the oily water far below and tries to measure the feat across the wide basin – maybe five hundred yards.

Turning on his heels, he moves quickly and quietly over the

362

vessel, learning its secrets, crouching below bulkheads, working his way forward, drawn by the drift of human voices and cigarette smoke. Ghosting through a low doorway into a dark interior, he breaks off to peer through a porthole. The BMW is stalking closer, accompanied by gunmen on foot, hugging shadows, searching for him, eyeing the ship and its closely moored neighbours, signalling to one another, reaching some silent accord.

Withdrawing, he treads carefully down a short flight of steps towards the growing sound of laughter, softening the ring of his shoes on iron. Pressing himself against a wall he looks in on a huddle of Greek crewmen playing cards and drinking in the galley, the peals of their banter concentrated by a harsh pool of light, bronzed and swarthy features floating in a nicotine haze. One player's bluff is called, he reveals his hand to raucous applause, Marcus slips by, steals the length of a narrow passage and ducks inside a dank darkish engine room. The engines are idle, but the enclosed space is oppressively hot. Perspiration streams down his body as he examines a rack of soiled boilersuits and a selection of greasy vicious looking tools. He sets to work.

Minutes pass, he presses on, climbing as he goes, surfacing to fore and peering over the port side. With a shock he sees his hunters and their car no longer there, the quayside empty, silent. No movement but the dusting of soft rain. Are they on board already? He looks round, expecting the worst. No one. No sign of them. And still no traces on the quayside below. He leans out, imagining his dark face will camouflage him. But the quayside chooses this moment to come to life, two, three, four figures materialising without a sound from sheer walls, flat roofs, narrow ledges, looking up at him, their faces, what he can see of them, devoid of expression. Marcus looks down, meeting their blank professional gazes in turn, dwelling on two men he recognises, the blond soldier whom he disabled with a ruse in the remote barn, standing cocksure now on a warehouse roof, and the dark rakish leader, who steps forward into the open.

'Time's up, Lieutenant.'

Lieutenant? Genuine respect, or flattery to soften him?

'Coming down?'

Invitation, or ultimatum?

'Time to go home.'

Same home you sent Annie? Marcus smiles, ever the fool. Lee

looks round with meaning at his men. When he turns again, Marcus is gone. His hunters drop to earth and sprint for the ship, swarming aboard, dispersing fore and aft, leaving young Baxter crouching by the gangway, preventing the fugitive from doubling back. A coded cry from Lee, and his men freeze wherever they find themselves. Impeccable timing. In the next instant a faint splash is heard below the bows. Lee's ears prick up. The black bastard's overboard, intent on trying his luck free-style across the port. Hurst and Williams are nearest. Lee barks an order, then radios Baxter, tells him to drive like hell across the river to the far side, just in case the son-of-a-bitch makes it. By the time he reaches his men the shooting has started – and ended. Williams, breathless, is holding four foreign sailors prisoner, spreadeagled on the deck. It's Hurst who's done it, turning to meet Lee's questioning gaze with a glazed expression, a man assuaged, spent firearm slack in his hand. Lee looks over the side. Far below, a man in a pale suit floats face down in scum and litter swilling against the ship. Head, feet and hands submerged, he washes back and forth, bullet-riddled, discarded.

'Get down and make sure.'

'You what? He's a dodo!'

'Get down.'

Hurst goes over the side, Lee watches him abseil down to the water. It's over. Mission complete. He experiences none of Hurst's climactic gratification, on this occasion not even light-headed relief that he has triumphed over failure. There's something sour about this one, a man of King's calibre slopping around in fouled harbour water.

'We've done it, Chief!'

Lee looks stonily at him, big innocent Williams, but says nothing, only tosses on the floor the four-inch ragdoll he's been carrying for this moment.

On the quayside the BMW surges from its hideaway and draws up sharply. Baxter has heard the shooting, a radio message from Lee confirms it. Leaving the engine running for the getaway, he gets out and stands in the cool rain, pensively caressing his cheeks like maturer men do, looking over the water, privately relieved he hasn't had to lay eyes on the night's handiwork.

A cyclist approaches through the drizzle, bent over handlebars, head covered with a seaman's rainhat, an old codger slow-pedalling, front light wobbling. Baxter turns his back so the potential witness won't see his face. As wheels whistle closer, there comes a shout of fury lifting over the ship, only too late for Baxter, who feels himself seized from behind and bundled with awesome strength to the quay's edge and flung away like a coil of rope. Even before the soldier hits the water, the cyclist is running for the car.

Beneath the ship's bows, Hurst has lifted the corpse from the scum by the scruff of his neck, flinging away the improvised dummy, a man's beige-and-gold suit stuffed and stretched with boilersuits.

Marcus drives off at high speed, fumbling with the unfamiliar controls, levelling off, measuring the impulses of the powerful machine like a man smoothing and restraining a tense horse in full flight. He checks the petrol gauge – plenty. No need to fill up. Little money left to spare anyway. The rest of Eugene McBride's contribution is in the hotel. Does he dare collect it? Sirens wail, blue lights like fireflies in the distance, growing rapidly. To the right deserted streets and railway yards, to the left the outstretched river, city lights on the far side. Mesmerised by the onrush of blue lights, he hesitates like a blind man at a crossroads, leaving it to the last moment to throw the car into a screeching turn, straightening up and gathering speed again to rush the bridge. The river spreads beneath him, ahead beckons the south side of the city, opening to receive him into its bleak midnight world, rain-doused roads, lonely churches, hollow buildings, a silent stadium, gas works. He flicks on the radio and drives in random patterns through the desolate nightscape in search of an idea – a way to survive the night, a way of smuggling from the hotel the things he needs to 'do it' twelve hours from now. He drives calmly, the shock of Annie's dying acting like an anaesthetic. He's alone again, dependent on himself, as he was the night he escaped from the hospital and drove the Landrover through Derry in search of a newspaper.

Sweltering in the tight, restricting boilersuit, he tears it open at the neck, letting the rain-flecked breeze rush through the gaping windscreen and cool him. Sirens fade behind him, and swell somewhere ahead. He switches direction, turns at a junction and cruises along an endless tree-lined canal, foraging for a strategy. Traffic is light, people thin on the ground, here and there a man wandering home, a young gang larking, a pair of lovers huddled beneath an umbrella, lone women lingering beneath street-lights, a motorist pulling over to address one. Marcus spares them little thought until, moments later, entering a handsome square and park enclosed by tall Georgian buildings, he sees more scantily dressed women exuding the same false ever-ready glow. Circling the square again, he rolls down his window and approaches two women of mature years embellished with tight clothes and loud make-up. They step back, nervous of the smashed windscreen, Marcus's black skin and intense gaze. He does another lap of the square and pulls over to talk to two young women, surer of themselves, unflinching. They want to see his money.

'I don't have it on me, but . . .' He presents a version of the truth. They cut him short and walk on. Discouraged, he is about to drive away when a taxi cuts in and draws up sharply. A woman steps gracefully out, opens her bag and pays the driver. She seems too well dressed and poised to be soliciting, but she remains on the kerb after the cab has gone, and something in her pose and the revealing cut of her stylish clothes makes him wonder if she isn't playing a dignified version of the role. Conscious of his own appearance, he opens his boilersuit further and straightens his tie. Easing the car forward, he slides alongside her. 'Pardon me if I'm making a mistake . . .'

She regards him coldly. She's thirty or forty. Skill and care have made an unremarkable face instantly appealing.

Marcus falters, then speaks decisively.

'I want someone for the whole night.'

She doesn't like what she sees, the windscreen, his state of dress, his fearful unfamiliar blackness.

'What would you charge?'

She quotes a steep figure, her face immobile, tinged with contempt, confident he will have to decline.

'OK.' He reaches across to open her door.

Her turn to falter. 'I'll take half of it now.'

Shaking his head, a grunt of despair. 'I'm not carrying it, and anyway it's not you I want.'

She frowns, suspicious.

'Get in and let me explain.' Taking the keys from the ignition, he reaches over to offer them. 'Please, get in.'

Something in his voice and manner breaches her defences. She takes the keys and gets in, leaving the door ajar. He explains roughly what he wants. She looks him dead in the eye.

'You're in trouble.' Rapid speech, full-blooded Dublin accent.
'Yes.'
'What have you done?'
'I'm an Army deserter.'
No reaction. Evidently she doesn't watch the news.
'What if the hotel stop me?'
'I've thought of everything.'
'What's in the case you want so bad?'
'My passport to freedom. Will you do it?'
Closing the door, she makes herself comfortable and hands him
back the keys.

In his bed in the Belvedere, Frank Mulraine dreams dreams of such
blandness and innocence that he wakens repeatedly to stay in
touch with reality. Listening to a pocket-sized wireless, he hears it
announced on the three a.m. news that he has been replaced as
leader of the hunt for British Army traitor Marcus King. He sits up,
reaching for a fresh packet of cigarettes. It comes as a shock hearing
it broadcast in the middle of the night, and described as a
humiliation for the distinguished detective, whose subsequent
disappearance is giving cause for concern. Also in the news, a
report confirming loose talk in the bar the previous evening – Dixie
Ragdoll Doyle discovering his wife and child dead in a bedsit on
the South Circular Road, and surviving an apparent assassination
attempt on the banks of the Grand Canal.

He sleeps again, a loaded automatic under his pillow. When
dawn, accompanied by distant thunder, filters through the
curtains, he half hears a news report which makes him sit bolt
upright – a night of shootings, a body in a city-centre car-park
identified by her father as Annie McBride. Gardaí believe Marcus
King was with her and escaped. A miniature doll discovered at the
scene suggests the work of Dixie Doyle. Road-blocks thrown
around the city, and reports coming in of more shootings at the
docks during the early hours. No reports of casualties, but one
more ragdoll.

Mulraine rises grimly, whiskey-dulled brain brutally awake.
Doyle on the rampage, not a pleasant thought, particularly as
Doyle may have seen him with McBride and King in Stephen's
Green and may only be waiting for an opportunity to present him
with his own special ragdoll. He may only have survived last

367

night because he never left the hotel. He peers round the curtain. The street is quiet under a leaden storm-filled sky. His work has always been perilous, but he had comrades to share it with. Now he's alone, in league with a Jamaican, a British Army deserter, the man he's supposed to be hunting, who, if he isn't already dead, may have abandoned his mission.

Stepping out of the line of the door, he carefully opens it, gun in hand. The corridors are quiet. Crablike, he withdraws, locks his door and picks up the phone. Waiting while the call is transferred to the room Marcus King booked under a false name, Mulraine finds himself wondering whether King and McBride sleep together, as some press reports suggest, and whether herself might answer the phone. And then it hits him – Annie McBride, the leggy girl by the swimming-pool, the jogger in the park, the fearless maid who tormented the Provos, led the security forces such a merry dance and recruited Marcus King to form such an outrageous duet, is dead.

'I'm sorry, sir, I can't seem to get an answer.'

He replaces the receiver. Where does a black man hide in Dublin? His coarse-veined hand shakes as he shaves, tracing the unfamiliar feel of his face, pared down with worry. A loud rap of knuckles on the door.

He barks, 'Who is it?' He goes through and unlocks the door. The night porter breezes in with a breakfast tray.

'I want you to do something for me, Liam, collect a suit from the dry cleaner's and even more important . . .' He presses into the young man's hand a brown paper package containing a cassette tape, to be posted registered mail at the GPO. He gives him more than enough cash to cover it, but Liam's face falls; he's going off duty now, he's been on all night. Mulraine closes the young man's fist round a crisp twenty-pound note, and cheerfully pushes him out of the door.

'Take that lovely young lady of yours out to dinner.'

Locking the door, he checks his watch – eight o'clock. In six hours' time he must keep an appointment with a man who almost certainly will not turn up.

Marcus dreams he's still in the Army, preparing for night patrol. Among the men he's desperately trying to wake are Charlie Winters and Robbie McLaren, both of whom he knows are dead.

The aim of the patrol is to seek and find the man who killed Bernie O'Rawe.

He wakes in a sweat, disorientated. Another bed, another building. He sits up, he can hear the voices of young children, his beard and separate moustache lie on the bedside table, Eugene's watch says eight-twenty a.m. His mind begins to clear. The woman he picked up, who calls herself Michelle and whose husband is in gaol, brought him back to this comfortable apartment in a tall modern block in the early hours. She asked him to wait in the car while she paid off the baby-sitter . . .

And Annie's dead.

He lays his head on his knee, closes his eyes, willing himself to believe it, the young woman who saved him in the remote barn, the comrade who shared his days and nights from Donegal to Dublin, and shared his vision. Did they really kill her, she who seemed immune to bullets? Won't she still join him later in the day to carry out the operation?

His eye moves inexorably to the chair where his shirt lies stained with her blood.

He hears them leaving. Rising, he wraps a towel round his waist, unlocks the door and ventures into the quiet apartment, which is painstakingly decorated and furnished, and enjoys views over the leafy district of Ballsbridge on the south side of the city. He steps out onto the balcony. Steady rain falls from a slate-grey sky, thunder echoes across a range of mountains to the south. Down in the forecourt, the woman who calls herself Michelle conducts her brood to school under an assortment of bright umbrellas. He had hoped she would have collected the case already, but he hadn't counted on her having children. He needs what's in the case, and now several hours will be lost, and with every minute the chances multiply of the Garda discovering his hotel room before Michelle.

The hours pass. He makes himself a sandwich and pours a juice from the fridge. He eyes the telephone, the urge to call Marcia almost overwhelming.

Noon. Something's happened, Michelle arrested at the hotel? He gave her the name of the church in case she was delayed. Has she given it to the police? And Eugene McBride, if they question him, will he stick to his promise and deny any knowledge of Annie's plans? Marcus shakes his head and emits a dispirited sigh.

He watches the television news: a reporter sheltering in the courtyard of Leinster House, Eire's Parliament, talks of this afternoon's major debate on Northern Ireland which will focus anger on Britain's refusal to consult Eire on matters affecting the province; the Northern Ireland Secretary has expressed concern that Dublin isn't doing enough to catch the alleged traitor Marcus King, who is believed to have escaped death during the night after a gun battle in the centre of the city in which IRA activist Annie McBride died; the IRA has issued a statement denying involvement, despite the presence of Dixie Doyle in Dublin and the discovery of two of his ragdolls; cameras home in on the car-park, dismal in the early rain, and the nook beneath the wall where Annie died; what were she and Marcus King doing in Dublin, they want to know, where is he now and what is he planning? And where has debunked detective Frank Mulraine disappeared to?

Suddenly they switch to London, a strangely familiar street front, an even more familiar figure emerging – Marcia! Engulfed by reporters as she leaves for work. Marcus watches, petrified. She looks drawn but calm, sustained by some inner knowledge.

'Where's your husband, Mrs King?'

'I'm afraid he's not at home at the moment.'

She retakes a step to gain space and height.

'What do you think of his behaviour, Mrs King?'

She seems unaffected by the jostling throng and firing cameras, she smiles. 'I'm proud of him.'

'You don't consider him a traitor?'

'My husband is a loyal subject of the Queen.'

'What do you think of him deserting the Army?'

'If he deserted the Army, he must have had good reason.'

'Do you think he's disturbed, Mrs King?'

'Marcus was upset about the girl.'

'The girl he killed?'

'Yes.' They jockey for positions and scribble vigorously.

'Some say he cracked up . . .'

Another reporter pitches in. 'Do you believe he's deranged, Mrs King?'

She meets the eye of every questioner. 'My husband valued the child's life, wanted to make up for it. Is that an indication of mental breakdown? I think Marcus has proved a little too sane for the Army.'

'Wouldn't you agree he's brought the Army and Britain into disrepute?'

'There is no finer officer in the British Army.'

She thanks them and descends amongst them to reach a waiting minicab. The cab driver, as though defending Royalty, tries to smooth the way. A shout from the turmoil: '*Will you be sticking by your husband no matter what?*'

Caught in the act of climbing into the car, she turns and raises a fist. '*I'm with him all the way, and I hope some of you will have the courage to join us.*'

Neighbours and passers-by applaud.

Marcus's eyes film over, the set goes out of focus. He gets up, a surge of energy pumping through him. It's time to go. This is the day he's been waiting for.

Resplendent in an amber suit, Frank Mulraine leaves the Belvedere with ample time to make the rendezvous with Marcus at the church. Pistol in one pocket, handcuffs in the other, he carefully checks the street before descending to the taxi.

'Whitefriar Street Church,' he says sharply.

The cabby opts for an oblique route along Parnell Street and Capel Street to avoid the rain-swept city centre, giving Mulraine ample opportunity to judge whether he is being followed. Reclining in the back, he looks round surreptitiously and soon becomes interested in a white Peugeot, and the dark glasses behind the misted windows. There's no hard reason for suspicion, but he has often had cause to be grateful to his gut feelings.

'I'm early. Could you manage a wee sightseeing tour?'

'No problem.'

'How about a run to the Phoenix Park?'

He expects the Peugeot will now go its own way, but it stays in touch, crossing the bridge and following the cab along the river. Mulraine's pulse begins to race, but he's not convinced.

'Take a left, will you.'

'There's nothing to see there.'

'Just do the block.'

The cabby turns sharply into a side street. Mulraine lights up a cigarette and looks over his shoulder. It's still there, keeping its distance, accompanying the cab on a fruitless circuit of a brewery. Doyle, he concludes, bent on demonstrating what happens to detectives who work too closely with the British. The cabby looks round.

'How are we doing?'

Mulraine dons his glasses and consults a trembling map.

'Change of plan; Heuston Station!'

The station is close by, the taxi turns into its narrow crowded forecourt. Amongst the milling crowds are a number of tall watchful policemen, rain dripping from their caps. As he pays the cabby, Mulraine watches the Peugeot go by in search of a parking space, then strides into the teeming station. Long queues of holidaymakers and luggage extend back from the railheads. Shouldering through the crush, he glances back now and again. When finally he catches sight of his pursuers, he detects two men who are decidedly not Provos, smooth neatly combed men in dark glasses and crisp summer suits. Mulraine falters, sharp tremors of recognition, the big genial Welshman Sergeant Williams, limping from his encounter with a fox trap, and that cheerful sadist Corporal Hurst, grim confidence ever present in his swagger. After the initial shock, Mulraine experiences a wave of relief. These aren't Doyle's men, not the assassins who killed Annie McBride, not assassins at all. Or . . . He tenses again, struck by a deeper logic. Relief evaporates.

He pauses beneath the huge departure board, long-distance trains to Cork, Westport, Tralee, and one leaving in eight minutes for Galway. Queueing for a ticket, he notes that his shadows have joined the queue almost directly behind him. The queue dwindles, two minutes to departure, he spends nearly all his cash on a single to Galway. Breaking into an ungainly run he passes through the barrier just as it is closing. Train doors are being slammed, a guard shouts. Panting and perspiring, he hauls himself into the rear carriage, glancing back in time to see the two men making a headlong dash for the train, flashing their tickets as they vault the barrier. He moves quickly to put distance between himself and them before the train starts, forging along narrow passages choked with seatless travellers and luggage.

A strident blast of a whistle, the train jolts forward, advancing in jerks, building momentum. He can't delay any longer. At the end of a carriage he wrenches open a door and turns to the nearest passenger.

'Wrong feckin' train! Would you close it after me?'

Leaning clear, he sees the platform rapidly running out, calculates the equation of his travelling body and the static platform, and jumps. Not a well co-ordinated man, he lands heavily, pitching onto his back. Instead of sidling out of sight, he finds himself winded on the floor, afraid that his pursuers have seen him, afraid to find them standing over him smirking. But the train runs smoothly out of the station, leaving a mercifully empty platform. Brushing himself down, the colour returns to his face, and he permits himself a chuckle. Two of Her Majesty's State ruffians set fair for Galway!

Limping slightly, he retraces his steps, hurrying now, afraid that Marcus King, if he's there, will think he's not coming. Pressing through the crowds at the entrance, he is dismayed to see a long queue for the taxis and curses his luck. Almost at once he hears a man touting for custom.

'Taxi anyone? Anyone for a taxi?'

'Yes!'

The young man in the cloth cap beckons him to follow, forging a path into the rain, Mulraine hard on his heels, the young man deftly flicking open the back door of his cab for Mulraine before climbing behind the wheel.

Mulraine freezes. The cab is a white Peugeot, its engine already running. The young man never showed his face. He backs away, prepares to escape, begins to turn and collides with a human wall, two powerful men almost lifting him off his feet and bundling him inside the car. Catching a glimpse of surprised onlookers, he longs to cry out, but a sharp jab in the ribs knocks the breath out of him. The car speeds away on squealing tyres, Mulraine wedged between the two men he thought he'd sent to the west.

'So you didn't fancy Galway, gentlemen?'

No one speaks, rough hands search him and find his gun. In the front Captain Lee doesn't even bother to look round.

'A grand treat you missed,' Mulraine informs his neighbours, 'the city flowing with good stout and the island-studded lake fairly leaping with perch, pike and salmon!'

No reaction, a vacuum of tension, the car stifling, rain-stippled windows obscuring the view. Mulraine suppresses a hoot of laughter, the violence in the air palpable. The cloth-capped driver – he recognises Baxter now – recrosses the river and follows a map to the sprawling Phoenix Park, pulling up on a rain-drenched avenue. Lee turns in his seat; Mulraine meets his eye.

'Where is he, Inspector?'

Lee's voice is low and taut. He manages a polite smile, the

patience of a man about to explode. Mulraine shivers, feels the blood rising in the attendants either side of him. Lee makes a supreme effort to stay calm.

'You've got' – consulting his watch – 'thirty seconds.'

Mulraine glances at his own watch. It's one-fifty. He is due to meet Marcus King at two o'clock. He knows that Lee will now stop at nothing, and he knows that he himself is incapable of enduring physical abuse. The best he can hope to do is win time for Marcus, proposing a devious route to the church, and pray the fugitive is flown.

'Ten seconds.'

'Pass me the map, I'll navigate.'

Lee shakes his head. 'Five seconds.'

Mulraine yields. 'Whitefriar Street Church.'

The entrance is on a main road, but the body of the church is reached by a passage tunnelling into urban brick and mortar, opening at last into an immense arched cave, dim and dusky, inhabited by solemn statues and winged angels, white-robed priests and silent communicants, kneeling, shuffling, jangling beads.

Marcus sits in shadow at the end of a pew, encouraged by Marcia's performance in London. She looked groomed, fit and full of fight. And unflagging in her support. He feels a weight lifted from his mind. Mulraine may be late, may even have betrayed him, and there's no sign of Michelle, and Annie is dead, but Marcia is with him.

Drawn to the forest of candles in the grotto, he picks his way among the shadows towards it. Slotting a handful of coins into the box, he selects four fresh candles, lights each in turn from the forest fire and stands them in vacant holders. Contemplating the first burning candle, he remembers Charlie Winters, dashing officer one moment, ablaze and footless the next, dying in Spiky's arms in a meadow in Ulster. In the second flame he sees Robbie McLaren, a teenager snuffed out in the blinking of a sniper's eye. Bernie O'Rawe appears in the third flame, spirit of Irish defiance, extinguished by the blunt face of his plastic bullet. He moves to the last candle. In its quivering flame he sees the young woman who should have been with him now, head lolling against the wall, eyes clinging to his, lips forming a final bidding, then her light suddenly gone, a vacant stare.

Absorbed in the flame, he doesn't hear footsteps approaching, quick and light, slowing, coming to stop behind him, waiting. The hand that taps his shoulder barely troubles him, and when he turns, he half expects it to be Annie.

'I'm sorry, I got lost.'

He takes the umbrella and suitcase from her. 'You got the money? You better go.'

She gazes at him, as if expecting something more. He touches her arm. 'Thanks. You've done great.'

She's gone. He heads unhurriedly for a long row of confessionals, each topped with a crucifix, lit up where a priest is in audience. He chooses a secluded unoccupied confessional and slips inside. Rummaging in his case, he sets out a hand mirror, spirit gum, hair spray and gloves. The light is poor, but he gums his grey beard and moustache into place and lightly resprays his hair. Then he finds his suit, dog collar and pistol, and begins to undress.

The church is awkward to find, eluding them as they circle closer. Nerves are stretched to breaking, Mulraine courts disaster by feigning only the vaguest of notions where it is. It's gone two p.m. when finally they draw up outside, wearing caps, berets and leather jackets. Lee orders Baxter to keep the engine warm, dispatches Williams to cover the rear and motions Mulraine to lead on.

Not normally a reverent man, Mulraine prays for Marcus as he leads the way up the long dingy entrance to the inner doors. Once inside, the church lifts to vaulted heavens, flickers with candlelight and resounds with echoes and murmurs. In order to hunt, Lee and Hurst are obliged to remove their dark glasses. Guns concealed, they separate, drifting forward pew by pew, scouring shadows, prying into confessionals. At any other time Douglas Lee might have felt fleeting unease about shooting dead a man in a church.

Mulraine finds himself alone in a long dark aisle, stained glass light anointing his feet. Slumping into a pew, he gazes anxiously, expecting to see the fugitive materialise at any moment. A mass is beginning, a priest's magnified voice intoning through the gloom, 'In the name of the Father, and of the Son and of the Holy Spirit . . .'

At last they emerge into daylight, pile into the Peugeot and take

375

off at speed, Mulraine the focus of murderous glances. Throwing the car through a succession of reckless turns, Baxter spots a disused yard and reverses into it. Even before the car has stopped, Lee and Hurst each have a pistol pressed to the back of Mulraine's neck.

'It was the truth, gentlemen,' blurts the detective, nerves beating in his temples.

'Lying bastard!' Hurst jabs his pistol deeper, Mulraine flinches, Lee is half crazed.

'When did you arrange it?'

'Yesterday.'

'Where?'

'Stephen's Green.'

'Time?'

'Six-thirty.'

'Shit!' Lee was there, he knows Mulraine's telling the truth. Switching the gun barrel to Mulraine's head.

'Don't make me do it, Inspector . . .'

'Swear to God – '

'Either you talk – '

'Captain, I'm not sufficiently heroic – '

'I'll only ask once . . .'

'Captain, you're many things but you're not – '

'What is Marcus King's plan, his purpose – what is his goal?'

Mulraine draws breath. 'I'd say he's abandoned it and gone to ground.'

He hears the metallic ring of both pistols being cocked simultaneously, bullets snug in the chamber, poised to split his skull.

'You've got till three. One . . . two . . .'

'Put away your guns,' says Mulraine icily.

A moment's hesitation.

'Your guns!' Mulraine livid.

Lee and Hurst exchange glances, Lee nods, the weapons are removed.

'His target' – Mulraine swallows – 'is Leinster House.'

'What?'

'The Parliament buildings.'

Lee frowns. 'What does he want in the Parliament buildings?'

'Today is the last sitting before the summer recess, and they're debating Northern Ireland. He and McBride had planned a guest appearance. I was to take them into custody after.'

Silence.

They're looking at the Ulsterman, awed and repelled. Attention turns to Lee, who has gone deathly pale, already haunted by defeat. Hurst vents his frustration.

'What the fuck are we waiting for?'

From Lee a hollow laugh. 'You want to walk in to the Irish Parliament and shoot him?'

'We might still intercept him,' ventures big Williams.

'That's a long word for you, Taf!' quips Hurst.

The two men begin quarrelling viciously. A glance from Lee quells them. He turns on Mulraine.

'How did he plan to get in?'

A deep sigh from the detective. 'McBride's father secured visitor's passes for the day from a TD acquaintance.'

'TD?'

'Member of the Dáil, the Irish House of Commons.'

'He's got a pass for today?' Lee looks at him in disbelief. 'You mean he's just going to stroll in?'

'You can't stop him, Captain.'

Lee stares into the rain, sinking into oblivion. Hurst is glowering at Mulraine. 'We ought to shoot you.'

'Boss. . .?' Resembling a French *ouvrier* in his beret and leather jacket, Williams tries to rouse the Captain. 'Boss, we got to tip off the Irish authorities.'

'And give ourselves away!' snorts Hurst.

'Anonymous-like, you bloody fool. It's our duty.'

Lee doesn't stir. He's out of it. Hurst seethes. It's left to Williams and Baxter to exchange knowing looks.

'A call-box,' whispers Williams.

Baxter nods and thrusts the car into gear.

A taxi proceeds along the north side of St Stephen's Green and turns into Merrion Street. Marcus is relatively calm until the building comes into view. Until now, this day and that building have been visions in his and Annie's mind. Now the hour has arrived, and he sees the building solid and permanent through a curtain of rain, standing like a stately home at the far end of a sweeping lawn.

His heart weakens. According to Mulraine's investigations, Special Branch men drift and mingle, alert for known terrorists.

There is also a contingent of police, and somewhere out of sight a small garrison of soldiers. However, since the most serious incident of recent times was last year's H-Bock protest which spilled over into the main chamber, security is believed to be discreet.

Outwardly relaxed, Marcus sits back in the cab, soberly dressed and dignified, an African or West Indian priest in his late fifties. The taxi turns off the road and pulls up at the steel ramps and low-level traffic signals just inside the grounds.

'End of the road, Father, I'm not allowed in.'

'I dare say the walk won't do me any harm.'

One of two colossal policemen rooted in the rain stoops to look in. Marcus tenses. How conscientiously are they looking for him? Paying the driver with his last note, he ducks into the rain, hoists his umbrella and meets the policeman's stern eye. Smiling benignly. 'Good afternoon, officer, I'm visiting the Dáil.'

The policeman touches his cap. 'Over there, Father . . .' pointing to the gatehouse. 'Sorry about the unseasonable weather!'

'You'll have to do better next time.'

'Sure if we'd known you were coming, Father, we'd have fixed you up with a spot of sunshine.'

Recalling Annie's coaching, Marcus steps across with slightly stooped deliberation to the glass-fronted gatehouse, occupied by a pair of uniformed ushers, who look to Marcus like capless policemen.

'Good afternoon, I wish to collect my visitor's pass.'

'Your name please, Father?'

'Reverend Robert Leymar.'

'Just a moment.' While the usher consults a list, his colleague studies Marcus, who turns aside to wipe his rain-speckled glasses. While he awaits his fate, he notices the low darkened dwelling crouching behind the gatehouse, and feels the eyes of soldiers on him.

'Just follow the road, Father. Go up the double steps and pick up your pass at Enquiries.'

It's a long walk down one side of a lawn the size of a football pitch, proceeding with measured stride beneath dripping trees, past statues and parked cars. A car comes up on him from behind; he tenses. It passes and picks a parking space. A young civil servant gets out and hurries on beneath a bright umbrella. In another car sit two men, well-built, well-fed, moustachioed – Special Branch. Again he tenses, they're watching him. His blood goes cold, he smiles, gives a little wave, stopping short of blessing them. Surprised, they reciprocate with a cagey nod.

The sun breaks free unexpectedly, sweeping the lawns, lighting up the massed windows ahead. The broad face of the building rises before him, massive, impenetrable. A tricolour flies aloft, snapping in the sun. He passes a gold-tipped obelisk, rose beds, an ornamental pool. The rain ceases, the sun beats down on the curving drive, leading him to a set of double steps draped in ivy. The entrance. He comes to a stop at the foot of the stairs. He doesn't have to go up, no one's making him. He could turn round and walk back out of the gate, hide in the city. And then? He glances over his shoulder, the gate, the trees in the square, the city – there's nothing there, no reprieve, no future. He's long past the point of no return.

Calling up certain images – Bernie O'Rawe's split skull, Annie's vacant eyes – he climbs the steps to a portico. Shaking his umbrella and folding it, he looks up to meet another usher. 'Can I help you, Father?'

'Please, the Enquiry Desk?'

'On the left in the Main Hall.'

As he crosses a minor hall, he feels the usher's eyes on his back, and instinctively registers the pressure of the pistol in his jacket. It's almost too late to stop him now. Through a set of double doors he steps into the lofty grandeur of the Main Hall, pausing beneath a column to breathe on his spectacles. The hall echoes with restraint, the tranquillity and absence of activity suggest that the Dáil is already in session. No troops, no police, only grand portraits and plaster busts looking down on him.

A mile away, a young British soldier is trying to get through to Leinster House from a public call-box. Two comrades form a queue outside, to prevent anyone hearing and identifying. Lee and Mulraine remain in the car, Lee silent, withdrawn, Mulraine smoking pensively as it begins to occur to him that Lee has no cause to hold him any longer. Glancing at the inanimate Englishman, he reaches slowly for the door, expecting Lee to lash out with tongue, fist or both. But he has the door open, and Lee remains insensible.

Suddenly, as Mulraine is halfway out, a hand like an eagle's claw catches his wrist.

'Tell me, Inspector . . .'

'Don't you think I've told you enough already?'

'. . . how a man like you lives with his conscience?'

'Painfully and fearfully.' Still held in Lee's grip. 'But you tell me, Captain, how a man like you lives without one?'

As Lee releases him, his voice falls. 'You misjudge me, Inspector.'

Mulraine gets out and walks rapidly away. The others return, Baxter excited.

'I finally got through. She thanked me. Obviously nothing's happened yet, but they're alert now, so if he turns up he's fucked!'

Lee stares out of the window.

'Back to base, Boss?'

No reply. They exchange looks, Baxter starts the engine, turns the car round and aims for the north.

The call is received by a switchboard operator in Setanta House in Kildare Street opposite the main entrance of Leinster House. It may be a hoax but, knowing she will face stiff questioning if an incident does occur, she makes rapid notes, recording time of call, caller's urgent tone, youthful voice and English accent, his refusal to identify himself and the scant but startling information that British Army deserter Marcus King has reserved a visitor's pass for today and is planning something. Planning what? The caller hangs up. The operator immediately puts through three calls to Leinster House, the first to the Superintendent, an ex-army man in overall charge of security, then to the Captain of the Guard, and finally to the on-site police. If Marcus King is in the building, closed-circuit cameras will soon locate him.

When Marcus presents himself at the Enquiry Desk, the usher observes, 'Wasn't it a party of three?'

'Mr Mason must be delayed, and Miss Murray won't be able to make it.'

The usher swivels the visitors' book for Marcus to sign, and fills in a small white card, printing Marcus's false name, the date and . . . 'Which Deputy will I put it under?'

'Sorry?'

'Which TD invited you?'

'Ah . . .' Annie tested him on the man's name and now it has deserted him: 'He, um, represents Wexford . . . Tom. . .?'

'Ah yes, Tom Gannon. There you go, Father. Enjoy your visit.'

Marcus clutches the pass.

'Just follow the main corridor to the Central Lobby.'

Resisting the urge to hurry, Marcus maintains a measured pace along the corridor, glancing up at a television screen monitoring events in the Dáil. The debate is in progress. As he reaches the lobby, a short, slim dapper man in a navy-blue suit overtakes him and hastens between a pair of pillars into an office, apparently responding to an urgent summons. After a moment's anxiety, Marcus's attention returns to the imposing marble staircase rising before him to a vaulted gallery.

'Visiting the Dáil, Father?' An usher checks his pass. 'Top of the stairs.'

He climbs, rejecting his own athletic muscles for those of an ageing priest. At the top he finds himself facing the main entrance to the chamber, his path briefly obscured by a Senator conducting a party of American Congressmen to the VIP gallery. They disappear into the chamber, an usher on the doors steps forward. 'Public Gallery you want, Father? One more flight of stairs.'

'Are you trying to get me fit?'

'You look pretty fit already, Father!'

He could have burst through to the chamber, but opts to reconnoitre the layout first. At the top of the final flight of stairs another usher takes his visitor's pass, presents him with a copy of the order papers detailing the day's business, and directs him into the Public Gallery.

'Sit anywhere you like, but no writing of any kind, I'm afraid.'

'Not even my maiden speech?'

'Ah well, that's a different matter!'

Summoned urgently to his office, the Super receives news of the anonymous call. Lips pursed, he considers a moment. The fugitive is known to be in town and is said to be mad, reckless and violent. The switchboard operator thought the call sounded genuine, and a visit from the desperado is not inconceivable. But to activate the siren could cause unnecessary panic. For a false alarm to violate the business of the House would be acutely embarrassing.

381

Instead, he puts the soldiers stationed in the basement on maximum alert, instructs the Gardaí to conduct a thorough search, stresses the scrutinising of closed-circuit televisions, and contacts the gatehouse at both entrances, warning them to look out for the fugitive. Finally a call is put through to Garda Headquarters in Phoenix Park requesting a detailed description of Marcus King.

Encased behind glass, and sweeping high above the Dáil in a horseshoe shape, the Public Gallery is crowded for this important end-of-term debate. Marcus stands at the back, looking intently down on the stately semi-circular chamber, gleaming pews of politicians descending in tiers like an amphitheatre to the open floor. One Deputy is on his feet, his voice carried by a public address system.

'. . . and would he not agree that the present British attitude is not only inappropriate, insensitive and frankly insulting, but is actually supplying the terrorists with propaganda ammunition?'

Marcus's attention crosses the chamber to focus on the man who rises to reply – the Taoiseach, the Irish Prime Minister. This is the man. Marcus studies him, dimly recognising him from television appearances, tall, heavy and vigorous, with ruddy complexion and hooded eyes, prominent beakish nose and wily intelligent expression, a man with a weary air of authority, one who's seen and heard it all before. But in a few minutes, Marcus vows, he will be in for a surprise.

With an Army officer's eye, Marcus takes rapid mental photographs of the layout of the chamber – the raised gallery opposite jammed with press, radio and television reporters and political correspondents, and the floor of the House below, the arena he must capture, carpeted in purple and presided over by an august figure seated on a throne – in fact the Ceann Comhairle, the Chairman of the House on his dais, attended by the two Clerks of the House and an official reporter at separate tables. Most importantly, Marcus notes the doors and gangways which give access to the arena.

Satisfied and strangely calm, he leaves the Public Gallery. The usher at his desk looks up, surprised.

'Caught short!' Marcus peers over the rim of his glasses, 'Is there a visitor's toilet?'

'You'll have to return to the Enquiry Desk.'

The debate fades, the stairs quiet, deserted, only the steady drumming of his nerves, counting down to the fast-arriving moment when he will burst into the chamber and set himself free. But when he reaches the landing, expecting to be politely redirected, the ushers at the doors of the Dáil stare at him transfixed, with expressions at once searching and accusing, trying to confirm something. Marcus tries to sway them. 'Is something wrong?'

Still they gape, throwing anxious glances towards the staircase. Following their eyes Marcus looks over the edge and abruptly retracts his head. Too late. They've seen him, armed soldiers in green berets, calmly mounting the stairs, calling to him: 'Father, will you hold it there a minute?'

He spins round, the ushers see his gun and pale, a passing secretary freezes. Marcus brushes past them, bursts through the doors of the Dáil and shoulders through a heavy curtain, colliding with a group of observers, plunging down a clear gangway, swooping towards the unsuspecting figure of the Taoiseach, conscious of the soldiers on his heels and the bullet which will stop him in his tracks at any second unless he's quick enough to claim his hostage.

'. . . I will, however, continue to prevail upon the British Government . . .' the Taoiseach falters mid-flow, distracted by the commotion behind him. He has time just to glance over his shoulder before being enveloped in a whirling embrace and danced violently across the floor of the chamber to the back wall. A soldier is bawling 'FREEZE', but Marcus, his back to the wall, has the Taoiseach trapped in an arm lock, held in front of him with a pistol to his head – an illustrious human shield. The House rises in panic, Marcus talks into his prisoner's ear.

'I'll release you soon as I can.'

There is no stampede of men and women, no mass exodus. The House stares as one in horror, unwilling to believe its eyes. The official reporter, Clerks and the Chairman have evacuated their seats, leaving the floor to Marcus, save for brave ushers at either door to Marcus's left and right. Keeping a reassuring grip on the Taoiseach, Marcus monitors and ignores everything – reactions of alarm in the pews, soldiers and Senators jostling in the Division Lobby, heads craning from the VIP Gallery, furore in the Public Gallery, and high above his head, breathing down his neck, a crush of faces leaning over the Press Gallery. Stay cool, Annie had said, and they'll settle down, wondering what we're going to do.

'What do you want, Mr King?' The voice of the diminutive Superintendent, trembling with authority.

'Get rid of those soldiers!' His deep West Indian voice quells the House. 'There's no need for them . . . Stay calm, no one will get hurt.'

Cleared of civilians, the surrounding Division Lobby belongs to soldiers planted at intervals, rifles aimed at Marcus's head.

'Get them out!'

'Out of the question! They stay!'

Marcus, low and menacing: 'Then put up their guns.'

A signal to the Army commander; another to the soldiers. The threat is withdrawn.

While the House remains on its feet conferring feverishly, Marcus guides his hostage sideways, makes him mount the dais and sits him in the Chair.

Cries of 'Shame!'

With his free hand Marcus peels off his beard, drawing murmurs from the audience. His glasses lie trampled on the carpet. Adopting a fixed stance, he places himself erect and still just behind and to the right of the Taoiseach, left hand resting on the Taoiseach's right shoulder, right hand holding the pistol, aiming it across his own breast at the hostage's head. The Taoiseach remains stony silent, inscrutable.

'I apologise to the Taoiseach . . .' he pronounces it more or less correctly 'Tee-shock', his voice tremulous but resolute.

Cries of 'Let the Taoiseach go!'

'. . . to all of you, and to the Irish people . . .'

Let the Taoiseach go increases to a tribal chant, waves of green order papers and foot-stamping.

'All I want . . .' His voice peters out, choked by the storm of hostility.

'What *do* you want, sir?'

The gravelly voice belongs to his impatient hostage.

'Give yourself up,' hollers the Superintendent, 'and I will personally guarantee . . .'

Anger flashes through Marcus. He hears Annie rallying to him – Keep cool, brother, hold firm.

'May I suggest' – a new voice, the Leader of the Opposition, a sober statesman-like figure, trying to attract attention – 'I suggest we hear what he has to say – '

'Not in this chamber!'

Dissension spreads.

'It's an abuse of this House!'

'Damn your House!' Marcus's voice rises like a bird. Visibly tightening his grip on the Taoiseach, he thrusts the pistol close to his head. Soldiers stiffen, a tense hush descends.

'Maybe it's time someone brought the war home to you.' Marcus's voice trails an echo around the chamber. 'You wouldn't think Belfast was two hours up the road . . . you seem to have plenty of time for injustice in South America and South Africa – what about South Armagh . . .?'

A Deputy leaps to his feet. 'What do you think we're debating today?'

Marcus rounds on him. 'You've been debating for sixty years! And your people are still dying, and my comrades are still getting blown up, and it's getting worse . . .'

He pauses for breath, sweeps the rows of faces with a steady gaze.

'What the hell have you been doing all these years, you and Westminster, parents of that bastard we call Northern Ireland? When are you two going to stop squabbling – '

'That's exactly what we're discussing today!'

' – and do something? Have you seen Ulster lately? A whole generation of Catholic and Protestant kids incapable of imagining a world without bombings, shootings, dead-of-night raids . . .'

His hand springs free of the Taoiseach's shoulder and points at his audience.

'You and Westminster have produced a tormented delinquent and you blame everyone else – Nationalists, Loyalists, the IRA. You and Westminster won't talk, and you'd rather your people perish and Westminster would rather my comrades get blown to bits than talk to the IRA! How many lives have you saved by not talking? Sixty years from now will it all be the same, same speeches, same injustices, bombers rearing bombers, mothers burying sons, soldiers burned alive, doctors pushing tranquil- lisers. . .?'

He returns his hand trembling to the Taoiseach's shoulder.

'Where else in Christendom do kids play stone-the-soldiers?

Where else do their Christmas paintings have helicopters hovering over the manger?'

The House is very still, he holds its gaze.

'Maybe you've given up, tired of statistics . . . there are no statistics, only dead people and people trying to live . . .'

His voice has dropped almost to a whisper. 'Bernadette O'Rawe is not a statistic . . .'

His eyes smoulder, his hand involuntarily digs into the Taoiseach's shoulder.

'I know . . . I killed her.'

Two or three soldiers, marksmen, have crept into more advantageous positions.

Marcus comes alive, points them out.

'I'm warning you, don't cross me! They've tried every means to silence me. . . I'll release your Taoiseach soon as I'm ready . . .'

'What do you want, sir?' cries the Superintendent. 'Our patience is running out.'

Marcus finds a smile.

'In coming here I hoped for a better response. So did Annie McBride – no terrorist, true patriot, who fought the Provos tooth and nail over the use of bombs, and would have been here today, denouncing the bombers and calling for a ban on bombs at least for a period of grace, had she not been assassinated in your city by British forces . . .'

Doubtful murmurs. 'Nonsense!' A voice from the back. 'The Provisionals did it, as well we know.'

'Were you there last night in that car-park? They were under orders to silence me too.'

'Can you prove it?' The question comes from above and behind in the Press Gallery. Marcus replies without looking round.

'Detective Inspector Frank Mulraine has the proof. He's another one they've tried to gag. Enough of that. I came here to send a message to my government' – He pauses for quiet – 'and I'll release your Taoiseach as soon as I've received a satisfactory response to three modest demands . . .'

London, 5.45 p.m.

A weathered row of terraced flats facing a park, the street jammed with double-parked press vehicles, television units, police,

386

onlookers, all waiting for the ritual of Marcia King's return from the nursery where she works.

A minicab is spotted coming from the direction of Stoke Newington, the crowd comes to life, swarming towards a focal point.

Marcia tenses, the reception much bigger than usual. Her heart lurches, something's happened.

He's dead.

He must be, yet she doesn't feel it. But then she never expected to, nature protects. The shock, because it's been so long coming, is not so bad, more like a long clean knife entering her belly. She and Jamie are alone now. Then with another jab she remembers that she's probably pregnant. Monotonously regular, she's missed a period. A conception that was her greatest wish all at once becomes a cruel twist of fate. A child she and Marcus made specially will never see him.

The cab slows, the driver sees the crowd. 'Bloody hell!' Then it strikes him. 'Do you think they know something we don't?' A glance in his mirror reveals her stricken face.

The cab draws up, immediately engulfed. Floundering in waves of nausea, Marcia struggles to find her feet, resolved to make no spectacle of herself, more for his sake than hers, even though he's gone, determined to hang on to her dignity until she's free to run screaming through the apartment. She tries to undo the clasp on her bag to get to her purse, but her fingers won't work.

'Forget it,' says the driver.

Marcia gets out of the cab with an absent air, jostled as though by the wind, only the rigidness of facial muscles betraying her terror. She makes slow headway through a forest of microphones.

'Have you heard about your husband, Mrs King?'

'Yes, thank you.'

'Did you have any idea he was going to do it?'

'No, I didn't.'

The police try to forge a path to the house steps, Marcia in agony to reach them.

'You approve of what he's done, Mrs King?'

'Of course.'

'Do you think he'll carry out his threat?'

She sways, a rush of hope – he can't be dead! Her legs fail her, someone catches her elbow and rights her, she laughs as if she'd merely slipped, and seeks a friendly pair of eyes. 'Is he hurt?'

'I'm not sure. Anybody know was he injured?' The question goes out to those around.

She reaches the steps, starts to climb, trailing reporters like a heavy cloak. She turns.

'I'm sorry' – holding her head – 'I'll be out to talk to you later.'

Once inside, she sags against the heavy front door.

He's alive! But where is he, what's he done, what threat might he carry out? Halfway along the hall she hears a phone ringing. She finds her legs and races up the stairs, fumbling her key into her apartment door. It's still ringing as she bursts in dropping her bags, ringing as she snatches up the receiver with a surge of expectancy . . . only to screw up her face in anguish at the sound of her father-in-law's voice. Then she begins to take in what he's telling her.

Replacing the receiver she moves trance-like into the living-room and homes in on the television. She checks her watch – just after six. Stooping to plug in the set, she switches on and steps back.

'. . . but this evening's news is dominated by events in Dublin where earlier this afternoon, British Army deserter Marcus King penetrated security at Eire's Parliament building and is still holding the Irish Prime Minister at gunpoint in front of a packed Dáil . . .'

Hand covering her mouth, Marcia sinks to her knees. Marcus dead was much worse and much easier than this. She feels more cut off from him than ever, terrified of what they will do to him.

The focus switches to Dublin, the roads around Leinster House jammed by motorists who've heard the news on the radio, crowds being held back by lines of police, soldiers glimpsed inside the gates.

Her phone's ringing, her doorbell's ringing, Marcia holds her head and screams.

Derry

A packed mess, soldiers from Marcus's company standing or sitting, staring at a black-and-white television screen, faces immobile, many open-mouthed.

They're looking at a reporter competing for space with rival reporters in the forecourt of Leinster House.

'. . . and it seems he got through dressed as a priest, his disguise *complete with false beard and grey hair, and armed with a pistol. We understand from colleagues inside the chamber that he has made three demands which must be met by the British Government before he releases the Taoiseach . . .'*

He glances down at a sheet of paper.

'This is the essence of the text I've received, I quote: "I demand a review of procedures for compensating families of soldiers and civilians killed or seriously injured in Northern Ireland, so that they no longer need to endure years of added suffering and suspense. Two: I demand the right of every soldier to attend the inquest of a civilian he has killed in the line of duty. And three: I demand an immediate ban on plastic bullets . . ." '

He concentrates on the camera again.

'It appears he's made a further call on behalf of IRA terrorist Annie McBride, shot dead last night in Dublin, for the IRA to abandon absolutely the use of bombs, and for talks to begin forthwith between the IRA and the British Government. Former Lieutenant King apparently stressed that the release of the Taoiseach is not dependent on these last two points . . .'

The scene switches to London, a senior reporter in Parliament Square, speculating on when and how the Government will respond, given that its hard line of no surrender to terrorism and blackmail will be severely tested by the Prime Minister's obvious concern for her counterpart in Dublin.

'He's bloody mad!'

A soldier, leaning against the wall of the crowded mess, has broken the silence, the corporal whom Marcus King reprimanded in the street for crudely frisking a local couple. At first no one dissents or agrees. Then a voice pipes up defiantly: 'Great! He's done bloody great!'

Heads turn to meet the impassioned face of David Spiky Rice, the lad who held dying Charlie Winters in his lap and whom Marcus ejected from his prison cell.

'Great?' sneers the corporal. 'He's making bloody monkeys of us!'

A row erupts, a few men ashamed of their former commander, others rallying to his defence.

'Shut up!' A soldier leaps to his feet hammering the table, knocking his chair flying – Bones, Marcus King's bitter young radio operator. 'He's a fucking genius!' All eyes are on him, he glares at them all, daring them to contradict him. 'Who always stood up for us, the ordinary shit-of-the-earth Toms what everyone else kicked around? Who taught us self-respect, who made us feel good, made men of us, men instead of robots?'

He points at them, squinting at them down the barrel of his revolving arm.

'He's fighting for all of us . . . and you know why they want to stop him?' – he looks fiercely into the eyes of his comrades – 'Because he wanted us to think! He was teaching us we're not too thick to think, that it's all right to think, that we've a right to think, a fucking duty! And some of us were beginning to listen . . .'

'That'll do.'

Heads swivel. The Major.

Bones breaks into a grin. 'Hello, sir! Your big day, sir! You got to take some credit for this.'

'Leave it out, Bones,' comrades counsel in whispers.

Draycott, the man who believed he'd broken Marcus King, glowers at the young hard-bitten rebel. 'Get outside!'

Bones moves slowly, preserving his pride, lip curled in anger, passing dangerously close to the Major on his way out. Once in the fetid passage, Draycott barks, 'What the hell do you think you're playing at, stand to attention!' The surly young soldier with the shorn head and the look of an urban thug springs into the correct rigid posture. 'That's more like it. There's good in you, Bones, and there's bad, but like Mr King you're beginning to show a worrying tendency to express the bad, publicly praising a deserter' – he pronounces the word as if it is something contagious – 'a man who abandoned his comrades and would rather deal with the Press than the Provos!'

Draycott taps him on the chest with his stick.

'We wouldn't want to end up like him, would we?'

A wayward smile: 'I wouldn't mind, sir, I wouldn't mind at all.'

Stormont Castle, Belfast

Seven forty-five p.m. While a British Army officer has been holding the Irish Premier at gunpoint for almost four hours, the world's Press has been gathering beneath the steps of the castle, waiting for the Northern Ireland Secretary to emerge with the British Government's response.

It's two forty-five p.m. in New York, after midnight in Bombay, six a.m. in Sydney, and although no television cameras have been permitted inside the Dáil, live coverage of activity outside the Parliament buildings is being beamed into living-rooms all over the world. From executives on late lunches in Ottawa to workers on dawn shifts in Tokyo, countless millions are learning of the drama being played out in Dublin; one hero, desperado or lunatic against the British Government.

Briefly distracted, the world waits.

The Northern Ireland Secretary appears, flanked by bodyguards at seven forty-nine p.m., stepping into the evening light with that air of imperturbability with which senior politicians contrive to turn calamities to advantage. Descending the steps he stops short of the bottom to stay above the rabble.

'Minister, has the Government reached a decision?'

'Minister, do you intend to give in to – '

Brushing questions aside, the minister launches into an impromptu statement.

'For obvious reasons we have been obliged to conduct discussions somewhat precipitately by telephone, since the Prime Minister is extremely concerned for the safety and well-being of the Irish Taoiseach. Naturally I share her grave concern; however, I also share her very serious concern about the consequences of allowing our democratic Government to be undermined and threatened by a fanatic gunman . . . because let there be no doubt in anybody's mind that we are dealing with a desperate man, a thug and a traitor who has flouted the rules of the British Army and disgraced his uniform, who has threatened the lives of senior officers, deserted his post and collaborated with the enemy . . . and all that before committing this appalling crime.'

He draws breath with barely a pause.

'If we were to allow him to get away with this, then the principles and freedoms which we in Britain hold dear would be as nothing . . . However disturbing and trying the circumstances, there can be no exceptions if we are to combat the evil of hostage-taking. Therefore, while expressing sincere and heartfelt concern for the Taoiseach, and while praying that good sense prevails and no harm befalls him, the Prime Minister wishes it to be clearly understood that the security of neighbouring heads of state cannot be the responsibility of the British Government, and that the Taoiseach's safety is a matter for the Irish authorities, whose security procedures were regrettably breached with apparent ease by the gunman . . .'

A dry cough momentarily breaks his flow, but he recovers quickly to deliver sentence.

'And therefore, for all the reasons I've stated, the Prime Minister wishes to make it perfectly clear that under no circumstances will her Government surrender to the ruthless demands of this fanatic. On no account whatsoever will any of his demands even be considered. Thank you.'

He turns to go back inside.

The press surge forward:

'Minister?' A broad Ulster accent, 'Do you consider any of his demands reasonable?'

'Certainly not!' The minister half turns. 'Compensation procedures are perfectly efficient, soldiers are already encouraged to attend inquests, and plastic bullets are a last-resort weapon used with great restraint by the security forces. We bend to blackmail at our peril!'

'Minister?' An American reporter stretches on her toes. 'What of allegations that you ordered Marcus King's death?'

Over his shoulder: 'Totally untrue, a tissue of lies!'

Dublin 8 p.m.

While huge crowds congregate at the gates of Leinster House, inside the Dáil Marcus is still on his feet, maintaining his vigil. He has removed his dog collar and his shirt is open at the throat. He has moved behind the Chair, loosely holding the Taoiseach by the back of his jacket collar, like a man at a kerb with an obedient dog.

The gun is almost out of sight, but it's apparent to those charged with security that the pistol barrel is close to the Taoiseach's neck. It would still be taking too great a risk to attempt to free him, but eventually the fugitive, however trained and fit, must tire, and then . . .

Marcus is tired, but doesn't appear to be. Whenever he flags, or concentration wavers, he draws from a rich store of horrific images. Although he stands straight and calm, there is something catlike in the way he watches over his prey.

The chamber is still packed, and all the galleries. Marcus has made no attempt to prevent anyone leaving, nor invited them to stay. He is at once alert and indifferent. Deputies, men and women, sit or stand, mingling, conferring, watching the fugitive, assessing his mood, debating his character and motives, his barbarity or nobility. They watch the Taoiseach, who remains steadfastly still, carved, inscrutable. Some slip away to the canteen, returning to find nothing changed. The green-bereted soldiers continue to mirror Marcus, loosely alert, untiring.

Marcus hasn't spoken since asking an usher at six o'clock how things were going on the outside, and seemed satisfied with the reply.

Something is happening, a huddle of senior figures in the Division Lobby near the curtained entrance throwing glances Marcus's way. Now they turn to face him, he meets their judicious gazes and they look away. They have news and are afraid to reveal it. The House senses something, a hush descends. The Tánaiste, the Taoiseach's deputy, clears his throat and addresses the House.

'I regret' – he corrects himself – 'I am obliged to report that the British Government . . .'

Marcus listens impassively. Eyes turn to him, afraid of his reaction, of the Taoiseach's reaction. By the time the Tánaiste is finished, Marcus is visibly shaken. But hardly surprised. This is the moment when he and Annie might have come badly unstuck, she determined to hold out to the bitter – even bloody – end, he reluctantly prepared to capitulate.

He sweeps the chamber with a look which makes it clear he's still in control. 'I'll have the Press down here . . .' He points to the first row of seats encroaching onto the floor of the House, traditionally left unoccupied. 'I want to talk to them.'

'Not in here!' a voice objects. 'Let's not forget where we are!'

An argument ensues, the Superintendent intervenes.

'Lieutenant, you mentioned Detective Inspector Mulraine earlier. Did you and he – '

Marcus is nodding.

The Superintendent gives a signal. Everything is calm, business-like. Moments later a burly silver-haired figure appears through the curtain. Escorted down the gangway, he turns when he reaches the arena and holds aloft a pair of handcuffs.

'This man is no traitor!' Mulraine's hoarse Ulster voice resounds. 'I knew that, that's why they removed me from the job.' He talks rapidly, impatient. 'The fellow wanted to express his regret about the girl and had the audacity to criticise the British Army. For his pains he's been hunted back and forth across the border like a rabid fox. If ever a man earned the right to a hearing . . . For God's sake, find him a space somewhere in this building.'

Brief consultations and it is agreed.

Marcus quietly apologises to the Taoiseach, who grunts an acknowledgement and is ushered away. Marcus is holding up his pistol in the broad palm of his hand, offering it to the Superintendent, who reciprocates with a grave nod. While Mulraine makes much ado of clapping the handcuffs on his prisoner, the Superintendent is curiously studying the firearm he is holding. Still warm from Marcus's hand, the pistol is exceptionally light. Plastic. A harmless toy.

9.15 p.m.

'Whose side are you on, Mr King?'

'Nobody's.'

Flanked by Gardaí, Marcus King sits at a long table facing a room dense with reporters from all over the world.

'How do you react to the minister's opinion that you're a desperate fanatic, thug and traitor?'

'I'm a reasonable man driven to a desperate act.'

Beside him sits Frank Mulraine. Marcus's right hand lies on the table, handcuffed to Mulraine's left. When Marcus illustrates a point with a flourish of the hand, he takes Mulraine with him.

'You haven't answered the charge, Lieutenant, that you're a traitor.'

Marcus sighs wearily, drawn, ill at ease.

'What's a traitor?' He spreads his hands, shrugs. 'A man who won't lie down.'

The questioner persists. 'A man who turns against his own country. Isn't that what you did?'

'I was proud of being a British officer and I believe I was a credit to the British Army . . . even if I did question what the Army was doing.'

'Since when, Mr King' – the reporter won't let go – 'do junior officers dictate Army policy?'

'I was never in a position to dictate.'

'What kind of army would you have if all the officers were like you?'

'A more colourful one.'

394

Laughter breaks the tension.

But the questions continue to be fired with venom, in whatever national accents they're delivered, probing and testing, trying to strip Marcus of his secrets and expose him for whatever he may be.

'Wouldn't you agree that your rebellion – '

'Why,' Marcus cut in, 'do you keep calling me a rebel? I was gagged, I tore off my gag. I was imprisoned, I broke out.'

'Aren't you avoiding the issue, Mr King? Most people will not be so easily persuaded that you haven't betrayed your country; in other words that you're a traitor.'

Mulraine chokes on his cigarette, scarcely controlling himself. 'This might be an apt moment to remind some of you that Lieutenant King has won more medals for bravery than any man in his regiment.'

The room falls quiet for a moment. Marcus takes a sip of water with his free hand and tries to ignore the television cameras.

'Mr King, or Lieutenant King' – a woman with a Scandinavian accent – 'which do you prefer?'

Marcus's smile conveys: whatever you like.

'Lieutenant, wouldn't you agree that you've been soft on the IRA?'

'Ask my men was I soft on the IRA. Ask the IRA.'

'Mr King' – distinctive French accent – 'what is the nature of your objections to the plastic bullets?'

'They're meant to be non-lethal. Surprising how many men, women and children they've killed – all Catholics incidentally. They're supposed to stop riots. I've seen them start them. They're supposed to be last-resort weapons' – he leans over and confers with Mulraine – 'twenty-nine thousand were fired in the province last year. That's a lot of last resorts.'

'Surely Ulster's a special case' – a tart Englishman – 'requiring special treatment?'

Marcus nods. 'That's what I say. It's a place that needs very special treatment.'

'How do you expect the security forces to defend themselves without plastic bullets?'

Marcus sighs pensively. 'The RUC and the Army face an impossible situation in Ulster. They deserve a more intelligent answer than plastic bullets. Plastic bullets are like treating a headache with a hammer. It keeps coming back.'

'So,' persists an Ulsterman, 'you'd leave the RUC and the Army defenceless?'

Without warning Marcus is on his feet, dragging Mulraine with him.

'There wouldn't have been any confrontation if I'd been in charge of operations in Derry on 12 July, and Bernie O'Rawe would be alive and we wouldn't be here talking . . .' Exhausted and choking with anger, he glowers into the faces of hardened reporters. 'Most people maimed and killed by plastic bullets have been passers-by. Ulster's not Chile or South Africa. I don't believe in the death sentence for the crime of being in the vicinity of a riot! We all deserve better than baton rounds. When are our so-called leaders going to get off their backsides?'

EPILOGUE

Dublin

Marcus wakes in a cold sweat. He never thought he'd still be having nightmares.

Where am I?

He sits up, heart pounding. Bare walls, dim nightlight throwing no shadows.

Prison. My second night.

He lies on his side on a top bunk. Leaning out, he can reach the window, scarcely more than an air-vent, and through the bars catch glimpses of stars, street-lights and spires.

He can hear a car crossing the night, going somewhere.

Hands in the pockets of his prison trousers, he steps into the exercise yard for the first time. Bare bricks and concrete, walls reaching to the sky.

On the far side laughter comes from a loose group of inmates, shuffling and smoking. They see him and fall silent.

He looks about him.

There's nothing to look at, only clouds. The prisoners are coming towards him in a pack, about ten men, different sizes and ages. He lowers his eyes to meet them. They stop short, blinking at him. He meets the eyes of those nearest. One long-haired man about his own age steps forward extending a hand.

'You must be . . . Pleased to meet you.'

He shakes the hand of each man in turn.

Footsteps, keys.

He looks up from his book.

The door swings open on oiled hinges. Enter the hefty warder, tossing a newspaper on the table.

'You've certainly put the cat among the pigeons.'

WORLDWIDE CENSURE FOR DÁIL RAIDER . . . DUBLIN FURY OVER SAS 'ASSASSINS' . . . KING SPARKS ANGLO-IRISH PLASTIC BULLETS ROW

'And you've a visitor.'

Marcus tenses – Home Office? Police?

'She's here.' The warder permits himself a smile.

Marcus gets up, looks down at himself, his drab uniform. He runs his fingers over his cheeks, shaven smooth, thank God.

He's trembling as the warder and two guards escort him at a measured pace through echoing gates and corridors, the warder whistling tunelessly. They cross close to a main wing, prison sounds intensify, and recede again.

The warder stops at an open door, motions him to go in.

'I'll be back for you. They said thirty minutes, but you'll be glad to hear my time-keeping's atrocious.'

He enters. There are two guards seated against a wall, eyes front. Marcia is standing with her back to him, contemplating a faded poster. She's wearing her pale grey Sunday suit, which, despite the journey, is perfectly pressed, crease-free. Knee-length, the skirt shows her fine mahogany calves and ankles. Her hair is shorter than last time, cut above the shoulder. She's wearing her best gold earrings. She carries a shoulder-bag and a white raincoat matching her shoes. Whatever it costs she always looks great.

She knows he's there. She's turning her head, looking over her shoulder.

He feels shaky, naked, waiting for rescue.

She comes, heels tapping. It's hard to look her in the eye and he focuses on her skirt, a glint of knee. Her hand lifts his chin. Their eyes meet. She draws his face down, stretches her arms around him. Relief rises like vomit to his throat. Sinking into her neck he breaks down, spasms of silent pain soaking her skin. Bent over her, he subsides like a broken tree.

With her finger she traces marks left by someone's crude surgery on his face.

She leads him to a table, they sit heads together, hands joined. His turn to lift her face. Her eyes are marked and darkly shadowed by sleepless nights and private crying.

Stroking her skin he dimly realises that Marcia, bravely and discreetly, has suffered most.

Footsteps, keys, the door swings open.

He looks up expectantly.

'Your request to attend the funeral' – the warder's shaking his head – 'I told you, not a chance.'

The warder leaves, locking the door.

Marcus picks up the morning paper again. PROVOS TO BOYCOTT McBRIDE FUNERAL

He slumps.

Keys in the door, the warder looks in again.

'Tell you what, do you want to see it on the box?'

He daren't hesitate, this man doesn't shower favours.

'That'd be great.'

'I'll let you know.'

He's escorted to a staff commonroom.

Several warders look up. Some are clearly not happy, others return his nod. The six o'clock news is underway.

'. . . but while no date has yet been fixed for the inquest, the Garda are intensifying their investigations, trying to establish whether the SAS were in Dublin and exactly who killed Annie McBride. Meanwhile, Detective Inspector Frank Mulraine, the man who has pointed the finger at the SAS, has been suspended from the RUC on full pay, pending . . .'

Suspended. Marcus sighs, his thoughts drifting to the detective who popped up as a gardener at Annie's poolside.

'. . . There was tight security in Rostrevor, County Down, this afternoon for Annie McBride's funeral . . .'

This afternoon. Marcus looks up with a start. The pictures unfold, a thin black cortège.

'. . . Despite the IRA disowning the young woman known as the Red Sniper, an estimated twenty-thousand-strong crowd followed in the wake of the hearse . . .'

Aerial shots show the cemetery and its surrounds straining to accommodate so many mourners. Marcus recalls the lush wooded landscape they crossed together to reach her home, the overrun moonlit garden where Annie blurted out that her mother was dead, the rough reception from Eugene.

On the ground they show a bright coffin with gold handles being lowered into the earth. Marcus shivers, he wants to tear the lid off and let the wind get to her skin. The coffin, brand-new and un-Annie, slips further. He wants to take her hand and wake her.

We did it, sister, we did it!

The camera homes in on Eugene, tall, ashen-faced, the slight figure of Deirdre hard by his side.

The coffin vanishes.

While Annie McBride is being buried in Rostrevor, on the other side of the province, in Derry, three masked men all in black are materialising in a back street to pay tribute.

Leaning an artist's impression of the Red Sniper against a wall and laying a pair of black leather gloves on the ground, they take three steps back to form a straight line and to observe, with the small crowd, a minute's silence. It's an act of double defiance, since not only are paramilitary send-offs prohibited, but in this case the IRA Council has turned its back on one of its own.

When the minute is up, the three IRA men raise their revolvers and loose three shots into the air over the picture.

Then, to the surprise of the crowd, the man in the middle whips off his woollen balaclava, revealing his face for the benefit of the lone photographer. The crowd stares as one, recognising the man whose wife and child were buried only this morning. He looks gaunt and spectral as he turns and walks away with a pronounced limp.

Late that night the same figure is climbing into the Bogside Cemetery. Keeping to soft verges, he walks slowly, a lone procession, taking cover each time the moon sails free.

Although he knew the RUC would be watching for him, he had considered smuggling himself among the mourners to appear defiantly at the graveside. But the sacrifice would have been lost on his enemies. In staying away he has committed himself to return to the war with a vengeance.

Threading his way among the dead he reaches a fresh grave. The moons spills over, illuminating the inscription on the small Gaelic cross. Even in his hardened state the words shock.

Wife and daughter of Dixie . . . beloved, irreplaceable . . .

Words of his own choosing, crude words which fail.

Even the final phrase falls short: Casualties of the war.

From inside his jacket he takes a crushed bouquet and tries to rearrange it in the dark. He curses, ashamed of such a wretched token for two people who'd received in life more than their share of wretched tokens. Despairing of repairing the bouquet, he tears

400

off the heads of the flowers and showers blossom over the ground.

Head bowed, he will stand here for a time, probably the last time.

Marcus is warned to expect no leniency. The toy pistol was a bargain if it saves him a few years behind bars, but he is advised to brace himself for three or four years.

When the ten-year sentence is delivered – to be served in Eire – the packed courtroom becomes a blur, friends and relatives dissolve, there's only Marcia, gazing back at him. It's in her eyes, the unbearableness of it.

As they lead him away, he twists his head to see her for as long as possible. She's smiling through her tears, nostrils flared, head high.

'You've a visitor.'

Visits are restricted and precious.

He follows eagerly, the long walk. Once a fortnight it's to see Marcia and Jamie, a uniquely distressing experience. Occasionally it's his parents, then Marcia's, once Elroy, and once, to his delight, Dominic, detouring on his way home to Kerry from Inishtrahull.

Today he finds a burly silver-haired man scarcely recognisable in cords, sweater and tweed jacket.

'The man himself!' beams Mulraine.

They embrace tentatively, then firmly. 'Jaysus, you're looking fit! This hotel suits you, I should have booked you in sooner.'

They sit and talk, Mulraine's heartiness a measure of his ordeal.

'I'd have been cosier in here with you. They fire-bombed my home. I saw it coming and we got the hell out in time. Barbara and the boys had a couple of weeks in Spain and are living with relations. Me, I'm helping the Garda with their enquiries' – he hoots with laughter and chokes on his cigarette – 'and two fellers follow me like flies in case anyone takes a shot at me, and I've to attend the trial of Michael O'Cinnéide, and I'm looking for work and a place we can live. Can you believe it! And I thought . . . well, hell, what did I think?'

He looks animated and exhausted.

Marcus pats his hand. 'Go easy on yourself.'

Mulraine lights another cigarette, smiles wryly. 'That's life for you. Stay with the flock and you're looked after. Stray and they cut you to bits.'

He looks directly at Marcus, they exchange knowing smiles.

'But sure it was worth it!' Mulraine slaps Marcus's arm and falters, '. . . wasn't it?'

'You're asking me, with nine years ten months still to go and Marcia three months pregnant in London?'

Marcus drifts with his thoughts. Mulraine calls him back. 'I'd say they could let you go early.'

'I don't even dare think about that. Anyway, whether or not it was worth it' – his turn to look Mulraine in the eye – 'it was right!'

The silences lengthen, the visit's nearly over.

'You know what gets to me?' says Marcus. 'Reading that they're still shooting off plastic bullets up North.'

'A hell of a lot less, my friend, and I'd say soldiers are starting to think on the trigger now.'

'What about before the trigger?'

Mulraine's sinking, Marcus calls him back. 'How's the inquest going to go?'

'Well, the Garda were intrigued by the tape and I understand the Taoiseach's heard it and is looking forward to making mischief with it. Evidence is accumulating . . . you know they found the BMW? Witnesses have come forward; remember the cabby who took you to the docks? I'd say they'll soon have enough to nail those sterling SAS chaps!'

Squeezing Marcus's wrist: 'Your evidence and mine will be crucial. Mind you' – waving his cigarette and frowning fatalistically – 'who's going to listen to two disgraced men?'

At the October inquest into the death of Annie McBride, two SAS soldiers admit to killing her, but they and the rest of the four-man team stress their intention was always to capture the fugitives, and that when called upon to surrender, McBride fired at them, leaving them no alternative – given her military record – but to use minimum lethal force.

As for the incident at the docks, the SAS men claim that even though Marcus King gave every impression of being armed, their intention to apprehend him remained constant. They tried to prevent his escape by shooting ahead of and around the imagined swimmer in the water, denying claims by two Greek sailors appearing as witnesses, who maintain that the SAS men retrieved the dummy and took it away with them for disposal because it was bullet-riddled.

The British Government admits conspiring to send military personnel into the Irish Republic to capture the traitor Marcus King, categorically denying the issuing of any orders containing lethal intent.

Detective Inspector Frank Mulraine's tape-recording, while causing considerable concern, is deemed inconclusive.

The Chief Constable of the RUC survives vociferous calls for his resignation.

No action is expected to be taken against any of the SAS men, nor any of their superiors.

In time, and after heartfelt thanks from his Prime Minister for his services to the province, the Northern Ireland Secretary will be relieved of that arduous and thankless job rather sooner than originally intended.

Although the Irish authorities express considerable consternation and anger, it appears the affair is drawing to a close.

Annie McBride is set to become an exotic legend.

Marcus King is about to be forgotten.

A safe cottage near Gweedore in County Donegal, a few miles in from the sea. It's early evening, Eileen Feeley stands in the doorway chain-smoking with boredom and expectancy. She has been waiting for two days, ever since the coded communication said to expect him.

As the sun slips towards the sea, she's climbing a tor thick with gorse, when she spots a car on the twisting road, coming from the east, vanishing and reappearing through the rugged landscape. Watching its progress, she stops with a jolt when she sees it turn onto the track and climb steeply to the cottage. Lifting field-glasses to her eyes she zeroes in on the two men climbing out. One she's never seen, but the other . . .

He looks up, shielding his eyes, taking a moment to be sure before giving a brusque wave. Glad, but apprehensive, she makes her way down. Many times she has imagined this moment, wondering is there a chance he'll be warmer with her, now that Mary and Josie are out of the way. After a respectable period of being cool and comradely, one night after dark will he come to her bed and take her with all the heat of those years of abstinence, and then sleep with her till morning?

The driver, smoking by the car, nods respectfully to her. She goes inside the cottage. He's standing over the open fire, gazing into the flames. She pauses, trying to read his back.

He turns unsmiling. He has changed. The old darkness is back, the hard line of mouth and jaw, the cold light of his eyes. Her heart soars.

'I'm sorry about – '

'Don't,' he says softly, sharply, 'ever mention them, ever. Do you understand?'

'OK, Dixie, there's no need – '

She stops herself. She wouldn't take it from anyone else, but he's beyond reason. Like a wounded tiger he's more menacing now than ever. One who has forsaken his conscience is more dangerous than one, like her, who never had one.

He has a week's deliberate growth of beard and his hair is cropped short.

'You're getting your hair cut too,' he says, 'and dyed. New identities, we're going to England.'

'When?'

'In time for Christmas.' He looks away into the fire. 'The Brits like their wars in other people's countries. Time they had a taste of it in their own . . .'

She nods patiently, as if she hasn't been suggesting it for years.

'When it's their women and children, maybe we'll get through to them, maybe they'll begin to understand that the Irish problem is a British problem.'

Silence, only the hum of the fire.

She wants to cross to him, welcome him with a back-slap, anything. But it's as though he's not there, only his lean outline and rasping voice.

With nine years nine months still to serve, Marcus seeks strategies for survival. Letters which take days to write are a beginning.

He's writing to a friend when keys turn in the door and the warder enters gravely. Chewing thoughtfully, the warder looks down at the swept floor.

Marcus puts down his pen. 'What's wrong?'

The warder looks at him as though for the first time.

'Something's happened,' said Marcus.

The warder nods.

'Back home?' Marcus breaks into a cold sweat.

'The elections, were you following the elections?'

'No.'

'Yer man's been toppled. The feller you held hostage is out, the other quare fellow, the Opposition leader, is in.'

Marcus retrieves his pen, searching for a suitable rejoinder. 'Are they blaming me for that as well?'

'Ah no. The nation wants a change of hat, that's all. However, you may be interested to know . . .'

Marcus has lost interest.

'. . . that the Taoiseach, the feller you held at gunpoint, has decided to fire a parting shot at Westminster. A pardon.'

Marcus looks up.

'That's right. You're going home.'